"MacLeod is one of the finest prose stylists around, and—borrowing as he does much of the melodrama of Victorian literature, along with the re-visionist modernism of later authors like D. H. Lawrence—his writing is unfailingly elegant, full of brilliantly realized English landscapes, deftly sensitive characterizations, luminously reworked fairy tales, and poetic elegies to lives and opportunities lost... Some of MacLeod's set pieces... are amongst the best fantastic writing today... *The House of Storms* is that uncommon thing, a sequel to be treasured as much as its precursor."
　　　　　　　　　　　　　　　　　　　　　　　　　　　　—*Locus*

"Tightly plotted... Full of detailed descriptions of landscapes and complex human feelings, this rich, leisurely novel bears some similarities to the more frenetic action of China Miéville, though the author's affinity to A. S. Byatt is even stronger. This is a major work by a master writing at the top of his form."　　　　　　　—*Publishers Weekly* (starred review)

"Ian MacLeod writes like an angel. He strings together ideally chosen words into sentences that are variously lush, sparse, subtle, bold, joyous, mournful, comic, or tragic. These sentences mount into perfectly balanced paragraphs, which in turn assemble themselves into poised and dramatically organic chapters. The reader is carried along effortlessly on the flow of MacLeod's prose, internalizing his vision as if in a dream... But it's on the character front that MacLeod truly expends his best efforts and achieves the most."　　　　　　　—Paul Di Filippo, *Sci Fi Weekly*

"The age of aether is still upon the world, and magic shines through the cracks of developing technology. It shines through MacLeod's powerful prose as well, illuminating the novel from within and driving it at a rapid pace... MacLeod's world and his novel are chockablock with ideas as intriguing as his characters and plots. He imbues his novel with exciting riffs from cyberpunk and war epics.

"MacLeod makes a frontal assault on both conservative and progressive politics, playing them out to a bloody and very bitter end. But for all the invention, all the playful intellectualizing, the author never loses focus on his characters and an epic arc of murder, madness, mutation, and war.

"In the end, as compelling as the plot may be, readers will find themselves slowing down, holding back, turning the pages with deliberate care. For the world that MacLeod creates, the characters who live there, the schemes and terrors they find themselves involved in are so real, so beautifully rendered, that readers will not want to leave them behind."
　　　　　　　　　　　　　　　　　　　　　　　　　　　　—*Interzone*

continued...

"The very vastness of the world that MacLeod creates leaves you breathless and a little lost . . . Ian R. MacLeod [is] a seasoned, gritty writer with a great depth of knowledge and understanding, who could teach us all a thing or two about writing a damn good tale . . . I was thrilled to be taken on an adventure into an alternative and yet highly believable world of magic. Not magic of the scar-faced wizard type, but believable, enthralling, science-cum-magic that you see in the splitting of the atom or a bright sunrise.

"At a quick pace I was taken into a place of guilds, civil war, love, and power. A place where the characters are well developed and interesting and, more importantly, highly believable and real. To me it was J. G. Ballard meets Robert Fripp. Intelligent and yet not pretentious, well written but not academic . . . The plot is twisting and complex . . . the characters are rich and diverse."
— *The Guardian* (UK)

"MacLeod's ability to tell a tale that blends history-in-the-making with the stories of the men and women who make that history renders this chronicle of love, war, and human aspirations a strong addition to any fantasy collection."
— *Library Journal*

Praise for
The Light Ages

"A meditative portrayal of an exotic society, fascinating in its unhealthy languor and seemingly imperturbable stasis . . . so powerfully recalls Dickens's [*Great Expectations*] that this affinity animates the entire work."
— *The Washington Post Book World*

"MacLeod brings a Dickensian life to the pounding factories of London in a style he calls 'realistic fantasy.' It's a complete world brought to life with compassionate characters and lyrical writing."
— *The Denver Post*

"A masterpiece of radical urban fantasy and of alternative history. Written in dense, cadenced prose, possessing a descriptive intensity rarely equaled in the speculative fiction of any period, this is very much a novel of nostalgia and loss."
— *Locus*

"Beautifully written, complex . . . With its strong character development and gritty, alternate London, this book . . . should hold great appeal to readers who love the more sophisticated fantasy of Michael Swanwick, John Crowley, or even China Miéville."
— *Publishers Weekly* (starred review)

"An excellent novel. Creative, original, profound, and stocked with utterly believable principal and secondary characters. In the end, however, the most captivating element of the book is quite simply the language . . .

MacLeod's prose manages to be both immersive and exquisite and manages an impeccable consistency of quality throughout." —*SF Site*

"A haunting and passionate evocation of a strange Victorian age twisted out of true from the one we know by dark magics and darker secrets . . . lyrical, compassionate, and complex, it should help to confirm Ian MacLeod's reputation as one of the very best writers working in the genre here at the beginning of the twenty-first century."
—Gardner Dozois, coeditor of *Wizards*

"Very much in the tradition of H. G. Wells, Aldous Huxley, and George Orwell . . . full of adventures and wonders . . . This really is an extraordinary book. You will enjoy it, and very much."
—Gahan Wilson, *Realms of Fantasy*

"The novel's industrial alternative London echoes Dickens in its rich bleakness and M. John Harrison's *Viriconium* in its inventive Gothic complexity. A gripping page-turner. A hearty read. Rising star Ian R. MacLeod offers an original political fable rivaling in ambition and execution the very best of today's new science fantasies."
—Michael Moorcock, author of the Elric novels

"Totally convincing and vividly written, this book invests the dark streets of London with a magic the reader will never forget . . . a brilliant writer." —Tim Powers, author of *Expiration Date*

"Really, I don't know what to say. *The Light Ages* is a wonderful book, a magical book." —Gene Wolfe, author of *The Wizard*

"Excellent. Ian MacLeod is rapidly becoming one of the contemporary stars of the genre." —Brian W. Aldiss, author of *Jocasta*

"*The Light Ages* is simply first-rate . . . The writing is instantly compelling."
—James P. Blaylock, author of *Thirteen Phantasms and Other Stories*

"Channeling Dickens by way of Coleridge, *The Light Ages*' magic derives as much from the high quality of Ian R. MacLeod's prose as any supernatural element . . . stands beside the achievements of China Miéville. *The Light Ages* is a must-read."
—Jeff VanderMeer, author of *Shriek: An Afterword*

THE HOUSE OF STORMS

IAN R. MacLEOD

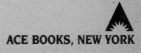

ACE BOOKS, NEW YORK

THE BERKLEY PUBLISHING GROUP
Published by the Penguin Group
Penguin Group (USA) Inc.
375 Hudson Street, New York, New York 10014, USA
Penguin Group (Canada), 90 Eglinton Avenue East, Suite 700, Toronto, Ontario M4P 2Y3, Canada
(a division of Pearson Penguin Canada Inc.)
Penguin Books Ltd., 80 Strand, London WC2R 0RL, England
Penguin Group Ireland, 25 St. Stephen's Green, Dublin 2, Ireland (a division of Penguin Books Ltd.)
Penguin Group (Australia), 250 Camberwell Road, Camberwell, Victoria 3124, Australia
(a division of Pearson Australia Group Pty. Ltd.)
Penguin Books India Pvt. Ltd., 11 Community Centre, Panchsheel Park, New Delhi—110 017, India
Penguin Group (NZ), 67 Apollo Drive, Rosedale, North Shore 0632, New Zealand
(a division of Pearson New Zealand Ltd.)
Penguin Books (South Africa) (Pty.) Ltd., 24 Sturdee Avenue, Rosebank, Johannesburg 2196,
South Africa

Penguin Books Ltd., Registered Offices: 80 Strand, London WC2R 0RL, England

This is a work of fiction. Names, characters, places, and incidents either are the product of the author's imagination or are used fictitiously, and any resemblance to actual persons, living or dead, business establishments, events, or locales is entirely coincidental. The publisher does not have any control over and does not assume any responsibility for author or third-party websites or their content.

THE HOUSE OF STORMS

An Ace Book / published by arrangement with the author

PRINTING HISTORY
Ace hardcover edition / May 2005
Ace trade paperback edition / August 2006
Ace mass-market edition / October 2007

Copyright © 2005 by Ian R. MacLeod.
Cover art by Steve Stone.
Cover design by Judith Murello.

All rights reserved.
No part of this book may be reproduced, scanned, or distributed in any printed or electronic form without permission. Please do not participate in or encourage piracy of copyrighted materials in violation of the author's rights. Purchase only authorized editions.
For information, address: The Berkley Publishing Group,
a division of Penguin Group (USA) Inc.,
375 Hudson Street, New York, New York 10014.

ISBN: 978-0-441-01539-9

ACE
Ace Books are published by The Berkley Publishing Group,
a division of Penguin Group (USA) Inc.,
375 Hudson Street, New York, New York 10014.
ACE and the "A" design are trademarks belonging to Penguin Group (USA) Inc.

PRINTED IN THE UNITED STATES OF AMERICA

10 9 8 7 6 5 4 3 2 1

If you purchased this book without a cover, you should be aware that this book is stolen property. It was reported as "unsold and destroyed" to the publisher, and neither the author nor the publisher has received any payment for this "stripped book."

For Heather and John
With love
And thanks for letting me borrow the name

PART ONE

I

When Greatgrandmistress Alice Meynell brought her son to Invercombe, she fully believed she was taking him to die there. Not that she had given up hope—*hope* was something she still clung to resolutely—but through the years of Ralph's illness she had discovered shades of meaning within simple words which, previously, she had scarcely known to exist.

She gazed from the car as it rumbled out of Bristol. It was a cold, grey morning, still cornered with night, and Ralph was shivering under his blankets, his breath as blue as his lips. That overnight train from London, and now they were being driven in this outwardly fine but actually quite freezing vehicle around the backs of yards which gave tawdry glimpses of a city which Alice had always felt to be more alien than many a far-flung reach of the Continent. The trams here went humming on high cradles which pressed their tips together over the streets like praying hands. And the buildings! Festoons of coralstone which the master builders grew and mutated, and which reminded her of dough creatures shaped out of flour and water. Everything twisted and curved and looking as if it was still growing, and in pinks and blues, like an explosion in a nursery. It was all so different from Northcentral's orderly grid. Slowly, in the better districts towards the dam at Clifton, the fantastic houses were coming to life, and servants were hurrying along the pavements to their day's work as the street-lamps blinked out. Then, in that quick way which could never happen in London, they were in open countryside.

Ralph's first sight of Bristol, and already it was gone. Even though the city would be within reach from where they were heading, Alice wondered, as she often found herself doing whenever they saw any new sight, whether her son would ever see it again. She gave an inward shudder. The clock, fevered and quick as his pulse, was always ticking. London, then Bristol, and now this tumbling landscape which the dawn had yet to touch as the lights of the car shone on bare hedgerows.

Before this, before that. Baden and then Paris. That place in the mountains. And doctors' surgeries. The glow of their vials. The glint of their glasses. Whispered, useless spells. The months and the shifterms sometimes condensed in her imagination to that one single protracted moment from a summer's afternoon back in London up on the Kite Hills—Butterfly Day, it had been, and she'd never felt the same about that particular holiday since—when Ralph had run up to her and he'd started coughing and she'd glimpsed flecks of blood amid the spittle in his palm. From there to now was like an endless flee-ing, and the times they'd spent in so many admittedly pretty and interesting places seemed like nothing but pauses to catch their breath before they started running again. Even a healthy child would have been wearied, just as she felt wearied her-self. And all to find that words like hope could be sliced into endless shades of nuance and grow so thin that eventually you could see right through them. But now, as they turned out from a valley and the rising sun suddenly poured from banks of grey cloud and twirled though the patches of mist, they were heading for Invercombe, and there they would make their last stand.

Ralph's breathing was more regular now. The sun was in his face, and Alice saw with a pang that this new day's light was glinting on the thickening down which was now covering his cheeks. Even though his illness had prevented him from living an ordinary childhood, Ralph was already becoming a man.

Sensing some change in her gaze, he turned towards her. There was a line of sweat across his upper lip.

'Is it a long drive?'

'I don't know, my darling. I've never been there.'

'What's it called again?'

'Invercombe.'

He nodded and looked again out of the window. A ghost of his breath pulsed across the glass from his lips. 'So this is the west.'

Alice smiled and took her son's hand, feeling heat and lightness. Now that the sun was properly risen, she was remembering just how pretty this western landscape could be, even on a late winter's morning. The way the hills never ceased unrolling. The sense that the next turn would reveal the sea. But she scarcely knew the west herself. Little more than honey-stoned towns in which she'd spent worthless half-afternoons in her younger, more difficult, days, sitting on a suitcase as she waited for a change of trains. But still, Ralph seemed happy as he looked out at the road angled down beside the huge estuary and the far hills of Wales. London, even the few days they'd spent there, and with its dense fogs and all the endless comings and goings, was unthinkable. Yes, for all the reasons she'd rehearsed, and for the odd, increasing sense that it had been calling to her in some vague yet significant way, Invercombe felt right.

'You really have no idea what it'll be like?' Ralph murmured.

'No. But . . .'

Ralph turned back to her, and together they chanted the phrase which they always did when they arrived at somewhere new.

'We'll soon find out . . .'

Trees parted. There were tall outer walls, a small gatehouse, a long estate road with a glimpse of some kind of castle or ruin across the parkland on the right, and then the land was rising through perilinden and evergreen plantation towards a stumpy lighthouse. No, that would be the weathertop.

Invercombe, Alice knew from her researches, had been here a long time. The Romans had possibly fortified this seaward command of the Severn Estuary, and there had certainly been a small castle here before it was sacked by Cromwell's armies. Then had come the years when the English landscape erupted once more into bloodshed after a lonely and obsessive man named Joshua Wagstaffe extracted a hitherto-unheard-of substance from the rocks he had spent a lifetime collecting. He named it aether after the fifth form of matter which Plato had surmised, and dowsing for it soon became the obsession of the Age. Aether persuaded corn to grow into bushel-sized heads on land which had furnished little but chaff. Aether made frozen axles turn. Aether bent the very fabric of the world. Aether, above all, was power, and the trade guilds understood that better than anyone, and, in their battles with the king and the church, took it as their own.

After the bloodshed of the co-called Wars of Unification, as the first of the Ages of Industry began, Invercombe was rebuilt, no longer as a castle, but, infused with new wealth and the abilities of aether, as a fine house on this precarious promontory; a veritable jewel of stone. A family by the name of Muscoates lived there for generations until their power waned and it was finally made part of a bankruptcy settlement, and drifted like so many things into the ownership of the Great Guilds. It became just one of many investments and holdings which were passed forgetfully from will to will, marriage to marriage, until it reached the hands of the Guild of Telegraphers towards the end of the Third Age, although it was doubtful if any of its great-grandmasters ever visited the place. Still, the place meandered on, and a use was found for it as a base for the development of a technology which was to become the wonder and wellspring of this current Age. The old water race was cleared, and a generator, new in itself, was built to feed Invercombe with electricity. A reckoning engine, also advanced for its time, was then installed, and a small but functional transmission house was constructed on the boundaries of the estate. From this early work, a new kind of electric telegraph, through which it was no longer necessary for skilled telegraphers to commune mind to mind, but through which ordinary guilds-people, at least if they were rich enough, could simply talk to each other as if they were face to face, was developed. It became known as the telephone, and by this great invention, the entire world was changed. But, and once again, Invercombe retreated from fame and from memory. It drifted, its halls abandoned in the chaos of the end of the last

Age of Industry, until it was granted in a life lease to a certain Greatmaster Ademus Isumbard Porrett.

Invercombe by then was half-ruined and seriously undermined by the swell of the sea at the cliffs beneath its foundations, but Greatmaster Porrett threw himself wholeheartedly into its repair. There were century-old records which Alice had studied recording how Invercombe's roof was remade, its generators repaired, and the re-establishing of its terraces, and of many gardens newly landscaped. Greatmaster Porrett even shaped an ugly transmission house into the battlements of a folly-castle so as not to spoil the view. All, to Alice's mind, a strange amount of effort to put in as a mere life tenant, but Porrett's most extraordinary improvement was a weathertop, the brassy dome of which she could now see placed like a squat lighthouse atop a brick tower on the south side of the hill above the water race. On the decks of sail-bearing craft, master mariners employed such devices to make the best of the winds, but the idea of a landlocked device to control the climate of an entire valley struck her as ambitious in the extreme.

The car swished to a halt on a semi-circular sweep of mossy gravel. With the quick eye of one who has long grown used to new arrivals, Alice appraised the tall windows and chimneys, the elegant gables, the stone-chased intricacies of glass. The house was even prettier than she'd imagined.

Signalling the driver to wait and glancing at her wristwatch—it was quarter to eight—she strode up to the front door and pulled the bellchain. She'd sent word a shifterm or so ago that she and Ralph were coming, but, as was her usual practice, she'd hadn't mentioned the exact time and date. Normally at this point the shocked face of some half-dressed maid would poke around the door. In the years since she had married Greatgrandmaster Tom Meynell, she had made it one of her many small personal crusades to ensure that all the properties their guild owned were properly maintained. That, indeed, was why Invercombe had first come to her attention. A relatively small estate, but the rows of figures beside it had indicated that it was sucking in money. It was that landlocked weathertop, which, it was explained to her, was too powerful to be fully decommissioned without ruinous expense. For whatever reason, for that odd device, or for a situation which seemed to guard the Bristol

Channel, or for the sense of a story which she didn't fully know, Alice had decided against condemning the place. And now she was standing at its door and Ralph was getting cold in the car and nothing was happening as the weathertop's greenish-gold dome glowed through the bare trees. She sighed and kneaded a twitch beneath her right eye. She was about to pull the bellchain again when she heard, or rather, sensed, a presence behind her. Slowly, she turned, fully expecting to find nothing but the illusions of her own tiredness. But a large Negro woman stood there.

'Welcome to Invercombe, greatgrandmistress,' she said, and made a curtsey. 'I'm Cissy Dunning, steward of this house . . .'

II

The first priority, always, was Ralph. She found him the best and the airiest room, fitted with barely used but century-old furniture and fine, sound-looking wood panelling. Even to Alice's eyes, the green and gold four-poster bed's huge mattress looked reasonably hygienic, and there were French windows to a southwest balcony with no appreciable draughts overlooking the fine gardens, and a decent fire already crackling in the grate.

She found a comfortable couch and had it shifted into Ralph's room as somewhere for her to rest and, if need be, spend the nights. Everything had to be checked, moved, aired, settled, sorted, explained, organised. Not just hours of it, but days. But the steward seemed capable and was difficult to fluster, even if she was female and a Negro, and her staff seemed to know their work, although there was no detectable sign of any change to the frigid weather engendered by that weathertop. And those *accents*. Little aspects of their manner and clothing, and the odd, faint taste to the water, which was strangely pleasant, and even seemed to enhance the flavour of her tea. Nothing was quite the same here, and Alice almost hoped to find some severe flaw in Invercombe's outward efficiency so that she could impose herself more easily on the people who ran it.

'Well? What do you think?'

She was sitting on the side of Ralph's bed. It was mid-morning, Eightshiftday, the fourth day since their arrival, and the fire was gently sparkling. All the ordinary and necessary events which she had stipulated had seemingly taken place, and she was in the odd situation of finding that there was little that she needed to attend to. Outside, although they got the best of the light here, it was yet another grey day.

Ralph smiled. He was sitting up, almost fully dressed, and he'd slept through his third good night. 'I like it here. I like the feel of the air. When will you let me explore?'

'Soon enough.' Exulted, she gave his hand a squeeze. 'But we mustn't rush. Only two shifterms ago . . .' That damn London air. Ralph muttering that his bones were burning. Even now, some of that weakness was still lingering. She leaned over and kissed his cheek, feeling the give of that new down. She smiled and sat back from him. 'I'll get you your books.'

Although many of the things she'd initially asked to be posted on from London had arrived, the textbooks through which she'd overseen Ralph's education hadn't. But long-dead Greatmaster Porrett had seemed to anticipate Ralph's needs in the surprisingly well-stocked library. The books were old, but, breaking open their pristine spines, Alice had concluded that little of importance had been added to the sum of human knowledge throughout this Age. Studying the fine, hand-coloured prints of flowers, both natural and aether-engineered, with their detailed Latin descriptions, and the avalanching pictures of rocks, would stand Ralph in good stead when he began the proper work of his induction into the Telegraphers, although Alice had never understood this male need to catalogue.

'Why are you smiling like that?' he asked.

Planning ahead. Thinking *when* instead of *if*. 'I'm just happy that you're happy.'

He studied her suspiciously. 'As long,' there was an up-down quaver in his voice, 'as you're happy as well.'

'Of course I am.' The local doctor, a character named Foot, had already called on her with his busy little wife, and so had the Reverend-Highermaster Humphry Brown, the parish priest. Of course, she'd go to church on Noshiftday morning just like any other respectable guildsmistress, but over the years she'd heard the chant of too many prayers and spells. She understood the stages the mothers of consumptives went through. The frantic agony of first discovery was followed by willingness to go anywhere, to do *anything*. It was often years before the guilty realisation finally came that you were simply making your child suffer more. Yes, consumption sometimes faded, but the only known way of alleviating it was rest and fresh air. Yet still you travelled and still you worried and still you paid in relentless pursuit of the finest kind of air, the purest form of rest. Your child's crises and remissions became the star by which your entire life was navigated. In many cases, as Alice had seen in spa towns and sanatoriums across half of Europe, this pursuit lasted until the child's death, or the mother's infection with the same disease. But the impulse to come to Invercombe had been clear and irrevocable. She felt none of the usual doubts.

She plumped up an extra cushion to support a book on botany and left Ralph to his reading. In the corridor, she checked her watch. Already close to noon. Back in London, her husband Tom would be heading for lunch at his club. In that dense fug, which was like the London air outdoors but ten times multiplied, over red wine and snooker and endless courses of stodge, listening to the same lame jokes and smiling at the same weary faces in their high-backed chairs, much of the real work of the Great Guilds was done. She decided that she would telephone him there before he ate. But first she must make herself presentable.

She turned along the landing to her own room, which lay at right angles to Ralph's, with windows opening to a balcony which hung giddily over the sweep of a large, secluded bay. Invercombe was disorientatingly full of such surprises, with odd angles in corridors and unexpected views of land or sea, and the house was positioned so close over the sea on this side that the damage its constant onrush was doing to the foundations scarcely bore thinking about, but it was all undeniably pleasant. She was even starting to wonder if, despite the continuing frigid air and flat grey skies, the odd comfort she felt here wasn't some initial symptom of the weathertop's awakening. She and Ralph had been greeted so calmly here, whereas in other places she'd experienced ridiculous fussing only to end up in beds which reeked of urine. Her suspicions of whatever it was that she suspected of Invercombe remained unfounded and unexplained.

Opening her balcony doors to the salt air, she shrugged off her green silk dress. Almost all her trunks had arrived now, and her clothes had been unwrapped and put away. Also here, a case of black lacquer set on the table beside the windows and glinting with the sea, was her gramophone. Setting the turntable spinning, she removed her earrings and waltzed, two and three, across the shining floor. She touched the steel locks of her portmanteau case and breathed the spell which triggered their release. Twin thunks—a mere emphasis of the music—and its sides unfolded on a velvet den. There was oil of bergamot from the sun-warmed sap of citrus trees. There were waxy distillation of ambergris, and special earths, and particulates of lead. Like a good wine, the contents were easily upset by travel, but as Alice unscrewed a bevelled jar of cold cream and dabbed a ball of lambswool to her face, she could feel that everything was already settling here at Invercombe. Scents of beeswax and almond and hints of rosewater mingled with the hissing sea as she turned two and three to the music in her chemise before the long mirrors of her wardrobes.

She studied herself left and right. The jaw, the neck, the profile and the timeless face and frame of a woman still entirely beautiful, if no longer quite young. Feet tiptoe light. Firm hips and bosom. Alice. Alice Meynell. Hair which had always been closer to silver than blonde, but which she could still afford to wear long. Clear, Classical forehead. Those wide-spaced blue eyes. All a matter of luck, really. Mere human flesh hung on accidents of bone.

Humming, she extracted her silver spirit lamp, struck a taper to its wick, and wiped a glass chalice with white linen. The record was clicking in its groove. Setting it playing again, then the chalice warming above the spirit lamp's gentle heat, she added oils, dashes of spirit, tinctures and balms, then Grecian honey. Stirred with a spoon of whale ivory, the resulting goo gained a frothy lightness which made it especially receptive to the final ingredient, which was aether of the purest charm. Still humming, dancing, and lifting out a small vial from the magic depths of her portmanteau, she whispered the part of the spell which caused its wyrelight to brighten, then squeezed the pipette and wafted the glowing tube towards the waiting chalice. Now, in a fluting voice, she chanted the main verses of her spell; sounds which she had refined with the avidity of the most dedicated steamaster. A pulse of darkness. Her song ended. The droplet fell. The potion was energised.

Sitting down at her dressing table, Alice kneaded her cheeks. Then she dabbed her fingertips into the preparation and began, always working upwards, to work it into the skin of her face. The sensation was tinglingly pleasant. Crackle, crackle, went the gramophone from the end of its song, joining with the faint hiss of the tide against the cliffs far below and all the rush of life which had brought her here to this moment, to this spell, to this place. She flexed her lips and blinked at the mirror. Then she worked on her neck and shoulders, and circled lightly across her arms and towards the scoop of her breasts, although there were other magics for the body.

There. She smiled more openly back at herself, completing the picture she wanted her husband Tom to see when she telephoned him. A hint of blue above the eyes, a dash of black across the lashes, then she cleaned her tools and closed her portmanteau and whispered the phrase which froze its twin locks. In every way, she felt refreshed. Amid its many other benefits, the practice of magic was far better than a good night's rest. She lifted her green dress back off its hanger and gauged, with a quick sniff, that it had absorbed just the right proportion of her personal scent. The record still crackled, and she realised that she was humming along as if it were still playing a tune. In fact—she cocked her head. What exactly had she been humming? It was dangerous, in any case, to murmur so carelessly when you were working with aether and the room, as she looked around, seemed caught in a stage of arrested movement. Hiss, crackle, the sound of the waves. As if, for one moment, the entire house had been breathing.

Realising that she hadn't replaced her earrings, she leaned before the dressing table to push the gold posts through the lobe of each ear. Then something terrible happened. As she studied herself and the bright scrutiny of the coastal light fell once again across her face, Alice noticed for the first time in her life that she was developing jowls on each side of her previously perfect jawline.

The telephone booth beneath the best stairs in Invercombe's inner hall was a small red-plush construction topped with a domed brass bell which looked as if it had been polished far more times than it had ever rang. It was part of the history of the house and her guild's own experiments, and certainly the earliest model Alice had even seen, although the booth inside was pleasant enough, for all that it was antique. Sitting down, she was confronted by a mirror, but in the softer downward glow of an electric bulb, she could almost tell herself that she hadn't seen what she had seen upstairs.

The bulb dimmed, and she felt the usual familiar give-and-pull resistance as she closed the connector and dialled the number of Tom's club with the pivoted brass post. Relays engaged through hidden cables which, buried below ground here so as not to spoil the beauty of Invercombe's grounds, broadened at that folly transmission house to head on towards the pulse and throb of a clearinghouse reckoning engine. She gazed at the mirror and felt something shiver, a break in reality. Her face dissolved, and then even the glass itself faded— or rather *widened*—and exhaled a mingled rush of male voices. She felt the sting of cigar smoke and heard the faint roar of London traffic; the portal to London was fully open.

A waiter leaned towards her from the distant booth to enquire to whom it was that she wished to speak, and she felt the breath of the door swinging shut as he went away, then heard the chuckle of a drink being poured—before her husband arrived and seated himself opposite her in the mirror.

'I thought I'd find you here at the club, darling.'

'You know me. Regular as clockwork.' Tom's tie, although doubtless recently reknotted, was already askew, and he smelled more of sweat than of eau de cologne. 'How's Ralph? I've been telling myself all shifterm that no news is good news, and you certainly seem to have taken enough stuff with you to that place—where is it? Inverglade?'

'It's Inver*combe*. And I've scarcely taken anything.' Alice looked playfully wounded as Tom gazed back at her with that familiar yearning look in his eyes. She needed his regard, especially after what she'd seen upstairs in the mirror of her vanity table. It was better than aether; a warm blaze. 'Ralph's settled in well. And I'm so glad we came here, even if I do miss you terribly.'

'You were in London for such a short time. And you've been away so long.' Tom's smile almost faded.

'Well, you know why. Needs must.'

'Yes, yes. And Ralph—I do understand that London's not the place for him.'

Tom gazed at her. He worked his lips. There were lines around his eyes now. He had Ralph's thick black hair, but it was receding at the forehead and greying at the temples now, although his jaw had been a little saggy even when she'd first met him. It was so much easier for men to grow old gracefully.

'Anyway, I've been missing you, darling.' He flared his nostrils as he breathed her scent, and vague commotions and the clatter of a passing London tram touched Alice's senses as she told Tom about Invercombe's peculiarities: the steward of the house who was female, and Negro; the weathertop, of the effects of which she remained sceptical; the odd accents: and Ralph, who had slept well and was working his way through the surprisingly good library and nagging her about exploring the place.

'That all sounds quite marvellous. I'm proud of you both. And tell Ralph . . . Tell him I'm proud of him, too. And that we'll soon be spending a lot more time together. There are so many things I want to share with him, Alice.'

'It's been difficult for us both.'

'And you seemed so gloomy when you left.'

'But I'm not now.'

'And you look . . .'

Alice, even though she hadn't allowed her chin to droop, raised it a little further.

'. . . quite marvellous, darling.'

Then they talked of business, and the news was hardly cheering. A construction contract was being delayed for supposedly technical reasons. Tom was all for allowing extra time for redesign, but Alice remained convinced they should pull out and take legal action.

'Isn't that a bit harsh?'

'We have to be harsh. Wouldn't they do the same to our guild?'

Tom nodded. He knew his own instincts were often too conciliatory, and relied upon Alice's strength and advice. Then they said goodbye, and his image faded, and the mirror darkened, and she could feel—doors slamming in an unfelt wind—the relays closing on them all the way back to London. It was time for her to lift the connector, but for a few moments she left the line open, and the black space of the mirror seemed to widen. Looking into it now was almost like falling. With a little more effort, she felt sure she might be able to enter that space; travel along the lines as something incorporate and then emerge at some far other end. It was an idea, a risk, an experiment, which she'd long toyed with, and then always dismissed as both too ridiculous and dangerous. But what better place than here, the house, the telephone breathed to her, to try? After all, isn't this where all this trickery with mirrors began? Releasing the connector, she sat back and watched herself reform in the glass of the booth's mirror. Raising a hand to touch the tender flesh of the jawbone, she could feel that gravity, which pulled down mountains and rolled the moon across the sky, was clawing the flesh off her face.

Leaving the booth, pulling on a coat, Alice headed outside. It was even colder than she'd imagined. Trailing breath, she crossed the front courtyard and then the bridge which spanned the gorge-like cleft over the River Riddle, and followed the path which wound up through the pinetum towards a smell of smoke. Bald-headed, handlebar-moustached, gauntlet-gloved, Weatherman Ayres was dragging curling black masses of a form of cuckoo-plant she recognised as hellebore into the flames of a bonfire in a clearing.

'Always have to keep pulling this stuff up, Mistress,' he called as he saw her approach. 'Have to drag the water race, too, at least twice in the spring.' It was ugly stuff—purplish and studded with venomous blue-black berries—and the flames leapt up from it with a gushing hiss. Remembering her face, Alice stepped back.

'I just thought I'd come and see how you and your weather-top were progressing,' she said. 'I was rather hoping we might have seen its effects by now. At the very least, for the benefit of my son . . .'

Weatherman Ayres tossed off his gloves and wiped his brow. Leading her up the muddy path of the gorge where pylons climbed from the wheelhouse below, he wheezed open an iron door into the weathertop's dry, amber light.

'Have you worked here long?'

'Best part of twenty years.'

'And you've never actually *used* this thing?'

'Well . . .' He gave a dial a thoughtful tap with a fingernail. 'Thing is, Mistress, it's never been turned off. So in a way it's always been running. Or at least, idling. Machines are far happier doing the thing they're meant to do than doing nothing.' His moustache curled upwards as he smiled. Slapping the gantries, stroking the lion-coloured bricks, he guided Alice around each level. Barnacled with conductors, feeding on aether and electricity, rose the weathertop's main device. This place, Alice decided, was either a humming shrine to industry or a vast confidence trick. But at least there was a shipshape sense of order. Up and up. Then at last they were at the top, and through another iron door into the cold air of the outer gantry. They were high above Invercombe's trees, and the drop down was impressive, especially on this side of the valley which fell all the way towards the turn and flash of the waterwheel.

The dome of the weathertop was pitted and stained. It looked like the surface of a harvest moon.

'Is it safe to touch?'

'Best not, Mistress.'

Looking out over the treetops through the clear, solid air, she laughed out loud, for the world whitened beyond the greys and shadows of Invercombe's valley. The fields were heaps of bed-linen. The towns and houses seemed made of paper. 'Why, Weatherman Ayres, it's been snowing!'

'Never realise here, would you?'

Not a heavy fall, it was true, but enough to transform the landscape. She stroked the cold handrail. The folly—a telephone relay house—was a white palace. That way, beyond the handkerchief fields, rose the Mendips. To the north, a dim glower, was Bristol. And there, a mere contraction of the haze, lay the place known as Einfell . . .

In Einfell, as every schoolchild knew, dwelt the changed, the deformed, those hobgoblins of industry who had suffered from over-exposure to aether and had taken on some of the attributes of its spells. Back in Ages less civilised that this, changelings had been burnt, or chained and imprisoned and dragged around like familiars or drays under the auspices of the Gatherers Guild. Now, though, and in these modern times, such practices were frowned upon. In Einfell, the changelings, the trolls, the fairies—you could almost choose whatever name you wished— took care of their own. And the guilds conspired forgetfully to allow them to dwell there because it dealt with the problem, and was mostly in their interest, and it was easier to forget.

Alice fingered the small scab of the Mark on the inside of her left wrist, remembering how she'd once lined up with all the rest of the local offspring outside a green caravan on her Day of Testing. An odd moment alone inside that wheeled shed, which had smelled of pipesmoke and sour bedlinen, as the guildsman dripped her left wrist with some glowing stuff, which, poor as she'd then been, she'd never seen before, but which even the most idiot child knew was called aether. And there you were. Your whole arm smarting and this blazing scab which would never really heal, which was called the Mark of the Elder. Many of the high guildswomen she'd subsequently encountered orna- mented their Mark with cleverly constructed bracelets, al- though for the rest of the world it soon became tide-rimmed with dirt and everyday life. But your Mark was never quite forgotten. It proved, as long as it didn't fade and you were careful and went to church and did all the things your guild expected of you and none of the things it didn't, that you were still human. But as for what went on inside Einfell's walls amid those who had changed, that remained a mystery, although, and more than most people, Alice Meynell had often had cause to wonder . . .

'Most people look in that direction,' Weatherman Ayres said, following her gaze. 'Not that there's much to see. Never have any dealings with them, but I've heard people sometimes go to them for help—cures, predictions. Though I doubt they ever get it. Place is a disappointment, by all accounts . . .'

She took dinner that evening with Ralph in his bedroom. The air felt warmly luxurious, yet beyond Invercombe the earth was sheeted with snow. She shared her discovery with him, and the knowledge floated over them as they played chequers. Ralph could beat her now if she didn't concentrate. He could even chat about his latest studies in his beloved sciences as he did so. Apart from the sad truth of those jowls, she felt almost entirely happy. It was pleasant to be sitting here in this odd, old house with Ralph—sheltered from the night, the snows, and as Ralph's words drifted and the chequers clicked, she even allowed herself to prod at the guilty thought that part of her wanted to keep him like this, trapped in a tower like a creature in those fairy stories of which he had once been so fond. But no; she really did want him to heal and to live a life away from her. She even half-believed that it could happen, now that they were at Invercombe.

Ralph grew tired, then slightly feverish. Feeling she'd allowed too much of her own restlessness to bother him, she plumped up the pillows, poured him a little more of his tincture, and watched the movement of his Adam's apple as he swallowed. Then he turned to her with the dark fluid still on his lips, and something that was not him was in his gaze.

She guarded the fire and dimmed the lights. She loosened his bedclothes and laid a cold cloth across his forehead. But he was still restless and lay awkwardly across his pillows. Such times, such feelings, were catching. Alice, who was somehow even more desperate than usual for Ralph to have a restful night, removed the wooden box containing his painstones. Polished and intricately veined, she'd avoided using them since they'd arrived here, but now she took out the third of the five strengths.

Ralph gave a bucking cough. His eyes skidded over her face. Another spasm was coming. She pressed the painstone's cool weight into his right hand and closed his fingers around it. Letting go, checking the sheets for telltale flecks of blood, a breath of sweat surged over her own skin. So many times she had thought, *Let it be me*. She thought it again now as Ralph's breathing began to ease. Within a minute—the painstone was that quick—he was asleep.

False alarm, really. She was over-stimulated, herself. Standing up, she glanced at the couch and wondered if she should spend the night here, but Ralph's breathing was regular, and he would take her presence as an indication that things were going backwards. When they were going *forwards*. Yes. Really . . . Kissing his cheek, breathing what was now the somehow indisputably male scent of his body, she left Ralph to his dreams.

Back in her own room, she avoided the dressing table mirror's gaze as she took off her shoes and then her jacket and lay down on her bed. She heard the sounds of the house falling towards sleep: Cissy Dunning's low, liquid voice; the maids' footsteps and bed-time whispers; doors closing. Ralph was growing. Soon, if things went in the way she sometimes permitted herself to believe, his voice would finish cracking and he'd be thinking, in the yearning abstract sense which came at that age but never seemed to leave most men, of the frictions of passion. Perhaps he was already pleasuring himself, although Alice doubted it; they lived too close for the signs not to be apparent. But he was certainly growing, whilst she—by the same unavoidable rules of unaethered physics and nature, as if one thing can never gain without another losing—was falling away from beauty.

She remembered how the first realisation of the power of her features had come from the attentions the old gardener had started giving her in the damp old house in which she'd been raised. *Have to be careful with* those *looks, my girl*, was all her aunt had muttered when she'd limped in, her dress torn. But at least she'd began to study herself differently in the mirror. Alice had always known that her father and mother had been a handsome couple, but, by questioning her aunt at unexpected moments and burrowing through the society pages of the old newspapers, she came to understand that her father Freddie Bowdly-Smart had been a 'notorious bachelor', that he'd 'played the field' (but what sport was that?) before settling on Fay Girouard as his wife. Fay had been an 'actress', although Alice hadn't then understood the implications of that description, other than to realise that her mother's fortune had lain in her body, her face. They'd married, and Alice Bowdly-Smart been born, and one clear morning Fay and Freddie had left her in the hands of a wet nurse to go out sailing on their swish new yacht. The tides had borne their drowned bodies back to shore a shifterm or so later, and she and her parent's money were given in trust to a maiden aunt.

The old woman had been as vague with Alice about the trust money as she was about most things, but the hints were already there in the poor state of the house and the decrepit servants and the watery food. The whole place, along with the debts which apparently went back into her aunt's youth and a lost suitor, was an object lesson in wasting gentility. Realising there was no inheritance, and dropping the Smart, Alice Bowdly had left the house after the death of her aunt and headed for the genteel city of Lichfield, which was the furthest destination she could afford on a one-way, third-class ticket. Once there, with a flashing smile and a glimpse of leg, she managed to obtain lodgings, but soon discovered that a smile alone wasn't enough to keep away starvation. But Alice submitted. She did whatever was necessary. Remaining detached was something she'd always been good at, and she reinvested the money she made and the contacts she gained in better clothes and better manners and, finally, a better place to live in the cathedral square.

In her early twenties, she moved south, by now a beautiful, modestly prosperous woman, towards Dudley, that wellspring of Midlands wealth and production. This time, she was able to set herself up in the most elegant district of Tipton, and to promenade the Castle Gardens. The affluent sons of higher guildsmen who managed the local slaughterhouses took her out on picnics, and Alice grew moderately expert at watercolour painting and playing the piano, and discovered she had a taste for the better things, and travelled somewhat, and learned a little French. She even received several offers of respectable marriage, but none of them was good enough for Alice Bowdly.

Soon, she was nearing thirty, and still dissatisfied, and still beautiful as ever. So she took the train to London, as Alice Smart this time, and dropped most of the ten years which were starting to weigh on her shoulders. Setting herself up in Northcentral in a small but extraordinarily expensive flat overlooking the ziggurat gardens of Westminster Great Park, and with the help of a well-placed grandmaster of the Guild of Electricians who became infatuated with her, she gained access to the all right circles. She made sure to dress and behave in an appropriately youthful manner, but still she seemed mature and compassionate beyond her years. To the men, she was everything the other society girls were not, and Greatgrand-master Tom Meynell was the biggest of all catches, and she was pleased to discover that she genuinely liked the man. Still, marriages within the Great Guilds involved monumental exchanges of power and wealth, whilst Alice could offer nothing but herself. Casting aside the grandmaster electrician, Alice glittered as she had never glittered in the summer that Tom Meynell finally proposed to her, and their marriage was the event of the season. She and Tom were happy together, and she loved the riches, the endless cars and carriages and corridors and lawns and lakes and servants, which were now all hers. She loved Tom as well, although the child which they both wanted was slow in coming. She used potions and took discreet medical advice, but she was ten years older than Tom thought her to be and her body, at the time when she most needed it, finally seemed to be betraying her. Then, after several false alarms, she was properly pregnant. She felt proud and ill, and the birth was everything she'd been dreading, but the child was perfect—a son, even—and Alice was happy as she had never been happy before. Ralph Meynell was all the good things about her, and the greatest thing of all was that he would never have to struggle as she had struggled.

In some ways, her appearance should have ceased to matter then. Women of the Great Guilds are permitted to sag a little once they have become maternal, and their husbands are expected to look discreetly elsewhere. But not Alice Meynell. She was the epitome of grace. And she had discovered by now that she had a far greater aptitude for the affairs of guild politics than Tom. Once his father died, she became his sole buttress and sounding board, and she was often able to tilt things in her guild's favour by using her soirées, her contacts, her smile. Alice didn't know quite when she had started to use the powers of aether in her cosmetics—it was a far more gradual process than that—but she never doubted, just as she had rarely doubted anything throughout her whole life, that she was doing what was *right*, what was *necessary*. Her fortune, and her guild and her son and her husband, all depended upon her being the legend of languorous grace which was Great-grandmistress Alice Meynell.

The years went by, unmeasured in her features by anything

more than a refinement of her beauty. Officially, she passed twenty-five, then neared thirty, and Ralph grew into a young lad, bright and eager and compassionate, although of course she missed the baby he had been, and would have had several more children. There were even a few false alarms. Then there was that hot afternoon on London's Kite Hills. Ralph had been nine, and feeling it was time—overdue, indeed—that he learned to swim, she'd taken him to the bathing pools there. Not that these chlorine-scented public places would have been her ideal choice, but at least the waters of the children's pool were shallow and safe. Or so she'd thought, although Ralph had stood rigid in the blazing water as the other children crashed and screamed around him, refusing to duck his head or strike out, and then complaining that his chest ached. He'd run off across the hilly parkland like a released prisoner when they left the pools, and she'd sat down in the shade of the trees to nurse her small disappointment. He'd started coughing when he ran back up to her. She'd been about to remind him that he should use a handkerchief when she'd seen blood gleaming on his palm, and their entire world had turned on its foundations. That same summer, Alice also realised that she was no longer fertile. Ralph—in a phrase which she'd merrily often thought without fully understanding—was everything.

So began this time of seeking, although she never allowed it to stop her from being Alice Meynell. She was still, to all outward appearances, a woman in the full bloom to her beauty. In the guild's great houses she even had to resort to the monthly charade of staining a few items of her laundry with blood, for she knew how gossip seeped up from below stairs, but she was Alice, Alice Meynell, and she made sure her presence was remembered as she and Ralph travelled the spas and resorts of Europe. She even discovered that distance lent her an extra sheen of myth and glamour. When she was in London, she planned her assaults on the soirées and dances with military precision. Arriving *here*. Not being *there*. Shamelessly flirting. Yes, she decided as she lay on her bed, it was more than ever necessary that she remain entirely Alice Meynell, and put a stop to these jowls which reminded her of the dreadful, dragged-down features of her ghastly, deceiving aunt.

Invercombe was dark, quiet. Shivering slightly from the

coldness of the floor, she crossed to her portmanteau and breathed open the locks and removed the stuffed pages of a fat notebook. In the electric glow of the table lamp, she spread its pages, which were torn, folded to near-separation, incomplete and stained—like a guildsman's book of spells, but snatched, borrowed, copied or found at small or large cost—across her bed. Alice's own neatly slanted green-inked handwriting mingled with the browned scribblings of men long dead, and scraps of eye-straining small print, and curls of hieroglyph, and fragments of strange illustration.

Through the night she considered questions and impossibilities. She breathed fragments of spells which caused the pages, many of which were infused with the remnants of aether through thumbprints and spillages, to rustle and stir. Oh, that they might all knit into a single magic carpet to bear her and Ralph and their troubles away! But instead she settled on something from an incomplete glossary; a small addition to the armoury of charms and spells which filled her portmanteau and might—no, *would*, for belief was always important—chase those sagging obscenities on her jawline away. And there was a correspondence in her being here at the edge of the very tidal estuary where the glossary assured her the thing she needed could actually be found. Reassembling her notebook, closing her portmanteau, she pulled on boots and her warmest cloak and headed down through the dark house. She spent a few minutes in the library, flicking through hand-tinted pages of bivalves and molluscs until she came to the entry she was looking for and tore it out, and left the house by a side doorway.

Invercombe's grounds were still filled with shadow. Only the weathertop had caught a little of the early light; it gleamed through the bare specimen trees as she descended the terraces where flagstones glistened with incipient ice. A strangely pleasant scent came from a dark green patch of what might otherwise have been merely grass. On impulse, Alice stooped to fan it with her fingers and the dew which dripped from their tips tasted sharply sweet, and here, at the far end of which sallow walk and the flatter expanse of the pleasure grounds, the pathways from the garden joined, leading through a gate past the mosaic depths of the seapool which was replenished with salt water, as she understood it, by hidden sluices from the surge of sea against the cliffs of Clarence Cove beyond Durnock Head. Walking briskly on around the looming headland, she discovered that the bigger rocks towards the Bristol Channel were dusted with snow—in the vague gloom, they looked like iced buns—and that the tide was out and the distant lights of the Severn Bridge, a trail of fragile arms like floating jellyfish, were still twinkling.

The image of the particular shell was clear in her mind, but the real life of the shore was messy and slippery and smelly. She unfolded a small steel knife from the pocket of her cloak and plunged her hand into a rockpool, which proved far colder and deeper than she'd imagined. When she lifted the first creature out, her sleeve wet and her fingers dripping, she saw from the different banding of its shell that it wasn't *Cardium glycymeris*—the mollusc she was looking for. Tossing it back, straightening up and wondering how best to continue her search, she noticed something quick and dark scuttling across the rocks. She felt a momentary thread of fear, but the shape was undoubtedly human.

'You there!' she shouted, for it was important when dealing with common people to establish dominance right away. 'What do you think you're doing here?'

The creature straightened. It had some kind of sack in its hand, and was dragging a rake. But it didn't move towards her, and Alice was obliged to risk her ankles on the greenish boulders which separated them.

'What's your name?' She kept up her haughty tone, but still the figure simply watched her. It was wearing a cap and an old and sodden-looking jerkin. More surprisingly, in this frigid weather, it was barefoot. A lad of Ralph's age or perhaps a little younger. Obviously impoverished, and perhaps dumb or simple as well. She was about to give up on the encounter when the creature blinked and licked its lips and straightened up a little more—closer, in fact, to Alice's own height than she'd have guessed—and spoke.

'I'm gathering cockles. My name's Marion Price and this is my bit of shore.'

So it was a girl. No *Mistress* or *Marm*. No curtsey. And *my bit of shore*, as if she owned the place.

'My name is Greatgrandmistress Alice Meynell. I'm from the big house—'

'Invercombe.'

Interrupting, even. But Alice persisted and unfolded the plate she'd torn from the book of shorelife to show the particular species of mollusc.

'Well? Do you think you'll be able to help?'

'That's a beady oyster. We generally throw them away.'

'I need one like this—see. The book calls them blood pearls.'

'Oh?' The shoregirl pursed her lips. They and her cheeks were reddened from the wind and the cold, although the effect was one for which many a grandmistress would have striven. 'You'll be disappointed if you want to make jewels of them. They don't last, although the children play with them happily enough.'

As if she were not still a child herself! But, even before Alice had had a chance to assure her that the blood pearl's very friability was the reason she wanted one, the shoregirl was hopping in a zigzag over rocks which would have shredded Alice's own feet to bone.

'You collect shells?'

'Cockles. We boil them up and sell them up along the market at Luttrell for about three shilling a bucket. We keep most of the weed to make laver bread.'

'You *eat* seaweed?'

'Of course.' Girl and woman studied each other from across the rockpool over which they were crouching, both equally amazed. 'You've never tried laver bread?'

Alice smiled and shook her head. 'Where are you from? Is there a village nearby?'

'It's called Clyst. It's just around that bit of headland. I live there with my mother and father. I have a brother. I have . . .' The shoregirl paused. 'One sister.'

Amid fronds of weed and the pulsing mouths of anemones, the girl's starfish fingers moved.

'And you do this every morning? Collecting cockles?'

'Not every morning. We do it whenever there's enough light and the tide's right.'

What a life! Dragged in and out across this estuary like a bit of flotsam.

'Now *this* . . .' The girl prised the shell off, lifted it dripping into the air with blued and wrinkled fingertips. Definitely *Cardium glycymeris,* but, split open with a quick twist of her stubby knife, there was no blood pearl inside.

'Does your family have a guild?'

'. . . Of course.' A slight pause in the wanderings of her fingers.

Alice understood. Here in the west, even the shoremen and coracle builders imagined themselves guildsmen. What light there was glowed up from the chilly water and across the girl's face, which had an unrippled stillness itself as she worked, deep and intent. Alice found her strange accent, her animal quiet, pleasantly soothing. A few more beady oysters sacrificed their lives. The hiss of the tide was getting louder.

'Shouldn't we be going? Isn't there somewhere further up the shore?'

'This is the best place. We've a few minutes yet.'

Another split, another fruitless mouth. Then, just as they were being surrounded by runners of tidal water, the girl extracted a bigger oyster. Quickly split, it revealed a wet ruby on its living tongue. Shoregirl and greatgrandmistress shared a glance of triumph.

'Is one enough?'

'It'll have to be.' The tide was chuckling around them. The shoregirl was already turning and picking up her sack and rake. 'No. Wait!'

The girl paused, and Alice considered her as she stood there barefoot in her ragged coat and the waters rushed between them. She had an odd feeling that this shoregirl might just add something to the workings of Invercombe. A little grit in the mill, most likely, but perhaps that was what the place needed. Having to cope with a raw new undermaid would be a suitably awkward challenge for Steward Dunning.

'How much did you say you got paid for a bucket of boiled cockles?'

'On a good day, three shilling.'

'And how many of those sacks does it take to fill up a pot?'

'Twelve or so.'

'I'll make sure you're paid twice that much if you come and work at Invercombe.'

Putting down her sack, the shoregirl wiped her hand on the side of her coat and stuck it out. Alice, as the tide drowned the rockpool and raced over their feet, was too surprised not to shake it.

III

On Noshiftday morning Steward Dunning sent word that she wished to see Marion Price. Outside the office door at the far end of a low whitewashed corridor, Marion corrected the straightness of her starched linen cap.

'Come in! You *are* out there, aren't you?'

She entered a small, cluttered room.

'Shut the door. Chairs are for sitting on, you know.'

Marion, who was certain she'd clanged one bucket too many or unwittingly ignored one or another of the endless instructions and prohibitions which were framed on the walls of the servants' halls, was determined to take her dismissal from Invercombe with some dignity and good grace. Things which she'd always taken for granted—the judging of each day by the smell and the feel of the dawn, the seasonal interlocking of tasks and trades, the coming and the going of catches and tides—were already starting to seem remote and bizarre. Here at this house, everything was so devoted to making each day the same, and she'd never been so well fed, or kept so warm, or realised that her existence counted for so little. Still, she tried to keep what she hoped was an appropriately solemn expression on her face as the steward sighed and her coppery, silver-threaded hair bobbed as she shook her head.

'It's possible,' she was saying, 'that I've been a little hard on you, girl. Of course, I didn't *ask* to have you taken on. My guess is that you had no particular desire to work here, either.'

'I've done my best, Mistress. I'm sorry that hasn't been good enough.'

'Now, now. Wait. You're not here so I can tell you *off*.'

'Mistress . . . ?'

'Being shorefolk, I don't suppose you've given much thought to a life in service. For me, it was what I always expected. The Dunnings have been in service in the big houses since my great-great-grandfather came here as a bondsman. Does that surprise you?'

'I'd never thought, Mistress.'

'There are still people who think us Negroes shouldn't be working as guildsfolk. In places like London they'll even preach it from the pulpits of churches.' Her round lips thinned. 'But anyway, you seem bright and capable enough. Fact is, I need all the help I can get to keep this place going . . .'

Marion's gaze strayed around the room as Steward Dunning talked about this and that aspect of Invercombe. The walls were covered with the usual framed needlepoint injunctions—A WELL RUN HOUSE SCARCELY NEEDS TENDING. DO NOTHING SLIPSHOD—and the steward's desk was awash with notepads and inkblocks and unspiked invoices, and a bean-shaped object of a kind which Marion had occasionally found in her wanderings along the shore. The children called them kidney beans, although they obviously weren't.

'You're not listening!'

'What? I'm sorry, Mistress. It's just—'

'Never mind. Maybe one day you'll rise to cook or steward. If that's what you want—and if you learn to say *pardon* instead of *what*.' She smiled. 'Fact is—and this isn't to go past these walls—the greatgrandmistress and her lad make an odd pair. Coming here out of nowhere and with no other staff and so little warning. So much money, all that travelling, and what have they got . . . ?'

Marion tried to consider this odd question. The fact was, she hadn't seen the greatgrandmistress since that day on the shore, nor the son who was also apparently staying here. 'Everything?'

'Girl,' the steward didn't even shake her head, 'there's no need to try to be clever. You must have heard how ill the lad is.' She sighed. 'And this, by the way . . .' Her pearly fingertips traced the kidney bean. 'This thing you've been staring at when you should have been listening to me—do you know what it is?'

Marion shook her head.

'It's from the Fortunate Isles. These beans are seeds and they drop from the palms and are bore all this way across the Boreal Sea.'

Thinking of white beaches, densely coloured flowers, Marion touched the kidney bean. This, she imagined, must be what a guildsperson must feel when they touch one of their own many strange devices—chalcedonies, whisperjewels, painstones, the spinet keys of a reckoning engine, numberbeads . . .

'Some final conditions,' the steward said. 'Firstly, this house runs on mutual respect and duty. Every single saying which cook has had framed—and which I've noticed you smirking at, by the way—is entirely true. And I expect all my staff to spend time with their families on Noshiftdays.'

'I haven't had a Noshiftday off, Mistress.'

'Well, you have one now. Wilkins has a wagon going up to Luttrell in about half an hour. See that you're on it, and in your best skirt and pinafore . . .' The steward's eyes travelled up and down. 'Remember, you're a representative of this house, and that people will look at you and imagine, may the good Elder help them, that you're the best we at Invercombe can manage. Your family—I'm sure they're wondering how you're getting on. Now you can go back to Clyst and tell Bill Price that Cissy Dunning sends her regards and says you're doing well enough, even if you still have to buck up your ideas a bit, can't you?'

'Yes, Mistress.' Curtseying, Marion realised that she hadn't done so when she'd first entered the steward's presence. 'Thank you.'

'Oh, one more thing.' The steward slid open a bottom drawer in her desk and wheezed open a tin. She held out a brown envelope. 'You might as well take this.'

'Mistress?'

'It's your wages, for goodness sake!'

* * *

It felt colder than Marion had expected as she sat on a bench at the back of a produce wagon with an assortment of stable lads, apprentice gardeners and undermaids, and the road beyond the estate was deeply puddled and the bare trees were dripping. Yet if it had rained at Invercombe, it had happened so stealthily that she hadn't noticed. She gazed back towards the weathertop. The idea that it could change the weather had been a story she'd been brought up on, then cast aside as a pleasant fantasy.

Set down at the roadside by Wilkins, Marion headed straight for the shore. After Invercombe's fiddly sense of things constantly in need of doing, she felt her spirits physically lifting. Here, if you yelled and waved your arms, the only creatures you startled were terns and gulls. Whooping, leaping, pausing only to drag off her new boots and socks, and then again to tear off her cap, Marion sprinted through the freezing, flecking mud. The tide was a neap one, big and cold and quick, hissing away from her even as she ran towards it, and at last her feet were in it, and it was sweet, effortless agony after the pinch of those boots.

She searched amid the rockpools for a kidney bean. The odds were impossible, but she was an inveterate shore-searcher. She'd found pennies, serviceable washpans, skirthoops, brooches, gluts of seacoal, fluted bones, fantastic scraps of machinery, lurid heaps of cuckoo-wrack. Once, washed down from Severn Bridge, had come the huge and hairy corpse of one of the gargoyles which crawled along those distant gantries as they endlessly painted them grey. But all she found today were a few scraps of prettily corroded glass. Straightening up, feeling the slap in her skirt pocket of the envelope Steward Dunning had given her, she quickened her pace towards the hunched and scattered cottages of Clyst.

The Price cottage's windows peeped beneath a low roof which was part slate and part moss. Ducking to save her head on the low lintel, Marion stepped inside. Mam was boiling up some underwear, raising it with a spoon as if to see if it was done. Then she saw Marion.

'I knew it!' Mam exclaimed, waving a steaming vest. 'You've got yourself sacked!'

It took Marion some time to reassure her mother that she really was still employed at Invercombe. Then Mam saw the new boots Marion had strung around her neck.

'What happened to your old ones?'

Marion shrugged, remembering the face cook had pulled as she tossed them towards the fire. 'I keep them for wetter weather now.'

'Wetter? But we've been half-flooded!'

'Anyway, I have to spend most of my time inside.'

' 'Course you do. Now go and get your dad and brother and sister for me, will you?'

There was a knack to recognising people across the shore's shining expanse. It came from the manner of a walk, their many different stoops and limps. And there was her sister Denise, dragging her sack and bending with that sense of surprised distaste. And there was Owen, poling across the shining mud on a wooden sledge known as a mudhorse. Marion cupped her hands to her mouth and gave an ululating shriek.

After their fishy hugs and expressions of surprise at how she looked, the three Price siblings found their father up by the little creek, polishing and restringing the fine blue glass floats of which he was so proud. By now a scatter of villagers and children had gathered around Marion. *Is there lots of gold in the house to polish?* someone asked. *Been learnt spells? Is that steward really an escaped bondswoman? How much have you nicked?*

This, Dad announced once they were back inside the cottage, was a special occasion. He beckoned Marion to the scullery, and she held up the boards over the pit where he kept his small trade. Unstoppering one of the brown rows of label-less bottles with his teeth, Dad tested it under his nose to check that the sea hadn't got into it. Sitting afterwards at the table, eating fried laver bread and herring, they all grew a little tipsy. Marion had never noticed before how grey their bread was, nor how diligently Dad picked at his teeth. She'd been sure enough of her family's needs to accept the greatgrandmistress's surprising offer, and had told herself that it was just another job, but being a maid at a big house seemed like an identity her family and the people of Clyst wanted to brand her with—and it wasn't *her*.

'All right, darling . . . ?' Mam's hand, gloved in calluses, kneaded her wrist.

'Your glass is empty, lass.' Dad brandished the bottle. '*That's* the trouble.'

'I'm fine. Did I tell you, by the way, that I've been paid?'

'Well then . . .' Dad banged down the bottle and rubbed his hands.

Marion knew it was the family's money. Of course, it would have been nice to go to Luttrell's only row of proper shops and buy Mam a new headscarf and Dad a cigar in a silver tube and Denise some perfume and Owen one of those compasses he was always eyeing—but she had a better proposal. In fact, it was the reason she'd accepted that guildsmistress's offer on the shore so readily. As she took the envelope out and laid it on the table, it felt as solid and certain as the weight of the money itself.

'I think,' Marion announced, 'that we should put this towards getting Sally a proper gravestone.'

She knew instantly from their looks that her family had never imagined such a thing.

'That's a *lovely* idea,' Mam murmured, squeezing Marion's wrist again. 'Quite, quite . . . Lovely.'

'The fact is,' Dad said after the long pause which followed, 'the whole thing's already sorted.'

'*What* has been sorted?' Marion was surprised at the harshness of her own voice.

'We've signed our Owen up for the Mariners Guild, just like I've always promised!'

'You're not upset, are you?' Marion was asked by her sister Denise as they shuffled about afterwards in the low space above the kitchen where they had both slept.

'Not at all.' It was true. Buying Owen a proper apprenticeship was the best possible investment the whole family could have made. And they never talked about Sally, even though she'd only been gone a year.

'And *I'm* going to be a proper seamstress. Did I tell you that? Nan Osborne's promised to train me up, and she can get me in at this guild-accredited academy in Bristol next year.'

'That's a lovely idea,' Marion said absently as she worked open a drawer and found it filled with her sister's things.

'You off with the quality at Invercombe and weeing into porcelain—who'd have thought it!'

'It should have been you, Denise. I could still try and put in a word.'

'Can you see me traipsing around with a duster and curtseying! But I *do* like your blouse . . .' Denise bustled forward. 'The way it's darted and tightened here and here.' Her hands brushed possessively over her sister's bosom.

'Really? I just thought it was too tight.'

Denise's startling blue eyes gazed at her sister with something briefly akin to wonderment. Her face, with its fine, high cheekbones, was flushed from the rum and being out on the shore, then framed with torrenting curls of blondish-brown hair. It was, Marion thought, the most beautiful face she had ever seen. At least, until she'd seen Invercombe's new greatgrandmistress. 'You still don't know much about the world, do you, little sis?'

By now, Marion had forgotten what it exactly was which she'd been searching for amongst her old things. Denise would have either thrown it away or appropriated it anyway.

'Any old scraps and buttons, Marion. Bits of ribbon like the one you've got unravelling from your dress. I know what those big places are like—useful stuff always getting thrown away.'

'I'll keep a look out.' Although, as one of cook's notices pointed out, BORROWING THINGS FROM THE HOUSE IS SIMPLY THIEVING.

'But if there's one thing above all, Marion, that you can help me with . . .' Denise looked surprisingly serious as she crouched by the tiny window and beckoned Marion to join her. She opened her jaw and prodded her fingers inside her mouth.

'Chun ya shuee?'

Blinking against a surprisingly rank smell, Marion peered down. Her sister's back teeth were black as lumps of jet. Denise had always had a taste for sweet things. A particular passion had been Bolt's Thunderbolts, huge gobstoppers layered like onions which changed colour as you cracked through them. Smear the red layers across your lips and it looked as if you were wearing lipstick.

'If you could let me have some proper toothpaste,' Denise said, swallowing. 'You know, the white stuff that smells like medicine. I'm sure that would sort it out. You *can* get me some, can't you?'

Marion realised that her return home to Clyst had turned to-day into something approximating to the family Noshiftdays which she'd read about in newspapers. That, or the rum. For Mam was half-asleep before the fire, Dad was humming and bumbling about without achieving anything noticeable and Denise, inspired by that blouse, was doing some vigorous taking-in. Marion found even the normally industrious Owen sitting on an upturned tin bath in their open-sided lean-to, staring towards the incoming tide.

'Congratulations,' she said.

He glanced up at her. 'Do you really mean it?'

'Of course I do. Now move up.'

It was growing dark. It had been, in fact, one of those days which had never been fully light—at least outside Inver-combe. Jewelled and grainy, the lights of the ships were glowing. Trade heading in towards Bristol, or out towards the entire world. To be a mariner on such a vessel, braided and buttoned and precise as the furnishing of its decks, had always been her big brother's dream.

'Have you been inducted?'

'No, but Dad really *has* signed the papers. They give you this yellow carbon copy which he says he's going to get framed. I can't thank you enough, sis.'

'It's not *my* money. Dad's been saving for years.'

'Well . . .' Owen laughed and shook his head. 'That's what he's always told us.'

In every sense, Owen was the biggest of the family; prone to plumpness even on the sparse meals they often ate, with a broad face, ruddy cheeks and a shock of sticking-up brown hair. It was hard to imagine him stuffed into gold braid and epaulettes, but he talked excitedly about his new guild, and he insisted that, whilst he would always protect its secrets, he would never forget where he came from.

'You do believe me, don't you, sis? I mean, I really won't change. I'll still eat eel cake and hate the bloody Excise Men.

I'll still throw plait-bread into the waves to keep the sea from wanting too many souls.'

'You're my brother, Owen. You're a Price. When I have to remind you of that, I'll get an oar and bash you over the head.'

It was easy to laugh into the darkness, even as the rattle of the wind on the roof became the stronger clatter of rain.

'Just wait, love,' Mam whispered, pulling Marion close as the whole family gathered in the darkness to wave her off. 'We'll get something nice fixed up for our Sally one day.'

Marion headed along the coast road as the rain worsened to sleet. There was, she knew, a quicker pathway around the headland which led by a gate up to Invercombe's gardens, but it was never a route she could have taken, either as undermaid or shore-girl. The road tonight was awash. Keeping to its bank, slipping occasionally, she followed it until it met with the smaller lane which led towards Invercombe's gatehouse. For a while, the sleet drove heavier than ever through the shrieking trees. Then, as if by the turning of a switch, it ceased.

IV

Exactly ten o'clock on a warm March morning at Invercombe in the ninety-ninth of this Age of Light, and each chime and bell and gong filled a separate silence in the house until another took up the long celebration of the hour. At first, Alice had latched on to this irregularity as something she might exploit. Now, she'd come to enjoy it. Ten o'clock and she spilled the purple-stained paper bag of hellebore berries into an engraved white retort from her portmanteau. Ten o'clock and she muttered the spell, and smiled as she watched them fatten and turn a glossy, appetising sugar-red. Ten o'clock, and she put on her sleek olivine coat and checked her face for the last time in her mirror and smiled at the renewed firmness of her jaw.

Outside, on her way to find Ralph on the south-west facing patio of the top terrace where he now liked to sit, she was amused to notice that it was barely half-past nine by the shadow which the sundial cast across the warm red brick of the wall above the main hall.

At the sound of his mother's footsteps, Ralph swung the circled image of his telescope away from the hectic stirring of a hedge where he had been watching the mating of a pair of sparrows and let the amplified gaze of his new possession, a genuine mariner's optic which Weatherman Ayres had recently given him, focus on a silvered fringe of hair.

'That's not quite such a nice thing to do, darling. Looking at people as if they're mere objects.'

'No?' Blinking, he removed his eye from the eyepiece.

'Well. Never mind.' Flicking back the rugs which covered his legs, his mother perched on the edge of his lounger. '*Such* a pain. I've got to see people in Bristol.'

Ralph nodded. It was a different world out there beyond these gardens and his library. He thought of his father, of the smoky London smell which came with him down the lines as they talked on the telephone, and bought the tickly urge of a new bout of coughing.

'I must be going.' Standing up, she gently kissed him. Nothing ever touched her. She was always so new and fresh, and she looked lovely as ever to him today as she strode off along the sunlit terrace where the spilling heads of giant bluebells nodded in the breeze as if striking their stamens to join with the chiming of all the clocks inside the house.

Alone again, he reapplied his eye to his telescope and drew the tripoded instrument in a blurring sweep across the valley. The air was astonishingly light, and this device, aligned and machined according to the principles of pure optics, was, Ralph thought as his gaze followed the gold-green stems of the lantern-flowers and the lactescent globes of moonivy, probably the only unaethered object in all of Invercombe. He had arrived, he was sure, at a new state of clarity here. For that, and for his improving health, he was entirely grateful to this new house. Weary as he had been at first, the place had seemed just the termination of another journey, and, as always, an opportunity for more reading and research. Knowledge, certainty, science had long been his bulwarks against fever, and they were also the surest evidence he had that the world—the real one of which, between fusses with blankets and bath chairs and trunks and railway stations, he had seen so little—really existed.

It had been maps which first drew Ralph. He had been an explorer as he retraced he and his mother's journeys across the dotted frontiers of Europe, then the inland reaches of Africa and the white boundaries of the Ice Cradle until a fresh fever took him and he fell into the *Terra Incognita* of nightmare. After that

bout, he turned instead towards the natural world. Everything in
life, he began to understand, was part of one intricate machine.
The petals of a flower had their relationship with the pollinating
bee which dwelt in its hive amid geometries which could also
be found in the crystals of rocks. As he turned the sleek, heavy
pages of the large expensive books his mother bought for him
and peeled back hazy layers of protective tissue to gaze down
at beautifully coloured and annotated plates, he often felt as if
some real part of him had left his bed and was wandering an incredible garden. This escape, where everything could be studied
and explained, was the exact opposite of his deliriums. Even his
own body, the very illness which kept him weak, was part of this
same pattern, and was thus neither wonderful nor terrible, but a
simple truth. *Primary pulmonary tuberculosis*; it was there in
the butterfly wings of the flayed lungs of its victims.

Chaos—unreason—rather than his illness, became the
thing to be kept at bay, and he hunted it down with the selfish
rigour of an invalid. He soon threw aside the need of the hand
of God the Elder to wind the mechanism which drove every
deed of nature, and with it the Biblical idea of a primal garden
where every species and genus had once supposedly thrived.
To him, Eden now existed only as a jumbled myth which was
entirely inappropriate to this Age of Light, although the image
of the first two humans, shy as fauns and naked even of their
fig leaves, was somehow harder to erase. He still found himself
gazing sometimes at old prints of Adam and Eve standing beside the fruit-burdened Tree of Knowledge. They were hairless
in a way he knew, from veiled references in the appendices and
footnotes of books on physiology, adult humans never were,
although he'd never yet found any illustrations against which
he could properly compare the things which were happening to
his own body. They often possessed navels, too, which was
surely wrong in the circumstances, and Eve also had breasts,
and nipples which she didn't always fully cover with a casually
raised hand. Sometimes, between her legs, there was even the
glimpse of a cleft. With his books put aside and the lights
turned out and the fire flickering and the treacly darkness of
spells and laudanum surging within him, she often still seemed
to hang there before Ralph like the reproachful ghost of his lost
beliefs. She sometimes even came to his bed to join him in an

embrace as the sweet ache in his belly brought the friction of release.

But now that he was at Invercombe, everything was clear. Here, and even though many of his precious books had gone missing in transit, he was provided with a library which was even better than the huge one at Walcote, the shelves of which were crowded with far too many novels and bound annual editions of society magazines for his taste. He'd known from the instant that he opened his first book on avian life here that it had never been opened before, let alone read. He was reminded of a distant memory of the time before his illness, and of being the first to walk across a white and seemingly infinite field of snow. True, the books at Invercombe were a little old, but Ralph knew that knowledge was unchanging. And there was an odd feeling—most unscientific, but still heartening—that these pages had been waiting for him, just as had this whole house. And he could tell that his mother was as excited by Invercombe as well, with its antique reckoning engine still apparently functioning somewhere down in the bowels of the house he hadn't yet reached, and its role in the development of his guild, and even a weathertop to keep the worst vagaries of the climate at bay. Something in him was healing by simply being here. Sometimes, heartbeat by heartbeat, breath by breath, new page by new page, Ralph could literally feel his body reknitting itself from disconnected islands of pain.

To get downstairs to the library, and unaided, was surely much like the proposal which Guildsmaster Columbus had once presented to Queen Isabella about the fabled continents of Thule. There were, as he walked out from his bedroom for the first time into the swaying emptiness of the main landing, the same familiar landmarks sunk beyond the horizon, which tunnelled on in the wan light for as far as he could see. It took days of retreats and setbacks to get further, but to Ralph it all remained one seamless voyage. Just as he reached the turn which had seemed impossible at the start, there were new obstacles which no cartographer could have anticipated. Like the edge of the world, he found himself facing the vast fan of the best stairs. But he wasn't deterred. Of course, there were murmurs of dissent from his mother, but Columbus had had the same from his crew. Stair by stair, he descended, until finally, more than a shifterm after he had first set out, Ralph found himself standing triumphant at the doorway of a library which was fully as beautiful as he had dared imagine.

For several days, the very act of sitting there and being surrounded by those tiers of unopened spines was enough. But slowly, his sense of himself expanded to possess this marvelous room. And climbing from bed, getting dressed and then heading off along the gallery and down those stairs was Ralph's equivalent of a long country walk. Sometimes his mother even let him set out alone, although he suspected that she hung back just out of sight in case he suffered a surge of dizziness. There was often this slight sense at Invercombe, in whispers, plays of shadow, the indrawn breath of the salt air, of being watched and followed.

Guiding the telescope, Ralph's circular gaze encompassed the thickening fruit of Invercombe's citrus grove. He could almost smell the ripening oranges and lemons which the weathertop nourished with warmth in the garden's most sheltered spot. Then up. Sometimes, he did that. Just let it fly and settle. Plants of incredible scent and power—red and white and green and purple, or all and none of those colours twirled together at once—glowed and frolicked from their beds. Previously, Ralph had had little concern for the wonders of plantsmasters' art, but now he was filled with a new curiosity. After all, and no matter how far the final creation might deviate from its origins, each had its roots in some natural equivalent. Cedarstone, he imagined, must surely contain elements of the redwoods of Thule. Sallow might once have come from the common parsley, and perhaps then also the rock samphire. Then there were the creatures which arrived, special delivery, stamped and sealed *Live Cargo, Addressee Only*, from the offices of the Arthropod Branch of the Beastmasters' Guild. Bees, flies and wasps were fine for commoner blooms, but when it came to the fiery tongues of the pyrepoppies, the trumpets of lanternflowers or fruiting moonivy, the insects of common creation simply weren't up to the job. These giant insects, mammoth things, furred and tusked, gaudily striped, massively prosboscised, were commonly known as buzzbugs.

Ralph swung his vision across a blur of treetops. And here was a hedge, and some grass with the dew still glittering.

Then something blue and white. Striped, in fact. Wondering what aethered extravagance he'd now alighted on, Ralph drew in the focus. The stripes became sharper, then vanished, then snapped into view again. Cotton; he could see the weave, and Ralph inched his telescope until he saw a boot, a hem, and that striped blue blouse again.

It was one of the maids. The sudden movements, the extending of that crease across her blouse, were caused by her bending and straightening as she hung out washing. Bit by bit, circular image by image, he formed a picture of her. Dark hair, almost black, but catching in the sunlight with serrations of gold. It was full and thick, and cut to just below the shoulder, although he guessed from the repeated flash of her hand as she pushed it out of the way that she'd have wished it shorter. He couldn't see her face—just the curve of her jaw and the glimpsed lobe of her ear which her hair quickly curtained again, but it was pleasant just to watch her. The items she was stabbing out on the line remained a white blur, but part of him sensed that it would be good to study them as well, discern their nature and stitching just as he had the criss-cross of those pinafore straps, and the sense you got of the shape of her shoulder blades moving beneath. But to concentrate on the washing would have meant losing focus on the girl herself. As another of Invercombe's clocks started ringing, Ralph felt more and more of his consciousness passing from his blanket-shrouded body, down his telescope, riding the light.

As well as on Noshiftdays, Steward Dunning now allowed Marion to go home on most mornings for an early breakfast at Clyst. Today, she'd awoken before four, dressed and walked swiftly out of the estate and along the main road and then across the shore to the family cottage, where the Prices were just rising.

Oh. It's you—as if she'd simply come from upstairs.

Then—*Isn't this the shift you get paid?*

The money in her pay envelopes seemed to have shrunk. As well as Owen's apprentice uniform, there were textbooks, special pens, special inks; special everything. The compasses she'd admired in shop windows at Luttrell weren't apparently good enough for a genuine Mariner. The pointer of the device he finally purchased swam in a sea of fluids deep enough to

bath a baby. Set with spells and calibrations, it twitched like a
live fish. Denise, too, was needing financial support to keep
on Nan Osborne's best side. And Marion hadn't been able to
bring herself to take one of the fat tubes of Pilton's Universal
Tooth Whitening from the sinks of the servants' washroom.

The hour after breakfast before Owen set out for the
Mariners' Halls at Luttrell was the time when he was supposed to study. One of the first mornings she'd returned home,
Marion had found him sitting outside in the open lean-to. It
was before dawn, freezing cold, and she'd been about to tell
him that there was surely a better place than this to work when
she saw that his big face was gleaming with tears.

'I'm useless, Marion! I can't even remember port from
bloody starboard. This . . .' He'd held up a page which looked
as if it had been used to quench his sobbing. 'It's not even
English!'

Marion prised the paper from his fingers. It was the text of
a spell.

'Owen, I shouldn't be seeing this.'

Dad knew a thing or two about navigation, and had certainly
picked up a few spells, but he would, Marion was certain, have
been horrified if Owen had asked him for help. She tilted the
page towards the fluttering lamp and tried to say what she
thought she saw, cleared her throat, then tried again. That morning, mornings after, as Steward Dunning, and although she
didn't ask the exact reason, came to understand that Marion's
presence at home was important, Marion found the appropriate
manuals on Phrase and Shape and Syntax amid the disorder of
Owen's satchel and, after striving to make sense of them herself, did her best to explain them to him.

The tides came and went across the estuary. The overwinter-
ing birds left. And Marion learned something of the referencing
of maps and the plotting of courses and the origins of terms like
fid and *buoy*. So, eventually, as their fingers went blue and their
books tried to fly away from them, did Owen. In particular,
there were knots to be studied. Piecing together the complex di-
agrams, her fingers trembling and itching and blistering as she
strained to get some scraps of old and tarry cordage to perform
the acts she willed with her eyes, Marion tried to get Owen to
understand. There were huge, decorative knots like golden

wasp nests, and there were knots so small and delicate that jewellers used them to secure strings of pearls. Then there were windknots. Without proper supplies of aether, they were particularly dry and difficult, and the endless uttering of spells hurt their throats as much as tying hurt their fingers, but sometimes there was enough residue of aether left in some ordinary bit of rope for the air around them to tense as if stirred by the passage of something huge and unseen.

It was a tiring way for her to begin a day, and it was a long walk to get back to Invercombe in time to attend prayers with cook and the rest of the maids. Even now, as Marion hung out the smalls which Steward Dunning insisted that, as part of her emphasis on self-reliance and discipline, every servant girl wash herself, her head still swam with mariner's spells. Those gently lifting sheets could be mizzens and topgallants; her vests were spitsails. She felt her neck prickle. There was a sense of lightness like the lifting of sweat in sunlight. Although the feeling wasn't entirely unpleasant, she was almost sure that she was being watched.

Up on the gantry of his weathertop, Weatherman Ayres caught a brassy flash. Looking down, he saw that Master Ralph was out on the top terrace, busily watching the Price girl from Clyst as she hung out her knickers on the laundry lawn, and he felt gladder than ever for giving the lad his old telescope. Fingering the dents of a ribbonspell, thinking warmly sexual thoughts of Cissy Dunning, he studied the Somerset landscape beyond Invercombe's grounds, which was still pooled in mist whilst Invercombe already basked in sunlight. Now, after years of waiting, he had a chance to stir this machine to its full powers and prove to Invercombe's steward that he could bring Invercombe properly to life, and perhaps gain her love in the process. Sunlight gleamed across his bald head and the weathertop's dome as he checked temperatures and barometric pressures and considered the correct phrasing of the spell he would use to edge away the coming bank of cloud. It glinted on Invercombe's many widows as ten o'clock finally ended in one last *bong*.

V

There had been some minor disappearances in the shifting of their possessions to Invercombe, especially of Ralph's books. Although, with the considerable contents of Invercombe's library to explore, he didn't seem to be missing them, Alice told Steward Dunning that, seeing as she was going to Bristol today, she would spare a few minutes to sort out the problem.

The Steward had levelled one of her looks. 'These things take their own time, Mistress.'

Oh, do they, Alice had thought. Then the train from Luttrell had been ridiculously late. In fact, the one that finally arrived at the little local station, in its livery and route, bore no obvious relationship with anything on the timetable. Still, they found a nice carriage for her, and the coffee she was served was sweet and strong and darkly aromatic, and she strode out from Templemeads and through the strange city feeling busy, happy, energised. Predictably, the knobbly phallus of the clock tower of Bristol Main Post Office announced a significantly different time on each of its six facades.

Coloured tiles inside and a huge waiting room. Long waiting benches. A smell of rubber bands. Trapped pigeons fluttering. She went straight up to the first counter and rapped hard on the bell, feigning impatience as she fiddled with the encrusted guild brooch she'd been sure to pin to her lapel.

'We shut at one, you know.'

'That's all right.' Alice glanced up at another huge clock, which hung its hands in an understandable impression of defeat. 'I don't have long anyway.'

'I'll have to get someone else to help you. This isn't my department, I'm afraid.'

And so on.

'Yes, Greatgrandmistress. *Most* unfortunate. We *do* understand. Have you a record of each mislayal? And do you have your petitioner's copy of form LIF 271/A?'

And so forth.

The Postal Guild was closely allied with the Telegraphers. Although the two organisations had gone their separate ways since the traumatic turning of this Age of Light, Alice could have reeled off a dozen names of senior guildsmasters with a foot in both camps. But she'd discovered long ago that it was useless to approach these great men about the work done far beneath them. Better by far to speak direct to the clerk, handyman or mechanic who could personally deal with the thing which concerned you, and to apply your immense leverage lightly. Direct threats of expulsion or advancement only left these creatures flustered, and Alice, although she believed herself immune from common vanity, nevertheless felt that she was doing them something of a favour by granting a few minutes of her personal attention.

'It's well after one o'clock now, greatgrandmistress. I most deeply regret that I simply won't be able to process this duplicate retrieval form until we reopen tomorrow morning . . .' In fact, the churches and clocks of Bristol were still busily bonging the hour, but this uppermaster, who was supposedly in charge of lost mail in Invercombe's postal district, was well into his sandwiches when she was shown into his office. The little room stank of potted meat, and apparently it was standard practice here for all of what were referred without any apparent conscious irony as *public services* to take half days on a roster which she suspected was entirely designed to confuse. The uppermaster twirled his carousel of rubber stamps.

He touched—and she really wished that he wouldn't, with those greasy fingers—the duplicate yellow sheets which she'd laboured to have created. Why did he stay here at all, if the place was closing? But she understood guild etiquette. This uppermaster was a sleeve-garter wearer, a wielder of those rubber stamps. It was no use asking him to wade amid catacombs filled with lost post. Anyway, he'd be useless at it. Sighing, still just about smiling, she left him to his lunch, and the empty post office halls to their pigeons.

Outside in the sunlit city, the odours of food mingled with old stone, bad drains, the frank reek of the open public urinals that the men here—and staring over the top at you—seemed suspiciously happy to use. The improbable buildings shouldered up to each other and the trams rattled high overhead and the people bustled, the affluent guildsmistresses mostly in fur coats of such nap and floss that Alice wondered if she shouldn't be feeling cold in her own thinner attire. But it was all for display, just like those incredible glassed-in balconies of billowing coralstone which leaned out from the first floors of houses, where you could see and be seen without the bother of ever getting your shoes dirtied. London, for all its clamour, seemed orderly by comparison, and she missed the certainties of its wide thoroughfares. After Lichfield, after Dudley, after all the many adjustments which she had had to make in her life, Alice liked to think of herself as flexible, but she had to confess that Bristol and the entire west were still taking her by surprise.

She found a cake shop with huge, gravity-defying constructions of spun sugar and whipped cream piled in its windows and went inside and waited, as even greatgrandmistresses must sometimes wait, to be served. The till was a huge instrument, incredibly polished, ringing up each purchase with showy glee, and then there was all the business of wrapping and a fuss over receipts, which were written by hand with tongue-extruding attention, and thumbed into several copies. Alice tried not to remember the duplicate forms at the post office. When it was finally time for her to be served, and once she had made herself understood to the strangely spoken assistant, she chose six individual cream tartlets.

Although it was nothing like as warm here as at Invercombe, many Bristolians were taking lunch in the cathedral square, and, as Alice found a bench beside a tall perilinden tree which was just starting to unfold its silver leaves, she had to admit that there was plenty to see. There were Spaniards and Frenchmen, whom you might notice in London as well, but never quite looking this at home, and many Negroes, and a spidery familiar dancing to a hurdy-gurdy, and glimpses of ships beyond buildings, and the clamour of gulls. As certain as she had ever been in a public place that no one was watching her, Alice laid her cakebox on the bench and unpicked its knot and extracted six glace cherries from their pinnacles of cream. A squirrel slipped down from the perilinden tree and took the offered cherries from her fingers. It nibbled them with a calm delicacy which suggested it had been fed from expensive cakeboxes before, then washed its whiskers and hopped away. Alice unfurled the grease paper package from the pocket of her coat and arranged the six newly red hellebore berries, which looked even brighter and more luscious, in their place on the tartlets. Retying the package, she headed gaily towards Brandon Hill, where Grandmistress Celia Raithby lived.

Alice supposed this business of getting to know people in the west had been unavoidable. She had been to a dance where flocks of ugly children had been allowed to eat and drink with the adults, then to vomit copiously across the parquet. She'd taken dinner with the dashing (or so he thought himself) Master-Enforcer Cornelius Scutt, who pomaded his grey sideburns and thought himself good with the ladies even though he was covered in age spots and was past seventy if he was a day. Doctor and Doctress Foot and the Reverend-Highermaster Humphry Brown, whom she'd thought she shooed away from Invercombe, had also circled and settled back again with the persistence of flies. It was all still somewhat irritating, but Alice knew, as she eyed the tall stalagmite grotto of the frontage of 28 Charlotte Street, that webs of duty and obligation fanned from here in Bristol all the way back through her life.

She wasn't quite sure when she'd first encountered Grandmistress Celia Raithby here in the west, but had come to detect something beyond dumb friendliness in the grandmistress's manner during a recent afternoon soirée in the green rooms at

Hotwells, which she still hadn't been able to get to the root of until Celia beckoned her away beneath the privacy of a leaning palm.

'So, so *nice* that us two girls are living close to each other now,' the woman had cooed. '*Great*grandmistress. Or perhaps I should say—' And she really had said this, fluttering her fan and expanding her bejewelled décolletage, for she looked the sort to read cheap romantic novels. '—plain old Alice Bowdly!'

Even then, it still hadn't all come back to Alice. After all, Cheryl Kettlethorpe had been as thin as this creature was fat, and it had all been a long time ago.

'Don't you remember, that pact we made as we sat beside Stow Pool?'

Of course, there had been no pact, but the likes of Celia— or Cheryl, as she now remembered—always liked to wrap up their demands in paddings of coy sentiment.

'We won't talk about it now. Not *here*, eh? But I think we girls should get together and have a proper chat. Oh, don't look so *worried*, dear . . .' She'd tapped her nose in that way which westerners liked doing. 'I'm the absolute byword for discretion.'

Now, Alice inspected the tiled surround of the front arch for something resembling a bell pull. All she could find was what looked like a brass cheese grater. She pressed the button beneath it, and was somewhat startled when a metallic approximation of Celia's voice crackled back at her.

'Do come in.' Something went *thunk*. The big door drifted open. 'Across the hall and you'll see a lift. Take it to the top floor . . .'

A lift—in a private house? But this was the modern Age, and Bristol was awash with electricity from the big dam at Clifton. The hall was all stars and moons, with glimpses through doorways of blotchy red furniture, and more of that cake shop marble. Unless this was all some immense bluff, Celia really had done as well for herself as she liked to pretend. Unnervingly, the lift clattered up beyond the top of the house into greater light, and Alice stepped warily out on to what she supposed was the roof, and was hit by a tempest of colour.

'There you are!' Celia Raithby beckoned Alice from an armchair. 'You've brought something for me!'

'Just a few cakes.' Alice laid the box on a glass table and shrugged off her coat and sat down and waited for her senses to finish reeling. The place was roofed with a tracery set with thousands of panes of multicoloured glass. Beyond, shifting with every slight movement of her head, lay a fragmented Bristol.

'I'm so glad I bought this house,' Celia sighed. 'This rooftop's such a comfort to me. The plantsmasters bring me their latest creations before they're made available to the public at large.'

There were white, dew-brimming, bowl-shaped flowers big enough to wash your face in. Lanternflowers glowed like brands. 'Doesn't it get a little hot here in summer?'

'Oh, no. All the glass is hydraulically removable. We're not quite as backward here in the west as you easterners think . . .'

'And that device on the door?'

'Imagine, to be able to talk to someone at a distance, and then just to hear their voice and no need to worry about whether you've just done your face. I understand the principle could work at longer range as well.' Celia chuckled. 'Just think, the whole world could be chattering away to each other whenever it wanted, instead of us fortunate few with our mirrors and telephone booths. But that would never do, would it?'

Alice had to agree that it probably wouldn't. She'd already gained a rough idea of the route Cheryl Kettlethorpe had taken to get to be Grandmistress Celia Raithby, and now she heard a lot more. Twice married and twice widowed, victor of several of expensive lawsuits against aggrieved relatives, Celia was certainly a fighter, although she hid that as well now as had the giggly young girl whom Alice had once encountered parading the streets of Lichfield in search of needy men. Sex had been the major currency then, and there had been far less flimflam about it, but Celia still seemed to see life in much the same way.

'My husbands, poor things, frankly weren't up to much in *that* department. And there was never the faintest chance of my staying as slim and petite as you still are, my darling. I can read my seamstress's measuring tape as well as the next woman.' She gave her motherly cleavage a pat. 'Secretly, most men yearn for a little extra meat on the bone, even if they're not always quite sure what to do with it. When I saw you, I thought—that's my old friend Alice Bowdly! But then, it can't be—because she hasn't changed! How *do* you do it, darling?'

Alice opened her mouth to say something about a strict diet, exercise, discipline, but Celia was already jingling her bracelets.

'Whatever it is, I couldn't possibly manage it. I'm weak as water when it comes to anything *nice*. And are there or are there not cakes in that box?'

The box fanned out, exhaling scents of sweetness and things dairy.

'We should have a drink as well.' Celia waddled over to a large, softly humming cabinet. Inside were glasses, bottles, trays. Popped, glugged out and fizzing, the wine added its own sweetness to the already cloying air. The wine had the colour of urine, and somehow hinted at the same scent. Here in Bristol, you were never far away from the pissoir. The bottle, Alice noticed, bore no label. Neither had the wine at the dances, and even some she'd inspected in Invercombe's own cellars. What, she decided to ask Celia, was the problem in the west? Was there a shortage of paper and glue because of all the stupid forms and receipts they so favoured? Were the Spaniards and the French ashamed of their produce?

Celia, who'd been avidly studying the cakes on the table, sat back with a look of near surprise dimpling her face. 'You really haven't heard of the small trade?'

'No.' Irritating though this woman was, this wasn't the time to pretend to know things she didn't. 'What is that?'

'Well, *there's* a question and a half . . .' Celia grew almost thoughtful for a few moments. Unspoken phrases played across her nimble red lips. 'It's a question of . . . As a matter of fact, it's quite hard to say exactly . . . But there are *rules*, aren't there? Silly rules—especially as regards the payment of revenue. Not that we shouldn't all pay our taxes. But there are limits, aren't there? After all, the rules wouldn't be so ridiculous in the first place if they didn't expect us to bend them . . .'

Slowly at first, then quickly, the fog was clearing. 'You mean this wine is contraband?'

'Alice!' Celia looked as if she was about to lean across the table and slap her wrist. 'You *do* have the *most* unfortunate way of putting things. Take a piece of advice from me and simply think of it as the small trade.'

Alice nodded. As was often the case, the euphemism told you far more about the subject than did any more direct phrase.

'Where to begin?' Celia's fingers danced across the tartlets. She glanced back towards Alice. 'But I think you should have first pick.'

Alice reached towards the vermicelli and angelica-flecked construction nearest to her, but a quick manoeuvre by Celia's doll-like hands presented her with the one furthest away. 'I'm sure this looks the nicest.'

Alice studied the baleful glare of the hellebore-cherry, then began, with cautious adjustments, and without the help of a spoon or a napkin, to consume it.

'All that rubbish about self-denial, eh?' Celia scooped up a tartlet from the middle row and ate it with licks and nibbles and small gasps of pleasure. 'You've done so well,' she murmured through a full mouth. 'I mean, I'm just a twice-bereaved widow, a mere grandmistress. But you're the greatgrandmistress of one of the major guilds. Yet you bear it all so lightly. And you have a family as well. Or at least a son, although I hear the poor lad's not quite as well as he might be. But all those houses! All that wealth! And such influence! You really must—oh, and this is just *so delicious*!—tell me everything about it.'

Between sticky bites, Alice did her best to keep up her side of the conversation, but the fact was that Celia wasn't interested in any subject but herself, and then how she and Alice were so *alike*, and what great *friends* they might be, and how they might now *depend* on each other. It was true, Alice inwardly conceded, that the disclosure of their mutual origins might cause Celia some harm, but not that much. Not with her husbands both dead and her life established here in the west, where the only standards were double ones. Alice, on the other hand, was still building her life. It was a work in progress. Of course, she'd been lax in not recognising the grossly changed Cheryl Kettlethorpe in Celia sooner, but at the same time she could detect no obvious desire for straightforward blackmail in this woman's florid manner. After all, she looked blissfully content here, surrounded by giant blooms and stuffing herself with tartlets. Did she really need any more money and status? More likely, she was somewhat lonely amid all the possessions she'd grasped from her dead husbands. Her desire for friendship, and with that extra *frisson* of a secret shared with a greatgrandmistress, was probably genuine. But Alice knew how these things went. Something always came up. Little favours. Even— for, on second thoughts, no one ever had quite enough of the stuff—straightforward requests for money. All of it couched in the usual this-is-what-friends-do-for-each-other banalities when underneath both sides knew that a knife was being held to your throat. She forced herself through a second tartlet in the certain knowledge that Celia would finish off the rest, pretended to take another sip of the dreadful wine, then asked if she might possibly be excused?

Alice extended the excursion by peering around doors and down stairwells, but it seemed as if Celia really had emptied the house of servants. Inside the palatial toilet, she vomited up the tartlets. The two hellebore berries, which she'd swallowed entire like fat pills, required several flushes and a wodge of toilet paper to sink. Heading back for the rooftop after rinsing her mouth and face, Alice really did feel cleansed. Her plans had assumed that she would consummate her spell several hours and many miles away, but now she was curious . . .

Celia was on her fourth and final tartlet, and the last red berry had already vanished into her cream-smeared mouth, when Alice sat down again.

'So we really are totally alone here?'

Celia sucked a blob of cream from her index finger. 'But there's no need for all this *secrecy*, Alice. I'd never tell a soul. In a way, you know, you remind me of my Clive. Did I mention that he was my second husband . . . ?'

And off she went again. Me, me, me. That particular husband had acquired his wealth from what she termed a colonial estate, which Alice knew meant enslavement under the burning sun for thousands of Negroes just so there could be enough sugar to keep the likes of Celia fat. It was all so typical of this city which lay around her, fragmented beyond the glass like the tipped pieces of a jigsaw. The notices on walls advertising bear-baiting and gargoyle fights. The coffee-coloured complexions of so many of the servants, and even lesser guildsmen, which told their own story. The ostentatious piety. The rampant bureaucracy. The small trade. Of course, it was all part of the rich pageant of which this great nation was composed, but, as she sat listening to Celia, summoning the white anger for the spell she was about to cast required little effort. Yes, she would stay at Invercombe and put up with as much as was necessary until Ralph was finally better, but she decided that there was something essentially rotten about the west.

'Sorry . . . ?' Celia licked glittering crumbs from the edges of her lips. 'Didn't quite catch that.'

'Just shut up and listen for a moment, will you, Celia? I want to make absolutely sure that I get this right.'

Celia perched her fingertips on her knees and leaned forward in her chair.

Alice took a breath. She cleared her throat. She felt almost self-conscious. The spell was guttural and arcane.

'Well . . . ?' Clearly puzzled, Celia sat back. 'I don't quite see . . . ?'

'It really doesn't matter now, Celia.'

'Hmm . . .' Celia tilted her ample neck as if considering whether she agreed. Then, almost imperceptibly at first, she started shaking. 'Hmm . . .' But now the sound was an animal one, wrenched from her throat.

Alice stood up. Celia was juddering, her hands clenching her chest and belly as if striving to rip out the source of whatever was happening to her. Her gaze, as her eyes bulged and her face paled beneath all the layers of make-up, roamed the flowers and the glass and the furniture. She let out a groan, and weird, luminously wyreglowing vomit pooled across her lap and bosom. She made to rise, but her legs weren't up to it and she keeled through the glass table, which sprayed in shards around her. Alice took a step back as Celia lay juddering in the wreckage and the characteristic Bristol smell of piss and faeces began to flood the rooftop air. Celia half rolled over through the glass, and blood also bloomed as the convulsions began to subside.

Alice picked her way around the mess. Celia was almost still now. Only her lips were trembling. Although the garden remained sealed from the outside air, Alice felt a swift, clean breeze passing over her, tumbling the elegant paper cups which had held the tartlets; some side effect of the spell which the pages she'd studied hadn't mentioned, but not unpleasant.

Half-kneeling, Alice studied Celia's face. The focus of Celia's gaze was inward, receding. She was nearing the final moment. But still her lips quivered. Was that not a word? Carefully, Alice parted her hair from around her left ear and leaned close to Celia's mouth.

'I thought we . . .'

Was *that* what she had said? And was *could be friends* the intended end of the sentence? Alice smiled warmly into the woman's dying eyes. It would make a suitably mundane epitaph. She studied the irises as they widened. Then, in a final foul exhalation, Celia was gone. Had she been thinking of her lost husbands? Was there emptiness? For a moment, Alice surveyed the scene. The plump stems of Celia's doll-like wrists were decorated with numerous bracelets. Breathing through her mouth, raising the left hand by its littlest finger, she eased one off. It was a thin hoop of silver set with tiny shards of beryl or ruby—expensive enough, but amid all this ostentation, no one would notice it. Putting on her coat, sliding the souvenir into her pocket, she crushed the second wineglass beneath her heel and left 28 Charlotte Street.

The morning's sunlight had vanished and Bristol seemed a different city as she took a cab to the Telegraphers' great guildhouse and transmission works, which rose across the harbour at Redcliff in the shades of the riotous growths of stone which were the colours of bruises. Genuinely cold now after the heat of Celia's rooftop, she stepped out in the eye-stinging grit outside the guildhall's front entrance. She greeted a tiered succession of lower and higher and upper and lesser and ordinary and senior guildsmasters before being ushered through halls and up stairways filled with a comforting, everyday hum. Not even for the arrival of their own greatgrandmistress did work stop here, and Alice was glad of that, and glad for the brightening glow of the telephone lines which fanned out from the high tower which was always a feature of the major edifices of her guild, although this one, being in the west, was more like a jet of erupting masonry. From up here, standing beside the antique but potent haft through which telegraphers had once communed, the darkening layers of windy western landscape already looked ensnared, entwined, enmeshed. Hers . . .

'You're not cold, are you, Mistress . . . ? We could always . . .'

She shook her head. It was a fine thing, to belong to this guild.

Down below, in a sea of relays, in the spooling copper ribbons of spells, in snake pits of wire and grommet, the great minds of the reckoning engines endlessly unspan their song. And it seemed not only right but necessary that she should use a telephone booth.

These little spaces. One place, endlessly duplicated and joined. Alice curled her fingers around the dialling handle and studied her face in the oval mirror. She tilted her jaw, but there was nothing to see. That blood pearl—and a mere fragment, so that she hadn't yet had to resort to searching the shore again—had done its work. She was composed, complete. But, even as she smiled back at herself and the small light overhead glowed on the silvered blonde of her comb-set hair, the red pearl swelled in her mind to the larger globes of the hellebore cherries and, like some bloody embolism, continued growing. She blinked, swallowing something which seemed to fill her throat. She was older, and it had nothing to do with her looks.

The light hummed. The chair, no matter how lightly she sat in it, ticked. She remembered the small animals which Jakob the gardener had once trapped in the grounds of her aunt's house. She'd sometimes come across them and had taken them out, cooed to them, tried to make them see and understand and properly love her like the pets she was disallowed and thus always craved. But they wouldn't listen. They were always too squeally and scratchy and afraid. So she'd killed them instead, carefully and slowly, and in many different ways. And as they died she would fix their little black eyes in her wondering, questioning gaze. Even then, she'd wanted to *know*, to *understand*, so that she could pinion that last moment of life and thus leave it for ever behind. But, just as had been the case this lunchtime with Celia, it remained a continuing mystery. Her hand played with the telephone's dialling mechanism, which, the thought occurred to her, mimicked the prototype at Invercombe. Buzz, buzz went the light. Tick, tick went the chair. This, she supposed, was the nearest one ever got whilst living to the essence of death. These endless little departures of the unforgiving moment.

She dialled Tom's private booth in his office at the top of Dockland Exchange. As always, he was delighted to see her, and even more delighted that she'd taken the time to visit his colleagues at the Bristol Exchange today. And it was a miracle, really, that Ralph was getting so much better. He really must get away from London and visit them. As Alice encouraged her husband in his vague plans, she thought how sweet it was that, despite all the years of evidence to the contrary, he still managed to believe that he could have days off like any of his common guildsmen.

'And how about that contract?' she asked. 'The one for the new eastern telephone line.'

'Oh, *that*,' Tom sighed, and quite a lot of the brightness seeped out of him.

Alice understood that things never happened with the simplicity with which they should, but still, the tale of cancelled meetings and misunderstood instructions with which he now regaled her sounded like a poor joke. Basically, the upshot was that Pikes the contractors were counter-suing and stood to make a better profit out of protracted legal action than they did out of actually doing any work.

'It's all a bit of a mess,' Tom said, shaking his head as he often did at the wrongs of the world. 'Of course, these things always look worse than they are. And I really shouldn't bother you with shop.' But he looked wearied, and Alice felt the same as they said goodbye and his ghost faded to be replaced by the falling darkness of the empty mirror. The connector was about to ping as it broke the connection, but she pressed it down and remained staring into the blackness.

The idea of making better use of the telephone no longer seemed like an absurd personal vanity. After all, it had been more than a century since the last great advance. And who better than her, as her guild's greatgrandmistress, to make the next leap? Now, it seemed, the entire spell—for a little more magic, she was certain, and rather than the clumsy intrusions of technology, would be all that was needed—was with her. Since she'd been at Invercombe, the final walls and uncertainties had fallen with almost absurd ease. Sometimes, it was almost as if the phrases she'd been perfecting had murmured themselves to her on the quiet breezes which passed along its corridors; although, Alice being Alice, and just like the magics in her portmanteau, they had in truth been acquired through considerable effort, industry and subterfuge. Certainly, she'd awoken once or twice recently as if startled by some presence in her room. But that whispering she'd heard was probably just the pulse of blood in her ears, or the tides which washed against the cliffs far below and infused the house. Perhaps, she'd decided, this is merely what artists call inspiration. But whatever it had been, she could feel it and Invercombe calling to her now, and the complex exhalation of sounds she now recited seemed to come, as with all the best magics, as easily as living.

There. As lightly as a diving swimmer submitting to the will of gravity, she felt herself being physically pushed towards the mirror. She and the emptiness within joined, embraced, and she poured along the networks which fanned out across Bristol. Unanchored as she was from the normal safe protocols which governed telephone communication, it made an exhilarating ride. A maintenance spell from the sorting machines at Templemeads took her down local lines into the patient arms of transmission routines where she was sucked across the city. She glimpsed bright little cars, and the silos of the sugar processing factories and the wrinkling flash of Clifton Dam. There were shipyards and jostling spars and funnels and flags. There was the jewelled cathedral. The streets were torrents of light, bearing along tiny specks which moved as if driven by some vast and indeterminate current instead of separate wills of individual people. Her scrutiny gathered and moved through junctions and relays, leaping switchbox to lamppost with the droop and rise of each individual telephone line until she came to Charlotte Street. It was all so easy! If she could have laughed, she would have laughed. If she could have cried, she would have cried. But she was scarcely Alice, and yet she *was*, and a small commotion was going on outside number 28, where servants were weeping, and guildsmen were doffing their hats. Drawing to the last droop of the telephone line which had borne her here, the ghost of Alice watched as Cheryl's body, wrapped in a red and blue bedspread, was carried down the steps towards the waiting black carriage.

Alice went straight up to see Ralph when she returned to Invercombe. He was out of bed and the curtains of his room were still open, although there was surely little enough to see out there beyond the faint glow of a few early lanternflowers. She brushed her knuckles against his cheek; this son of hers who was growing up. 'We really must get you a razor.'

But Ralph never looked quite as pleased as she expected when complimented on his becoming a man.

'Your father says he might come down,' she added. 'I wouldn't get your hopes up too highly, although I'm sure he'd love to.'

He nodded. 'I was thinking that I might get properly dressed tomorrow. You know—go out into the garden. There's so much I need to study.'

'I sometimes wonder if that isn't how you wear yourself out. Not everything has to be understood and explained. You do know that, don't you?'

He gazed back at her. She saw his throat working. He was suppressing something, but perhaps it was merely a cough. 'I sometimes think *you* try too hard as well. I mean, look at you today—I can tell you find it exhausting.'

'Well, I do, but . . .' Quickly, fully formed, the idea came to her. 'But there's something you can do to help me, darling. I mean, getting better isn't just about wandering around gardens and knowing the names of flowers. You've got to learn how to meet people as well.'

'People?'

'I was thinking just a few local dignitaries. It would just be a dinner here, downstairs. It's about time this house had some other visitors than us, isn't it?'

Alice kissed Ralph goodnight. Heading down the corridor to her own room, she was met by a tray-bearing Steward Dunning.

'I know you didn't ask for anything, mistress. But cook thought . . .'

Alice *was* a touch hungry. And thank the Elder it was plain, simple food. Cinnamon toast, a ripe red apple—although even these things had a innate richness here in the west. The ordinary milk was close to what easterners would have called cream, and the tea steaming from the white porcelain pot smelled as seductive as ever. 'That's most considerate.' She made as if to hold out her hands and take the tray, and then to be struck by a thought. 'And this wonderful tea, by the way. It isn't the mixture that I had brought up from London, is it?'

'Well . . .' The steward gave the carpet a sideways glance.

'Oh, I'm not complaining. I was just hoping cook might let me know the name of the suppliers so that I can order some myself.'

'I'm not sure that *supplier* is exactly the word for it, Mistress. You know how these things can be.' The steward's gaze was frank now. If she hadn't been holding the tray, she'd probably have tapped her nose. Alice smiled and nodded. She understood.

'Did you find time to visit the post office, by the way, Mistress?'

'Oh, yes . . . I think I made some progress, but the place was almost shutting by the time I got there.'

'Well, never mind. These problems eventually sort themselves out here in the west. It just takes a little patience . . .'

Alice went to bed early that night. She gazed up into the sea-swelling darkness after she had turned out the light and remembered the times of her childhood, that damp old house. When she'd finally discovered that all her inheritance had been lost or wasted, she'd lured her aunt to the falls at the bottom of the gardens. It had always been her favourite place, with that sense if you stared at the waters that they were hanging still and the rest of the world was moving, although her aunt had seemed to float far more easily than she sank as Alice struggled to drown her. It had been like wrestling a huge, angry frog until the moment came when, after all the thrashings, the surface of the waters had finally subsided. She remembered those dulling eyes, that gaping mouth, that vanishing moment of departure from life, before her aunt's dead body had turned and floated across the pool.

Then she was walking the path around Stow Pool in Lichfield on a smoky autumn evening. Here, surely, was her good friend Cheryl Kettlethorpe. She quickened her steps, certain that there was something vital they needed to discuss. But Cheryl was elusive, and she was wearing a fur coat which was the colour of the twilight, which deepened and darkened as the light fled from the lake until, when Alice finally caught up with her, all that was left was chill, misty starlight, and a nagging sense of something unsaid.

VI

As the shifterms turned towards April, Invercombe was tremendously astir. Everything in the grounds, to the urgings of the sun and Weatherman Ayres's weathertop, was growing, stretching, swelling. Yellow kingcaps shone at the margins of the green pool. Ferns uncoiled in the pinetum and the pyre-poppies beside the walled gardens began—much too early—to blaze and glow. In the linoleum dark of the servants' halls, Steward Dunning had to preside over angry meetings. Master Gardener Wyatt complained of unseasonable bugs and late plantings. Cook was upset for having to serve forced rhubarb when they should still have been subsisting on potted. Even Wilkins was fretting about his drays. Cissy could have listed a good dozen problems of her own, but she kept silent as Weatherman Ayres started to bluster about how all this would have been mutiny on the ships he'd sailed, then cast her varieties of the same longing glance he had been giving for most of these last twenty years.

Now, there was to be a dinner. After much consideration, Alice had invited Doctor and Doctress Foot, Enforcer Scutt, Reverend-Highermaster Brown. Local worthies. Dull or interesting, depending on your view of ditchwater, but useful nevertheless. This would be nothing like her grand soirées and dances, but it would be the first formal dinner of Ralph's adult life, and antique dinner services and jorums were decanted from their wrappings and found to be cracked or crazed, and vital ingredients of condiment and cutlery were discovered to be missing. But Alice strove to remain calm and swanlike; whilst, beneath the waters, all was mad paddling.

There was the ordering of Ralph's first formal suit, and she saw, as the tailor she'd summoned from Bristol ran his tape across Ralph's shoulders, how her son was shaping into a man. She also suggested he try a little of the wine she'd selected from Invercombe's maze of cellars. It turned out he'd drunk so much spirit and morphine over the years that he was almost immune to intoxication, but nevertheless she showed him how to water it by the amount which was expected at dinner of a lad—young man, really—of his age.

Then the sixth day of April, an Eightshiftday, arrived, and it seemed that nothing was ready. Alice strode the house, checking flower arrangements and sympathising over minor crises in the kitchen whilst surreptitiously scanning the ingredients cook had gathered, many of which bore no labels. She even visited the weathertop to impress upon Weatherman Ayres that the weather at Invercombe this evening should be warm and clear.

Ralph was half in and half out of his new clothes when his mother entered his room and her gaze took in the knotted ruins of his tie and cummerbund.

'This stuff should come with some sort of manual.'

'Your father's not so very different.' She shook loose his bow tie. 'Raise your chin. Under and under and then in.'

'How can I manage this on my own? Couldn't you perhaps get one of the maids . . . ?'

'The poor things are all much too busy.' His mother, a red spill of his cummerbund shining in her hands, was watching him carefully. 'And I'm sure you'll be fine if I just help you with this. Here . . . It's a bit like wrapping a bandage. Put your arms up. Now, turn towards me.' Ralph revolved. The cummerbund obediently encased him. 'And you really shouldn't worry about this evening, darling. The people, quite seriously, do not matter. Just think of it as a couple of hours you're spending in a slightly different way to the way you'd probably ideally be spending them. That's what I do. And you really do look the part.' Her hands smoothed him. He felt the cool, familiar sensation of her close presence. That fresh-linen scent of hers which never really changed no matter what perfume she was wearing. 'I'm so, so proud of you. And this . . .' She went to pick up something she'd brought in without his noticing. 'It's just something you might find useful.'

A blue plush-covered box, somewhat lopsidedly weighted, embossed with an *R* and an *M*. The sprung lid leapt open. Inside were the glinting components of a shaving kit.

After his mother had left, Ralph addressed himself to the mirror. The razor was a Felton—he'd seen the adverts on placards at railway stations—but this model was gold-plated. And was that big stud on the ivory handle of the shaving brush really a diamond? Running the water, humming to himself in the way that he imagined men were supposed to, he assembled the razor and began to shave.

Apart from the blood leaking onto his collar, the face which peered back at him when he'd finished seemed little changed, and, for all the mess that he had made, Ralph decided he could do little to improve on the effect. He paced the room. He considered looking at his books. He decided to go outside.

His strength was gaining. As long as he took his time, he scarcely felt any of his old breathlessness these days. This, he decided as his new patent shoes creaked down through the valley in the fading brilliance of the late afternoon, must be exactly what being well feels like. The absence of any significant ache in his chest or head or limbs was almost eerie—it was as if he'd left something vital behind. Vistas he'd previously only witnessed foreshortened through the lens of his telescope revealed themselves amid all the scents and murmurings of evening which even the finest optics could never convey.

The lemons were yellowing, and oranges were oranging, wafting their sweetly bitter odour from the citrus grove. And there were poppies pyre, already. He cupped his hands around their petals to feel their slow warmth. It was quite impossible to tell here where nature ended and artifice—and then magic—began. The sensation, after the orderliness of his books, was giddying. The garden continued descending. He

was into a territory as unfamiliar in its own way as that which
he would soon have to face back at the house, but one he
found much more inviting. He was beyond reach of the sunlight, which now glowed only on the weathertop and the varied greens of the specimen trees which climbed towards
Durnock Head, and the air felt cool and green. He imagined
the aeons it must have taken to form this valley. Water crashing down and down. He could almost see and hear it happening. His thoughts unravelled so much better out here than they
did when he was reading books.

Beyond the parterres, the garden continued descending. It
was as if he'd already stepped down into deep, still water even
before he glimpsed the dark gleam of the stew pool beyond a
turn in the pathway. Then there was movement on its far side;
a concentration of the twilight, a shifting of the grey. His
mother was out walking, although in a fur coat he'd never seen
her in before, and which would surely be ridiculously warm
on an evening such as this. Still, he felt grateful for her presence, and yet suddenly somewhat alone. He opened his mouth
to call to her, but at that moment one of his previously obedi-
ent feet chose to miss a step. He tumbled forward, skidding
his hands and dirtying his shirt on the mossy path.

The jarring taste of shock still filled his head as he climbed
back to his feet, and his mother had already gone from sight.
It was probably time to get back up to the house in any event;
face the people. The whole sky seemed to pulse and glow—a
darker, bigger weathertop—as he made his ascent.

'Ralph? Darling . . .' His mother's shape emerged from the
statuary. 'We've been looking everywhere.' She wafted over in
a beautiful green dress. 'And *look* at you.' Plucking a globe of
moonivy from a wall, she raised its soft light to inspect him.

Ralph saw the smears of moss across his shirtfront. 'I'm
sorry—it's just that I saw you from across that big pool a few
minutes ago. When you were out walking . . . In that fur
coat . . .'

'Fur *coat*? What *are* you talking about, darling? As if I've
got time to be wandering about the gardens on this of all days.
I should never have let you shave on your own. You've got a
couple of specks of blood. Hold steady.' She said something;
less words than a splashing of the fountain. '*That's* better.' And

then again, her hand on his shirtfront, and the moonivy gave an extra pulse of light. Once again, his shirt was stainless.

'The guests are here. You really *do* look the part, I just wish you hadn't chosen this of all evenings to decide to do your exploring . . .'

The west parlour was lit by numerous candles which doors open to the faintly gleaming garden barely stirred.

'Her death was so, so sudden.' Doctress Foot, a small, busy woman, with a mind far livelier than her husband's, put down her spoon. Her fingers toyed with a lustrous beetle brooch. 'Celia was the sort of person I always missed when she wasn't there.'

'I seriously thought of coming to the funeral myself,' Alice said as she signalled for the soup plates to be taken away. 'Of course, we'd met. And I did feel an immediate affinity with poor Celia, and felt that we might have become friends. But I feared that to attend her funeral might have seemed . . .' She considered her choice of word. '. . . presumptuous.'

'And how are you finding the west, Greatgrandmistress?' Enforcer Cornelius Scutt, resplendent in the blue and braid of his dress uniform and smelling somewhat of mothballs, enquired.

'I'm not sure that I *have* found it. Or at least, not until tonight. With you, my friends, and here.' She raised her glass, touched it to her lips. 'I suppose I *do* still find the use of bondsmen which you espouse a little . . .' She tilted her head. '. . . unusual.'

'Your presence,' said Enforcer Scutt, who could scarcely draw his rheumy eyes from her, 'is more than ever welcome here in the west, Greatgrandmistress. It will help save us from the ill-founded criticisms which emanate all too easily from London and the east. People who have never visited and do not understand the colonies . . .'

'Oh, I do realise,' Alice said, 'that bonding provides work and security for many who would otherwise live as mere savages . . .' Through the sorbet and on into the pâté, she continued to enumerate the arguments in favour of the custom she'd always thought of as pure slavery. But there was the undeniable economic need for sugar and cotton, and the labour-intensive methods which were required to produce them, whilst even the Bible acknowledged slavery as a necessary condition of mankind. And were we not all, in one way or another, bound inescapably by birth and circumstance to our role? She aimed the last question at Steward Dunning, who had come in to help supervise the changing of the table's arrangements which the serving of lobster entailed.

'Well, yes, Greatgrandmistress. Although it's hardly for me to say . . .' The steward retreated, her true opinions kept well beneath the surface, and Alice, who'd feared that her approach on the subject had been too subtle, felt sure that she had made her point. The fact was that westerners, even the freed Negroes, were instinctively defensive about bonding.

The main course was duck, prepared over many days to cook's special recipe. Tasting the delicate flavours and most probably illicit spices, Alice would have liked to have raised the small trade, had she not tried it before, and had seen the poor effect it had. Not even Enforcer Scutt, who was supposedly in charge of preventing it and was now studying her cleavage, was remotely comfortable on the subject.

'I never realised before I came here,' she said instead, moving on towards what she imagined was a lighter topic, 'that Invercombe was surrounded with so many tales and superstitions. It's almost as if the house recruited them. Although I must confess I haven't seen any ghosts yet.'

'Oh, but there *is* a ghost,' said Grandmistress Lee-Lawnswood-Taylor, who was predictably over-dressed in red tulle, and was drinking her wine with a restrained avidity which, along with the barely-disguised threads of broken capillaries on her nose and cheeks, Alice had noted before. 'Not that *I* should presume to say . . .'

'Please. I'm most interested. Do go on.'

'Well, it's said that you can sometimes see the guildswoman Greatmaster Porrett was betrothed to wandering the grounds.'

'Really? You mean that grandmistress he never married? But I thought she never came here. Isn't that correct?' They all seemed to be taking this far more seriously than Alice had intended. 'Isn't that the whole point?'

'I think,' Enforcer Scutt breathed to her right, 'that that *is* supposed to be the whole point.'

'How charming—you mean the ghost of someone who never actually came to Invercombe haunts this place!' This time, just as she had for most of the meal, Alice avoided the enforcer's rheumy gaze. With men like him, there was no need for conscious flirting. In fact, it would be self-defeating when she knew she already had him in her hands. 'In London, our ghosts are all . . .' She paused, genuinely searching, for once, for a phrase. She looked for assistance towards Ralph who sat at the far end of the table and seemingly at the edge of the darkness beyond the candelabra. She'd been paying him far too little attention tonight, and he seemed pale. 'My son Ralph here, with all his considerable knowledge of the sciences, could perhaps offer an explanation. Couldn't you, darling?'

'I would imagine,' Ralph said, in a voice so slow and yet oddly emphatic that she wondered how much he'd drank of the wine, 'that ghosts, if they had to exist at all would exist, of necessity, outside what we think of as time.'

'Really, dear?' It was as if he was contradicting her, although she had no idea how or why. 'I'd have thought, with all your knowledge of the natural world and your logical bent that you'd have—'

'Or perhaps a house can be haunted as easily by things which have yet to happen as by those which already have. From what I understand of its history, Invercombe has experienced nothing more remarkable or unfortunate than many another house. And yet . . .' Ralph blinked as if surprised by his own words. His face seemed as transparent as the flames which hovered over the table between them. His wide, white forehead glinted with a bony sheen. Yet, with these doors open, it was still pleasantly cool in here. The night weather, just as Weatherman Ayres had promised, was perfect, and Alice had planned a promenade along one of the garden's many walks after dinner, but now she felt the first twinge of alarm about her son. Was Ralph simply tired? Was he just drunk? And why on earth had he been dirtying his best clothes by running about in the garden? His gaze, red-rimmed, and not quite seeming to focus, wandered the table, settling at first on the full red wine glasses, then followed the movements of a dark-haired maid who was clearing away the sauce-smeared plates. It was some moments before Alice recognised her as the girl she had encountered on the shore. Steward Dunning had done a good job; she now moved with the sort of grace you could never train into a maid if it wasn't there already. And she was a shapely enough thing, too. Pretty, even. Ralph, Alice saw, was still watching the space by the door even when she left the room, and she felt a small surge of relief. Perhaps he wasn't ill. Perhaps there was a simpler, easier explanation.

The meal moved on. With the admittedly excellent food and wine—for cook really had excelled herself—the guests grew more voluble. These people, Alice thought, only talked about London as somewhere they visited, marvelled at, left. With the many things they would and wouldn't discuss, and the way they ate and drank and the accent and the thinly educated veneer of their voices, they seemed to her essentially clumsy and naïve. Alice had heard from Tom this very morning that Pikes had won the first round of court cases in London, and it was in Bristol that the recalcitrant contractors had their main office: of course it was. That explained so much to her now.

The lime sorbets produced from Invercombe's own fruit were sprinkled with a thin, chive-like herb she'd never encountered before. It was called bittersweet, and cook grew it in cold corners of the gardens because Invercombe's balmy weather was otherwise much too mild. Sharp, irresistible sweetness flooded Alice's mouth. She'd lost track of the conversation, and Ralph was now actually holding forth with some vehemence.

'But if the Lord made the earth for mankind,' the Reverend-Highermaster Brown then purred in denial of whatever her son had been saying, 'why would he leave it desolate and unpopulated for all those thousands of years. Granted that current thought acknowledges that the seven days of creation may not be *days* in our modern understanding of shiftdays—'

'Don't you see!' Ralph's unsteady gaze swept the table. 'The universe isn't like that. We must step aside from our natural desire to place ourselves at the centre of all creation and accept the simple evidence of our senses. The natural world has changed immeasurably. How, otherwise, do you explain the clear imprints which have been found in rocks of species of plants and even of animals quite unlike those we know of now?'

'Look—you have, may I say so, a point.' Doctress Foot, who'd been quiet for most of the meal, suddenly spoke. 'Indeed, I always say, don't I,' wavering, she inclined her small head towards her husband, 'that my own small studies of the world of insects, small though they are, do show—'

'But those are just *beetles,* my darling. It's an interesting hobby for a guildslady and so forth, but they hardly count as evidence of anything. Permit *me*—' Doctor Foot leaned forward past his wife '—to explain, young master. All of England was once inundated. There were probably swamps where we are now—a wild and uninhabited landscape beyond the small, fertile area which the Bible terms the Garden of Eden, and modern scholars have located within the fertile crescent of the lands of Araby. There may have been tropical birds flying above the very air where we sit. Quite possibly, hippos—'

'But where did those birds come *from*? Why do they have *wings*? How did they learn how to *fly*?'

'I'm sure their mothers taught them to do so just as any good mother would. Isn't that so, Greatgrandmistress?' the Reverend-Highermaster Brown put in, and was swivelling his irritatingly benign gaze towards Alice when a barking laugh drew it back to Ralph.

'And where does this air come from? Can you tell me *that*? Was it all made just so for us, and then left never to change?' Ralph's own breathing, Alice couldn't help noticing with gaining alarm, was quick and shallow. 'What about the sun, eh? The stars? Were they all just plonked around the heavens like ornaments on a shelf to make the sky look pretty by—by the hand of a supposed God?'

That *supposed* rang awkwardly in the air. In this company, you did not question the existence of the Elder, whose Son himself had been a member of the guilds; firstly of the Carpenters, and then of the Fishermen. Still, if she put an end to matters now and got Ralph reasonably quickly up to bed, the guests would all pretend that, like their stupid superstitions and rampant smuggling, they hadn't noticed.

'I think you should go upstairs now, dear.' Alice knew she was treating Ralph like a child again, when the whole point of this gathering had been that he wasn't. Still, he nodded and obediently raked back his chair and stood up. He coughed, swaying slightly, and wiped his mouth, a wet comma of hair clinging to his forehead. Then he swayed again, and leaned forward against the table, his splaying hands bunching the cloth, rattling glasses and condiments. Alice jumped up and moved swiftly towards him. This was worse than she'd feared, but still, as she caught his arm and saw the starbursts of red which had flecked across the table, she thought at first that they were spillages of wine, not blood.

VII

Ralph was sure he would soon have won his argument. Even as he was helped from the west parlour, he felt a sense of exultation. He was sure, as he was peeled from his jacket and unwound from his tie and cummerbund, that he was entering a new and certain world. His ears were singing and his head was spinning, but he could almost smile up at the faces of his opponents in logic as they came and went around the huge green and gold fortress of his four-poster bed.

'I always bring my bag with me, Mistress. A few potentially useful medicaments . . .'

'Then get it.' His mother's voice was unusually harsh.

Time hung around him. He smelled the silk of his mother's dress.

'I'll get you your painstones, darling.'

Ralph felt pleasantly lazy, lying here. Moving shadows and the voice of Doctor Foot returned. Rough, disconnected hands touched his face, then hooked into his mouth and opened his eyes. Then came the cold, familiar touch of a stethoscope on his chest, although this one seemed to be some innovative device, which was sucking out air. Bucking, coughing, he fought against it.

'Definite signs of toxaemia, Greatgrandmistress. No, no. I wouldn't use that painstone . . .' He felt his palm being prised open. '. . . the spells might conflict.'

He smelled the doctor's bag. He was falling towards its syrupy comforts as it opened. Endless bottles were nodding their tall cork heads and twisting their thin blueglass necks as they fluttered around him. Then something brimmed against his lips, and a sticky spillage spread dark roots across the snowfalls of his sheets.

'It's aethered?' His mother's voice. 'A spell?'

'I think that's the minimum necessary.' Doctor Foot cleared his throat. Brightness glowed into the twin moons of his eyeglasses. There was a faint rain of spittle, and Ralph felt some vapour stirring, roiling, climbing up his throat. His heart constricted. He had no energy to do so, but, once again, he was coughing. Then the spell was incanted again, and there came a kind of rest.

He found himself beached in daylight, half hanging out of his bed. His books were stepped and waiting on a bright square of carpet. Coughing, he urged his hand to reach towards the embossed leather cover at the top of the nearest pile. The book flipped and skidded. He had no idea of its contents, but he craved the cool bliss of its numbered, annotated plates. The thing was impossibly heavy. Perhaps this was the Book of Knowledge from which all others were mere extracts, its pages made from the pulped wood of that tree in the Garden of Eden. Perhaps he would soon see Eve.

Waiting for another wave of sick weariness to break and expend itself over him, Ralph finally lifted the book and prised open its cover. Then, pausing to regain his energies, he turned through pages of guild dedications and blank sheets towards the waiting truth. Insects? He smiled dizzyingly. Strange, really, that a book which encompassed everything should begin there. But every system of classification had its problems, as he knew only too well. So; Lepidoptera—butterflies. And why not? And, after all, and even in the book of everything, you had to start somewhere.

'Ralph. You're nearly falling out . . . And you shouldn't be reading.'

He was surprised at how easily his mother could move his body back to the middle of his bed. Then there were all the other things she did for him. Summons and instructions issued by her cool fingers to which his unthinking flesh responded. Cold air and rubber and porcelain. The shock of a sponge. And new sheets, new pyjamas. All he needed was that cummerbund and tie again.

He croaked, 'I'm sorry . . .'

Her lovely face loomed before him. She looked immaculate; clean and fresh. It was only the mess of the fever he could already feel leaking its way back into his body which spoiled everything.

'You mean about the night before last's dinner?' Questioningly, lovingly, she tilted her head. Her cool fresh hand was stroking his cheek, and lingered there in a subtly different way. After all, he had shaved, and this sensation of touching was new and different for them both. 'You were ill. People understand. In fact, Doctor Foot will be back here soon this morning. I know he's a bit of a bumpkin, darling, but he seems to know his job at least as well as those expensive charlatans in Harley Street. And it's important that we keep a proper watch over you.' Her gaze roved his face. Those grey-blue eyes. Like diamonds. Underwater. At the ends of the earth.

He swallowed and worked drying sand back into his throat to speak, but her fingers sealed his mouth.

'Sssh, darling.' Her breath stirred his face. She was so close to him now that her features blurred. He felt her lips settle against his. Then she was gone.

Slipping in and out of awareness. Concentrating, between wet spasms of coughing, on breathing. Conscious that words were being said. Pages in a play.

'I don't care right now what your worries are, Doctor Foot.'

'Still, Greatgrandmistress. There's a limit to the power of the spells which might help combat his fever and ease his breathing. It's a question of the amount of aether of this strength of charm we can use.'

'If you're talking about caution, about money, about the regulations of your own guild—in fact, about anything—I'm sure that I can—'

'No, no, Mistress. It's not like that at all. If I were to use more aether than this in a potion, if I were to introduce the amount you're suggesting into his body, it would take him over beyond the control of any guildsman. Your son would become a changeling.'

A long pause in the dialogue. Ralph, with an effort of mind, turned the white, empty pages.

'Would that save him?'

'It would just mean even more agony and uncertainty. Far more, in fact, than either of us dare imagine. We'd be treating a monster. And your son would then be beyond my help . . .'

The light was fading. He heard the bubble of a humidifier, and tasted its herbal breath on his lips. Pains flared and were gone. The fire in the grate had been replaced by a pug-nosed creature with a glowing mouth which squatted on the tiles as if it was preparing to jump. Its tweezering legs were crawling over him. Its arid grin was searing into the foul sump of his lungs. Then came a moment of clarity, with his mother lifting him and placing water to his lips, and the agony of swallowing.

The wings of a fan brushed over him. The fire still grinned and squatted on insect legs. His lungs and the humidifier bubbled. He felt his mother's movement, her touches and sighs. The empty moments flapped by him one by one, pure and sharp as empty pages of his endless book. Then he sensed a presence behind him, and turned the next page and laughed out loud at what he found there. For he was up on the Kite Hills, and the bitter taste of the bathing pools were still in his mouth, but all fear had gone and London slouched grey below him as its sooty breezes bore up the many kites that sailor-suited lads, watched by their adoring mummies and nannies, were flying. Big and bright, huge butterflies caught in the warm hand of the wind. Yes, this was Butterfly Day, and Ralph laughed and ignored the rawness in his throat and let the slope take him as he ran. People smiled and waved. The fact that he was wearing sweat-soaked pyjamas didn't seem to bother anyone. Then, as if the kites had shrunk or he had become a giant, their sails surrounded him. Ralph held out his amazed hand and felt one of them settle there. Paper-dry and light, it spread its wings to the sunlight, and the part of him which had studied the blissful pages of so many books recognised the creature instantly. Not a kite or even a butterfly, but a moth. *Biston betularia,* the peppered moth, which was small and unremarkable and common, although he remembered now, with a strange push of extra knowledge which seemed to ignite some new fire inside him, how there were often two illustrations of this creature in books on Lepidoptera; a darker, blackish variety, and one which was greyer-flecked and light. This moth, here at the smoke edges of London, was of the darker kind. Ralph studied it. A sense of power and knowledge was gaining on him.

He scanned the huge slope of dry summer grass which separated him from his mother as the moth twitched its near-black wings in his palm; an emissary from the world of science and certainty which he now so wanted to share with her. Carefully, cupping the tips of his fingers over it so it couldn't escape, he began to ascend the slope. The distance was huge. The sunlight was blinding. Gasping, he looked along the shimmering benches, but the effort of climbing this burning space had left him confused. Smells of ice cream and tramped earth. A harsh metallic taste of dread. He coughed and tried to steady himself, cupped fingers still bearing the precious load of his peppered moth as the kites hung and the gritty sweat burned his eyes and the trees swayed. Bicycles and boaters and picnic baskets and the shouts of gimcrack sellers and all the empty faces along the benches were sinking into looming dark. But there she was! Sitting on the green wooden bench exactly where he'd left her, and wearing a silver-grey fur coat. He waved, shouted, ran, stumbling through the airless heat towards her. She was smiling. Her face was a cool flame, and the rest of the Kite Hills retreated as he approached, until her features suddenly changed, and what remained of Ralph's rational mind saw another face—red-eyed, blue-lipped and gaunt—inside the blood-fogged glass visor of what was surely a diver's brass helmet. The lost moment contracted. Something was wrong, and breathless fathoms of pain engulfed him until, just when he was sure that he could bear it no longer, there was no pain at all.

VIII

Alice found herself staring at the grandfather clock in the great hall. *Now* she understood those dull-eyed mothers she'd seen trailing across the Continent revisiting the places which had failed them, lost and black and alone. For she'd do the same. She'd visit every spa and sit in every hopeless waiting room and drink the blood-threaded phlegm of every victim until she finally possessed Ralph's disease. Then at least—and instead of this terrible impotence which, after two sleepless days and nights, had made her flee Ralph's room—she could share. She'd take his pain from him and make it entirely her own.

This was far too quick. Not long ago, he'd been wandering the garden. Arguing. Reading. Eating. And it had never been this bad. Not ever. She should never have come to the west, this dreadful place . . . She couldn't simply stay. She knew she had to do *something*. Dry-eyed, her face hurting, Alice hurried outside.

'Mistress . . . ?'

She turned and saw Steward Dunning running across the gravel towards her.

'Mistress, where are you going?'

Alice didn't know. But wasn't it a simple enough request— a horse, to ride? 'And I want nothing done here. You hear?

Nothing. And make sure Doctor Foot stays awake. And these skies—tell Weatherman Ayres to get rid of this damn sunlight . . .'

Summoning a horse from a flustered Wilkins, Alice rode out from Invercombe. Already, the sky above the weathertop was greying. It looked like filthy milk as it bloomed and each clop and fall of the mare's hooves, the tink of the bridle, was an affront to the air. Then she was struck by the odd thought that she hadn't telephoned Tom since Ralph had fallen ill, that his father would be busy in London whilst his son, to his mind, still laughed and walked and grew better. She gave a barking laugh, and the mare twitched her flanks. The sky had drawn the light from the land, and she had no idea where she was, or where she was going. Then she came to a sign at a crossroads. **Einfell**—it seemed beyond all logic that this was where she was heading, but at the same time, it was something which had always lain unadmitted in the back of her mind since she'd first come here to the west. Ahead lay the realm of the changelings. Indeed, and despite everything, she almost had to smile to think that she might soon see Silus Bellingson again.

Here were big hedges of a kind which might surround any large and relatively private establishment, and then a nondescript set of gates, and she dismounted. There was silence. No birdsong. She pushed at the gates, which swung inwards. She tugged the mare's bridle, but the previously compliant beast wouldn't budge. Hooking the reins, she headed up the grey-white path.

On either side lay shadowed woodland, then she was facing a lake of parkland with a low building islanded at its centre. Pushing against the thud of her heart, she walked towards it. The building was of the grey concrete which had been briefly thought to be modern near the start of this Age, now weather-stained, and its brassy swing doors gave soundlessly to the pressure of her hand to an anonymous interior, and a wide, shining desk, although there was no one behind it. After all, just how desperate would you have to be to visit this place?

Alice heard the small frictions her shoes made against the polished floor. *My son is dying.* The thought, far more true and shocking and terrible than anything she had ever experienced, engulfed her. Then she became conscious of something standing in the doorway behind her. A cowled figure, like a friar. It couldn't be. And yet . . .

'Is that really you—Silus?'

Long hands, whiter than ivory, fanned and shaped. *I might ask you the same. Has time forgotten you, Alice?*

She shook her head, then forced herself to take a step closer to her old lover. 'My son is dying.'

'People rarely come to Einfell on happy occasions . . .' His voice, although recognisably still his, had become slurred and lisping. Gesturing along a corridor, he turned silently, and Alice followed, wondering how much he remembered, felt, knew. There were numbered doors, and more glimpses of those green lawns squared on the walls like endless versions of the same painting. Whoever had made this place must have loved ordinariness. Then they were in a room, a mere office, and Silus was seated behind an empty desk and motioning with those changed, strange hands which had once caressed her that she should take the chair on its far side. There was another window at his back, giving a view across more of the lawns towards the woods which seemed to lie beyond in every direction. The light meant that Alice could see nothing but shade inside his hood.

'Should I still call you Silus?'

'You can call me what you wish, Greatgrandmistress.'

'You know that I'm a greatgrandmistress?'

'Wasn't that the whole point of your life, to become who you now are? And then that you'd never need to tell people how you got there?'

Dimly now, there was a face inside the shadows of the hood. But it was scarcely Silus at all. Scarcely human, indeed.

'I've been staying at a house not far from here. My son's been ill for so long that I've forgotten the time when he wasn't. But I've been searching, and I really thought that Invercombe might make the difference. There's a weathertop— I gave orders . . .' Her eyes strayed from the pallid shape inside the hood, and her cheeks tingled with something cold. Alice Meynell realised she was crying.

You fear your son's dying?

Tasting salt, she nodded.

'As you can perhaps imagine, Alice, you're not the first to visit Einfell in grief. Or expecting miracles.'

'It's not a miracle. I just need to give him back what's . . .'
Mine?

No. She shook her head. *I could let Ralph go, Silus. I could let him fly or fall or be anything. If only . . .*

Silus chuckled, although it was an immensely sad and alien sound; the hiss of winter trees. The hands reached to the hood, lifting it back, and Alice was forced to meet those eyes, which were entirely of the same colour as today's sky, yet still somehow human. That, far more than the distortions of his skull-like face, was the most terrible thing of all.

'Why should I help you, Alice, of all the people in the entire world?'

'You were always a good man, Silus.'

Again, that wintry chuckle. *If I'd been a good man, Alice, I wouldn't be here now. I had a wife, a life, children. I had a career. I even believed, may the Elder help me, that I could have you and still keep their love for me . . .*

'You were scarcely the first man to ever—'

But I loved you, Alice. I think that was my real mistake.

Alice supposed it probably was. In those first difficult months in London, she'd needed a lover of wealth and influence; someone whom she would have to pass beyond, but nevertheless an essential stepping stone along the shining way to becoming what she was inevitably becoming. Grandmaster Silus Bellingson of the Guild of Electricians—a handsome man who prided himself in being both faithful to his wife and family, and yet still charmed all the ladies—had been the ideal choice. And an easy lure. Of course, after a few months when Alice had been sufficiently established in London to decide that it was time to end things and pursue Tom Meynell, Silus had resisted. She remembered the night that she had agreed to meet him late in his office beneath the smoking towers of London's main power station, and how, unable to resist bragging about his guild's prowess, he'd led her past the huge halls of the generators, and slid back the doors of the secret cabinets wherein enormous quantities of aether sat quietly roaring light and dark from their quart-sized vials . . .

'It wasn't arrogance, Alice—not all of it. It was love.' *I believed . . .*

'And what do you believe now?'

'Is your son really dying?'

'I would never lie about such a thing.'

'No,' he sighed. *For all I know about you, I don't think you would.* 'But you imagine that because the guilds once used my kind to mend problems which lay beyond their spells—and used us badly, it has to be said—and because of all the myths and rumours, we Chosen might also be able to help mend your son. But humans aren't machines, Alice. And Einfell is as real as you are, as real as this day, and as real as your son's illness. There is no Goldenwhite. It's not some mythical place, and the good health you wish back for Ralph isn't like some broken flywheel. You, Alice, of all people, should understand that there is far more to the imminence of death than that . . .'

She studied the room. There was a metal four-drawer filing cabinet set on a shining grey linoleum floor beneath off-white walls on which were hung a few faded photographs of Age-old faces. You're right, she thought, gazing back at the changeling through her blurring sight. I know exactly what the nearness of death is like. This is it.

'Then why,' she said, 'don't you simply send me away and be finished with whatever game you're playing?'

Without making the slightest motion, Silus shook his head. 'I can't. And there's *something*. The Shadow Ones—'

'Shadow Ones?'

'They live in Einfell's far woods. They are . . .' He paused. 'More changed than I am. Closer to the pure stuff of whatever it is that aether seems to strive to make us become. And they have been restless lately. After all, by the end of this year, this Age will have lasted a whole century . . .'

'You're saying that—'

No. I'm not saying anything.

A fresh wave of loss broke over Alice. 'What can I possibly?'

'I think you should leave.'

'Ralph could be . . .' *Dead already.* She let the terrible thought, unspoken, escape from her.

'I think you should go back to Invercombe.'

Alice nodded and stood up. Silus stood up, too, and opened the door for her with his long white hands. Beyond the office, far along the corridor, she thought she glimpsed another of the creatures, and a face of terrible charcoal, but it was too quickly gone for her to be sure. Then she was outside and alone. Why had she come here? What had been the urge, the point? And what had Silus meant about the Shadow Ones in the woods? When she reached their edge, where the trees brushed the clouds in threads of dark, something in their tumbling shade called to her. Despite everything, she had to know what lay beyond.

There were objects strung amid the trees. Cooking spoons and forks jangled to her passage. Scraps of ceramic and curtain hoop turned and flashed. The way beneath her, which had now become more certain, was paved, of all things, with dinner plates. Then she came to a wider space, and there was movement, although it seemed to her at first that it was merely a cloudy settling of the greyness amid the trees and the summonings of her own confused feelings.

What would you give, Greatgrandmistress . . . ?

Alice blinked, paused, swayed. Was she really hearing, seeing? Then a shape, part human but entirely grey and ragged, loped towards her across the sere grass, and another, quick and light as a shadow, whispered behind it. Something else rustled the trees. For a moment, Alice was surrounded, and the sound and the feeling—frightening, and yet queerly musical, like a yearning song you might hear in a dream—thrilled through her. These things had faces, yes. They had mouths and eyes. They even wore scraps of clothing which rustled and jingled just like the woods which surrounded them, although they were all impossibly thin and quick and faint. Despite everything, Alice smiled. She reached out a hand towards them, and felt momentary touches against her flesh like the falling of the lightest of silks. These Shadow Ones, she thought with an odd rejoicing, are the true changelings. They are so infused with aether that they have become almost pure spell. And how sad and typical of Silus, that, even in becoming what he was, he should stop halfway.

What would you give . . . ? Again, that question. Then they rustled away, and Alice, standing alone once more in the clearing, noticed that a small and ancient transmission house lay at its far side. It was abandoned amid the peculiar statuary just like everything else which had been placed here, but she found herself stooping inside, and dusting leaves from the screechy metal chair, and rubbing a dried-up rag across the mirror until her reflection filled the grimed glass. The antique heaviness of the fittings reminded her of Invercombe—of course, this was where those first telephone messages would have been sent, for you could hardly have just *one* telephone booth. Here was another relic of her guild's great history . . .

Her attention regathered in the dulled brightness of the mirror. Alice Meynell. Neither old nor young, but eternally beautiful. Through all her anxiety about Ralph, and although the booth had been long disconnected, it really did seem to her for a shivering moment that some kind of exchange took place.

IX

Ralph strode through the summer grass across Durnock Head, dwarfed by the widening horizon as he approached the Temple of Winds.

'Come on!' he called down to his mother as she struggled to catch up with him. 'I'd say you were tired already if I didn't know you better . . .'

'Quite frankly, I *am* tired, darling.' Alice was surprised at the spinsterish wheeze in her voice as she finally eased herself down beside him in the shade of the circular bench. 'After all, I'm not quite as young as you . . .' She smiled back at him as brightly as she could manage. Strands of windblown hair clung to her wet neck. And her bones, the bones which had always carried her flesh so well and which she had stupidly imagined would faithfully bear her through the rest of her life, were aching. *Our children*, she remembered the phrase from somewhere, *are the messengers of our mortality*. But she'd never imagined that the message would come this suddenly, or so strongly.

Doctor Foot still urged caution, but it was apparent to everyone that Ralph Meynell wasn't just mending—he was healed. It was no longer a matter of what he or Alice did or didn't believe. He was fit; impossibly, yet quite demonstrably so. Her heart might be thudding, yet he wasn't even panting, and the entire time since his recovery now felt like the climb she'd just made up Durnock Head; of trying to catch up with him and never, ever quite managing. She remembered her return to Invercombe on the grey Noshiftday of her visit to Einfell, and the sight of Steward Dunning beaming and hurrying out of the house. Dragged helplessly up the best stairs, Alice had still been entirely unable to make sense of the woman's gibberings. But all the windows had been open in Ralph's room. In fact, every single, simple order she'd given had been countermanded, and Alice was a moment away from striking the steward across her fat Negro face when she realised that Ralph's eyes were open and that he was looking at her with a bemused but essentially happy expression on his face. The fever, as she laid her wondering hand on his stubbled cheek, no longer poured out of him. He truly was past the crisis. A day later, he'd been sitting up and eating with almost worrying greed. The day after that, he'd been striding about the house as he rarely ever strode anywhere. And look at him now, little more than a shifterm later.

None of it made sense. Steward Dunning and her maids might take a mere miracle in their stride, and Ralph could put the whole thing down to his beloved science, but Alice still felt confused, as well as tired and breathless, as she sat in the Temple of Winds. He mind still wrestled with her trip to Einfell, her conversation with Silus, and her glimpse of the creatures he'd called the Shadow Ones.

I should have brought some of the textbooks up here from the library . . .' He was up from the bench and pacing the boards of this windy chapel to lost gods, his renewed and deepened voice ricocheting off the domed roof. He was saying how the books often spoke of the *best, most typical specimens*. As if there was something wrong with all the others! As if they, too, didn't have their story and meaning—although meaning was a word he detested almost as much as all those pious phrases about *evidence of design* . . .

Alice, bemused and exhausted, decided she should make the most of the opportunity to rest and enjoy the view. Soon, they'd be wandering around this headland and inspecting the leaves of some trivial plant individually and in pointless detail. Ralph's

good health had come upon her so suddenly that she hadn't
had time to react. Before, she'd always taken responsibility,
she had been in charge. The old Ralph had been essentially
stationary. She'd known that if she left him in a room, he'd
still be there when she returned, but this new son of hers was
dragging her about like a dog on a leash. Sometimes, it was
hard not to feel just a little resentful. And she had so many
other things on her mind. Tom was floundering over this dispute with Pikes and she desperately needed to get back to
London, if only for a few days, to steady the ship.

'You know, you can tear out the relevant pages of the books
if you need them. After all, they're ours.'

'I suppose so,' he conceded, almost frowning. 'But the
pages are arranged in a hierarchical pattern, and that pattern
isn't just in the books. It's out there . . .'

And off he went and, soon, off she went as well, out from
the temple's shade to examine each blade of grass for length
and breadth and hairiness and make tedious notes. It was like
unpicking some tiny, pointless knot. And meanwhile her guild
was haemorrhaging influence and money. Yes, she admittedly
enjoyed her own occasional early morning searches for a particular flower or plant or insect, but they were nothing like
this. Most frightening of all, Ralph's plans were blossoming.
He wanted to look at shells next, and the insides of rocks.

Alice slumped down on the billowing greensward and
squinted back towards the house. Invercombe's greens, its glistening waters, its windows and chimneys; all looked so triumphant, so solid—yet her entire world was askew. Then,
looking down the north side of valley where the headland dwin-
dled and where, beyond the parterre gardens, Invercombe's
grounds took on a more practical bent, she saw the white flap of
washing, and a female figure stooping and rising, and a plan began to form in her head.

That lunchtime, Alice went in search of Cissy Dunning. The
house was cool, quiet, softly creaking and ticking, caught in
its usual slur of hours. Guessing the steward would also be at
her lunch and thus probably in her office, she headed straight
there and entered without pausing or knocking, as was her
habit with servants.

'Ah, Mistress . . .' Cissy half stood. Her cheeks were crumbed and greased. 'It's been *such* a beautiful morning.'

'Hasn't it?' Alice sat down facing the steward and took a breath. 'I've been up Durnock Head with my son. But you mustn't let me stop you eating your lunch.'

'I'm pretty much finished.' Cissy Dunning dabbed her face with her napkin. The fact was, she half suspected that this beautiful, if slightly windblown, woman wanted her to continue eating because she would be at some minor disadvantage with her mouth full and butter on her face. The greatgrandmistress, on the other hand, scarcely ever seemed to need to eat. Or sweat, or excrete, either . . . Cissy cleared her throat and tried to meet that penetrating blue gaze. These weaselly thoughts always seemed to come when Alice Meynell was around. It wasn't that she didn't trust the woman, who had treated her fairly, even if she seemed to relish being unorthodox. It was more as if there was some other kind of standard by which Cissy should be judging her, but which she'd never been able to put her finger on.

Perhaps she's an angel, she thought. *Perhaps that's what it is. After all, she looks like one.* And she certainly acted the part, if that meant behaving in a way which you could never quite understand. And *something* had come to this house recently. Cissy, who'd always wondered what it must have been like for the onlookers outside Lazarus's grave, now almost felt, after the shock of seeing Ralph Meynell sitting up in his bed, as if she knew.

'This really is the most extraordinary time,' she commented.

'I've never seen Ralph this happy, this active—and I'm certainly not complaining. But I think I—*he*—needs some help . . .' Then Alice leaned forward somewhat, and her smile grew quite dazzling.

In what she was coming to think of as the old times, Cissy would have certainly resisted what this pale, graceful woman was now proposing. To put Ralph Meynell and Marion Price together, who, for all their vastly differing backgrounds, were of opposite sexes and almost the same age, was asking for trouble by all her normal standards. But it seemed to her now as if many of her old certainties were already crumbling.

'Her local knowledge would be useful from Ralph's point of view. That, and being fit and able and—and I think I'm right in surmising—reasonably intelligent. And I would guess that she knows quite a bit about the local wildlife. Certainly more than *I* would ever want to know.' A small gesture of the hands. That smile again. 'I want no opportunity to be held back from my son this summer. There will, of course, be many other summers now that he's so plainly recovered. But, and to be frank, I doubt if they will be quite the same as this one. My husband's a powerful man, and Ralph must move out from his shadow, if he is to prosper and thrive. This autumn, he will enrol at our Great Academy at Highclare. There will be study and duty, and he will be catching up. Catching up not just because of his illness, but because my son is the son of a greatgrandmaster and must therefore expect to exceed those he finds around him.'

'You make it all sound rather harsh, greatgrandmistress.'

'I don't make it sound that way, Steward. That, I'm afraid, is how it is.'

Cissy glanced at the kidney bean on her desk which, had it been anyone other than the greatgrandmistress sitting before her, she would now have picked up for the small comfort of its shape. But what, after all, was more natural than allowing two young people to spend this summer together?

•

X

The Temple of Winds was joined in dawn by the variegated tops of the specimen trees, and their greens and silvery-blues were mirrored and enhanced in the seapool. Within its still water there then came a hint of genuine movement; the flash of a shirt. Voices followed.

'Every single living thing is different. That tree is shaped like no other. The splay of its branches, the pattern of its bark—everything's unique.'

'And I thought it was all the work of Master Wyatt.'

Ralph laughed. His voice, after several months of wavering, had settled in a lower octave. 'With or without Master Wyatt!'

His and Marion's reflections glowed from the seapool as they sat on its stone surround and Invercombe unfolded into full daylight. By Ralph's standards, they were up ridiculously early. He'd wanted to make a particular study of the differing way the flowers opened their petals along the various aspects of the valley, and the effect that had on their orientation and shape, although Marion had merely shrugged at the mention of quarter past four and said she was up by then anyway. In many ways, she was hard to surprise. But then, sometimes, when he said the most obvious thing . . .

'You know, I'd really like to get to the libraries in Bristol. There must be some decent enough facilities in the guildhalls.'

'I've never been.'

'I suppose not. The Great Guilds—'

'I mean Bristol.'

'Don't you mind?'

She shrugged and looked away. Ralph's gaze, as they sat by the seapool, was drawn to the precision of her reflection. To the angle of her jaw, the dark gleams in her hair. To the point where the cuff of her blouse settled against her wrist, and the blue vein he could see there entwined around the glittery scab of her Mark. Every living thing, he reminded himself, was unique. But some, perhaps, were more unique than others.

The way Ralph saw the world now, everything was inextricably linked in ascending tiers of complexity and adaptation. But the implication of this pyramidal view, starting with the dumb rocks and narrowing up in increasing specialisation through mosses and slimes and then plants towards the animal kingdom, where beasts raised themselves to their legs and began to demonstrate the abilities of reasoning, was that, somewhere, there had to be a peak. Marion Price, he thought, still staring at her image in the dark depths of the pool, could well be it.

Apart from her breathing, she was as quiet as the seapool itself. There was a stillness about her, and then a suddenness and unpredictability to her movements. *Any moment now*, he thought, hoped, *she will turn and look at me*. But instead her left hand wandered as if with a will of its own across the lip of the pool. Her fingers dipped the water, shattering the whole valley into spreading circles of ripples. Ralph almost wanted to complain about the lost vision. But perfection has many facets, and the rise and fall of a disturbed fluid, obeying rules of surface tension with which he was broadly familiar, had never been so elegantly displayed.

As they headed out through the swing gate from Invercombe and along the path which wound towards the shore he could feel the day warming and expanding around him. He'd seen marvellous vistas on his journeys across Europe, but had mostly been separated from them by panes of glass and the blurring sense of being ill. This was more like the instant of stepping outside from a car—the sudden bustle of a street in a strange city. The world was so bright, so large, and everything was becoming so clear. More and more now, with his gathering strength and his renewed wonder at the start of each bewitching day, he felt like the God he no longer believed in.

He couldn't have asked to have a better guide to the shore than Marion. She had names for every type of plant and creature, which, even if they weren't technically correct, he even found himself using in the endless notebooks they were now compiling. *Pulmrose. Witches' purses. Cutthroats. Bootlace weeds.* And she knew about habitats as well. Not in the general sense of the men who annotated the plates in Ralph's books, but the exact type and nature of the life which dwelt in the individual rock-pools, and how and why they differed. Ralph could crouch with her for hours watching the slow growth of a worm cast, the wavering tentacles of a sea-urchin, the death-struggles of a shrimp, or Marion herself.

Now, dark against the shore-dazzle of sunlight, she turned back towards him.

'You should try walking barefoot,' she said, hopping to demonstrate as she peeled off boots and socks. Ralph, who'd forced himself to read the odd novel as part of his education, had previously wondered what all the fuss was about women's legs and ankles.

'Doesn't it hurt?'

'Your feet'll keep a lot dryer. And it'll save your shoes.'

Ralph shrugged, sat down. He'd always associated bare feet with beggars and urchins, but it felt better right away. In fact, the sense of air and sun on his bare toes was quite delicious. 'This is much better!' He took a few steps across the shingle, hobbled, winced, sat down again. 'No it isn't!'

'What a fuss you're making. Look . . .' She skipped, pirouetted. Ralph, as he watched Marion Price twirling and laughing barefoot on the shore, her hair fanning, dismissed any remaining doubts that she was the pinnacle of all creation. Then she gave a yelp and collapsed on the rock close beside him and began ruefully massaging the soles of her feet. 'Look . . .' She held up a foot.

Ralph looked. The toes were decorated with bits of sand

and shell. The two big ones, he noticed as she wiggled them, pointed upwards with a happy, eager tilt. 'Seems fine to me.'

'I used to be able to walk the shore barefoot all day. It never bothered me. I suppose I've been wearing shoes for too long.'

'That makes a difference?'

'Your skin hardens. It's like . . .' She stretched her legs and gazed out towards the estuary where sails, funnels and spars were drifting on the quivering air. 'Like the men out on those boats. Their hands get tougher than leather from working the ropes.'

'I don't think I'll never get tough feet like that. I mean, I can't imagine the last time a member of the Meynell family walked barefoot unless it was to step into their bath.'

'What are you saying—that I should have tough hands and feet because my father has?'

As was so often the case, Marion was already ahead of him.

'It doesn't work like that, though, does it?' she continued. 'If we became the way our mothers and fathers are, all of my cousins at Stipley would have only three fingers on their left hand just the way their dad has.'

Splaying his feet, laughing, the sunlit world expanding around him, Ralph felt the wet sand oozing between his toes. Marion wandered ahead. He loved the way she walked when she was on the shore, always looking, stooping, searching—so alert. She reminded him of some seabird. She found something. Lifted it, laughing.

'Look—Ralph! I've found a kidney bean.'

He had no idea what a kidney bean was, but he stood up and ran towards her through the hot light to share in her discovery.

I've never been, he thought, *so happy*.

XI

London, Alice thought as she prepared to leave her Northcentral townhouse, had come as a shock. It was as if something in the west had left her amazed like some stupid bumpkin by sights she'd long grown used to. But her car was waiting, gleaming and darkening in the flash of Hallam Tower, and she let the great buildings and the morning's traffic pass her by. Part of her thoughts were still with Ralph, but today she had other fish to fry.

Dockland Exchange, almost old enough now to be picturesque, still soared over the docks. If the story of her guild could be rewritten, Alice would certainly have chosen a different location for its main halls. Sometimes, she even permitted herself daydreams of taking over the halls of the Beastmasters or perhaps even the upstart Toolmakers along Wagstaffe Mall, but today such hopes were far off. And she supposed, as she stepped out and looked up through the turning cranes at the great, tall edifice where her husband worked, that there were advantages to be gained in having your head office close to the real means of production. Wealth, she knew as she stepped over slippery spillages, was essentially a messy business, and had little to do with marble halls and courtrooms.

She took the lift, but nevertheless stopped at many floors, unannounced at first, although word that the greatgrand-mistress was about had soon spread upwards. Uppermasters and highermasters scurried amid the clatter of typewriters, air-tubes, message trolleys, ribbon-reads. As always, she made a special note of those most knowledgeable and hard-working; such men were useful to her guild, but then again, they could pose a threat.

Tom had already been long at his desk when she reached his wide top office. Club luncheons and morning walks had their parts to play in the smooth functioning of the Great Guild of Telegraphers, but these were difficult times, and she felt a twinge of pity for him. He looked measurably older now, and had been unable to properly sustain an erection last night despite their long separation. If he carried on this way, he'd be in his grave even sooner than his father. But this, Alice decided, as she laid her hands on his shoulders and kissed the thinning hair on top of his head, this was the difficult end of a difficult Age. Everyone would have to make sacrifices.

'I really must get down to that house of ours in the west.'

'Of course you must.' She straightened up, removed her gloves. Light gleamed on the paintings and panels. Up here, London was bright, blue-grey. 'As soon as you get the chance, you must take a proper rest, darling.'

'And you say Ralph's much better.'

'He's not just better, darling. He's *mended*, and he spends all his days out on the beach. He's even made friends. Honestly, darling, you'd hardly recognise him. Otherwise, I would never have left him and come here.'

Tom sighed and smiled. 'At least something's going the right way.'

She sat by his desk, and they began to talk business. The figures prepared for her by the reckoning engines hadn't been done in quite the way she'd asked, but nevertheless they told the expected story. Profits were down. Costs were up. Pessimism was always more infectious that optimism—you only had to listen to the conversations in the clubs—but the Telegraphers were suffering even more than the other Great Guilds. Alice had taken her eye off things far more than she'd imagined during Ralph's illness, and this was the price they were paying. But she had plans.

'Let's go outside. I've something I want to explain to you.'

Out on the balcony, the tart London air rushed over them. From up here, the huge roofs of the warehouses seemed to be climbing over each other in their eagerness to get to the crowded river.

'Strange, you know, that old Grandmaster Pike should die in the way that he did,' Tom, who wasn't looking at the city at all, was saying. 'I mean, to fall from a balcony. It reminds me of that chap who was talking of buying into some of our shares a few years back and restructuring the board. What was his name—Digby? No, *Drigby*. He died in a fall as well, didn't he?'

Lightly, but unblinkingly, Alice met her husband's gaze. 'What are you thinking?'

'I don't know really,' he sighed, his eyes drifting from hers to follow the movement of a crane towards a ship. 'People dying, I suppose.' There was a long pause. Tom's eyes, he studied without seeing the clamorous scene below, seemed lost and strange. 'These are hard times for us, Alice. But everyone says we're the luckiest couple on earth, especially now Ralph's properly mended.'

'And we are. And we will be.' Alice composed her profile and let her eyes glitter in the wind. 'We own, as you know, a lot of land on the east coast. It's poor stuff mostly, and we lease most of it for grazing at a few pennies an acre. Of course, it was where we were supposed to be siting that new telephone line that Pikes were supposed to have built, but I think there's something else we can do with it . . .'

She'd planned this moment, had envisaged it happening much as it really was now out on Tom's balcony, although things were almost spoiled by a sudden swirl of London wind as she tipped out the contents of the envelope she'd removed from her pocket. Light and dry and green, the stuff almost scattered from her palm before she managed to cup it. But there was still enough left for Tom to dab his wetted finger into her hand when she prompted him to taste it.

He pulled a face. 'It's almost sweet—but it has a kind of edge to it. What's it called?'

'Bittersweet. People in the west occasionally use it as a herb. But it never grows that well there. It thrives, you see, on poor soil, cold conditions. It's a practical crop for us to grow on that land along the east coast.'

'For what?'

'Do you know how much sugar cane we import each year from the Fortunate Isles to feed England's sweet tooth?'

'But I'm not aware that there's any kind of shortage.'

'There isn't.'

'You're saying this could be grown and marketed as a substitute . . .' Tom swallowed, his cheeks still working and his eyes watering slightly. He saw her point; he always did. They made a good team—she with her ideas and subtle influences, he with his hard work and determination. Bristol would have less trade and London would have more, and the Telegraphers' Guild would profit enormously . . .

'I've had a little research done,' she continued. 'You'd be amazed at the uses bittersweet can be put to. Not just cakes and chocolates and for stirring into tea. Scents and cosmetics as well—meat pies and cheeses—especially anything that's been cheaply made—all benefit from a little sweetening.'

Still, and perhaps it was merely the effect of the admittedly harsh taste of the raw bittersweet, he looked doubtful.

'If you think, darling, that the costs—'

'Alice, it's not the practicalities which worry me. If you of all people say that we can, I'm sure we'll be able to sort things out. I'm not so much concerned about bittersweet failing as I am about its success—and what the consequences of that might be.'

Sometimes, Tom could be as strange and stubborn as Ralph. But it was already far too late for them to back out, and she knew he wouldn't let her down. Effectively, the planning documents were already approved and merely required his signature. The deed was already done. But Tom didn't need her to explain all of that to him. He'd work it out himself.

Late that same evening, after a day's hard catching up with her own paperwork, and when the exchange had emptied of most of its staff and even Tom had gone home and she was certain she would not be disturbed, Alice entered the private telephone booth on the topmost floor. It was pleasingly odd to sit in the place where her husband had so often spoken to her, and there was a dusty, leathery smell in the booth which she'd noticed during their calls. She glimpsed herself in the mirror as she opened the connector. It was as if some part of her was still out there, waiting.

She dialled, and, with what was now practised ease, breathed her new spell, and surged down the great vein which ran through the centre of Dockland Exchange to its subterranean reckoning engines. It would be good to involve these machines more closely in the development of bittersweet, but she knew they were fallible. It wasn't their fault—nothing ever was—but the economic data they received, especially from the west, was corrupted by all the fudge. One day, she silently promised this whirling mesh of information, the world outside will be exactly as you imagine it is. Logic will reign. Your predictions will be perfect. But now, she headed on into the national network and leaped east to west across England from relay to transmission house until she reached the *here* of Invercombe's telephone booth, which seemed to her, and more than ever now that she was away from the place, the most specific here of all.

Alice regathered herself within the distant mirror. She could hear clocks ticking. Slowly, ghost limb by ghost limb, she slipped from the glass, and then out of the empty booth. Beyond the best stairs, where the simulacrum of her gaze caught in one of the house's many mirrors, there remained only furniture and long evening sunlight, but she no longer felt the crisis which she had first experienced to realise that she both was and wasn't present. The inner hall was deserted. Flowers hung in vases, momentarily scentless. She made the effort. Yes, that was better. The best stairs breathed in silent ascension. Her presence held. Slippery and invisible as a shadow within a shadow, Alice drifted forward. The simulacrum of her gaze caught in one of the hall's many mirrors. There was nothing for her to see, but she no longer felt the crisis which she had first experienced to truly realise that she both was and wasn't in the place she imagined. *I am*, she thought to herself, and would probably, if such a thing were possible, have chuckled, *getting better and better at this*. The combination of movement and keeping focus was still the trickiest part. To concentrate on that old oak chair, this marble bust, then the distinctive swirl of wood on the panelling of the far doorway, it was necessary for her to fill herself with each factual solidity before she moved on from it.

Drifting forward in pauses and dashes, she entered the dim, whitewashed corridors of the servants' halls, and then passed down through workrooms and storerooms. Invercombe grew cave-like in its depths, with pillars of glossy rock curving into darkness where salt air pulsed out to the beat of the waves. Strung across the roofs, wavering faintly like the feelers of some enormous lobster, were rubberised, red-coated cables. A swishing and a buzzing filled the air. Here in its musty alcove was that old reckoning engine, ticking with lazy agitation through its local streams of data within which—and this was still amazing to consider—she herself was now represented. Deep in this basement, underground but still lit through by archways with the glow of fading daylight where the Riddle cut the valley at its deepest, two fat, laterally placed generators squatted and growled like angry beetles. But their turning wasn't the main source of the noise, which came from outside where the buckets of the waterwheel were chanting *yes, yes, yes*, as they filled and turned.

From here, she could have gone further into the honeycomb of Invercombe's sea-bowels, but instead she looped up along the pylons towards the glow of the weathertop. For a moment, she *was* electricity, and then she was the weathertop's outer gantry, where the soft green of all Somerset lay in one direction and the valley and the gleaming Bristol Channel lay in the other. And there was Weatherman Ayres, looking down towards the path which led to the orchards. Alice followed his smiling gaze, and saw, humming and swaying and topped with a dotted red head-scarf, the round, unmistakable figure of Steward Dunning. She was bearing a heap of silver-fronded sallow in a big wicker basket back from the physic garden. Really, this was a job for cook, but Invercombe's steward looked entirely happy. Indeed, Weatherman Ayres's gaze, of which Alice was now part like the silver throw of an invisible spiderweb, had a warmth and a hunger to it which had little to do with the prospect of tonight's supper, no matter how fine it would inevitably be. These, indeed, were strange, abandoned days.

Alice drew back to the gantry of the weathertop. At other

times this was as far as she would have dared extend herself from the telephone booth, but the loveliness of the deepening evening was in her as well, and the trees of the pinetum were beckoning. In a mere simple leap, she slipped from branch to branch, shade to shade, then slid down towards the cascades, and passed through the fronded mouth of the grotto, and the peculiarities of the specimen trees. She reached to the seapool. It would be pleasant just to float here in this blood-warm salt. But from there a final fence rambled its way around Durnock Head, and it was set with a gate, which was her next obvious destination. Then she moved across the long shadows of the rocks towards the gaining scent of the sea.

The tide was far out and the sense of life here was very different, away from Master Wyatt's control. It fought and hunted and consumed itself. Far out across this shining expanse, three figures moved like wyreblack flames. On a twist of sand, a broken limpet shell, a hank of old fishing net, the white bones of a gull splayed across the blazing sunset. Alice drifted towards them.

XII

The lights of the Severn Bridge were just starting to glimmer as Ralph helped Marion and her father push their surprisingly obdurate boat into the rising tide. Ralph, as he heaved, was no longer the frail greatgrandmaster-to-be of other years. With his ragged clothes, with his browned skin and sun-bleached hair, he'd come to look more and more like the other figures who wandered the shore. So did Marion, although she was merely slipping back to a natural state. Soon, dark-haired, barefoot and swiftly busy, both full-grown but still impossibly young, even their appearances had grown somewhat alike. The other shorefolk who waved and chatted to them would sometimes ask if they weren't perhaps related?

Mud slipped under his feet and knees, and then, with a sucking rush, the keel slid from them. Ralph, as he attempted to catch and climb into it, was surprised by the sudden light-ness with which the boat skipped away from him, and fell headlong into the deepening water. A momentary panic as salt-bitter water rushed into his mouth and throat, then Marion was helping him up.

'Can't swim, eh?' Her father chuckled. 'And I thought you said you'd been on lots of boats.'

More carefully, as Marion helped steady the boat, he climbed in. He was soaked, but the air and the water were too warm for any discomfort, and it hardly seemed worth explaining that the ships he'd sailed in had possessed ballrooms and promenade decks. This was a different kind of sailing entirely, just as it was another kind of living, and it was amazing how easily the weathertopless sail filled even on a night this still.

Each day now had an easy rhythm. In the mornings, Marion and Ralph often investigated the rocks on the seaward of Durnock Head. Apart from its geological significance, it was a marvellous landscape for climbing, and for Marion, much as for Ralph, this summer was a chance for her to experience the freedoms of a childhood she'd scarcely known. As the air across the Bristol Channel grew impossibly clear and the ships became toys you could cup in your hands, they would begin to unprise the shale, each layer breaking with that sense of newness which only the *chink* of a hammer could create. Sometimes, they would discover a scatter of shells, some would be recognisably like the ones they found every day on the shore, whilst others would be strange. Or they would find worm-casts, or odd things which looked like giant woodlice. Ocean drawn back to ocean, they wetted the facets in nearby pools, and Ralph imagined he was moving beneath the waters of some lost sea.

They often went to Clyst at lunchtime, but the other Prices scarcely saw the vast distance which Ralph had travelled to sit at their kitchen table. Ralph's skin was tide-marked with salt and sunburn, and he had a decent knowledge of the shore, even if he did give some of its creatures the strangest names. He'd even absorbed a little of the western accent. Only Denise asked the sort of questions which you might expect to have answered by someone high-guilded. But London was a shrug. Paris was a smile and a vague shake of the head.

By mid-afternoon, the heat drove them to the fragrant shade of the citrus grove, or they headed down Invercombe's dimming stairways to the cool alcove of its reckoning engine. Once oiled and brushed of dust and rust, and peeled of their cobwebs, the device's tumblers and levers still moved with the slick ease of all good machinery as Ralph and Marion attempted to input the information they'd gathered about life on the shore into punch-cards. The work was considerable, but he was sure they were making progress.

Now, the evening had settled into glowing night, and they were reaching deeper waters where the air changed its moods and scents. Ralph glanced at Marion's father—her dad, as he'd come to think of him—who was nudging the wooden tiller with his calloused fingers. Marion, meanwhile, was holding the boom rope. They both had this careless manner when they were doing the work of shorefolk, although Ralph had known long before tonight's dunking that this was deceptive. The skills they possessed were as complex as any of the Great Guilds, and considerably more fascinating. He'd been out with Marion's brother Owen on a mudhorse to help clear and collect the salmon traps. He'd helped Mam strip willow switches, and he'd headed with the whole village on magical nights when everyone went eel-trapping, pushing the fizzing chemical lights beneath the thigh-deep water and steering the sleek, undulating bodies into whispering nets. Ralph had done all of these things, and rejoiced in them. And soon, it would be Midsummer, and he already knew this Midsummer would be marvellous and entirely different, for the plans and the preparations were enormous. Even tonight's voyage was part of them, although he still didn't know quite how or why.

There was darker water now, so clear you could see right down into bottomless nothing. Marion's dad was murmuring instructions, checking the distant landmarks. The Temple of Winds was just a glint of moonlight. Lights scattered north towards Avonmouth clustered as if drawn on strings towards the tiara of the Severn Bridge. Big ships hung tall across the waters, sleepy-still as they waited at anchor with lights at their topmasts, or churning ablaze through the main outer dredgeways as they went about the business of the guilded world. You could see inside the lit windows of their cabins, and breathe the smoky rush they bore from their weathertops and engines.

Marion tugged the boom. Laying a quick hand on Ralph's knee, which sent a warm shudder through him, she squeezed past to take the rudder. Dad leaned over the side, peering into the depthless waters. He then began to stir a stick of driftwood and mutter something until threads of faint luminosity started to form. Was this some phosphorous effect? But Dad was still muttering, almost singing, words too quick and slurred for Ralph to catch. A glass float—sparkling blue, a mirror of the night—bobbed up. Dad lifted it into the boat. A thin strip of tether, then a thicker stream of rope, followed.

Ralph helped pull whilst Marion coiled and stowed, with the exquisite press of her forearm coming and going against his back until the rope lay coiled wyredark on the floor of the boat in the gaining light of the rising moon. He'd just witnessed, he realised, the casting of a spell. But now a crate was emerging and he was too absorbed in getting the thing over the side. He had to lean so far back against its weight that he feared they'd be capsized. Then, in a final rush, the crate was on board.

Gushing slats revealed the green shapes of bottles. Dad gave a wide grin. 'Nothing but the best for this Midsummer, eh? Now—let's get back to shore and have this stuff hidden before we run into the bloody Excise Men . . .'

XIII

Greatgrandmaster Thomas Meynell finally arrived at Invercombe on the last train of the eve of Midsummer. Next morning, he felt exhilarated, and he wondered as he wandered the corridors just how many other discoveries Alice had been quietly nurturing amongst their guild's possessions—but none, he decided, could be quite this glorious. It was hardly surprising, he thought, looking into rooms where air and sunlight wafted through open windows, that Ralph had recovered in this place.

The doors of bedrooms breathed open. This room, surely, was Ralph's. There were stones and books and shells, although there was no sign of the lad. This one, around the corner, was certainly Alice's. Glancing back, he decided to risk entering it. Last night, both claiming tiredness, they'd slept in separate rooms. Yet he felt much closer to his wife here as the sea air washed in through the open French windows and light glowed across the black leather sides of her big portmanteau. He smiled and touched its immovable locks, and glanced again towards the door.

There were things about his wife which, secretly, Tom had long known. That she was perhaps a little older than she claimed, for example. Or that her guilded origins weren't quite as exalted as she liked everyone to think. His father had had his doubts from the start—he even used the phrase *gold-digger*—but, for Tom, that slight aura of evasion and mystery had always been one of the many things which he'd found so impossibly attractive about Alice.

Here was the mirror where she prepared herself, although he'd never seen her look anything less than perfect, not even in the wildest moments of their passion. In fact, she was even *more* perfect then. He felt his cock stirring. He recalled the secret, magical things which had once been so precious to him about their sexual life. Her wiles and abandonments. The first time she'd astonished him by bowing unbidden to take him into her mouth. Love—sex—was both simple and extraordinary. Like a song he hadn't heard in years, it all came back to him. Last night really had been nothing but weariness. Now, it would be like old times, resurrected by the inescapable magic of this house.

His gaze strayed along the perfume vials to the green velvet case where she kept her jewellery. He slid it open, running his fingers through glints of sapphire and pearl as he thought of how they had lain on Alice's skin. A chain snagged, but he managed to untangle it, and was laying things back in some approximation of the Alice-like neatness when his knuckle brushed on something, and a drawer underneath, which had shown no previous sign of existing, sprang out. There was an odder mixture of stuff down here. Even the finer bits, like this silver bangle set with bits of green stone, seemed much too brash for her. And this brooch was surely cheap paste—extremely cheap, if he could tell. And this hatpin had been corroded by long exposure to air and rain. And here was exactly the kind of brass button his father had once favoured for his waistcoats. Then a fine diamond earring; but just the one, and missing some of its gems. And surely this was simply the catch from a man's zip fly—but perhaps here lay the edges of another secret about Alice of which Tom wasn't entirely ignorant. After all, we all had our histories. He didn't begrudge her that. Why, he, too, had had his long-lost passions . . . Then, as if summoned by the thought, he discovered a silver teardrop strung on a thin gold chain. It turned and flashed as he held it before the mirror. It was a fine piece—expensive, too. Not that he hadn't wanted to spend more on dear, sweet Jackie Brumby,

but this graceful chain and pendant was probably as extravagant an item as any laundry maid could safely wear, even if she
had had to keep it hidden beneath her blouse as their own private secret. But how he'd adored the way it swung and glinted
between her naked breasts as they made love.

'You slept well?'

Turning, Tom slipped the chain from his fingers, closed the
velvet drawer.

Alice's voice, her whole presence, was cool and lithe.

'I think it must be this country air.'

She smiled. 'That's what people always say, isn't it?'

'And I was thinking I might move my stuff in here and
sleep with you tonight.'

She'd done up her hair in a way he especially liked, loosely
caught at the back by a long-fingered tortoiseshell comb to
display her fine neck and ears. Her legs were unstockinged
and her bare feet were lightly entwined in espadrilles. Slipping her arm into his, she led him downstairs and into the gardens. Up there on the left is the famous weathertop—well,
darling, it *should* be famous, anyway. That way, the promontory known as Durnock Head. Over there, those fairy turrets
disguise the very first telephone transmission house ever built
by our fellow guildsmen. Why, the place could be a museum
of some significance, were it not far too beautiful! They
reached the Lebanon walk, where the cooler air was threaded
with cobwebs. There had been, Tom couldn't help remembering, a minor spat with his father about the authorising of some
papers just before the old man had died from some spasm of
the brain whilst out riding one of the unicorns at Walcote.
Even on this glorious morning, the thoughts, like some
aethered darkness cast out by the sunlight, wouldn't go away.

*I've done a funny thing, darling. It's not much, really—but
you know those documents we talked about a shifterm or so
ago? Well, fact is, I still haven't signed them. Oh, it's nothing to
do with the planning process or that new plant of yours or our
guild. It's just—and I know this is entirely stupid, my dearest
Alice—but I simply want to be able to tell you I haven't signed
them, and then for you to smile back at me and say it doesn't
matter. And I'd sign the papers then, anyway. I'd sign the
bloody lot of them. Told you it was stupid, didn't I? I just want*

to hear you say you love me whether I sign those papers or not. But, as they crossed the bridge over a lily-studded canal, Tom found that he was unable to say any of those things.

'Ahead of us now, darling—this wide space—is what we call the pleasure grounds . . .'

Long trestles had been laid across the grass and were being covered by blazing tablecloths, and then by an endless stream of tureens and serving plates which were being borne down the valley from the kitchens. And pies the size of wagon wheels. Cakes of all colours and varieties. Pyramids of oranges. Scented mountains of peaches . . .

'Nibble away, dear. It'll all be eaten at midday when the locals arrive.' Her hand, butterfly-light, settled on his waist. 'It's a shame none of this can yet be made with bittersweet. Cook just uses it as a decoration. You know, you really are getting a shade portly.'

And then she was off, chiding or laughing with the servants, kind and compassionate, beautiful and wise: the very picture of the mistress of the house. Pushing away the shining image of Jackie's pendant, deciding that all his worries would probably settle into decent order if he just spent a little longer here, Tom looked about for Ralph. The shock of how tall his son had grown, the breadth of his shoulders, the length of his sun-tinged hair and the sense of warm health he exuded through his scruffy clothes, was even stronger this morning than it had been during their brief encounter the night before. *You really are a man now. I'm so, so proud of you.* But once again, the things Tom wanted to say to those closest to him wouldn't come.

'This is quite a show, eh? Anyway, Dad . . .' Ralph smiled, as anyone would, at the busy scene. 'I'm pleased you've finally come down to Invercombe.'

'You called me Dad . . .'

'It's just a word people use around here. I suppose I've picked it up. You don't mind, do you?'

'I quite like it.' Tom felt layers of ice breaking somewhere within him. *Dad*—perhaps it signalled the start of a new ease between them.

They wandered the lawns, Ralph happily pointing out this or that landmark or variety of tree, Latin names tripping from his tongue as easily as the pleasant burr of his new western accent. His son was fuller than ever with suppositions and theories, and Tom was breathless by the time they'd climbed the steps to the lip of the vine-fronded grotto which looked out across the pleasure grounds, but Ralph didn't pause as he talked until, finally, as the first of the locals began to appear, his gaze lingered on a particular dark-haired maid who was helping erect more trestles to support the seemingly endless tide of food. Tom had noticed her as well. She was exceptionally pretty—no, beautiful was the word—and the way Ralph was looking at her, that mixture of awe and longing . . . She glanced in their direction, and waved cheerily in a gesture as warm as the sunlight. Tom smiled to himself, to think that his son might be finding love. He even allowed another brief, illicit thought of dear, lost Jackie who'd left service and died so inexplicably . . .

'What I'm really after is evidence of specialisation—inherited adaptation to local conditions. I have this idea, you see, Dad, and I think it might be important to how we view life as a whole. I can't quite fully explain it yet . . .'

The scent the mouth of the grotto breathed out at them was cool and earthy.

'This really is an excellent place for study,' Tom agreed. 'After all, there's so much of our own guild history here. Those old devices—you really must show me. By the way,' he continued, quickly changing tack with the slight fall in his son's face, 'I've left the new prospectus for Highclare in your room. Your mother suggested I bring one down personally. Apparently, the post here's a little unreliable.'

'Highclare—that's our main academy, isn't it?'

'It's where you're going this autumn. Hasn't all this been . . . ?'

'I honestly hadn't thought, Father.'

There goes *Dad*. It was ridiculous, really, that Alice had never got around to mentioning this, with all the time she'd had with him here.

'Although I suppose it makes a kind of sense that I go there,' Ralph conceded.

'Well, that was what we thought. Your mother and I.'

'Of course.'

'And all of this is assuming that you're still as well as you seem to be—I mean, fully recovered.' Briefly, Tom could almost hate Alice for the way she'd foisted the task of breaking the news about Highclare to Ralph on him. But after all, he was Chief Telegrapher, and she'd simply and discreetly left the path clear for him to have the sort of man-to-man conversation about the future which any better father would have had already with his son. As always, it was his fault, not hers. For not being here. For his stupid obsessions. And he so admired Ralph for the dignified way in which he was taking this. He wasn't even asking to be reassured about what Highclare, with its cold dorms, its initiations and muddy pitches, was really like.

'I'm sorry.' Ralph's eyes, unfocused, met his father's. 'I suppose this was due to happen. I mean'—he gestured vaguely—'how could we be here in this lovely spot without the Telegraphers? And I know I have responsibilities. It's just that—well, it's come as a surprise. And I think I'm close this summer to discovering something important. You understand that, don't you?'

'Yes,' Tom agreed as they looked at each other blankly. 'I think I do.'

The picnic in the pleasure grounds was due to start at midday, but time amongst the shorepeople, and with the sole exception of the tide, was always *about*, which generally allowed a good hour or two's leeway. So it was a little before ten when the first arrivals tumbled through the swing gate which they had never dared use and up the paths into Invercombe's amazing grounds, and it was considerably after one-thirty when the main procession finally arrived. By then, the great pies were in ruins, cook had had to summon up many more batches of sausages and there was a chronic shortage of lemonade, but there was plenty of almost everything else to go round even if the scene of sunlit jellies and ravaged hams looked more like a battlefield than a picnic, and there was much lobbing of bread rolls.

Denise Price, who was this year's Midsummer Queen, arrived in a flower-bedecked chair surrounded by rose-petal-tossing swarms of children, although her acolytes scampered ahead at the first whiff of food, and she, after a little hesitation, and hungry herself, soon tucked up her train and ran to join them. Afterwards, sated and somewhat jolly, people headed in ragged groups back towards the Midsummer Market which always took place in the dray field up towards Luttrell. The presence of Invercombe's great-grandmaster and his beautiful mistress this year was a bonus. Many even commented— although well out of earshot of Denise Price—that Alice Meynell was today's real Midsummer Queen. She browsed the stalls of fruit and knotted hanks of herb and aromatic cigars and cheroots, along with the ubiquitous stacks of labelless bottles. People were proud that she was here, and grateful for her interest, and answered all of her many questions with a frankness which they probably came to regret.

A ram was slaughtered, a fire was lit, and savoury smoke drifted with the deepening evening. An old sail was stretched between the spars of two beached boats, and shapes began to flow across it. By the third reel, it became apparent that the cinematograph involved pirates, and laughably unlikely looking ships, and some kind of quest for treasure, and the occasional sword-fight. The flickering captions were haltingly echoed by the audience, either reading for the benefit of themselves or those around them. After much confusion about the order of the reels, the tale reached some kind of ending, and it was time for the main business of any Midsummer night, which was dancing, to begin.

The band was a liveried mixture of the various local guild academies. Sashes and uniforms were much in evidence, and Owen Price soon discovered that his new mariner's outfit made him a much greater prize amongst the girls than he'd been in previous Midsummers, whilst, and just as every year, every boy wanted to dance with Denise. But even the Reverend-Highermaster Brown wasn't short of partners tonight, for many of the women reckoned he was worth a quick spin for the good of their souls, although his roving hands were a blessed nuisance. Cissy Dunning, dazzlingly dressed in a swirling skirt of greens and oranges, coaxed Weatherman Ayres to join her. It would have been observed by anyone who was sober enough to notice that she was the only Negro amid the main throng, although there was a small gathering of darker-skinned local servants and employees who danced and drank together further down towards the beach.

Faces gleamed with mutton fat and excitement as an avenue of flaming willow branches was formed, and laughing couples ducked its blazing tunnel. There was a special cheer for Owen, who emerged with two girls. Another for Denise, who'd told all her evening's many suitors that she was saving herself for Bristol, and went triumphantly alone. There were other odd pairings that night. The maid Phyllis and Stablemaster Wilkins from Invercombe, although, after all their dancing, Weatherman Ayres and Steward Dunning came by now as less of a surprise. But Gardenmaster and Mistress Wyatt ducked the flames for the first time in twenty years, as did Bill and Mam Price. Then came the greatgrandmaster himself with his lovely greatgrandmistress, whilst their son, to no one's particular surprise but his own, went under arm-in-arm with the younger Price girl with whom he was so often seen.

It was approaching midnight, and parties were deputised to light the bonfires. You could watch the progress of their torches as they headed off along the shore and up the hillsides under the rising moon. Durnock Head in the north. The cliffs at Yaverland and High Reston to the south. This ceremony was being enacted by many communities, and the first fires came from across the estuary along the hills of Wales. Then the headlands of Hockton flickered, and their own furze fires caught. Soon the entire coastline was braceleted with stars, and those who stood on Luttrell shore on that night felt for once as if they were at the very centre of something, here the midnight of Midsummer in the ninety-ninth year of this Age of Light.

The seapool gleamed. The full moon was still up, but here in the lee of Durnock Head the night had a surprising, inky density. Nothing moved. Then came voices, footsteps.

'I'm sure those cinematograph reels were the wrong way around. The sword-fight at the end definitely belonged somewhere in the middle. Otherwise, how could that big pirate with the striped jersey still be alive?' Ralph laughed. His voice felt almost used-up, but pleasantly so. 'He'd already been made to walk the plank.'

'Perhaps he swam under the ship and climbed up the other side and back on to the deck,' said Marion, who'd seen such things happen before. Her dress was loosely hitched above her knees. She was carrying her shoes. 'Did you see that pirate who looked like Weatherman Ayres?'

'Perhaps he really *is* a pirate.' Ralph shook his head. It didn't seem so unlikely, and he wanted to say more. About how the shorepeople cheered the Spanish pirates and booed the English Enforcers when it was supposed to be the other way round. And how the jumbling of the reels had allowed the cinematograph to end with the definite impression that the pirates had won. Then he rounded the path and saw the dulled shine of the seapool, and his head span. Even with the tolerance he'd acquired from spirit-rich medicines, he was more than slightly drunk. Or he had been until they entered the shadow of this valley, where the air was cooler and no longer tinged with smoke. He was conscious of the scuff of Marion's footsteps. The whole day, in a stream of flags and flames and buntings, seemed to have dropped behind them on the path.

He climbed to the edge of the seapool and walked, swaying, balancing, along its stone lip. Marion watched him, and he tried to laugh, but this really was much more difficult than he'd imagined. He made a final dash to the steps at the far side.

'It's deep. Good job you didn't fall.'

'Yes . . .'

'You really should know how to swim.' Marion climbed to the edge of the pool. 'I'll teach you.' When she was beside him, she did the most extraordinary thing Ralph had ever witnessed. Loosening the tails of her blouse, she unbuttoned it. Then, her shoulders and bosom barely covered by her chemise, she began to loosen her skirt. 'Just do what I do.'

Ralph, too surprised to do anything else, followed suit. Until that moment, the night air had felt warm. Now, he was conscious that he was shivering.

'This is how shorefolk swim,' she said as she stood in her white underthings. 'Enough for modesty, but not enough to slow you down. I'd take off that vest as well if I were you,' she added matter-of-factly as she laid her things on the pool's dry edge. 'It's not as if it's covering anything in a man.'

Ralph did so, although this felt nothing like stripping before the gaze of nurses and physicians.

'This is an ideal place to get you started. The currents out in the channel can be strong.'

Ralph had never seen anything more beautiful than Marion as she pushed back her hair and slipped one foot and then the other into the pool's surface. There were submarine steps, which she slowly descended, meeting more and more of her reflection, knees, then thighs, then back, until the water covered to her shoulders and she merged, arms wavering outstretched, into the flickering moon.

'Is it cold?'

She laughed, turned. 'You'll have to find out . . .'

Soft weeds nudged his toes. It *was* cold, but at least it gave an excuse for his shivering. He descended until he felt a wintry compression against his ribs. 'What do I do now?'

She swam towards him, hovered tantalisingly beyond the steps.

'Just push out as hard as you can. I'll catch you.'

Ralph barely hesitated—she made it look and sound so perfectly easy—but water instantly boomed into his ears and rushed into his nose and mouth. Then he felt her hands on his arms, and stars and the indigo night burst around him.

Marion nudged him back. He scrabbled back to the steps and gulped and coughed.

She floated away. 'That was good.'

'*Good* . . . ?'

'Now. Let's try again. Try kicking harder with your legs and feet.'

This time, she was further away. He was certain he'd drown long before he reached her, but she looked so impossibly lovely, her hair wet and the water lapping her shoulders, that Ralph wondered briefly if mankind didn't have an aquatic origin. But the thought was too complex for him to deal with. He kicked out instead.

Once more, the surface closed over him. Once more, and just as he was certain that he would never breathe again, Marion's hands drew him back to the surface.

'Better still.'

His coughing subsided.

'And again.'

Marion, this beautiful sea-creature, this siren, this lovely mermaid, was taunting him. But he was determined not to give in. Time and again he pushed towards her. Time and again he sank. But the process got no worse and she, after a while, stopped retreating and hovered near the middle of the pool. After pushing off, he sometimes began to get glimpses of her from above the surface as his arms and feet crashed around him, and even a vague sense of movement. He was making progress, he was sure of it, and the more he believed, the longer he seemed to be able to keep his hands doing something which approximated to swimming. It was as if he was being borne up in this element more by the power of thought than anything he was actually doing. There was, Ralph decided, a spiritual element to the art of swimming. But a more straightforward problem was starting to worry him.

He didn't know about Marion's underwear, but the Jermyn Street outfitters who'd made his had clearly never envisaged that he would wear it whilst attempting to swim. The cotton flapped and chafed. More alarming still, and midway out on a journey towards Marion, the rubber waistband slid abruptly from his buttocks. Reaching to grab it, he instantly sank.

'What happened?' Marion asked when she'd finally hauled him to the surface. 'You were doing so much better.'

'It's these underpants.' Even as he gasped, they were making further progress down his thighs.

She smiled. The moon smiled with her. 'I rather lied to you, Ralph, about shorepeople wearing underwear to go swimming. Most of the time, we don't wear anything.'

'But . . . ?'

In truth, Marion could have informed Ralph that adults and older children rarely swam at all unless it was necessary to prevent themselves from drowning, but instead, she slipped the translucent straps of her chemise from her shoulders and gave a downward wiggle. Ralph's underpants, which were already at half-mast, descended in sympathy and he liberated them with a final kick. He gave a laugh. He hadn't even realised until that moment that he was floating unaided. *This really is a matter of belief*, he thought as his underpants went wavering and darkening towards submarine caverns. Marion, more prudent than he was with valuable clothing, swam to the edge of the pool and slapped a wet heap of cotton on its edge. Ralph, by raising his chin and kicking hard, found that he was still afloat. *People could fly like this as well*, he thought, glimpsing her breasts as she turned and swam back towards him.

The underpants had obviously been the problem. Now, by aiming at a particular part of the seapool's stone lip and pushing out hard from the steps, Ralph found that he really could swim. Relishing his new freedom, he crashed to and fro for a while, but he was conscious that the night had thinned overhead and that the moon was dimming; conscious, too, how noisy and clumsy his efforts still were. Paddling back to the steps, he crouched half-submerged and caught his breath and watched Marion swimming.

Almost dawn now. As on the days of his earliest risings, he noticed how the world seemed to hang there half-formed, greyed and misted as if it were being rethreaded by swirling invisible hands. The light grew milky soft. The stars hazed and retreated. Water sluiced Marion's shoulders and feathered her fingers. The surface twisted and rippled about her, but scarcely ever broke. Ralph was reminded of steel, then of mercury. And she was all of these things. Liquid and solid. Real and unreal. As she dived down with a mere flicker of her feet and the elements joined, it seemed likely that she would never return. When, a long time later, she did, her eyes grazed him, the rocks, the dim shapes around him, all in calm and equal measure. *I'm part of this as well*, Ralph thought, as she shook back her hair in a burst of droplets, and the thought was a joy to him.

He heard a sound. It was watery and clattery, and he imagined at first that it was the day's first bird. But it was no song he recognised, and it seemed to come from the pool itself. His eyes were drawn to its source just as Marion swam to it. One of Gardenmaster Wyatt's buzzbugs, it must have alighted here under the impression that the seapool was as solid as it had briefly seemed. Marion cupped the creature in her hands and bore it towards the steps. Limb by limb, she emerged. Ralph, when he thought back at this moment, could honestly say that he'd somehow managed not to consider how the difficult business of their both getting out of the pool naked might be achieved. But as he climbed from the shallows and crouched down beside her as she laid the half-drowned creature on the grass, it turned out to be this simple.

'You sometimes find them on the shore. The children like to collect their wings.'

This one's were yellow, flecked with brilliant greens towards the apex and spur. Its compound eyes were lapis. Its antennae were hanks of ostrich feather. Large and intricate as a tin toy car, all it needed was a windup key, but it was bedraggled. For a while, Ralph regarded the buzzbug with fellow-feeling. Then he looked at Marion. Her right knee was raised, and the other pressed into the grass as she supported herself against her heels and on the bend of her toes. Everywhere, she was beaded with streaming droplets of water. He studied the changing textures of her skin. Olive-coloured and dotted with small hard-to-see freckles across her arms and neck from all these sunlit days. The rest of her body was far paler, almost translucent, as if she was also being formed out of the same tremulous grey stuff as the morning. Water broke from her hair. Pausing to join with other droplets, it traced the shape of her back, or trickled forward more quickly down the incline of her right breast towards where the skin of her nipple darkened and puckered to fall in small, precise drips. Ralph's view of Marion as the pinnacle of creation was entirely reaffirmed as he gazed at her and she gazed at the buzzbug. Nature, science, survival—whatever it was that governed this world—had invested so much in the shape of the human female.

Ralph kept his thoughts on these somewhat abstract planes partly because it was the way his mind usually worked, and partly because he was uncomfortably conscious that his penis was exerting a strong upwards pressure as it tried to escape from beneath his left thigh. Concentrating on willing the thing down didn't help. Neither, after a while, did science.

Marion gave a shiver, and a droplet of water scurried down her forehead and broke from the tip of her nose. Soon, another would break from her right nipple, then shudder and regather according to the laws of surface tension, friction and gravity. The drips were a little slower now, and the widening spaces on her skin between the droplets had the look of being almost dry. Marion sniffed. She turned to him and smiled, and Ralph knew from that smile that she'd known, had always known, that he was watching.

'You're beautiful,' he murmured.

'No,' she said. 'You are.'

Once again, Ralph was amazed. She shifted her stance and touched him on the chest, drawing a small cold shape, a hidden hieroglyph, through the droplets there. Ralph shivered. He could scarcely breathe, and his penis, giving up patience, finally leaped up jollily between his legs, but she smiled at that as well, and then laid her hands against his waist as if they were still swimming, and drew him to stand, and stood herself. They were so close that the water which broke from the hollow of her neck trickled across his toes. Then her breasts nudged him and her arms closed around his back. They were both trembling almost uncontrollably as he felt the full long shape of her body, and then her mouth, against his. For a moment, she tasted like the seapool, and was cold as the morning, then she was warm, human and alive. Their teeth clashed. Their breath shuddered. He felt the rumble of her laugh.

'I've never done this before . . .'

'No . . .'

Her hand sluiced water from his back. Then it travelled forwards. So lightly that he almost cried out, she traced the shaft of his penis. Then she drew him down towards the dew-wet grass, and he felt the shape of their meeting hips, for they had both studied nature for too long not to know what they were doing. Of course, it was nothing like either of them had imagined, but still it was far better than anything done for the first time should ever be.

Across Invercombe, different but similar scenes were being enacted. Gardenmaster and Mistress Wyatt were tumbling hungrily amid the heat of a crushed bed of pyrepoppies. Cissy Dunning, after wishing Weatherman Ayres a brisk goodnight, had been halfway down the hill from his weathertop when she'd turned back. She was breathless by the time she'd returned to the iron door and banged hard on it. She still had no idea what it was that she wanted, but Weatherman Ayres did, and he drew her into the humming light, and nested his fingers in the back of her hair and pulled her mouth against his so quickly that her body was pushing back before she could think to say no. Across the shore, and in the Price family cottage, and deep in the dunes, where Owen no longer needed his uniform and Denise had given up saving herself for Bristol, bodies moved together. Shoremen, shorewomen, fisherfolk, masters, mariners, seamstresses, nurses, innkeepers, matrons and marts were all joined in love. Even up in the house, to which they had returned arm in arm and drunk on the day, Greatgrand-mistress Alice Meynell was now astride her husband amid the tousled sheets, and her timeless body gleamed as she smil-ingly urged her husband towards the peak of pleasure for the last time in his life.

Ralph awoke. It was extraordinary, really, that he'd fallen asleep. Daylight was streaming over the specimen trees. He sat up on his elbows. Marion had slept as well. She was sleeping still, her face and hair mingled with the daisies. After a long time of drinking in these moments, he stood up. Looking down at himself, he noticed that a little blood had stuck to his thigh. Nature was so contrary. He padded over to the seapool. He pushed out, swam, trying to break up as little of the mirrored morning sky as possible with his strokes. It was easy now. The water bore him just as her hands had done. He stepped out into a place where the sun already fell and shook the water from his limbs and let the sun warm him. Marion had turned slightly, her left arm moving up across her face to show an uptilted breast and the light nest of hair in the hollow beside it. But she remained asleep.

He noticed something black lying nearby. The buzzbug she'd rescued had died, and its colours had leached. These things never lived for long, but its loss still saddened Ralph as he crouched down beside it. Even in a moment as lovely as this, death was always waiting. In fact, death was essential to everything, and was beautiful in itself if only one could step back far enough from the self-involved process of living. The buzzbug had stood no chance of surviving. It had died because it was too big and blundering . . .

Ralph stood up. A thought, almost a memory, a recollection solid and yet hard to place, had struck him as he cupped the dead creature in his hand, and was striking him still. He shook his head. He gave a small chuckle. It wouldn't go away. It was just *there*—small and large and entirely obvious, but with im-plications which shot off in so many directions that they left him dizzy. Sacrilegious though the notion was, the thought was as beautiful as Marion as she lay there on the daisied grass, and this seapool and the golden morning captured in it. In fact, it was them, and they were it.

So simply and elegantly that he felt like crying and then physically hitting himself for never having thought of it before, the thought, the idea, the evident fact, explained exactly why all things were as they were. Striding along the lip of the seapool, Ralph leapt down and ran along the path towards the shore where the outward tide was gleaming and the air was vibrant with gulls and salt, sunlight and decay. Arms outstretched, laughing, he danced across the wet sand.

XIV

Trams swept in at the pinkly ovoid entrance of the south side of the Bristol Merchant Venturers' Halls and trundled out at the north. Mid-building, visitors disembarked from the swaying, sparking carapaces into a cavern of polished marbles, jewels and coralstones which would have appeared cool in any other weather. This morning, though, the gleams were like the sheen of sweat.

Weatherman Elijah Ayres—although the Elijah part sounded odd even to his own ears when he presented himself to the duty clerk, and Cissy still called him *Weatherman* even at the peaks of their passion—was borne towards his meeting by a churning carpet of electric stairs. He whistled to himself. Staunch, red-faced Bristolians glanced at him as they ran fingers around wet collars. No one, really, should look as happy as he did today. But he'd put a chalked board up on Invercombe's parterre steps, just as he did every morning now, promising *Rain at Four*, and he'd instructed Marion and Ralph to keep an eye on the instruments until he returned, and he was already looking forward to that cooling downpour, and then, later, to the scented slopes of Cissy's breasts . . .

He knocked on the ornate door. A voice, and he entered a long, wide meeting room where dark cedarstone shone in swirls, and the air, stirred by several hopeless fans, smelled of stale eau de cologne. A wilting group of men were alternately studying and wrestling with maps which the fans attempted to lift.

'I think, Weatherman Ayres,' said Greatmaster Cheney at the furthest end, 'that you know most of us here.'

He did, or at least he'd heard of them. Senior-this and grandmaster-that—he wasn't quite taken in by the nods and smiles, and paused to consider his choice of chair before he sat down. Close enough to contribute, but to remain at the edge of the group; that should do the trick. But still, there was an astonishing mixture of guilds here—even more than he'd have expected. He was intrigued, and a little wary, but these people needed him, otherwise he wouldn't be here. He gave an easier smile towards Grandmaster Lee-Lawnswood-Taylor, who owned lands which bordered Invercombe, and for whom he'd kept back the hail from his crops.

Greatmaster Cheney was a big man, grey-eyed and bristle-haired, said to be happier supervising the milking of his cattle than the workings of the Actuaries of Guild. 'The sooner we get this done,' he sighed, 'the better . . .'

Palms were wiped across trousered thighs.

'From what we've all said, I don't think there's the remotest disagreement that we've all seen a significant downturn of the levels of trade. Of course, we must all deal with losses and crises—even as sad as that which has afflicted the younger greatmasters Pike over here with their beloved father.' He nodded towards two similar-looking guildsmen in young middle age whom Weatherman Ayres hadn't seen before. 'But what is alarming about this particular downturn is not so much its extent as its universality.'

A pneumatic drill began jammering down towards Saint Stephen's. For some reason, Weatherman Ayres's attention was momentarily rooted on a beautiful Cathay vase which sat, gleaming and glowing, on a side table. It seemed like the only cool thing in this room, or city.

'I know that we've probably all taken our own measures. But I put it to you that they're not enough to save the westerly counties from tipping into recession. We need to do *more*, gentlemen. Yes, I know we have all in the past found some necessary extra

profit—and, indeed, no little comfort . . .' He paused to smile.
'. . . in the small deliveries with which Weatherman Ayres and
his fine device have been able to assist us. But the small trade in
anything is no longer enough. We must think large.'

Greatmaster Cheney scattered a handful of neatly holed
stones across the table. Normally, numberbeads were strung
abacus-like on a rack by which a skilled operator, by whispers
and finger-blurring clicks, could still exceed the operation of
the fastest reckoning engine. But these were bigger. 'Our vessel,' he began, 'is called the *Proserpine* . . .'

The last individual word the weatherman noticed was *our*.
Instantly, as he picked up one of the numberbeads, he was not-
ing the configuration of *Proserpine*'s sails and the horsepower
of her engines and style and manufacture of her weathertop,
which was a Woods-Hunter out of Dudley, one of the most
venerable makes, if a tad slow in the bidding. High-waisted,
narrow-hulled, she was designed for speed and the bearing of
light, expensive loads. Beyond the fug of this meeting room, he
was sure he could detect harbour smells of bilge and fresh
paint. Tuxan was a port he'd never visited, but he knew it lay
on the mainland of Central Thule. Not that it was the sort of
place which an Englishman, or any white European, would
wander too freely. The Mexicans had never forgotten the ravages Cortez had inflicted on them and were proud of their regathered empire—proud and protective of their bloody
magics, as well. Even now, and although sites like Tenochtitlan
had long been dowsed as rich sources of aether, they were reluctant to trade with the rest of the world. In any case, the problems of mining, extraction, distillation and transport had long
proved near-insuperable. But money was money. And trade
was trade. And aether, above all, was aether.

On the current schedule, the *Proserpine* would be fully refurbished and loaded and ready to embark on the high tide by
early September. Against the Trade Winds, admittedly, and
aether was a problematical load, but there was no reason to
imagine she'd encounter difficulties as long as she was out in
the Boreal Ocean before the hurricane season, and kept shy of
the trade lanes and Enforcer ships. With luck and a good
breeze, she'd be outside the Bristol Channel and quietly waiting for a pilot before October set in.

'Our agents have negotiated with the Emperor a price of five million pounds in gold for the entire load,' Grandmaster Cheney said. Outside, the drilling had stopped. Even the fans seemed to have slowed their endless nodding. 'On current market values, and allowing for the cost of the *Proserpine*'s refitting, we estimate the cargoes residual value here to be something in the region of thirty million. Of course, there are technical problems. I gather that every spell on the ship needs to be rephrased and set in perfect pitch or the presence of that much aether will corrupt it. But I firmly believe she could be brought to our shores before winter. Of course, she'd need the right sort of conditions for her arrival that'll keep the Excise Men blind. Here, Weatherman Ayres, is where you come in. We need your best weather—or rather, your worst—for the unloading.'

'There would be no problem.'

'But I understand that Invercombe now has residents?'

'There's a lad and his mother—she's Greatgrandmistress of the Guild of Telegraphers, very much an easterner, and certainly not the sort we'd want looking over our shoulders. But she's away now far more than she's here, and the lad's a decent sort, and he'll be gone off by then to his big academy.'

'Forgive me for saying this, Weatherman, but this is more than just summoning some wafts of mist to unload a few barrels of porter. We are discussing, all of us gentlemen, a far more difficult and expensive project than any of our previous endeavours. The entire estuary must be cloaked in fog. And then the *Proserpine* will need to be unloaded as quickly as safety permits—then sunk, I suppose, in deep water, and with a spell cast over her to keep her out of mind until it ceases to matter to the likes of us seated around this table.'

Weatherman Ayres smiled. Thinking of Cissy, he licked the sweat from his moustache.

XV

Marion and Denise were walking the shore. A breeze was coming in from Luttrell, but not enough to extinguish their mirrored shapes, and the tide was warm as tea.

'I can't believe I'll be in Bristol this autumn,' Denise said.

'You almost sound sad.'

Denise smiled back at her sister. She was wearing a sun-hat—Invercombe's greatgrandmistress had made a considerable impression on her and she was striving to keep her complexion fashionably pale—but she looked more than ever like herself, her hair gleaming copper-red, her fine features dark with joined freckles, her eyes shining. 'No. I'm not sad . . .'

They walked on, happy in each other's company in a way they rarely had been when they were younger. Happiness for Marion was like good health had been for Ralph; in fact, the only surprising thing about happiness was how unsurprising it felt, and she wondered what particular shade of life the Marion Price of before this glorious summer had existed in. It had been a kind, she decided, of waiting. She chuckled and gave the water a kick so that it splashed across her bare legs.

'Tell me again, Marion, that thing you were saying about how creatures were made.'

'It's all very simple—'

Denise laughed. 'You said that before.'

'It *is*. The way creatures die, the number of offspring they produce, is governed by how good they are at surviving. How strong they are. How well fed. How fertile.'

'That's common sense.'

'Denise, it's *all* common sense. We're all different. You and I—look at us—even though we're sisters. It's the same with every living thing. That starfish is different to that one over there. So, if one creature has traits which make it particularly good at surviving, chances are it'll have more offspring. And they'll live longer as well and have more offspring of their own. Given enough time and enough variation, any characteristic can change and develop. Taller, smaller. Longer or lighter bones. Better ways of walking or swimming . . .'

'That's it? It doesn't sound like much.'

That was part of the idea's glory. 'There's clear evidence—there's a species of moth which is much darker in cities. It doesn't get seen and eaten by the birds so easily.'

'Sounds a bit harsh to me, as well, Marion. All this stuff about creatures having babies and dying as if that's all life is. You'll be telling me that this is something different from the word of the Bible next.'

Marion swung her toes deeper through the limpid tide, glimpsing wormcasts and razorshells, the darting shapes of her own toes. Things developed. They evolved. *That* was the true beauty of creation: there was no need for the Elder's interfering hand. Still, she sensed in her sister's blank resistance the looming of a far bigger hurdle than she and Ralph had ever discussed. Not that anyone would ever care what Denise thought, but then there was Doctor Foot and the Reverend-Highermaster Brown, and all the unreasoning and set-in-its-ways rest of the world. And Denise was right. Ralph's theory *was* harsh. Adapt or die. Adapt, in fact, and die anyway. *I'm walking*, the thought suddenly came from somewhere, *in this place I know so well, and the tide will soon be over my knees, but I have no idea where I'm going . . .*

Ralph's bedroom back at Invercombe was a changed place. Books sprawled in teetering heaps. And every shelf, every space, every spare bit of floor, had gathered a collection of some kind of object which he and Marion had found. Dead insects, both natural and aethered. Chippings of rock. Scraps of plant. Skulls. Broken-spined drifts of worn-out notebooks. Everywhere, above all, there were shells. Goose barnacles withered on their dead tethers. Keyhole limpets and ormer shells. The windows remained open throughout most of the day and night, and their ledges too were heaped with drying tresses of horn wrack and sea belt, and what there was left of the floor was glittery with sand, and the room smelled of the shore. But the place seemed complete this way, as if Invercombe's picture rails had always been waiting to be decorated with the spongy yellow egg cases of the common whelk. Learning for Ralph was different. Everything—*everything*—made sense in this new way they were looking at the world. It was as if they were reshaping it, making into something clearer and better.

'One tip, though, sis,' Denise said. 'If you and Ralph really are planning to sell this idea to the world, it'll need a good, catchy name. All the best things have one. Think of aether . . .' A slight pause. 'Or Pilton's Universal Tooth Whitening.'

Marion laughed. 'You're right.' She fished in her pocket and drew a tube out.

'Thanks. You didn't steal this from Invercombe, did you?'

'Of course I didn't. Why would that bother you?'

'It wouldn't. But it would bother *you.*'

'Ralph gave it to me.'

'Well. *There's* a surprise.'

'Shall I take it back?'

'Of course not!'

The water was cooler now. Soon, she would have to get back to Invercombe. She and Ralph had measurements to take for Weatherman Ayres; a duty which would only come to a lesser maid—a shoregirl, even—on a summer day such as this, when the ships hung upside down in the Bristol Channel and Durnock Head, but for the wyrelit beacon of its Temple of Winds, had been swallowed entire by the blue of the sky.

'I'm happy you're happy with Ralph, sis,' Denise said eventually. 'But, well . . . The fact is, I don't want you to end up in Alfies, and Mam's too embarrassed to say anything, so it's about time someone took the effort to explain—'

'*Alfies?* Denise, what on earth are you on about?'

Denise took her sister's hand. 'Come on. We'll sit by the dunes.'

Marion acquiesced. She'd already guessed what Denise wanted to say. Since that first perfect Midsummer night together beside the seapool, it had become a source of some difficulty and no little frustration between her and Ralph, and she knew enough to understand premature withdrawal was hardly a reliable contraceptive.

They sat in the tussocky grass, and Denise produced a small cork-stoppered jar. It was as dark as Pilton's Universal Tooth Whitening was white, and lightning-flecked if you shook it. She explained the spell Marion should chant at the first sign of her bleeding, and the different one she should always whisper to the full moon. Little things really, but Marion found it amazing to hear of the way her sister's words mingled the seasons of her own body with cold grey spheres of rock turning in space, and the flow of the tides.

XVI

It was a hot, heavy afternoon when Alice left the house of Enforcer Scutt, but Bristol, even greyed, still had an edge of lightness, almost of unreality, in its coloured tiles and extraordinary over-leaning shapes of the houses, which seemed to have bulged and risen like cake dough. She glanced up, briefly smiling, at the arched window of the enforcer's bedroom in case he should have arisen from his sprawled snorings. But that was hardly likely, and in Cornelius Scutt she was convinced she'd found someone who lay at the fulcrum of the west's mendacity.

Past these gingerbread houses, and a sweetshop on the corner, she turned towards the plainer reek of the docks, which were even messier and more ancient than London's. Churches and almshouses mingled amid confusing fingers of water so filled with ships that they seemed like dry land. Bigger magics were practised with this heavy industry, and the air resounded, amid all the other sounds of engines coughing and barrels rolling and chutes spewing and pallets being dropped, with the oddly accented cries of western spells. Here was a spiked trap for kingrats which, her endless curiosity driving her to explore the dark as well as the light places, gutters and piss-smelling alleys, she almost stepped on to. Here were festering, whispering clumps of cuckoo-nettle. There was no way of telling that this place was in recession, although Alice knew that it was. She gazed over the jangled rooftops at the smokestacks and silos of the big sugar importers: BOLTS, KIRTLINGS; their names shimmered huge upon sooty walls. Big players, certainly, but everything here was stuffed rigid with pomp and restrictive practice, and set ready to fall at the slightest push.

Cargoes of this and cargoes of that. Swarthy men and peculiar accents. Wafts of alien spells and smells from strange vessels. Negro crewmen and dockhands, physically fine specimens with no evidence of obvious maltreatment or the lash. Freemen or bondsmen—it was impossible to tell, although their presence here seemed subtly wrong to Alice in much the same way as Cissy's did at Invercombe. An easterner at heart, she still thought that black skin equalled slavery. What would happen to Bristol's economy, Alice wondered idly, if that prop were kicked away? Smiling, she reached the Bristol Exchange. They were almost used to her now, and after she'd dealt with all the usual bowing and scraping, and had drunk a cool glass of dilute limeade to get rid of Enforcer Scutt's aftertaste, she settled herself inside a telephone booth with little fuss, and firm instructions that she should on no account be disturbed.

As always, there was so much to be done. There were contracts and investments in the west to be redirected, alliances to be forged or broken, and the first commercial processings of bittersweet to be supervised. More than for herself or for her guild or for Tom, it was for Ralph that Alice now felt as if she was doing all these things. Not quite, perhaps, the Ralph who picked over rocks at Invercombe with that shoregirl and was fuller than ever with science and some new theory of his, but the man he would soon become. He'd be knowledgeable and powerful and handsome. He'd be loved and feared. Almost, in fact, herself made male.

With her routine calls finally finished, she decided to stay in the booth a while longer and practise her recently refined skills. Doing so, calling up the spell, she was drawn, as ever, towards Invercombe. Even before Weatherman Ayres brought the late afternoon rain, the garden's colours had a gloss, a glow, a density, and the buzzbugs already shone like huge glow-worms beneath the deep-cast shadows of the trees. Their minds, as Alice brushed against them, were thoughtless—scarcely minds at all—but the sense of being *here*, the fragmented hues, was impossibly strong. The conflagration of scent, shape and colour of a particular flower was something they yearned for as nothing else in their sharded, spinning worlds and Alice, in all her human complexity, basked in the absolute moment of entering a pyrepoppy as a timeless sharing of mutual need. Then she wafted on across the parterre gardens and up through the pinetum towards the beacon of sunlight which was the Temple of Winds. Beyond that, where the land fell away in the cliffs which guarded Invercombe's northeast side, a small boat was moving by twitches of its oars.

Ralph, bare to the waist and below the knees, felt cool escapes of sweat from his back and armpits as they entered Clarence Cove. Marion had dragged off her blouse once they were out of sight of the shore, and was wearing scarcely more. He knew, loved, how her skin changed shade, but now only subtly, in the places her vest and hitched skirt kept hidden. They'd dutifully taken swimming costumes with them, but by now they were used to swimming brown and naked as seals.

They dragged back the oars and stilled the boat. Ralph looked up at the portion of the house which peered from the top of the cliffs, which was just one coral cluster of chimneys and the balcony of his mother's empty room—for she was in Bristol today—although it was hard to shake off the sense of their being watched. The sea sucked and boomed. The entire cliff face beneath Invercombe was honeycombed with caverns, although he and Marion had been warned by Cissy never to attempt to go below the level of the generators in the house. Real caves were slippery and dangerous, and as likely to be vertical as horizontal. Ralph peered over the boat's side as the last of the ripples settled. The sea here really was astonishingly deep. Clear as well—the sense was almost vertiginous. Sunlight blazed through the water and was slowly lost.

'This'll do . . .' Marion unpeeled her cotton top. Then, balancing so well that their boat scarcely bobbed, she stepped from her skirt and knickers. She was so beautiful, yet a shadow fell briefly over Ralph. *The thing about summers*, he thought, *is that the deeper you get into them, the less there is left.*

'What about over there?' One of the caves in the cliffs looked more than wide enough for them to row their boat inside. There even looked to be a sort of natural jetty where they might manage to clamber out.

But Marion shook her head. For a moment, he thought, and as far as it was possible, her as she was, to seem that way, she almost looked slightly uncomfortable. 'Anyway,' she said, 'I'm too hot to row any further. Let's just dive in from here, shall we?'

With a kiss, she was gone, and Ralph was momentarily alone and looking down as she swam away from him towards the cool deep. Struggling, rocking the boat wildly, he followed. Once, in the distant time of not-so-long-ago, he'd never have believed that anyone could dive at all, but he'd left the old Ralph far behind, and only Marion, feet flashing and kicking through the swarming dark, lay ahead of him.

They rose, gasping, towards the sun, then dived down again. Deeper, this time. Their ears sung with lost guildsmen's spells and dimness pushed at their eyes. Beneath was a moonlit place with a darkly white sea floor and flickers of fish, inkstains of weed. Then Ralph saw the bones of something lost and huge. Not some sea monster, but the remains of a ship. Slowly, rising to the air and kicking down, they gained their bearings. Marion found a green pendant amid the sprawled wreckage. Ralph, an encrusted marine implement which still whispered, when he touched it, of stars and sand. A boiler, its furnace lit with a cold inner fire. Fronds of weed, a temple of pale flames and rising banners, wafted about them.

Ralph felt, as his airborne lungs tugged at him with increasing urgency, a near-religious awe. Then Marion swam above him, and the light shone over her limbs and her hair wavered across her face amid the dancing weeds, and she gave him a siren wave. The scene was almost ridiculously beautiful, and he felt clumsy and lost as he hauled himself once again to the surface and clung to the side of the boat. Marion's head popped over the other side. He was still gaining the necessary energy to climb back over the gunwale, but she was scarcely breathing hard.

'I wonder,' he gasped, 'how it got wrecked there?'

'Probably wasn't . . .' She flipped back her hair. 'Sometimes pays to sink boats when you've finished with them.'

'Why would anyone . . . ?'

But she was already climbing into the boat. As they lay eating the oranges they had picked earlier from the citrus grove—which had grown incredibly warm, as well as stickily sweet—they talked about all the new information they would need to catalogue back at Invercombe—species and phylums, every gathered bit of their shore—to create an unanswerable case.

'You know . . .' Marion launched the emptied white hull of an orange from the side of the boat. 'All those things that went on a century ago when the Age changed. Haven't people been saying that it should change again soon? Yet nothing's happened, has it?'

Ralph's gaze travelled with the sunlight along her thigh. He thought of her hands bunched in anger. Or waving flags. 'I can see you on the barricades.' He really could. *Ma-ri-on*. He could even hear the chant.

'No, but . . . What I mean is, perhaps it's us—this theory. Every Age is different, and ends differently, and perhaps we're what will cause ours.' She shifted her legs and picked pith from her teeth. 'But what we need is a *name*. Something people won't forget, like a brand name.'

As usual, she was right, and whilst Ralph struggled with the distractions of Marion's body and the afternoon beat down on them, they considered *Mutual Selection* and *Species Change* and then *Species Development* and then *Habitual Development* and finally *Habitual Adaptation*, which still didn't seem quite right, but was at least clever in the way it played on the meanings of both habit and habitat. So Habitual Adaptation it was, and at last there was a faint haze of cloud over the cliff top towards the chimneys of Invercombe, although Ralph's thoughts were too distracted now by the shining divide of Marion's breasts. His fingers traced the silky flesh. Her ribs rose and fell as she chuckled and her nipples tautened as she half-heartedly pushed him away. A shiver of breeze nudged their boat. He kissed her shoulder. She tasted bitter-sweet. Of oranges.

'Don't you sometimes worry,' she murmured, her face so close to his that she was a lovely blur, 'that we're being greedy?'

But all he wanted to do now was run his tongue around her ear. Was everything he was feeling merely base instinct? Was the joy he felt now that she'd assured him it was safe for him to come inside her merely a tingling of nerves? Nature was nature, and they were part of it, here and now, and why would they ever want to escape?

It was just possible, they discovered, although hardly comfortable, to make love in a small boat. It was partly comical as they worried about splinters, yet wonderful as well as Marion drew up her legs and the sky darkened and the sea gasped and shuddered as he entered her and the boat rocked and the air moved warm and chill across his back.

Ralph lay beside Marion when they had finished. An oar pressed against his thigh and he was stuck with pieces of pith, and the sky was almost black as a new breeze hollowed Clarence Cove. Habitual Adaptation. It would have to do. In fact, as Marion's salty, orangey scent mingled with that of the storm and the first raindrops struck his skin, it was the only thing in his world which didn't seem entirely perfect.

Refreshed by her virtual journey through sea and sunlight and the cool of Invercombe's caves, Alice returned to the Bristol halls of the Guild of Telegraphers and the heat of the afternoon, but decided, as a further refinement, to attempt to delay the moment of re-entering her physical self. It proved easier than she imagined to simply hover there in the glass amid the booth's humid brass and leather. She studied the seated form of Great-grandmistress Alice Meynell. The fine architecture of throat and neck. Blue eyes which were cool and warm and unflinching even as they gazed into the booth's mirror, which she saw, with a shock of both surprise and understanding, was entirely empty.

Alice drifted, observed. Yes, she was beautiful. Even that slight sagging of the cheeks had been entirely banished this summer. But an odd thing was happening. How could it be, in this draughtless booth, that a few silvered wisps of her hair could be seen to stir? Passing and repassing herself, she tried to make it happen again. Fine as smoke, the strands drifted to her invisible will. A further effort, although it was nothing more really than the realisation that such a thing might be possible, and Alice saw, hovering as if drawn in palest reflection from the silvered shadows within the mirror, the ghost shapes of her own hands. As she turned them, admired, the smile on Alice Meynell's face grew yet more lovely and enigmatic.

XVII

Tom had escaped London's heat to spend a few last listless days beside the sea at their great estate of Walcote when Alice finally came to visit him. After all his recent discoveries, it was a moment he'd been dreading, but had also been longing for. She arrived in a long green car which she drove herself, and she felt as lightly beautiful as ever as she embraced him at the top of the marble steps, linen-fresh from her journey as no one else could possibly be. It really was as if nothing had changed and she was just as she'd always been, but everything was different and he was sure he knew it meant the end of him when, later on in the red splendour of the westerly hall, she bore in a tray of cakes.

'Try these, darling. I think we're really getting somewhere. Even the glaze and those candied fruits contain absolutely no sugar.'

Tom looked at her as she perched on the chaise longue. He longed to mention those papers—the papers they both knew he hadn't signed—but it was still beyond him.

'Well? Doubting Thomas—aren't you going to at least try them?'

Will you as well? The question blocked his throat. And she was so bright, so beautiful. He realised that he loved her still. Loved, when he should have hated. That was the worst thing of all.

'Later, darling, and if there's time, I'll show you how our plans for the first bittersweet processing plant are going. There's a partition in the reckoning engines which I've had set aside especially to recreate a three-dimensional version of the finished design. You can dial its number from any telephone booth and wander the place as if it's already made.'

This project, he wanted to tell her, had never been what all of this was about. It was about love, and about their lives and lies. Had she come to his father in Walcote bearing something like these miraculous cakes—was that how he'd died? Tom still really had no idea of how much he knew of the truth. There was Master Pike, for example, a decent man by all accounts for all that they'd been adversaries, and that fashionable widow in Bristol, and people in Dudley and Lichfield. It seemed too much—too rich—like these cakes, but part of him now understood why she had done all of these things. For Alice only ever did what was entirely logical and necessary. Giving her body for money—well, that was always a shame upon the man rather than the girl, to his mind. Even killing his father; Tom could rationalise that as well. After all, the man had been a block to her progress, just as he himself had become now. Something had to give, and he understood it would never be Alice. But why, the thought kept coming back to him, had she had to kill poor, sweet Jackie Brumby? What crime had she committed, other than sharing his bed long before he and Alice had even met?

'These cakes are just the start. But I was thinking, darling, we could have a bittersweet party.' Her laugh was unchanged. 'Now, *there's* a phrase to conjure with! We might just set a trend.'

The *we*, Tom felt sure, was the we of their guild, to which she was entirely dedicated, rather than of the couple he'd once thought them to be. But she was making it easy for him now, with these cakes in all their glistening sweetness. She was avoiding all unpleasantness, and being entirely herself. Tom selected the cake which seemed most familiar to him, the one with a cherry and white icing of a type which he'd enjoyed as a child. He bit through soft layers and chewed and pushed the cherry around his mouth and gazed back at his lovely wife.

There was nothing but melting sweetness, but as he swallowed there seemed an odd tang.

'Try another. I'm told these vanilla slices are a great success, although they're really not my cup of tea.'

Dutifully, Tom ate everything she suggested, and each time his mouth flooded with anticipatory saliva, although his heart and stomach remained hollow, and when he'd finished he was surprised to find that he was able to stand up and follow Alice back down the crisply echoing corridors when she announced that she had things which needed doing back in London. He walked her down the sweeping steps of Walcote and heard the sounds, distant seas, of splashing fountains and his feet on the gravel, and hugged his wife tight and hard, twisting his mouth from her offered cheek to the greater softness of her lips.

'Are you all right, darling? Are you sure nothing's worrying you?'

'Nothing. Nothing at all.'

He stood on the drive long after her car vanished beyond the first silver line of perilinden trees. That bitterness was still in his mouth. It was there in the morning as well, when he awoke surprised and also somewhat disappointed to find himself still alive. But even without Alice's help, he realised the man he was couldn't possibly function in this world. What was to be done, he supposed, was the business which he'd read about in books called *putting one's affairs into order*. Once he'd sorted through his desk, though, and given each of his personal servants a necktie, there didn't seem much else to do. Life and responsibility seemed such a small thing, once you started casting it aside.

The weather was hot, and Tom took to riding the fine unicorns and sleek horses from Walcote's stables harder than he had ever ridden them before. He rode recklessly beneath the low boughs of forests. He leapt hedges and brooks. Still, he survived. Visiting the tree in the estate where his father had been found contorted, presumed at first to have died in a fall from his horse, and then from some embolism of the brain, he discovered a nearby gravestone commemorating the body of Greatgrandmistress Sarah Swalecliffe-Passington and the unicorn she'd loved to ride. Both the Passingtons and the Swalecliffes were his predecessors in rank, if not direct relatives, and he knew the story of how Sarah's father had committed suicide by walking into the cage of the hunt dragon when his guild's bankruptcy became apparent. It had always seemed to Tom that there was a nobility in that act. He even considered repeating it, but the cage would have to be put up and the dragon ordered out of season, and what message, apart from his own madness, would such an exploit send?

Tom knew he should speak properly to his son, but whenever they had faced each other on the telephone, he could only ask stupid questions about Invercombe's wondrous weather. He couldn't tell Ralph about Alice; she was still his mother, who'd cared for him and given him life, and in their combined hands lay the future of his beloved guild. He couldn't talk to the lad about love, either, for what the hell did he know about that? Ralph, in any case, seemed to be at least as obsessed with this theory of his as he was with that pretty young shore-girl, which was surely a misplaced priority.

It was when he was out riding and had stopped at the graveyard of Saltfleetby's local church that the idea finally struck him. He'd hoped to find Jackie's tomb, but he had no idea where she lay, and, thinking how the dead so easily outnumbered the living, he'd simply been wandering amid the smaller tombstones when he noticed two names etched in the stark sunlight. JOHN AND ELIZA TURNER, who'd both died before his Age of Light had even begun, but had lived a decent number of years. He didn't recognise the seal of their guild, but the inscription as he parted the grass described Eliza as *a decent guildsmistress* and John as *a master ringwright*. Tom wasn't sure what being a ringwright would involve, other than that it would be the respectable work of one of the simpler guilds, but as he stood up and surveyed the peaceful dead, and thought how easily people forgot what was really important in their lives until it was too late, Tom knew exactly what message he would send to his son. He remounted and rode briskly on towards Folkestone beach. It was shimmeringly empty up-shore from the beach huts and the afternoon had grown so hot that he had to wrap his hands with a handkerchief as he went picking up a dozen smooth stones.

Back in London next day, the heat was even more intense.

The streets smoked and the cables of his guild buzzed and glowed between the buildings with all the traffic of commerce. He knew now what it meant to put one's affairs into order. He had the papers he'd destroyed—which authorised Alice's plans—reprinted and resealed, and delivered to his townhouse by puzzled lawyers in the sour heat of the evening. After he'd signed them, which he was determined would be his last act as greatguildsmaster, he noted with pleasure that the last of the bitterness had gone from his mouth.

Dismissing all his servants, he retired to his bedroom and drew up the sash windows to let in the dead air. The sky hung low and blank, and pulsed bright then dark with the circling of Hallam Tower. A storm was surely brewing, and the house lay quiet as he sat on the edge of his bed and stared at his open bedroom door whilst the dark hours slid by until finally, as the air above London stirred and cooled with incipient rain, the shape he loved and awaited began to form.

XVIII

That shifterm, the weather was developing a will of its own. Weatherman Ayres had noted his readings and examined the daily reports of the Bristol Meteorographic Office and scanned the forecasts in the newspapers, although that was mainly so he could chuckle over them. Mostly, and like any good weatherman, he felt it in his bones. He'd taken in his blackboard for the season—for the weather could be deflected, encouraged, even slightly delayed, but it should never be confronted, and there was no point in making promises you couldn't keep.

What was coming was far bigger than anything of his conjuring. He'd pictured huge banks of cloud churning up over the mid-Boreal Ocean, and had sought news of *Proserpine*, and the processes of her fitting and loading. Then came the evening when the storm reached its arms this far from the Antillian Sea and he stood out in the electric dark on the weathertop's outer gantry as the weather front poured in across the south of England. His skin bristled, but he knew his weathertop was earthed and aethered like nothing else in Elder's kingdom. There was no safer place for him to be standing.

His feelings about Invercombe were now tinged with the sad and happy expectation that he and Cissy would soon be leaving. After all, they were no spring chickens, and, now that they'd finally admitted to all the years they'd wasted in avoiding their feelings, it seemed the only sensible thing to do. There was a feeling, as well, that this summer was unrepeatable. Many times, Cissy had commented on how perfectly the house had run itself in recent months. The bath water always ran hot. The floors all shone. The linen was whiter, the pans brighter—every task was easier than it had any right to be, and Weatherman Ayres had had the same feeling up here in his weathertop. Levers you tried to pull the wrong way resisted, then slid in the other direction like knives through warm oil. That time when the lad Ralph had been ill, the anemometry wheels had almost taken his hands off in their eagerness to turn. But, whatever this storm was now, he urged the *Proserpine* to ride the clear breezes of her aftermath towards England for her unloading. Not that they hadn't saved, but even Cissy, who always bridled at the prospect of a big delivery taking place near Invercombe, admitted that it would be nice to have the extra cash.

It was an enticing prospect. Both of them living in a nice house in some better part of Bristol, perhaps Saint Michael's Hill or Henbury, and she decently retired. A young lass to do the fetching and cleaning; someone for Cissy to boss and befriend. And a white balcony for them to sit out on during warm evenings. A cellar, as well, for a few bottles of the best vintage of the small trade. And jewels and dresses, too—things for her to wear when they paraded together along Boreal Avenue.

Trees silvered. Windows banged. Clouds were moving. There were no ships left out in the Bristol Channel, and he was glad for that, for this was like no other storm he'd ever witnessed. Sweat oozed from him. His teeth and eyeballs felt cold. The light was greenish, it was purple, then it was no light at all. The weatherman's moustache began to writhe and twitch. If he'd had any hair on his head, that would be stirring as well. He wished he could chuckle at the thought, but his mind was filled with strange, uneasy calculations about just how well-earthed and magicked this weathertop really was, and what sort of weather front this was, to be stirring so far across the Boreal Ocean from its tropic origins.

He'd thought that there was no sound left in the world, but

now, at its vanishing, he realised there had been one. He was so used to the waterwheel's chanting that its stillness felt like a blindness. Suddenly, after all his years of faith, the weatherman had no confidence in his weathertop. Cissy was right; he shouldn't be up here. But it was too late now, and the blackness was spreading. It filled his eyes and his thoughts. Then, in a roaring blast, the first thunderbolt shattered across Invercombe.

XIX

Nothing, perhaps, but the shadow of a shadow.

For a long while, Tom Meynell found it hard to be sure as he gazed at his bedroom doorway. As the air grew fitful, raising the curtains, he was reminded of the prophets and madmen with whom he'd never have thought to compare himself. Stare at one space for long enough, and the thing you most loved would eventually form. The wind surged, the sky boomed, longing for rain. And there she was. Alice.

He said, 'You're not really here, are you?'

'I'm not. But . . .' She moved from the doorway more clearly into the room. It was hard to see what she was wearing, other than that it fitted her beautifully. But, with her, that was hardly so very strange.

'I'm glad you've come, Alice. I've been waiting.'

'Don't tell me.' She was standing before him, partly outlined and partly translucent in the stormy wash. 'You want to ask me a lot of questions.'

'Not really.' It was true. 'But *this* is extraordinary—whatever it is that you've managed. I'd say you were a ghost, but I know you're not.' He noticed consciously for the first time that she was carrying a small glass tumbler between the tips of her joined hands.

'I'm merely using the telephone, darling.' A smile of acknowledgement at the word *merely*. 'I know it probably seems like more.'

Surely there would be possible commercial uses to this discovery? But Alice was Alice, and quite what it must be like to be in one place and yet wander at will in another currently escaped Tom. 'But this storm. What would happen if there was a lightning strike to one of the transmission stations? You know how the relays lock. They can be down for days . . .'

But she just smiled and shrugged faintly as the curtains flared and flickered through her, for risk was part of what she was.

'Can I touch you? Is that possible? I mean, you're holding that glass.'

She considered. 'But you must do so slowly, and tell me where.'

He chose her left cheek, and then, greedily, also the push of her hair. She was so silky smooth. Almost grainless. Angel flesh. She was just as he remembered.

'I suppose you know why I'm here.'

'I think so.' He laid his hand back on the bed. 'I've been waiting . . .' Raising it, he made a clumsy gesture, and was unsure from the chill he felt whether his fingers had brushed through some part of her or if it was merely the sense of the storm. 'For I don't know how long. It'll come as a relief, to be honest. I've had enough.'

'I'm so sorry, darling.'

He nodded, and wondered what the word *sorry*, for Alice, meant. 'I've signed those papers, by the way. The thing was becoming a farce.'

'Not that they mattered.'

'I don't suppose they ever did.' They shared a smile. The air tasted sharper now. The light was growing bluer. 'Although I've always wondered about my father—'

'I thought you said there would be no questions.'

'Is this how you came to him?'

'Oh, no. This is something I've only been able to manage after years of what I suppose you might call experiment. Thanks mainly, I think, to that lovely house. It seemed to teach me to speak. But don't ask me how. Or why . . .'

'And tonight, if you're not here—I mean, that glass really *is* . . .' He trailed off at Alice's look. After all, the woman he loved was entitled to retain some of her mysteries.

'Will you drink it?'

'I ate those cakes, didn't I?'

'Ah, is *that* what you thought! But imagine what would happen, if word got out that you'd died after sampling bitter-sweet.'

As always, she had a point. 'But, even now . . .'

'That's why it's important that you die in recognisably the same way that your father did. People will imagine some odd inherited weakness. And you *have* been behaving a little . . .' A pause. Heavy on the carpet as falling marbles came the first few drops of rain. '*Unusually*. All that riding. And giving things away.'

He studied the glass. The fluid inside was as darkly translucent as she was. 'What's it like?'

For a moment, she was fractionally uncomposed. 'Darling, I don't know.'

He nodded. The rain was washing through her now, patting the backs of his hands. He thought of Jackie, and wondered, if his death would be the same as hers, and if it would bring her closer to him, and why he had ever left her.

'I'll take it, Alice. But I want you to promise that you'll never do anything to hurt Ralph.'

'He's my son, darling. I never, ever would.'

On this one thing, he decided, he must persist. 'But I want you to swear.'

'On what?'

'I want you to swear on yourself. On your beauty and mystery. On everything you are.'

Alice did so solemnly, her chin raised. She was a spell, a swirl of dark and rain.

Carefully, Tom took the glass from her ghost fingers. He raised it to his lips, and drank. Alice was closer to him now. Closer than ever. More beautiful as well. Her infinitely blue eyes, as he fell bucking and gasping, were the last things he ever saw.

XX

Work across all London had stopped for the morning and the telephone lines laid like ribbons of night as people lined two and three deep along Wagstaffe Mall to watch a large funerary carriage drawn by plumed black horses go by, with Ralph and the guild's grandmasters walking behind in slow procession amid the muffled toll of bells. First there was a public ceremony in Northover Chapel, and then a so-called private one beneath in the extraordinary onyx crypt of the Telegraphers' Guild. Ralph, standing at the spread wings of a golden eagle to make his address, had expected to find himself nervous before this lamp-lit sea of faces, but he found that he didn't care. Of all the people here, only his mother, unique and angelic and proud in her loss and quite, quite beautiful in widow's black, mattered to him, and he realised that all he felt for his father was a dim sense of the loss of the diffident but essentially decent man he'd hoped he might eventually have come to know.

Ralph had been sitting in Invercombe's library on the morning after the big storm. The sky had cleared and the pavings outside were already dry, but the moaning, restless air had flapped at the spread pages of his notebooks until he'd got up and closed all the windows. The papers seemed to grow more chaotic as he attempted to reduce and collate them. More than ever, he was becoming conscious of how little he knew.

The house was incredibly quiet. Every single clock seemed to have ceased beating in the aftershock of the storm. Then, sensing someone standing at the library door, Ralph had felt a surge of unease. It should have come as a relief to him that the figure was no one more surprising than Cissy Dunning, but there had been a look on her pleasant face he'd never seen before, and she'd said nothing until she'd settled herself down by him and laid her hands upon his knees.

London's shops had reopened by noon after the funeral, although there was an extravagant stand-up banquet beneath the frescos of the Hall of Great Guilds. Ralph, who'd previously talked to waiters and explored corridors on the few such occasions he'd attended, was endlessly buttonholed. There was High-clare, his new good health, something about his father being a great loss, then, invariably, how marvellously his mother—who was surrounded by black flocks of mourners—was taking it.

The day ground on. There was a meeting for him to attend high up in the Dockland Exchange. He'd only previously glimpsed this committee room through closing doors, but now he was expected to sit at the head of the table, and required to endorse many documents. *What's worrying them*, the thought struck him as his name was endlessly blotted, *is that I'll die before I reach my majority*. He thought of his father, sitting in this same chair, surrounded by the same or similar faces. Then he thought of Marion, of the shore-scents of her skin, and wondered if it was ever possible to get close to someone after being this far away from them. For the first time since his father's death, he genuinely felt like crying.

His mother, who'd been absent at the start of the meeting, came in, changed into a different black outfit which showed off the glow of her hair, and the effect she had upon people's faces like the play of sunlight. The arrangements which had just been enacted had been prepared in case of such an eventuality many years before, for Ralph could not be formally invested until he had been trained and inducted as a telegrapher. Meanwhile, a trusteeship was in place. His mother, of course, would be its chief.

When the meeting dispersed, he stood beside her on the balcony of his father's empty office and was surprised to note how much taller than her he now was. That small difference of inches seemed far greater than the drop from the balcony, where all of the docklands and most of London lay below.

She gave a sad laugh. 'All this life and bustle. People stop for a few hours. They think of it as an early lunchbreak, and quietly ask each other who it is that's died this time. Then they go back to work.'

'You'd tell me that was the way of the world.'

'Oh—it is . . . The duty engineer here said he thought it would be wrong for telegraphers to be working normally at all today, but I said . . .' She sniffed. Her hands brushed her eyes and came away glittering. 'But I told him the best tribute he could make to Tom was to get everyone working.' She sniffed again, then smiled at him. 'Come on, I'll show you . . .'

She took him down through clamorous reckoning engines and the extraordinary spectacle of lined banks of chalcedonies glowing like phoenix eggs. *This*, he thought, *is how my father and I can get closer*, although it was hardly a comfort, today of all days. His only consolation, here in places where Marion would have been hopelessly lost, was his mother. She was his helpmate and support. All these years of telling him about *people* and *duty*; now, and after the farcical false start of that meal back at Invercombe, he finally understood.

Next day was for the ceremonies which acknowledged his new status as Greatgrandmaster-In-Waiting. Striving and failing that morning not to cut himself as he shaved, Ralph thought the face which stared back at him from the mirror already seemed changed. He had to wear another new suit, and shoes which were torture after all the slow marching and standing of yesterday. And that was before the chains and caps and capes. In a final flurry of bells and guild reliquaries, he was presented to the prime haft at the pinnacle of the Dockland Exchange. Thorny and black, the thing absorbed the cloudy sunlight and all the sounds of the docks. There were similar objects at Walcote's famous Turning Tower and at offices such as Bristol or Preston, all of which he would have to chant through using arcane spells during days of magnificent procession once he'd come of age. But to touch the haft now and without the necessary preparation, he was quietly warned, would probably wreck his mind. It was a sobering thought, on this most sober of days.

Back at last at their townhouse, his socks removed and his feet throbbing, he took dinner on a tray with his mother that evening. The first fire of the year twitched and snapped in the lilac room's grate. Just the two of them; it was almost like old times, and he appreciated the gesture and her presence more than words could say.

'You did so well, darling,' she told him. 'Everyone was saying so. And not just in your earshot. Or mine. Or so I hear, anyway.'

'Being stared at. Now I know how the beasts at London Zoo feel.'

She smiled and laid aside her tray. It had come out more bitterly than he'd intended. 'Believe it or not, that's something you get used to. But then I suppose the lions do as well—so think of yourself as a lion. And you, darling, hold the keys to your cage.'

Did he? It seemed an odd thing to say.

'And you look so *healthy* now, darling. The very last bit of your disease really has gone, hasn't it?'

'I suppose people were commenting on that as well?'

'That's hardly a bad thing in itself.' She paused. Drifts of fire-light played over her lovely hands. 'After the death of your father—the sudden way he died, which was so like what happened to your dear grandfather—wouldn't anyone be concerned?'

Ralph understood the meaning in the blues of her eyes. After all, he'd spent the entire summer studying the complexities of inheritance and the thought had certainly struck him that he, too, might well be destined to die in apparent good health from some sudden spasm of the brain.

'You shouldn't worry, darling. I know you have your father's dark hair, but in almost every other respect, looks, mind and bearing, you're far more like me than him. Everyone says so.'

Ralph returned to his food. Somehow, he believed her.

The day after, with his mother detained in London by phone-calls and meetings about the trust fund and some odd new herb his guild was apparently developing, Ralph took the train back to the west alone—or at least unaccompanied, for every porter and steward and stationmaster seemed anxious to make an impression on him. It was evening by the time he reached Invercombe, and the house was coolly dark and knowing as it loomed in the twilight. Inside, it was entirely empty. Apparently Marion and most of the other maids were in Luttrell, celebrating some feastday of their guild. There was no sign of Cissy, either, this being the time of day which she spent privately with Weatherman Ayres.

Pricked by a long-delayed curiosity, and ignoring the continuing itchy and irritating sense that he wasn't alone, Ralph headed down stairways and along storeroom corridors towards the cellar rooms. For the first time this year, he had to click on the recently renewed lights to find his way, and the old reckoning engine ticked to itself in its whitewashed bay, lazy relays flashing a corroded sea-green, seemingly dreaming not of Habitual Adaptation, but of messages unsent, cries unheard. Ralph, in a sheer animal instinct he'd heard of but had never previously experienced, felt the hairs on the back of his neck rise like a dog with its hackles. But he pushed on.

Beyond the last of the glowing lightbulbs, where the bricks gave out, the tunnel nevertheless continued, dipping down. Hands laid against the clammy rock, he ducked along the passage. The floor went down in dips and slants. His feet skidded, then encountered a step, studs of crumbling cement. The passage seemed entirely dark, but, as his eyes grew more accustomed, a faint light still glinted across the black, wet stone. He studied his hands. The black stuff, the slime, was almost certainty organic. Even down here there was life. He thought, as he moved on, of knotted tubercles which had grown and faded in the darkness of his own lungs. Then he tried not to think of anything at all. The salt air, the unmistakable boom and suck of the sea, drew and pushed at him, and Ralph felt as if he was on the lip of some new revelation when, beyond an angle of this cave or passage and in the very last of the light, his progress was blocked by a heavy iron gate. It creaked away from him, then held on a heavy chain. All he could see beyond was darkness. All he could feel, hear and smell was the living song of land against sea.

Sighing, frustrated and afraid, he ran and clambered back up the tunnel and followed the winding, widening stairs. The sun had set. Even in the main part of the house, he now had to turn on the lights to find his way. The place remained deserted, and his London luggage still lay where it had been left in the hall for the non-existent maids to put away, although he discovered that ghostly hands, most possibly Wilkins, had borne some kind of wooden crate up into his bedroom. Imagining yet another portion of his belongings had finally been spat out from the ruminations of the western postal system, he glanced at the tag. Invercombe's address was written there in what he was sure was his father's handwriting, and it was stamped on the day of his death.

Tearing off the seals and wrapping, all Ralph found inside was a heap of pebbles. His first thought was that his father had been behaving at least as oddly as several people had hinted before he died. His second was that he'd sent him these stones in a clumsy attempt to help him in his geological researches. He didn't know which was more sad. They were flints of the sort which abounded on the blue-grey shingle beaches of the southeast, and he was wondering what to do with them, when, in the puzzled process of reaching deep into the box, his hand brushed against one.

Like putting a needle into the middle of a record, or the disorientating surge of a crossed line on the telephone, the sense was immediate. Information flooded into him, then, as he drew his hand back, it instantly stopped. It took a moment's more rummaging to locate the stone. Balling it in a loose sheet of paper to avoid the rush of data, he bore it to the glow of the nearest lampshade. There were no signs, no seals, nor the characteristic hole in the middle, but this was nevertheless some kind of numberbead, and Ralph placed his hand upon the pebble more deliberately, and let the message from his dead father unfold.

XXI

The Western Chambers of the Ringwrights' Guild lay in a narrow street in Bristol's Old Town. Pillared buildings which had seen better days and endless generations of pigeons huddled around each other in cobbled courtyards, turning their backs away from the coralstone fantasies which had proliferated elsewhere. Ralph studied a browned brass plaque.

'I suppose this is where we decide not to go in.'

'But it would be a shame to have come this far,' Marion said, and he had to agree.

Inside, and up creaking stairs, they entered an office set with long cases of ancient-looking files. A tuning fork stood on a desk. Ralph gave it a ping.

'Yes?' A small, stooped man emerged and peered at them through wire-framed glasses. 'Yes?'

'I'm Master Ringwright John Turner. This is my wife, Mistress Eliza. We've just arrived in Bristol this morning from Kent.'

'Looking for work, I'd guess?'

'We'd like to get our bearings—'

'Most wise. I'm Master McCall of the Second Harmonic.' He offered a hand. Ralph took it, wondering if he'd missed some essential curl of the index finger in his researches into the life of this guildsman his father had given him.

'I'm afraid my, ah, guildcard was stolen.'

'Some light-fingered bastard in the east, eh? Over there, I hear that it happens all the time. No problem. Now, if you'll just permit me . . .'

The most extraordinary moment came when Master McCall unfurled a long printout. Running down columns of names, humming Ss and Ts, Master McCall's browned finger finally alighted on Msr J TURNER (E: SPSE) IDCT KNT GH. OTVE 1ST, then the same long unique number Ralph had carefully memorised from his father's numberbead.

'Here's a temporary pass. Valid for six months. Get your photo retaken sometime and bring it back in and we'll turn it into a real one, but there's no hurry. Lost your tools as well, did you?'

'Some . . . We've left all our luggage back at Templemeads.'

Master McCall heaved shut his ledgers. Unhooking his glasses, he polished them. *This is when it comes*, Ralph thought. Some obvious bit of protocol he'd missed. 'Problem is,' he said, 'you can take as long as you like to settle here, but I can't promise you'll find any work. It's as hard here as it probably is in Kent. Not that I don't think you've done the right thing, moving west, but you're the third chimer I've had here this last shifterm. Quite a lot are just passing through, mind. There's better work to be had out in the colonies. Thule, the Fortunate Isles, maybe even Africa. That's where I'd be putting my money . . .' He chuckled. 'If I had any.'

Ralph nodded. He glanced at Marion. *Chimer*, he supposed, was a play on the name and function of this guild.

'Places to stay—I'd recommend Sunshine Lodge if you want something cheap and not too scummy. Maybe the Lascome, if you're really stumped for cash. And stay clear of the east side of Redcliff at night . . .' Master McCall gave the temporary guild-card a thudding stamp and waved it towards Ralph. 'And welcome to Bristol.'

They took late breakfast in a nearby chophouse, calling each other Master John and Mistress Eliza in loud voices now just for the fun of it. He was dressed in a leather-patched jacket and a pair of trousers he'd borrowed from Wilkins. Marion wore a loose homespun shawl and a long tweed skirt. As far as it was possible for him to judge, the couple he'd glimpsed in the plate glass windows of the shops they passed on their way from Templemeads Station fitted in with the morning crowds. Not that anyone seemed to notice, in this smoky racket. Marion had taken the full day's leave she'd accumulated in her work as a maid. Only yesterday, Ralph had been endorsing more of the papers which his mother regularly sent down for him. Was endorsing different to signing? He didn't care. It was just so marvellous to get away from everything—even Invercombe, and the stress of trying to make sense of all they knew about Habitual Adaptation. He loved this stale bread and chewy meat. He felt, genuinely, like a different person—and as if a huge burden had been lifted. For these moments alone, to be drinking warm beer in a Bristol chophouse with Mistress Eliza who was also Marion, he was eternally grateful to this father.

They tumbled out, nearer than ever to shouting, laughing, or waltzing with the barrow-pushing old ladies who were heading towards Upmeet Market. They counted out what change they had left, which was mainly Marion's. Ralph was unused to money, and he felt far more nervous entering the pillared blue ceilings of Martin's Bank than he had at the Ringwrights' Chambers. Here there was the busy sense of purpose and wealth and mystery. An army of clerks peered like hermit crabs from glassed alcoves before which many Bristolians were queuing.

Babies squalled. Grandmistresses cooed to extraordinary dogs cradled in their arms. Businessmen in bright cravats frowned and studied their watches. Ralph looked around for other common guildspeople like John and Eliza Turner. There were enough here for them not to stand out, but not very many. He tried to imagine what his father had left here. Surely people like ringwrights used savings clubs or tea-caddies. More likely, perhaps, than money was a deposit box and a note which would make sense of this whole masquerade.

'My name's John Turner. This is my wife Eliza. We've just arrived this morning from Sevenoaks . . .' He was sweating, and he knew he was saying too much, but where did you start when you had no idea what you wanted?

'You have an account?' the blond-haired clerk in high collar and long cuffs drawled.

'I have my guildcard if you need proof of identity, and I was wondering—'

'You want to make a withdrawal?' His pink eyes unfocused, the clerk was already punching figures into the till-like device beside him. 'How much?'

Ralph had no idea. He looked at Marion.

'I think we could do with three pounds and ten shillings,' she said, then to Ralph: 'After all, we've got our room at Sunshine Lodge to pay for.'

'In that case, if you'll . . .' The clerk was reaching for a withdrawal slip when he noticed the till's display. His expression changed. He glanced at Marion. He looked Ralph up and down. This was already taking longer than any of the other transactions, and the queue behind them was getting restless.

'You *did* say *three* pounds and *ten* shillings?'

'It might be useful,' Marion leaned towards the window past Ralph, 'if you let us know the state of our account.'

'I'll write it down.' Even this simple process took longer than Ralph, or the people waiting behind them, might reasonably have expected. When the note was passed through to him, he understood why.

Marion was the first to gain her composure. 'I think in that case we might as well round that withdrawal up to five pounds, don't you, dear?'

It was merely necessary for Ralph to duplicate the signature he'd seen recorded in numberbead on the withdrawal slip to take the money, and then they were outside. The day had gathered an impetus of its own. After all, why not really have a room at Sunshine Lodge, now that they had the money? The place lay behind the sugar factories where the air was smoky and sweet. Asking for directions, they were sent along a wide, litter-strewn street. Spars and funnels rose at the far end. Other couples were also wandering, some trailing children or hauling luggage, others arm in arm and mismatched in age and dress for reasons which Ralph was slow to guess. Sunshine Lodge had little to distinguish it from many other optimistically entitled boarding establishments.

'I wonder what Lascome's like,' Marion murmured, struggling to open the window after they'd been shown up to room 12A by a woman in a hairnet. Ralph laughed. He jumped on the bed, which shuddered alarmingly. There were voices from other rooms, people coughing, and a greasy, indefinable feel to the air. By rights, it should have been a dreadful place, but it was theirs. Giving up with the window, Marion came over to him. He undid the knot of her homespun shawl. He touched her hair.

'Well, Mistress Eliza?'

She leaned down to kiss him. Soon, their hands were greedily on each other and the moment was as sweet as it had ever been as they rocked and gasped and the bed rocked and gasped with them. They were alone and they were together, experiencing for the first time the pure recklessness of being in a big city where no one knew them and no one cared. Back at Invercombe, these needy times now came most often as they were outside in some quiet spot in the gardens attempting to make sense of all their data, or down in the reckoning engine's cool darkness where Ralph grew distracted by the inner vein of her arm or the pulse in the hollow of her throat, and their lovemaking seemed stolen from that bigger purpose. But here everything was different, and Ralph was sure he heard other cries through the yellowed walls. The sounds of love were the spells of a guild which all humanity could share, and Marion was so, so lovely, and her flesh was an endless territory. Her nipples had grown broader and darker, he was sure, and she gasped and almost pushed him back as he took one in his mouth and felt it harden. Women, in their passions, were as changeable as this late summer weather beyond Invercombe, and it was a stormy Marion who pushed back avidly and almost angrily against him; who bared her teeth and looked at him, in the very instant when she should have been closest, from far, far away.

They lay back, gazing up at the ceiling's blotched, intricate stains.

'Just how much is four thousand five hundred pounds really worth?' he asked eventually.

Marion chuckled and the bed chuckled with her. 'Enough to buy a lifetime in this room.'

It was a pleasant thought. A ship sounded, loud and close enough to buzz the glass of the window.

He laid his hand upon her uptilted thigh. 'I never thought I'd understand my father. But I think I do now. I mean—look what he's given us. This name. This money. It's like a door.'

'My dad hasn't earned that much in his entire life.'

'It's a lot. But at the same time . . .' Ralph paused.

Marion laid her hand across his. 'I know what you're trying to say. A lot to me—but not to you.'

He had seen items of this amount recorded in guild printouts as a shifterm's interest on a single account. But that money belonged to the Telegraphers. Personal wealth of the sort you could put in your pocket and spend was much rarer. In fact, he imagined four and a half thousand pounds was as much as his father had possessed, or at least had been able to pass on to him without anyone noticing. Yes, it was a little, but it was also a lot, at least if you were a ringwright, and he felt a growing excitement as he lay beside Marion. What his father had given him truly *was* a door, a way towards a life entirely different to the one which Tom Meynell himself had had to live. And he and Marion could walk through it.

'Don't you see how it all adds up? He wanted me to escape. He knew about you, and he wanted it for both of us. *That's* the message in that pebble . . .' Thoughts which had crossed his mind now became real. It was as if everything—Invercombe, his recovery from illness, Habitual Adaptation, their love for each other, even something his mother had said to him about having the key to his cage—had been leading to this. 'We really could become Master and Mistress Turner.'

'And where would we go?'

Ralph gazed at the ceiling's brown stains. There was something familiar about their scatter and shape which reminded him of his journeys across maps in the times of his illness. He was reminded, as well, of a hand of bananas cook had shown in the kitchen, and the huge, hairy-legged spider, bigger than any buzzbug but apparently a natural species, which had emerged. And then of the kidney bean Marion had once shown him on the shore. 'We could go to the Fortunate Isles. You heard what Master McCall said. I mean—do you really want to spend the rest of your life as a maid, or even a shoregirl?'

There they were, those islands, laid in all their intricate variety across the stained ceiling of room 12A at Sunshine Lodge.

He thought of fruits and insects and birds. He thought of proving Habitual Adaptation across a canvas far bigger than the shore. The silence stretched. The shapes seemed to recede back into mere stains. Was Marion really so fond of the life she'd had, or the one she was now living? 'I mean, we don't have to be *together*. I'm not—'

'No, Ralph. It's not that. I'd love to go with you, there or anywhere. It's just . . .'

'Just what?'

He heard her sigh. Propping herself up on her elbow, she laid her hand across his chest. 'Just nothing. But there's one place in Bristol I want to go to. And I want you to come there with me . . .'

Bristol's grander buildings—hotels, houses, shops, monuments, guildhalls, factories; it was often difficult to tell—were extraordinary. Sphinxes and lions, luridly veined or solid glass, emerged from the pluming masonry. One structure, the Great Hall of Wheelwrights, splashed and shimmered across its entire frontage with dripping terraces of fountains. Another seemed from its spewing pipework to have been built inside out. Trees of coral-stone buttressed clouds of marble, whilst down on the streets hollow-eyed beggars shouldered for space with guildsmistresses trailing black-skinned servants bearing rhubarb-red parasols. Marion led Ralph around the edges of busy markets, then on beneath washing-strung tenements. Had she been here before? He was entirely lost. They reached a gateway to what he assumed for a moment was a public park, for people were picnicking there. No London cemetery was like this.

'People call this Bristol Boneyard,' Marion said. 'Mam was the only one who came when Sally was taken here. Seems there's no room left in Luttrell Church, at least if you're a Price. Apparently, it's a common problem—not enough space . . .'

Many of the grave markers on the lower slopes were tall and narrow, like stone telephone booths. Others were not particularly miniature versions of Bristol's private and civil architecture. Monuments in the shape of flames, or formed from red crystal, or built like Cathay temples, or Egyptian pyramids, or propped by Mughal elephants, competed for sunlight and attention. Framed photographs were favoured, and skulls and bones

were as popular as cherubs, but Bristol Boneyard was crowded
with the living as well. Some, those who weren't picnicking,
laid flowers, or knelt in contemplation, whilst others wandered
from stone to stone with what looked like nothing more than
idle curiosity. There was a great deal of touching going on, as if
people suspected some of the more incredible tombs really
were made out of plasticine or jelly. Then Ralph noticed that
whisperjewels were inset as the focus of many of these mau-
soleums. He crossed the greensward to touch one, and the face
of a young man smiled up at him. In another, a toddler laughed.
In a third, an elderly cleric cleared his throat and began to explain in measured tones what was wrong with the world.

As they climbed, the graves grew less opulent. There was
room here for Bristolian lads to play football, with leaning
stone goalposts provided, and the path itself, Ralph noticed,
consisted of the remains of old monuments. Inscriptions and
guild scrolls came and went. With them, sometimes, came the
faint pressing sense of some aethered message. Blurred faces,
half-words and unknown longings tugged at him.

They came to an area which was mostly a field, but where
the raw earth was piled in one or two places as if by large and
industrious moles. Here and there were a few square, modest
stones. Scattered more commonly amid the grass, if you looked
more closely, were wooden stubs not much bigger than the ones
Master Wyatt used to mark his plantings. Marion counted left
and right. She crouched down.

'I know this is the worst possible place to take you after all
you've just been through, but—'

'No, I understand. But do you want me to leave you alone
for a while?'

She shook her head. 'I don't know what I was expecting.
This is just . . .'

Ralph looked about him. It was a beautiful spot, looking
down at this city and the rise of Breedon Hill.

'Sally was almost nine years younger than me—I don't
think Mam and Dad ever expected . . .' She fanned her fingers
through the grass. 'We used to share the same bed. Everyone
loved her and spoiled her. Then, one morning, she started saying she had a headache. Then she was sick. She just got worse
so quickly. She was gone in a day.'

'I'm so sorry, Marion.'

'No one ever really wanted to talk about Sally at home once she was gone.' She stood up, brushing her hands and knees. 'It used to bother me that there was no marker here. When I got my first wage envelope, I thought it could help buy one. It was a stupid idea.'

'Listen. Some of this money—'

'Don't be ridiculous, Ralph. I don't want it, least of all now I've seen where she is.'

Ralph nodded. Back in London, a statue of Greatgrandmaster Thomas Meynell was being moulded and cast in preparation for unveiling around Christmas.

Meeting Doctress Foot at the Hotwells Pumproom had been the pretext of their journey to Bristol, although the waiter looked at them even more critically than the bank clerk had before leading them to her table. High tea, at a cost which would have bought you a whole shifterm at Sunshine Lodge, was already laid, whilst a string quartet sawed, parrots, echoes of the Fortunate Isles, fluttered overhead and a small stream made its way between the tables. The lanternflowers at Invercombe had faded, but here they were still so bright that it hurt the eyes to look directly at them. Doctress Foot was wearing a hat of a plumage which the parrots must have envied. Her small, eager face shone with excitement.

'Listen—should I call you Master, or is it now correctly Greatgrandmaster?'

'Ralph will do.'

'Look at you! When my husband said it was a miracle, I thought he was exaggerating.'

'This is . . .' Ralph hesitated. 'Marion Price. She works at Invercombe. She's been helping me with my studies.'

'Yes, yes.' Her smiling eyes moved to Marion, to Ralph, back to Marion. 'And you look well together, if you don't mind me saying. I'm so *pleased* to have the chance to talk. Listen, shall I be mother . . . ?' Doctress Foot poured the tea. Her own passion, she explained, her eyes still scurrying between them, was beetles. She'd collected ladybirds as a child, had drawers and drawers of the creatures now. She admired their fangs and horns, loved their characteristic beetleish independence. The problems presented in their classification were enormous. They were, by common consent, the largest of all the living orders.

'Doctor Foot,' she continued, 'always likes to say they're the Elder's favourite creature because he made so many. The thing is, he means it *literally*. My husband thinks that God just sat there like some draughtsman and came up with this or that shape of wing. You, Master Ralph—and Mistress Marion as well—you of all people, will appreciate his skills as a physician—but he does sometimes seem to look at things in a rather—and I don't want to say *simplistic*—way.'

Ralph wouldn't have gone quite as far as to think of this quaint woman as a fellow spirit, but he was nevertheless pleased to find how she responded to his concept of Habitual Adaptation, and how well it fitted her pinned and catalogued trays. Insects from nearby locations often had forms which were essentially similar, but varied according to the precise nature of their habitat. Further afield, continent to continent, two species of beetle which lived in essentially similar ways might have jaw parts the function of which was almost entirely identical, but which were entirely different in the details of their construction.

'Listen—' She fluttered through her handbag. 'I've made notes. And these, look, are what I've found to be the best libraries and collections. Just mention my name.' She smiled. 'Or say I'm the Beetle Lady . . .'

'I think,' Marion chuckled into Ralph's ear as they left Doctress Foot and hurried back outside into the bustle of a Bristolian afternoon, 'she's worked out that I'm not just your assistant . . .'

Camouflage, Ralph was thinking, was one of the simplest yet most extraordinary examples of Habitual Adaptation. In Hotwells, for example, he and Marion had stood out in their dowdy yet practical clothes, whereas Doctress Foot, in that hat, had fitted in perfectly. And perhaps that explained the plumage of the peacock as well, which otherwise had been bothering him. There was so, so much still to be done. At the guildhalls they now visited, they received the anticipated stares, but, at the mention of the Beetle Lady, they were allowed to share hallowed rooms of dusty knowledge. The records of the Arthropod

Branch of the Beastmasters' Guild were amongst the most spectacular. Colours fluttered out from hand-tinted pages, whilst the reading room was supported by sculpted pediments of locust and tumblebug. If a configuration of insect could be imagined, it seemed that life had had a go at trying it out somewhere—but Ralph, as they filled in requisition after requisition and books were unchained from their alcoves, found himself concentrating on the varied fauna of the Fortunate Isles. They signed their chits *J.* and *E. Turner.* They promised to give their regards to the Beetle Lady.

Ralph and Marion wandered Bristol as the guildhalls withdrew to their evening ceremonies. People were eating out, and the markets were busier than ever. Pigs and geese were being herded. There were sellers and hawkers everywhere. Walking hand in hand, they examined bags and shoes and useful things, debating what John and Eliza, fresh up from Kent, might choose to buy. That scarf for Noshiftday, that tie for evening promenades. The great ships moaned over the tram gantries as they left on the tide, and many walls were scaled with posters promising *A Fresh Start, A Way Ahead.* Leaving last shifterm, leaving tomorrow. All skills and ages needed. *Good berths.* Smoke and sails and the faint tingling stirrings of weathertops as breezes were summoned over the handkerchief-waving crowds. Bound for the Fortunate Isles, bound for Thule.

In their happy absorption they almost missed their last train and had to run to Templemeads. Hot and breathless, they collapsed on a carriage bench just as it pulled out. But a cooler breeze began soon to play through the open carriage windows. This, Ralph felt sure, as Marion leaned against him and the train picked up speed as he stared out at the shadow-pooled landscape of the west, was the beginning of a much longer journey.

XXII

Invercombe's gardens had changed. Fir trees ruffled their golden-plumed boughs as Weatherman Ayres, secretly testing and recalibrating his weathertop for the coming of the *Proserpine*, inflicted quick rains and flurries of cold and midday mists on the valley, which often spilled down across the shore and caused confused circlings amongst the migrating geese and avocets. Cissy, too, was uncharacteristically irritable, chiding her undermaids about the blooms of damp which had appeared on the walls of the peacock room before retreating to her study to try once again to compose the letter of her resignation. Decisions, she decided, were simple things. What was hard were the deeds which brought them into place.

One way or another, Ralph was also leaving. He'd already been fitted for the clothes of a Senior Apprentice, and had been a reluctant interviewee to a fawning contributor to a periodical call the *Highclare Alumni Gazette*. Every morning now, and again after luncheon, the west's previously unreliable post system bore him requests from strangers for alms and references, and more papers to endorse. He was set to leave for Highclare on a Fiveshiftday, the first day of October, and he knew that he and Marion would have to leave for the Fortunate Isles before that date.

The Isle of Pines was by far the largest and heavily populated in the archipelago, but for that reason it interested him the least. Hispaniola, too, and even Arawak were too civilised for their purposes, both as students of natural history, but also as fugitives. It was the smaller islands where there was less cultivation of sugar cane which would demonstrate more precisely the supreme mechanism of Habitual Adaptation. Eel Island. The Isle of the Holy Spirit. Crooked Island. Ragged Isle. The names rang out to him, although proper data on the flora and fauna of these lesser islands was impossible to find. All he'd discovered in Bristol and in Invercombe were confused generalities about lizards and pineapples and giant turtles, then rubbish about boiling lakes and chackcharnis—which were red-eyed elves—and birds smaller than your thumbnail. It was confusing, but it was also encouraging. Here, he was sure, lay untouched natural landscapes just waiting to be catalogued and explored.

He found that Marion now was both diffident and different. After all, she was leaving a far more substantial life behind than his had ever been. She had less time to spare now to help with the cataloguing, and their love-making faded. She felt uncomfortable, he knew, about the deceit she was inflicting on her family. Still, it was strange and exciting to open the pages of the *Bristol Morning Post*, and to scan together the advertisements promising a new life. They settled on the *Verticordia*, which was offering *Good, Simple Berths* for a departure on the very last day of September. She was bound for Penn Island, which was one of the smallest of the Antilles, although they both agreed that they would only stay there for a few shifterms before moving on. Being a ringwright was a peripatetic occupation in any case. They talked of travelling island to island, and of Ralph really acquiring the skills of his trade, studying out on the deck with dolphins leaping at the prow, although their aim was always to prove and perfect the theory of Habitual Adaptation. Ralph agreed that it was better that Marion make the journey to Luttrell and withdraw the necessary cash to buy their tickets from the shipping agents.

It was useless now to attempt to finish organising their summer on the shore either in his notes or through the reckoning engine, and in any case he was too distracted. He wandered the gardens. He strode the shore. He walked the roads. He visited the Temple of the Winds. The weather was so variable. Surely Weatherman Ayres could do better than this? He took a detour up around Durnock Head one morning, hoping to be able to look down on Clarence Cove. It had rained heavily in the night, and the earth clotted his boots, although the sky had since hollowed and the view from here was absolutely sharp. Rather to his surprise, a couple of the undergardeners were at work up here. For some reason, they were diligently removing a portion of drystone wall.

As he paused to chat with them, Weatherman Ayres came briskly over the edge of the hill, wiping a handkerchief across his forehead. 'Well—and I thought you'd be busy with packing.'

Ralph smiled and shook his head. There was another gap, he now noticed, in the wall in the next field along. Together, they formed line a which led towards a small track which wound around the side of Durnock Head to the Luttrell back road.

'What should I call you now, technically, by the way? It can't still be just Master, can it?'

'I like Ralph. That's what I always tell people.'

'*Always*, eh?' The weatherman worked his lips. 'Then you're off to that academy, just like Marion's brother.'

'That's right. Although,' he felt compelled to add, 'Highclare and a local Mariners' Academy are probably a little different.'

'I'm sure they are.' Hands on hips, squinting, Weatherman Ayres studied the rolling landscape, which was mottled now in browns and darker greens. 'And when exactly, if you'll pardon me for asking, is it that you're leaving?'

'My mother's picking me up next Fiveshiftday.'

'Quite late to be leaving for a first year, isn't it?'

'Well,' Ralph said, wondering exactly where this conversation was going. 'This isn't my first year. Well, it is, but I'm already a year late, if you see what I mean.'

Weatherman Ayres, although for some reason still looking rather doubtful, nodded. 'And you know what they say about Telegraphers?'

'What?'

'That you should never trust them with a secret, because they've probably heard it already.'

Ralph grinned. He hadn't heard that one.

'And when you leave, and when you get to be in charge of your guild up in London, you'll remember how we do things here in the west?'

'I will. I promise. Although I'll be back to Invercombe many times before then. I promise that as well.'

'Sure you will, lad.'

The weatherman wiped his brow again, sniffed, and walked away. As Ralph left the men to their peculiar work and gave up on his search of Clarence Cove, he thought again of his and Marion's plans, the times and meeting places, their journey to Penn Island in the Fortunate Isles aboard the *Verticordia* in that decent berth. It certainly wasn't his intention to permanently sever all contact with England. He imagined that he'd probably telephone his mother after a few shifterms, and that she, eventually, would be understanding. After all, wasn't she an independent spirit herself? After two or three years, his theory of Habitual Adaptation proved and perfected, he and Marion would be able to return home on their own terms. Then, he would be quite willing to study the tenets of his guild and assume his responsibility as greatgrandmaster. In fact, he would welcome it. His mother would be at his side again by then, and so would Marion. From that exalted viewpoint, Ralph was sure, he'd be more than ever grateful for the things he'd learned about the ways of the west.

XXIII

It was the last day of September, and the end of Marion's old life. That morning, after prayers and breakfast with the other undermaids, she picked up her brush and bucket and went as usual to clean the grates. Ralph had taken to sleeping in later, and his mother was away, and the house seemed cold and deserted. As she bent down in the west parlour to pull out the ash tray, a wave of nausea came over her, and she was lucky to make it as far as the cloakroom by the best stairs before she threw up, even though she knew that using guests' facilities was against all the rules. Marion rinsed her mouth and looked at herself, framed in the clarity of this ornate mirror. *This,* she told herself, *is the life you've made*. She returned to her duties, brushing and burnishing the grate, although today she found herself lingering over the polishing, breathing the deep, ammonia smell.

'Penny for them, eh?'

It was Cissy Dunning, and Marion stood swiftly to execute the light curtsey which it was necessary to give senior servants when you were in the main part of the house, although her head swam a little as she did so. 'Sorry, Mistress. I didn't hear you coming.'

'I wish everyone could always keep as busy as you do. You're feeling all right, by the way? You look a little—'

'I'm fine, Mistress. But thank you for asking.'

'Well. That's good.' Cissy kneaded her hands. A clock pinged. Another bonged. Soon, it would be eight in the morning. 'I suppose Master Ralph'll be packing today. And I just wanted to say that I have no objection to you helping just as soon as he's up and you've finished with that grate.'

'Thank you, Mistress. But I have a half day. I thought I'd probably go home.'

'Of course. And—well, I know that this is a difficult time for you. I do understand that. If you need to talk, now or later, you will come and see me, won't you?'

Marion nodded. 'I will, Mistress. And thank you.'

Cissy smiled, hesitated, then turned away. Sighing, Marion returned to the grate.

By eleven, when she had run out of duties and excuses, there was still no sign of Ralph emerging from his bed. Balling her apron into a laundry basket, she headed down the back corridor, eased open the east door and ducked through the flapping washing to the path which led towards the main gate. The wind moaned. The sky churned. She was leaving Invercombe without warning or notice. She was the very worst kind of undermaid.

Ralph awoke from some complex and unremembered dream. He rang for breakfast to be brought up to him, and picked at it before putting it aside and getting dressed. Noon, but only the weathertop seemed clear—gold-etched; a collage cut from a different painting. This was the day. Marion already had the tickets for the *Verticordia*, which departed Bristol for Penn Island on tomorrow's morning tide, and they would meet at nine tonight at Luttrell Station to catch the last train.

There were two tasks of packing, and he started with the easier one, albeit with far more items, for the journey to Highclare he would never take. The new cases his mother had ordered for him smelled sweetly of leather and shop displays. Shirts and jackets. Ties and sports gear. It seemed important that the Ralph who was heading to Highclare should have everything he needed. His gaze settled on a big pelican's foot shell on the mantelpiece. Lifting it, he wondered why it was that gastropods always unwound their shells clockwise. He put it to his ear, and smiled, and laid it on top of his shirts before buckling up his cases. Then it was all done; folded and sorted in the way which his mother had taught him through their long European journeys from hotel to hotel, and far better than could be accomplished by some ignorant porter or maid.

He dragged out a loose canvas bag from the space beneath his bed; it was something he'd found down in the house's cellars, and perhaps even Master Turner might be expected to travel with something better, but it would have to do. What, anyway, could Ralph possibly bring with him to the Fortunate Isles? His clothes were either too smart, too small, or worn out and ruined. His books—well, he was coming around to his mother's point of view that they were purely information, and he knew that, once he started choosing, he'd be unable to stop. The shells, the feathers, the leaves, the driftwood, yes, they had all been recorded—or, if they hadn't, it was too late. Yesterday evening, and after days of wrestling with the decision, he'd filled this same canvas bag with his father's stones and carried them down to the shore. The tide had been pulling out, and he'd thrown them far out across the restless water towards the cloud-swirled hills of Wales. He saved the numberbead with his father's message until last, but he'd held it so many times now that the information had almost drained. Apart from a faint echo, it was just another stone. He, after all, was becoming the real John Turner.

Ralph opened up the bag. He flipped in a few punchcards, although he knew they were riddled with errors. At the end of the day, even bringing his hard-won notes seemed essentially pointless, when there was a new world to study out in the Fortunate Isles. He gazed at a neat annotation Marion had made. He couldn't even remember the day they'd written this, or the particular rockpool. It was all drowned in a gleaming generality of seawater, and then of Marion leaning over to look at what he'd written. *Shouldn't we say this as well?* He'd never stayed in a single place for this many shifterms before, or experienced the sense of time passing so vividly. And now it was gone. All of it. Almost at random, and somehow angrily, he stuffed in a few notebooks and clothes. The whole house was dark and quiet apart from the sound of the wind's booming. Cloud-shadows, each one darker than the one before, careered across the sky, and the sea beyond looked dangerous and un-welcoming. There were no ships out in the channel. Where *was* everyone? Even in his preoccupied state about his own plans, Ralph sensed that something odd was afoot. But he must speak to his mother.

The temperature within the house was dropping notch by notch. Even downstairs within the shelter of the telephone booth, the air felt inexpressibly cold as his image in the mirror faded, and that of his mother, who always answered calls herself when she was at any of her houses, took his place. She was at their London townhouse, and the air seemed considerably warmer there, and bore faint wafts of polished woods. She was still wearing black, but in a way which was so restrained now that you scarcely noticed it. He imagined it was already becoming the colour of the season in tearooms and salons.

'How are things going with your packing?' she asked.

'I'm pretty much done.'

'What's that sound?'

'Oh, it's just the wind.' Ralph had imagined that lying to his mother would be the most difficult of all the things he had to accomplish today, but he felt extraordinarily calm.

'Is it as cold as it seems there? I wish I'd put on a cardigan just to speak to you, darling. But I always did wonder just how much of the summer's good weather at Invercombe was down to that weathertop, and how much was just sheer luck. There's *something* about Weatherman Ayres, haven't you always thought—a little secretive, a touch shady?'

'. . . I suppose.'

'Anyway, I should be down there by tomorrow lunchtime. If you could tell that to Cissy and cook. I thought we'd drive about halfway back in the afternoon, perhaps stop for a meal somewhere around Oxford.'

'That would be nice.'

'And I know, darling, just how difficult this is for you. And I don't mean Highclare, where I think you'll actually cope extremely well. But this is an enormous break in your life. Everything that's happened this year—your father dying.' She paused. Ralph could hear the distant rumble of London traffic. 'And I know how fond of the house you've become. And that maid.'

Ralph nodded.

'Oh, you don't have to say *anything*. I know it's useless me telling you at a time like this that I understand. You feel as if you're the only person ever to experience these feelings, and in a way you are, because that's how life works. But things move on. Time never stops. Sometimes, indeed, you have to leave something behind for a while before you can appreciate how important it is to you.' *Or isn't.*

Ralph blinked and shivered, unsure whether he'd really heard that last phrase. And his mother was dimming from him now, greying and receding like a misting mirror. She looked oddly distorted as well, less than the real woman he knew she was. In fact, a kind of wraith. Then he realised what it was: in the meeting of hot and cold air within this booth, a fog was forming.

He said, 'I'm not sure this line is going to hold much longer.' A sweat of condensation was gathering on the dialling handle underneath his palm. 'Or even that this is safe.'

She chuckled. 'But I just wanted to say, darling, that there are times when I feel as if I've been a bit negative about the life we high guildspeople must expect to live. You know—visits, people. But it's also quite marvellous and privileged and thrilling. You hold *influence*, Ralph. You hold *power*. And that will never fade . . .'

There, though, the conversation ended, and Ralph left the booth and re-entered the gloom which had gathered inside the hall. Any other day, and he'd certainly have gone up to Weatherman Ayres to enquire about this weather, but he sensed that he wouldn't be welcome. Perhaps it was just autumn. Perhaps it was just the house. Perhaps he was simply missing summer.

He flicked through the morning's post. More papers to endorse, although he couldn't bring himself to do so. Then he noticed something familiar about the handwriting on a smaller envelope and slit it open. It was from Doctress Foot, explaining all the new insights which Habitual Adaptation had given her into her collection, and how she'd do whatever she could to promote it against *the forces of silly unreason*, by which Ralph wondered if she didn't mean her husband. He smiled. It was nice to have an ally. In a PS, she mentioned a hitherto-unheard of species of beetle. Brown-backed and stubby-antlered, it was reported to be rampant in the cane fields of Arawak, where it was gleefully consuming all the new sugar cane shoots. Surely here, she suggested, was good evidence of a fresh adaptation of a species to a new environment? It was an interesting thought, but to Ralph this beetle's appearance sounded too sudden. More likely, he thought, it was the work of man rather than unalloyed nature. He laid the letter back on the silver tray and went into the library. It was too dark now to read properly without turning the lights on, but he sat down for the last time in his favourite chair.

Cissy Dunning climbed the path towards the weathertop as the trees in the valley streamed like wrack in a storm. The wind pushed and pulled at her in cold, sudden swerves.

She found Weatherman Ayres striding the inner gantries, puffing a cheroot and whistling a thin version of the same song the wind over the weathertop was screaming. There were several barrels on the lowest deck, red-stamped with what, although she couldn't read the guild's language, had the look of prohibitions and warnings.

'All just part of what's necessary,' he explained as she caught her breath.

At least it was warmer in here, but her skin crawled and itched from the electric air. 'What on earth are you up to, Elijah Ayres?'

'Just that delivery I mentioned to you.'

'You said that would be shifterms yet.'

'You know how these things change. Remember that big storm that blew out all the bulbs on the chandeliers? Well, we were just catching the very edge of it. One of the worst hurricanes in memory to hit the Gulf of Thule, and the *Proserpine* was caught pretty badly just as she was being fitted and loaded.'

She ran her tongue around her teeth and sighed. She'd heard this before, which was the worst of it. 'Ralph Meynell's still here, and he's acting oddly. And I really should never have agreed with that mother of his that he and Marion Price should spend time together in the first place. And *she's* coming in the morning, for Elder's sake.'

'We'll be well done by then. And the lad won't trouble us, not down in Clarence Cove with the sort of night I've got brewing. And it'll be the last, I promise you. After that—'

'Yes, yes.' She rubbed her temples. 'A whole new life.'

'You'll see, Cissy,' he said, hands upon her hips now, eyes as brightly alive as the dials around him. 'You and I, we'll be the swank. We'll be the gentry.'

He smelled sharp and matchy as he leaned forward to kiss her, of something more than clean oil and cheroots and electricity. She held him away. 'You and I need to do some talking.'

'We've said it a million times, Cissy,' he murmured. 'Now is the best time for us to leave Invercombe.'

'That's all well and good. The fact is, I've composed my letter of resignation, and I'll be handing it to the greatgrandmistress when she comes tomorrow.'

'That's wonderful, Cissy.'

'So I'm retiring, and I really do think, may the good Elder help me, that you're the most sweet and strange and infuriating and fascinating man I've ever known. But what I've been meaning to say to you is to do with all this nonsense we've been telling each other about jewels and fine houses.'

'Cissy—'

'No. *You* listen and let me have my say for a change. Look at you and look at me. Look at your hand. Look at mine. Look at the colour of our skins. It might be all right for us to walk arm in arm here at Invercombe, but just how many couples like us do you see parading Boreal Avenue?'

'That's the—'

'I *still* haven't finished. Dreams are fine things, and so is love, but no amount of money on that ship is going to buy you and me the life of the guilded gentry. So what I'm saying is, yes, perhaps we could have a garden and maybe even a maid, but it'll have to be somewhere quiet where people can talk as much as they want but they don't need to bother us. A nice little cottage in Cornwall, I was thinking. I've always loved a rowdy sea. They mind their own business there, and Cornishmen don't really have tails. We can wander the cliffs and talk about all the places you say you've been to our heart's content. Now. How does that sound?'

The fog was thickening as Marion reached Clyst. It swirled with her into the cottage kitchen, where Mam was boiling up some more underwear.

'Hope you're not expecting any kind of dinner yet. Everything's to pot, what with Owen and Denise off at the end of the shifterm—and isn't it about time you got paid?'

Sitting down at the long family table, Marion studied the burns and the scarrings where Dad, much to Mam's irritation, had used it as a workbench. She'd left a note back at Invercombe which Cissy wouldn't find until tomorrow, asking to make sure her severance pay was forwarded here.

'I went to Bristol with Ralph recently,' she said eventually.

'Did you, eh?'

'We took the time to go up to the B—the civic cemetery. I found Sally's grave.'

'Won't have moved on its own, will it?' Mam was still avidly stirring and inspecting the smalls, her face wreathed in steam.

'I just wanted to say . . . Well, it's a lovely spot and I don't think you need worry about buying a stone marker. I think you should save the money.'

'Ha! As if we had any . . .'

Marion subsided. All she was doing was worrying at her own guilt. It wasn't that Mam had given up thinking of Sally—neither had Dad, or Denise, or Owen. She was there in their silences, and the shape of a rock or a turn of the wind. She was there in Mam's face now as she studied the laundry and licked her lips and rubbed her hand down her skirt and pronounced that it was probably time to get a bit of dinner going.

They didn't live badly; Marion realised that now. They had food to eat, shoes when they needed them, a roof for shelter, the dignity of knowing who they were—in fact, a whole way of life. Being shorefolk really *was* a kind of guild, and a good deal better than many. You didn't need the certificates and stupid oaths and daft ceremonies to believe in what you were.

She helped Mam lay the table, then Dad and Denise and Owen returned. Dad ate his food in quick pecks. Marion knew the signs; with a fog this dense, there would be a delivery tonight in which he and some other local men had been enlisted. Owen, on the other hand, was talking about all the things he'd need to do before he went off to Bristol. He seemed relaxed and confident. Now he'd reached a basic plateau of the level of knowledge required to become a mariner, he understood that the rest was mostly the window-dressing every guild put up to make their work seem more daunting than it was. Marion had still been toying with the idea of telling her family that she was heading with Ralph for the Fortunate Isles, but Dad was already leaving the table and Owen had forms to complete and Denise was working on embroidering her apprentice piece and Mam had yet more laundry to boil. It seemed a shame to disturb any of them in the purpose of their lives.

'Things going all right at the big house?' Denise asked her later as they sat together on her bed upstairs and she threaded last bits of crimson into a waistcoat. 'Isn't Ralph supposed to be leaving?'

'His mother's picking him up in her car to take him to Highclare Academy tomorrow.'

'Shouldn't you be with him, then?' She bit through a thread. 'Last night together, all that sort of thing?'

Marion shrugged. Her gaze travelled towards the orange box where she had buried the tickets for the *Verticordia* amid old clothes and bits of forgotten schoolwork.

'Hold that candle for me, will you? There . . .' Denise flattened the waistcoat out. 'Not bad, as long as you don't look too hard at the back. Don't you think it's about time, by the way?'

'For what?'

'Time you admitted to someone what you're doing.'

Marion tried to frame an innocent question.

'Just stop it, will you! A good job I haven't got any scissors in my hand or I'd stick them in you right now, Marion Price. Dad may be too busy fretting about the small trade and Owen polishing his new badges and Mam boiling her pants, but anyone with any sense can see you've had a bee up your bum these last few shifterms. And do you really think I don't take the trouble to have a good occasional rummage through what's left of your things?'

'You've seen the tickets?'

'Of course I've seen the bloody tickets! But why are you calling yourself Mistress Eliza Turner?'

Marion nodded. It was a relief to be able to confess to someone, and at least she knew now that Denise could explain everything to Mam, Dad and Owen once she'd left. Still, when she'd finished, Denise continued to look at her somewhat disbelievingly.

'It's *true*, sis—you've seen the tickets.'

'You haven't told him, have you?'

Marion blinked.

'Didn't you take that potion? You, of all people, Marion!'

'I think it was before that.' She sighed. 'It might even have been the first time. After that, we tried to be careful.'

'How many months?'

'Three.'

'And you haven't seen a physician?'

'I've felt fine until recently. Now, I'm starting to dread breakfast.'

Denise chuckled. 'They always say that's the sign of a healthy baby. Ralph has no idea?'

'None.'

'That's men for you. They only grumble as if it's your fault when you get your monthlies. Still, it'll have to come out if you and him are going off to this island, won't it?'

'I've thought about telling him—I've been so close. But he's been through so much. His father's died. And then, when he started talking about our going away, I didn't want to make him feel as if he had to do it. I wanted him to feel that he was starting a life with me because he wanted to. Not because of some . . .' Marion trailed off. She was still having problems with the word *baby*.

'Of course, the other reason for not telling him is that it might put him off the whole idea entirely.'

'That's not Ralph.'

Denise sucked her teeth. 'You're lucky if you're right.'

'You don't know how much he's giving up to do this. I don't think he realises himself.'

'And if it doesn't work out?'

'I'm not helpless, Denise.'

It grew dark. Owen called up the ladder to say that he was going out. Dad had slipped off already and wouldn't be back until morning. In the kitchen, Marion kissed the top of Mam's forehead as she dozed before the fire, and worked open the cottage door. The wind outside had stilled, and the air tasted of salt and smoke. It clung to her face and clothes in greasy droplets. Faintly, up along the edge of the shore, bonfires were glowing. Nights such as this, before a big delivery, the shoremen put up as much smoke as they could to help with the fog Weatherman Ayres was creating.

She turned to Denise. 'I hope you find everything you want in Bristol.'

Her sister chuckled. 'They say my academy's right beside a toffee factory. But who'd have thought it, eh? You running off with a greatgrandmaster to some tropic island. They'll be singing songs about you, Marion, soon as word gets out. But you'll let me know, won't you?'

'Of course I will.'

The two sisters hugged. More by touch than sight, Marion made her way up to the shore road. Even there, it was difficult to keep a proper sense of direction. She wondered about Ralph, but decided that she didn't have time go back to Invercombe. She passed haggard trees and glimpses of unrecognisable walls, until she finally reached a swirl of light and lampposts of Luttrell High Street. Rousing the ticket clerk at the station, she bought two single tickets for Templemeads with what money she had left from her withdrawal from the Turner account. The platform was deserted, but there was a fire going in the waiting room. Marion sat down on the bench. She waited.

Sore and breathless, clambering towards what he thought was the shore path, Ralph found himself one step away from falling into the scummy depths of the seapool. Dull lights. A thicker smog of smoke plumes. The canvas bag banged his leg. Then, he was sure he glimpsed Weatherman Ayres hurrying out of the fog before the night closed in again. Just when he was thinking of retracing his steps, and then wondering how he could possibly do so, he found the coast road. From there, it was somewhat easier. Then, unlit, hooves muffled, a big wagon came by so suddenly that he was nearly run over. Pushing himself up from the hedge, he coughed and wiped his mouth and wandered on.

Luttrell was a changed town, and his recollection of the station's exact location was as vague as the fog itself. He passed muddy yards, the too-close moan of balehounds, then, quite literally, fell over a porter's wooden handcart. Marion had said she'd buy the tickets, but the platform was empty, and for a moment his heart froze, but he entered a waiting room, and there she was, sitting amid its slightly brighter smog. Their clothes felt wet between them as they embraced, and she tasted like the night—a colder kind of flesh than the Marion he was used to. He was late. Loud and insubstantial, the train was already arriving, its carriage lights flickered like scenes from a cinematograph. Ralph turned unthinkingly left towards first class, but Marion took his arm and drew him towards third.

Three lads climbed on at a station called Aust. To Ralph, what they were saying was almost incomprehensible as they sat splay-legged on the hard benches and shared a narrow-necked brown jug, but it became apparent that they were asking him and Marion where they were bound. *Got no tongue, has he, yer master?* Not particularly liking the way they were looking at Marion, Ralph assured them that he had, and the lads burst into eye-bulging, thigh-slapping laughter. *Well ark at im. Proper lush. Fancy some o this?* The reddest-faced of the lads was holding out the jug on the hooks of his fingers, which Marion took and drank from, and passed on to Ralph.

'Go on, John.' She wiped her chin. 'Elder knows when we'll have anything else.'

John? Then he remembered. The stuff—some kind of cider, but thick and slippery—caught in his throat. What a way to travel, wheezing and patronised by boozy marts, but at least the fog slowly cleared. In lights and yards and back-to-back houses, Bristol finally arrived.

They passed beggars and wandering widows around the fringes of Templemeads Station as they debated the quickest and safest way to reach Sunshine Lodge. They trudged vaguely north. Warehouses and railings formed dead ends amid kingrats and dragonlice and slurry and mud.

'You've got the tickets?'

Marion gave her coat pocket a rustling slap. A few minutes later, when at last they were amid houses, she put her hands to her mouth and scooted off down an alley. Ralph put down the bag and felt the cold city air nuzzle against his skin as he listened to the sounds of her being sick.

'It's that ghastly cider, Marion. You should never have accepted it.'

'No, it isn't. It's . . .'

'What?'

'We're nearly there.'

They'd the reached the street with its steeply cambered cobbles. Couples sloped past, loud and bleary. The same woman in the same hairnet unhooked the same key at Sunshine Lodge. Putting down his bag, weary beyond weariness, Ralph gave room 12A's light switch a cautious prod. Surprisingly, the bulb glowed, although it did little to add to the look of the place. Peeling off her boots and socks, Marion slumped on the creaking bed. Ralph sat down on the other side, facing the wall.

'I need to find a bathroom.'

Marion and the bedsprings chuckled. 'Look under the bed. I imagine there's probably a bucket.'

There was, but he couldn't bring himself to use it. Feeling his way down the unlit stairs, he ended up using an outside wall which smelled as if it was solely maintained for that purpose, but told himself as he climbed back up that he'd have to get used to these things. Marion seemed already asleep, curled up and fully clothed. Not wanting to turn off the light, he lay down on top of the greasy blankets beside her, his back bowed by the droop of the mattress. This was nothing like the summer room where they had made love. Even the stains on the ceiling had changed. There was no sign of the Fortunate Isles, or any recognisable sea or continent. This was the landscape of his fever dreams, deformed by illogic. Then the light blinked out as a distant generator stopped humming and the night went black. Somewhere not far off, but much too loud and long for the sound to be happy, a woman was laughing. Marion was softly snoring. Her breath smelled of vomit and cider. He rolled over, swallowing back the urge to cough.

His skin itched. He wished he'd brought more of his notebooks. He wished he hadn't thrown away his father's stones. What sort of message was it, anyway—to send your son the life of a lesser guildsman, when his father had always been resolutely proud to be a telegrapher? Or perhaps there was no message, or one which he'd misinterpreted in this childish desire to avoid responsibility. Ralph sighed. The bed sighed with him. But he couldn't go back. He was here and he was with Marion. They must face their future together.

He closed his eyes. Tried to think of white beaches and transparent oceans filled with teeming evidence; beautiful fish. He strove to sleep.

Weatherman Ayres was convinced that there was nothing to beat a good delivery, no matter how much Cissy complained. After all, she was as happy to accept the better vintages, the fresher fruit, the cash-in-hand, and to his mind, there was an essential rightness about the small trade which the ordinary stuff of life often lacked. Even the arrival of the *Proserpine*, whose sponsors and investors went all the way up to the big-noses of Hotwells, had a feeling of decency. To him, smuggling was a moral obligation, and he'd probably have done what he was doing tonight even without the substantial packet he was getting for his troubles, although admittedly that helped.

The men hallooed as he and one of Wyatt's more reliable undergardeners rolled the barrels of explosive to the shore where a big rowboat was being readied. Someone waved a brand. They loaded and pushed out, dipped oars, and passed around a flask of the best stuff, which was sharp and tart and sweet, and just what this night needed. Ghost-like, they slipped out through the swirling dark. Weatherman Ayres trusted these men as he would never have trusted any fancy mariner. There was Scobie and Jack and Little Paul, and there was Bill Price, who was father to the girl Marion. They eased the boat into the tide's deeper rush, certain in the knowledge that no other vessels would be about on this black a night. Back at Durnock Head, wooden hoists were being erected. Wagons would be waiting on the back road.

Deeper darkness lay ahead, although the smell of the ship was the first thing to catch their senses as they approached the rendezvous; that, and the slow throb of her engines. There she was, spars looming out of the mists, the *Proserpine*, which had been in the weatherman's dreams since he'd held that number-bead in the Halls of the Merchant Venturers. He glimpsed faces over her side, and ropes snaking, and Weatherman Ayres told himself as he and his crew climbed aboard that this would be just like any other delivery.

The captain, a Spaniard named Convertino, hobbled out of the fog as they were stood on the tilted deck. 'Glad to be finished with this journey, though it seems a shame to lose the ship, even if she is an old thing—sunk already according to her records . . .' He had greying hair tied back from a lineless face. The sea did that to some people; puffed them up instead of etching itself into them.

'I'm Weatherman Ayres. This here is Bill Price, Jack Petty, Pete Scobie . . .'

But there was no time to be lost. Immediately, they set about the business of hauling up the aether from the hold with the help of some of the crew, who proved to be a weak and subdued lot, even for bondsmen. As a rule, the weatherman disapproved of this as a way of running a ship, and he saw nothing tonight to change his way of thinking. The signs of their inexperience were in saltsores on their limbs and the scars on their hands. Still, they'd be getting a wage for this which would buy them their freedom.

The aether wasn't in the caskets or barrels he'd expected, but big jars embossed with tongues and dragons and symbols which no English guildsman would ever recognise. They gathered on the deck like fat terracotta idols as the weatherman helped lower the explosive through the main hatch into the emptying hold. The floor was smeared with oil and bilge and the straw of packing. Ignoring the glower of the remaining pots, the weatherman propped the barrels against each of the bulkheads, then picked off their wax bungs and tamped down their fuses. The wound strips of cordite shone like glowworms in his hands. The envelope containing their unique spell had come plastered with warnings that it shouldn't be unsealed until the moment the fuses were to be activated, but he'd memorised those twists of phonetic hieroglyph days ago, easy as you like. They sang in him now as he climbed back up to the main deck.

A murmur in Spanish, and the anchor was raised with commendable quiet. After a brief conversation about draught and displacement, the weatherman took the wheel and pushed forward a slide valve. The engine shifted its beat, and the *Proserpine*'s list increased. If ever a ship needed sinking, this sorry vessel was it. As he eased her forward into the channels, he thought of fragrant sheaves of tobacco and gleaming bottles and the scents of oranges and bananas in cool caves on summer nights. That, not this, was the real small trade. The Mexicans ripped out people's hearts at the tops of pyramids and offered them to the sun, for Elder's sake. No wonder the itch to say the ignition spell was churning inside him.

The streamers of mist were still dense enough to shroud the prow, but he knew they were entering Clarence Cove from the changed smell of the water, the slip of the currents, from the echo of the silences around him. The *Proserpine* creaked. He eased back the screw to dead slow as he edged towards the swish of the caves. He signalled to ready the anchor. Even then, the sudden bulk of the cliffs surprised him. Waves sucked and washed. A voice shouted. A flaming brand was waved. Ahead was the stub of decking constructed on the lip of the largest sea cave, which would be destroyed like all the other evidence once this job was finished. The ship dragged to a dead halt. Silence now, but for the gulp and moan of her engines, then even that stilled. Then came the squeak of oars.

Crossing the deck, the weatherman watched as ropes were tossed and the *Proserpine* was berthed for last time. Rowboats bobbed in the space between the ship and the cliffs. It was a matter now of winching these pots overboard and bearing them up through the caves to the passage which opened in the middle of a field and then down to the wagons. For all of which this fog needed to hold for several more hours, although, oddly enough, it seemed to be thinning.

The weatherman tasted the air. Puzzled, he stroked his damp moustache, which was as reliable a gauge as any. He rehearsed the weathertop's settings. The *Proserpine*'s spars were showing clearer above him now. He could even see the ragged tip of her mizzen against the nodding cliffs, and the individual faces of the men in the boats below him. But there was no wind—and the air hadn't shifted. Odd, indeed, although he imagined it was another effect of this damn cargo. Not that it mattered as long they got the winch working and the night held, although here was a lesson to be learned that this stuff wasn't worth all the money he'd heard mentioned at the Halls of the Merchant Venturers. *They* never risked their limbs and their freedom on darkly freezing nights such as this. Neither would he. Not again. The last thing he'd do, the very last thing, would be to cast the spell which sent this ship down to join the others which rested in this cove. And Elder bless her. And good riddance.

But the fog was definitely clearing. The wet cliffs were glinting as the ship rose and fell, and brightness was gathering at her stern out towards the entrance of the cove—gathering so strongly that he'd have said it was dawn if he hadn't been certain it was the middle of the night. Then he heard engines, and thought for a moment that those of the *Proserpine* were somehow stirring, but now there were also flashes and shouts. The effect, he suddenly realised, came from a bigger ship's weathertop pushing back the fog as she entered Clarence Cove. So stupid. So obvious. And not the sun's rising, but floodlights churning through thinning scarves of white to spear the *Proserpine*'s ragged spars and the scurrying figures on her deck. Not one ship, either, but two; the gun-pricked prows of a pair of brassy white Enforcer vessels.

'Every man off! Quick!'

No point now in stealth and silence. Even the bondsmen were running. There were gun cracks, heavy splashes in the water, the crump of bone meeting deck. The man at the prow of one of the Enforcer vessels was adding to the confused racket by shouting incomprehensibly through a loud-hailer. In the pomp of his sideburns and uniform, it could only be Enforcer Cornelius Scutt. Weatherman Ayres looked about him. The deck was already empty and the bright-lit water between the *Proserpine* and the sucking cliffs was aswarm with oars and boats and splashing limbs. He waited. The rowboats were pulling off, bodies were being hauled in or towed. Not that he imagined that there was any way of escape from this cove, but he wanted to be sure that everyone was well back before he did what was necessary.

Weatherman Ayres licked his lips. He touched his moustache. He thought of Cissy, and of Cornwall, and of evening walks with the sea-pinks waving along the gull-wheeling cliffs, and afterwards in their fire-lit cottage and the gingery smell of her flesh. But he was glad now that he'd ignored the warnings and opened that envelope, just as he was glad in his life for so many things. The phrases of the ignition spell were in him, and they were waiting. They took no effort at all to sing.

XXIV

The entrances to Bristol docks funnelled down through tighter and tighter conjunctions of jostling, shouting, lower-guilded humanity, and the raw grey day above stirred with conflicting breezes as the weathermen on the big ships tested their devices. Flags furled and fell, sails filled and stilled, and the chalked board above the eastern access announced that the *Verticordia* would be departing at 2:30 that afternoon, which was considerably later than Marion and Ralph had expected. Leaflets were pressed into Ralph's hands as they pushed their way back out towards the road. The clammy print promised *New Lives, Fresh Starts, Fine, Easy Work* and *Verdant Pastures*. At least half of Bristol seemed to be leaving England, or trying to. Glancing over towards the first-class access, its shining black gates topped with lions, Ralph remembered other voyages; the carpets and the panelled cabins and the greetings of the captains.

He picked at his eggs and fried sea-potato, which he'd never tasted before, and had no particular wish to try ever again, as they took late breakfast at a dockside café. More money, he thought, although he didn't say it, squandered.

'I just keep waiting for something to start,' he said. 'I mean,' he studied his chipped mug of tea, 'this isn't what we came for, is it?'

Marion gazed at him from her own scarcely touched plate in that odd way she'd been doing increasingly lately. 'Perhaps things haven't finished ending yet.'

'We'll probably look back on this in ten years when we're in London and—'

'London? What do you mean?'

'It's not as if we're going to spend the rest of our lives in the Fortunate Isles, is it? We have a theory to prove, and we must return here to do that.'

'What happens to Eliza and John Turner?'

He shrugged. 'Perhaps we'll have finished with them.'

There was still plenty of time before boarding—whole hours of it—and they decided to go back to the public reading rooms of the Arthropod Branch of the Beastmasters' Guild. It was a relief, in any case, to return to Bristol's bigger byways, with their swept streets and milling hats and carriages, and newsboys shouting something about *Arrests*. As before, they were admitted beneath the hall's insect-winged pillars as Master and Mistress Turner, who happened to know the Beetle Lady.

Their wait for the clerk's return after they had presented the requisition forms for the dozen books Ralph imagined they might have time to look at was longer than he had expected—perhaps poor service was something else you needed to get used to when you belonged to some lesser guild. Marion sat down on a bench and began kneading her ankles. This was taking far too long, and he was just starting to worry when a more senior-looking figure emerged.

'Master, Mistress Turner? Would you mind coming this way?'

Passing the glass cases of giant insects which might have been enlarged models, or real examples of the more extravagant work of the craft of this guild, they were shown into a small office, and the guildsman who introduced himself as Highermaster Squires asked if they'd been long away from Kent.

Ralph, unwilling to break whatever remained of the credibility of their identity, assured him that they hadn't.

'And you know the Beetle Lady? A fine student is Doctress Foot—especially for someone who isn't a member of our guild.'

Highermaster Squires, grey-haired, podgy around the cheeks and belly and thin elsewhere, seemed an amiable enough sort. His desk, Ralph noticed, had six legs. As did their chairs, the arms of which were carved into the shapes of maggots. Guilds, in their inner intricacies, really were the most extraordinary organisations.

'Would you like tea?'

'To be honest,' Marion said, 'we're pushed for time. We're taking a ship on the high tide.'

'Leaving, eh? And our humble halls are the place you choose to visit. I'm flattered, I must say. Especially as you both know as much about natural science as you plainly do, judging by the books you've requisitioned. Both this and last time, although I can't say I don't think you're wasted in the Guild of Ringwrights, if you don't mind me saying.'

'I'm sorry. I don't understand.'

'It's easier than you think, you know, to tell what people are researching. You'll be surprised at what you can pick up by looking through requisitions, and the Beetle Lady also mentioned something. Although she seems, dear soul, a bit confused about your names and rank.'

'I can assure you,' Ralph said, 'that it's us she means.'

'Oh, good. Or *mostly* good anyway. But the thing is, this idea of yours, this supposition, this theory—what is it that you call it?'

'Habitual Adaptation.'

'I've heard worse.' Standing up and jingling a key, Highermaster Squires unlocked a cabinet. Inside were books, notepads, rolls and sheaves of paper. 'This, for example.'

Humouring the man, Ralph took the offered book. It was small, cheaply printed. Dimly embossed on the card of its spine was the title *On the Force of Natural Development*.

'Or this . . .'

A dry ribbon-bound curl of loose pages, hand-written, illustrated with fine drawings of the eyes of insects in all their varieties. *An Argument Towards A Better Understanding Of The Processes Of Life On This Earth*.

'Beautiful hand, don't you think?'

Another volume was merely a compendium of the varieties of bee, but someone had flagged an appendix, and then drawn a black line through each of the seemingly offending pages. And *The Principle of Selection*. And *Life: A Query*. And *The Origin of the Variety of Species*.

'Ah! You're beginning to understand?'

Ralph's head was spinning. His chest hurt. He felt empty and weak.

'In a way, I'm not so surprised that you don't belong to one of the guilds which actually deal with the processes of life. Although I must say it's an achievement to have got as far as you have, and yet so young. If you were to attend one of our academies, and no doubt a plantsmaster would tell you the same, the first glimmering of any thoughts in *this* direction would be laughed at and crossed out before they could lead anywhere. It's a kindness, really. Although some things seep through. Hence my little collection.'

'You're saying it's not true?'

'Not sure that that really enters into it. But, since you ask, I imagine it's probably correct that hereditary characteristics are governed by a mixture of random change and natural competitive forces, although I must admit I still have some quibbles with such matters as the appearance of chicks' beaks at the same time as the evolution of shells, or the question of which came first, the bee or the flower.' He shrugged. 'That sort of thing.'

'You're telling me it's suppressed?'

'What I'm telling you, Master Turner, is that our study of how the natural world functions must reflect the real needs of human society. A hothead, for example, might use your theory to argue that we humans are descended from apes. And where would that leave the unique concept of the sacred human soul, and our beloved church, and people's dearly held beliefs? Then again, if life is always in this state of change and flux governed by little more than who lives the longest and has the most babies, should that not also apply to human society? Where would that leave the guilds, all the succour and certainty and stability which they provide? I appreciate your disappointment. But things are as they are. I understand, for example—and if this is any comfort to you—that there are similar necessary constraints in other fields of study . . .'

They left the halls. So much for Habitual Adaptation being Ralph's unique insight, although it did at least reaffirm his conviction that he was right. Neither was he alone any more. He owed it to these others—the authors of those lost books— to do something. Back in room 12A, Ralph paced the floor and ground his fist into his palm. He remained determined.

'We can't give up now, Marion. This is all the more reason not to.'

'Who said anything about giving up, apart from Higher-master Squires?' She was sitting on the bed. The tip of her nose seemed pale, and part of him longed to touch it; to change things—magic them away.

'In a way, everything makes even better sense. Yes, we can be Master and Mistress Turner, but we will also need all the power and might of my guild to force this business through when we return.'

'*When* we return. You keep saying that today. I mean, if you want so much to be Ralph Meynell, why bother to leave England in the first place?'

'We need *evidence*, Marion. We need to collect and collate—'

'Is that all this is about?'

He realised she was near to crying, which was hardly like the Marion he knew. It was disappointing, really, that she was reacting like this, at the time when he most needed her strength.

'Listen, Marion. You're a shoregirl—you don't understand how these things work.'

'I thought you were leaving England because you wanted to be with me.'

'That as well. But what's important at the moment is—'

Standing up, she pushed past him so quickly that the bed was still sighing and rocking after she'd slammed room 12A's door. Ralph shook his head at the dimming of her footsteps and the bang of Sunshine Lodge's front door; women really were quite different creatures. He didn't do her the favour of going to the window to see her standing out in the street. Leaving rooms, the dramas of arguments in general, had al-ways struck him as empty gestures. She'd be back soon. Was bound—would have—to be.

He lay down on the bed. He gazed at the ceiling. Stains and blotches. Not a landscape of any kind. Perhaps there were two room 12As, and perhaps he and Marion were in the other one at that moment, joyously making love before embarking on their sunlit journey towards a chain of beautiful islands where all the workings of the world would make sense. He stared at the door, willing her to come through it. He checked his watch. Less than an hour left. The loading gates would be open already, the third-class families teeming through to get the best berths. And she had the tickets, he remembered. Perhaps she was down there already. He decided to go outside and check.

The crowds were already gone, and the ship he imagined to be the *Verticordia* was in plain view across the sprawling yards. The smoke from her tall, rusted funnel fluttered and blurred. Her topsails sank and filled as if they were breathing. But there was no sign of Marion. He hurried to the ticket office.

'Turner? Turner?' A clerk ran his fingers down the boarding list. 'Not Turton? Tyler?'

'But can't you check the issue of the tickets? They were purchased through your agents in Luttrell.'

'No, no—if you had tickets, you'd be on this list. Everything's telephoned through to us, see.'

'But we *have* the tickets. I've . . .' *Had* he ever seen them?

'Our rules are very strict. If you had tickets, then you'd be on this list. We do have a few left—second class, not third.'

Ralph stormed out of the office. Marion would surely be back in room 12A by now. His breath ragged with the taste of the sugar factories, he ran up the streets. He ascended the stairs, then had to go down again to ask the woman with the hairnet for the key, although he realised by now that that meant Marion couldn't be there. Grabbing his bag, he stumbled back outside into the brightening street. He still had twenty minutes. Perhaps half an hour. There was this annoying sensation that Marion was either a few steps behind or ahead of him. But he couldn't stand here, waiting for her to backtrack or catch up. He needed to buy fresh tickets to replace those which had seemingly vanished into thin air.

He limped quickly towards Martins Bank, the loosening contents of the bag swinging and dragging against his leg. The bank's halls were quieter today, but he recognised the palely fringed face of the clerk who'd served them before, and headed up to his window.

'You have an identity chit? A guild badge. Addressed service bills? A chequebook? *Any* form of identity?'

'Surely you remember. Myself and my wife—John and Eliza—Master and Mistress Turner. We're ringwrights. My wife—she's dark-haired, attractive . . .' Ralph licked the sweat from his lips. 'We had more than four thousand pounds in our account when we came here last.'

Now, the clerk was nodding. 'Of course.' His fingers played over the keys of his device. It gave a cheery *ping*.

'I'd like to make a withdrawal.'

'Not possible, I'm afraid.'

'But you just said—'

'There's no money left in the account.' There was a look of pity on the clerk's face. 'It's all been withdrawn. I can give you the printout . . .'

Ralph hobbled back across the shining floor and out through the early afternoon crowds towards Sunshine Lodge. For Marion might still be there. It was all quite ridiculous and amazing. How they'd laugh about it, once the real explanation—which was surely so simple, so obvious, but taxed his intellect far more than it had ever been by Habitual Adaptation—became clear.

The sky turned and hazed. How he hated the west and the dragging of this canvas bag as he stumbled up the cobbles towards Sunshine Lodge and looked at its grimy windows. A ship's horn sounded. Perhaps it was the *Verticordia*.

He climbed the steps and shouldered the front door until it gave into the soupy gloom of Sunshine Lodge's hallway. The woman in the hairnet was sitting in her customary seat. She shook her head when he asked for the key to 12A. It wasn't on the hook. Look—she pointed.

Ralph pushed by her. He scrambled up the stairs. Room 12A; the number was on the door. He pushed it open. And she was there—sitting on the weary bed, but somehow different, and dressed in darker clothes than he remembered.

'Ralph . . .'

He felt a surge of joy, then of puzzlement, then of falling relief, as his mother, her face beautifully framed by hair the colour of winter sunlight, turned towards him.

PART TWO

I

The land had long possessed much of whatever consciousness eventually became focused in the spillage of stone which became known as Invercombe. It had lived to many rhythms. To the passage of the tides. To the slow comet of the sun. In flurries of sunlight and in falls of dark, it had taken and retaken the sea, and basked in the change of the seasons. Small movements of life had flickered lighter than the shadows of clouds, but some had dug tendrils into its earth, and some, quicker yet, had come and gone to their own inexplicable purposes. It had been dim witness to the growth and sculpting of trees, then to their death and the white coming of near-endless winter. In its own slow way, it was part of the earth's rising and giving beneath the grinding outreaches of ice as the estuary reshaped itself.

As the deeper colds departed and meltwaters churned the estuary and the far hills lost their endless caps of white, the quick shapes of living things returned. Trees grew and billowed and fell and were renewed in their tangling decay. Quicker yet, more beasts came and went. Some of these beasts did odd things. They felled the trees. They dug stones and fired them in cairns which, much later when their heat-crackled remains were found, would be puzzled over by historians and

termed *burnt mounds*. From these, and for the first time, a little of the land's consciousness was released. It was used
blindly at first by these odd beasts, in that it was used at all.
Later, when a crown of larger stones was hauled up the cliffs
of what became known as Clarence Cove and embedded in its
headland, their ceremonies grew more elaborate, were associated with gods and magic and the pulls of the moon. Still,
though, the land did not understand, and when that crown and
the people who had built it fell and were long-buried and lost,
it remained uncomprehending.

Time, above all, was an alien element. Even as the channel
grew alive with increasingly elaborate vessels and the wooded
earth seethed and divided itself into clearings, the land remained
aloof. Then, more of its trees were felled, and its grasses were
grazed by grey-white beasts. The stones and timbers which the
other creatures laid upon it grew more elaborate, climbing upon
each other into fortifications which briefly almost mimicked the
cliffs of the cove in their grandeur before, as always, they fell
away. The land gave and the land took back, and the land remained unchanging even as it changed. Nourished by flesh and
faeces, washed by the rain, heated by sun and splintered by frost,
burrowed by worms and beetles, eroded from beneath by the sea
and haloed by gulls, all the things which came and went did so
in their own inexplicable ways, but still the land remained.

It was called Inver-Durnock by now, in some variety of
sound and spelling, and the valley, like all valleys in that part
of the world, was known as a combe. From that, the name of
Invercombe grew, and seeped into the headland as well, although Durnock Head stood so large and proud that it kept its
own name. At this time, had the land been aware of it, the
beasts called humans discovered more about the substance
which their ancestors had once crudely extracted from their
heat-crackled stones. They called it aether, and they used it to
construct the most elaborate yet of the heaps of stones which
had guarded the head of the valley. Decorated with bright
enamels, cosseted with spells, spanned by the long, delicate
ribs of beams and arches of the first fellings of the fabulous new
trees which the Guild of Foresters was now growing, the house
became a miniature of the aethered wonders of London and
Bristol and Preston and Dudley. It rose, proud itself, although

as light as shadow-chased sunlight to the land's regard—mere windless air. Still, the aether which suffused the house from its keyplate to its highest chimney carried echoes of the same consciousness which the land possessed beneath, and these echoes caused it to experience something resembling curiosity.

Slowly, although to the land nothing seemed slow, it and the house mingled, and then spread also into the gardens which, aether-infused themselves and greenly hungry, enlarged in increasing elaboration across the valley. The Ages, for the little they meant, came and went. A white Temple of Winds arose on the spot on Durnock Head where upright stones had once bared their teeth. House, garden and land were dimly conscious of a new profusion; a calling of wills which it saw no particular reason to dispute. It was aware, certainly, of a gathering complexity. This, too, it welcomed, inasmuch as it welcomed anything. It breathed now not only to the rise and fall of seasons and the clamorous sea, but also, in a shadow-light evanescence, to the manifold tides of life, purpose and machinery.

The valley became a stepped garden, fed by pools from the River Riddle. Above it, a waterwheel churned, and flour was ground from the new golden fields of the west, and bread was baked in the ovens beside it and borne fresh to the house. Wines filled the cellars which the new builders rediscovered and enlarged. Instead of arrow-slits and cannon, frail swallows-nest balconies of curlicued iron leaned towards the sea. Invercombe had always been a pleasant place to arrive at, and a difficult one to leave; generation on generation, a family was happy there, feeding the fish which grew to incredible size in the stew pond, or walking walled gardens at night to the fantastic glow of the moonivy. Perhaps it was *too* happy there, for, as the First Age became the Second and telegraph lines and railway tracks spread across the country and the cities swelled under their palls of smog, its influence began to fade. Gaslight never reached Invercombe, and the nearby grand-masters and mistresses who called on the place smiled and exchanged glances as they flicked the dust from their chairs and decided to perhaps not come again. Invercombe grew wilder in its ways. Its tall chimneys grew nests, and smoked intermittently like tall old men in hats. There was drink and suicide.

The family faded, and Invercombe finally drifted into the accounts and inventories of the Great Guild of Telegraphers. Coloured sunlight still fell through the magnificent hall windows, but it snagged now on streams of dust.

Age changed to Age. New technologies came into play. One summer, men arrived, and Invercombe resounded once more to the sound of spells and hammerings. It was nothing like the grand days, but it was light and it was life. For the first time, as well, Invercombe found itself re-energised by a substance called electricity, and then connected along tiny wires which looped across the countryside to a consciousness which was both greater and yet part of its own. The men soon went away, and the talking reflections which they had gathered of themselves in mirrors faded, but Invercombe was no longer alone. Granted on lease to Greatmaster Ademus Isumbard Porrett of the General Guild of Distemperers as compensation for a marriage contract on which it had reneged, its roofs were remade and its chimneys straightened. At night, Invercombe's windows gleamed as they had never gleamed before, and in daylight all shadows were banished. Then the valley was warmed by a weathertop, which expressed the land's will as much as it did Greatmaster Porrett's as it battled grey skies and fought back rain. Fogs might sweep down the Bristol Channel, but all that lingered over the stepped floral gardens and specimen trees was the same delicate mist you might find hazing the background of a Renaissance painting. On hot summer's days, when weather was made perfect and the light grew as burnished as the aethered brass which had drawn it, Greatmaster Porrett endlessly strode the weathertop's iron gantry as he gazed along the estate road for a sign of the arrival of his lost bride.

Beyond Invercombe, England grew sleek and prosperous. This was the Age of the telephone and the gramophone, it was the Age of boisterous new rhythms and dance crazes borne over from the Fortunate Isles on the sweet winds of trade. Spices and chocolates; the mally and the jag; werrysilk dresses weighted at the hem to fall sheer as water and almost as clear; excavations in Egypt; ambitious new settlements on the wild mainland of Thule. The zoos were filled by monstrosities, and scandal became as fashionable as cartouche wallpaper, and fashion was everything, and money was everywhere, and the parties were endless. This was the Age of Light, when the streets of the great cities glowed as they had never before; when trams sparked and ghost-visions of cinematographs flickered on the screens of the picture palaces which supplanted the music halls of old. Motor cars became as common as carts, and the complex telegrams of old which had had to be sung guildsman to guildsman, haft to haft, were replaced by the telephone. It was the Age, too, of information and money, of the clever machines which bore the commerce of the nation with a speed and accuracy with which no human brain could compete, and to which Invercombe, through the tiny turning of the small intelligence of its own reckoning engine, sang along.

Greatmaster Ademus Isumbard Porrett was found one winter's morning by the last of his servants, standing frozen to the gantry to his weathertop, staring down the estate road for the guest his icicled eyes still seemed to believe would come, even though it was known that she had been dead since almost the start of the Age. He was buried in its grounds to his own instructions in an unmarked grave, and Invercombe reverted to the Guild of Telegraphers. Once more, it lay forgotten, if not quite entirely neglected. A skeleton staff was established. Sometimes, to the scurryings and workings of the creatures which the house and the land still did not understand, mists were summoned, or seas were calmed, on nights when tiny craft flitted like water-beetles across the estuary. Things changed, and time passed, but everything remained essentially the same.

Then, the house sensed a new stirring as the cold of a particularly long winter, which it felt now in the damp bones of its old stones, began to abate. The arrival of two new creatures seemed to be the trigger for all this activity, although it still knew little of cause and effect. It knew little, as well, of the ties which kept these busy beasts apart or together, and understood only that the larger and older of many species—those which flew and those which burrowed as well as those which put stone upon stone and spell upon spell—fed and protected the smaller and newer of their kind, and often killed other species in order to do so. So in many ways it found little that was unusual about Greatgrandmistress Alice Meynell, and yet it also sensed that she was unique, and the stones and the land spoke to her as they spoke to all of Invercombe's residents, not because they cared that she heard or wished to communicate, but because they could not help but sing.

The summer was a warm one. Invercombe basked and exhaled. The gulls on the cliffs of Clarence Cove hatched their eggs and glutted themselves on sprat, and the one of the creatures which had come to the house near to death recovered, and spent much time with another of its kind which had been born nearby on the shore. To Invercombe, the weight of each incident was the same. Then came the pinprick instant of a lost aether delivery, and Invercombe was emptied once again, although the telephones that long winter rang with word that the Age of Light was ending, that east was turning against west, and even Invercombe began to sense a slumberous change.

II

In the beginning was the song, and the song was all and the song was everything. Klade, happy though he always told himself he was, sometimes looked back on these unremembered days of his earliest childhood as a time of lost content. Slowly, within the song, he'd become aware of individual voices, presences, shapes. Ida's hands, which were rough and giving. Then Silus's voice, and the white shape of his face. Walls and ceilings, and light spinning through windows, and the clear image and scent, perhaps his first true memory, of Blossom standing over him above the bars of his cot, swaying and weeping and crying and singing through the broken petals of his face. For Blossom was the song as well, and the song was neither happiness nor sadness, nor was it hunger or warmth, but it was all of those things, and it was the rucked feel of his sheets as well and the Farmers lowing each evening to their cattle across the thistled fields. The song was the rubbery taste of a teat pushed into his mouth, and the hot gush of need which followed, although Klade knew that that was a later memory—something he'd made up himself in the times when he'd begun to explore Big House in which he lived, and opened a spill of bottles in Kitchen.

He was growing, changing, and time was passing, but the song was always there. It was bigger than Big House, or Garden, or the Woods into which he must never stray, for that was also where the Shadow Ones dwelt, and the song there was at its brightest and fiercest. *The song is you, and the song is us*, Ida would murmur in the way she had, which was different to sound or seeing. *You, Klade, are the Chosen.* Blinking. The dark geometries of her face. *And so are we . . .*

Chosen. Rambling amid the seedheads in Garden, picking the silvery bark off the trees, Klade swilled that word around his mouth just as he did the pebbles from the bed of the Impassable Stream which he sometimes sucked for their slick coolness. *Chosen*, he was *Chosen*. He liked the feel and taste of that. *Chosen, Chosen, Chosen . . . !* And so was this sun and so were these clouds, and so were the tiny mud-grey fishes which slipped away from his fingers in the stream. The water sang as well as it slipped sweetly cold through his fingers, and he sang with it, and laughed through the pebbles with which he'd filled his mouth. Standing up, he could see Big House, the crooked finger beckon of its chimney and the greyed panes of its windows. Garden wavered, delicious with the scent of nettles, and here came Silus with his white face and the odd draw of his lips which made trembling shapes in the air like the waft of the clouds. Klade tried to perform the same trick himself, but found that his mouth was still blocked by the hard glinting coolness of those pebbles.

The song changed and lifted him. The song pumped his back. The song was a spew of stones. Time, then, was passing inside the grainy windows of Big House, which he was on no account to lick with the swollen thing inside his mouth called a tongue and which Ida didn't have. Then there were voices—winter voices, although he knew it all went back to the singing river and those pebbles. This, he'd now been firmly told, was to touch something. This, he'd been told, was to listen. This was taste, which again was different. And this, Klade, is colour, and this, Klade, is scent. There are your hands, fingers, which you must use rather than your mouth to explore, although the fire he was squatting before on his three-legged stool in Big Room had no fingers and was still touching him with warmth. The fire was good, but at the same time the fire was dangerous, and he was to sit here, but no closer, as he listened to the winter voices wafting through the door.

Even his name—Klade. Whenever has anybody been called such a thing?

That was Ida, whom he could hear with or without the door being open because she had no tongue and the sounds she made came only in his head.

'Blame Blossom if you like—it was just the first noise he made. But he's unique. Why on earth should he have a name that's been used by someone else?'

But we're making him too unique. You've seen how confused he gets. Things he can and cannot hear. We should never have said yes and gone to Saint Alphage's . . .

'You're talking as if I had a choice, Ida. Whatever it was that Alice Meynell wanted, she certainly wasn't going to let Klade grow up and live an ordinary life. You haven't met her, Ida—not close up. She's . . .' Here, whatever Silus was saying— and he'd been striving recently, Klade had noticed, to use his mouth to say as many things as possible even though he found it awkward and it made a warm rain on your face—drifted into song, and the song was lost to him, as dark and strange and dangerous and enticing as the flames of this fire. *We can't give up on him, Ida . . .*

But it's just—I sometimes despair. Even though I love him so deeply. And even if we have no choice.

'We must strive to be practical. That's the thing which is most important. And probably also the hardest. Who knows what the future will bring—but he's part of it.'

After all, who would have him now?

'He's perfect. He's unique, and he's ours. He truly is Chosen. It's too late for regret. Think of how *we* came to this place, Ida . . .'

So much of that and many other things made little sense to Klade. But the world was growing, and so was he, and meanwhile he must study. Study tasted like spiders and dust. There was even a room for it, set high in a corner of Big House where the beech tree tapped the windows, and in summer you could hear the nesting swallow chicks chirruping as they learned their part of the song.

'Now, listen. Say it slowly. Take your time. My name is Klade.'

Klade did, but Silus shook his head. Klade could feel even as Silus made his mouth into a smile that he was sad.

No . . .

'I don't want you to talk as I talk, Klade. Open your mouth properly. You shouldn't slur or spit.'

But that's . . .

'I know, I know. It's my fault. It's the way I've been changed.' The grey in Silus's eyes, the song in his head, dimmed. Other aspects of the song—the birds, the tap-tapping beech tree— welled up around Klade. Ida was moving outside in Garden, and he knew that she was listening. Or not listening—for to listen you used ears; the part of the song which was sound. So perhaps not listening at all.

'You should speak, I think . . .' Silus said.

And perhaps not. Perhaps this is even more confusing. 'Speak as you hear Ida speaking. In your head.'

With that clarity. 'Does that make any sense?'

'Yes.'

Ida, in Garden, snapped the dry stem of a teasel, the feeling of it mingling with that of her flesh.

Yes.

From then, it was easier. Klade was to make sounds in his mouth rather than inside his head. Like birdsong, yes, although we are not birds, Klade, we are the Chosen, we are the Children of this Age. And you are not to put stones in your mouth, no matter how cool and sweet they taste, or, even secretly, to lick the windows.

Then, with spring, arrived the fluttering things which smelled like the corner of the house where its walls bulged and the rain trickled in. Things which Ida would cup in her awkward hands or place on her rough lap and stare at for the longest time. They were called books and these, yes, Klade, are letters, words. *They're a special part of the song.* With summer, the cows came charging into Garden and the Farmers escaped with them, mooing and chomping amid the hazy flies and trampling the nettles until the Ironmasters came in as well to shoo them off with the paddles of their big hands still glowing from the forge.

Summer was a good time. Summer was sitting with Ida on the old bench in the butterfly heat. Summer was for books. Summer was learning to read. She'd point a black finger against the grainy shapes. *Cow Bird*. Then *Dog*—which was like *Cat*, but which he'd never seen until Ida showed him. How they laughed when she made it stand in the middle of his head and wiggle its tail! Yes, he soon knew these things, and the special shapes they made when you squashed them up like flies between these things called pages. But—man, woman? What is sad, Ida, about those words? And how do you spell Chosen?

Klade was, long before he discovered the phrase, a *voracious reader*. In fact, he was a voracious everything. He gobbled things up, and no longer just pebbles, for voracious meant eating without eating. Gobbled Big House. Gobbled the sun-flecked attic. Gobbled Garden all the way to the Woods where the Shadow Ones dwelt but not beyond. Gobbled the long space they called No Through Road, which went all the way to the Ironmaster's Forge in the one direction, and absolutely nowhere in the other.

He loved to sit in the Forge's mad heat and glow, with all the huffing of the furnace and the shouts and the clamour. There were two Ironmasters, with their flat red faces, their huge shoulders, their blistered, greying, clanking arms, but there might as well have been one of them. Like the image you saw when they doused the heat of their metals into the lovely, scummy surface of the water butts, they were joined in the heat and the glow and the steam. They made big sounds to go with their hammerings, but the words which came from their mouths were nothing like the ones Klade read in books, or that he was supposed to make. Ida told him that they were *Endlessly chanting the spells they'd learned in their apprenticeship*, which meant some secret and distant part of the song he still didn't understand.

In a corner at the back of the Forge, near where the Impassable Stream laughed and rattled, Klade found huge sheets of words which had somehow escaped from the books Ida was showing him, and then been piled and tied and tightly squashed, and lived in by mice who'd left their mousy stains and smells. Fascinated by these browned pages, unpicking his way through holes and droppings, Klade discovered many words about these creatures called *women* and *men*, whom Ida and Silus and Blos-

som mostly called *Outsiders* when they called them anything at
all, and who were not Chosen. They had things called Births.
They had things called Marriages. They had things called
Guilds. They had things called Deaths. Some of these Outsiders
liked to have themselves squashed into pictures in these pages
just like flies and dogs. They were always in shades of brown—
the colour of mouse pee, in fact, even when mice hadn't peed
on them.

Einfell, he understood, was a particular place, and there
were other places which lay elsewhere with names like London and Preston and Bristol where the bricks of many houses
and the Outsiders themselves were all piled together and
clambered over each other like the woodlice you found if you
peeled away the walls of Big House when Silus wasn't looking. Outsiders were everywhere.

There was this machine. It came from the nowhere end of No
Through Road each Tenshiftday afternoon and into the Fold
Yard beside the New Barn, which was where the cats lived.
The machine had a face on its front with something like eyes
which glowed with bits of sunlight when it was winter but otherwise were entirely blank. It spat and clucked, and there were
these big letters down its side. *A. Brown. Taunton. Grocers
And Suppliers*. Then, watching, watching through the weeds
and the cobblestones, the side of the machine put out a wing
as if it was a beetle in the sunshine, and Brown stepped out.
Not all of Brown was brown, though. Bit of Brown's face were
very red, and there was sparse gingery stuff on his head which
he kept rubbing. His eyes were red as well; and white, too, and
blue. The cats came prowling and purring with their tails up
around Brown's legs and he tutted at them with what seemed
like every last bit of his attention. The funniest thing was,
Brown worked his mouth as he petted the cats, and clicked
and licked with his teeth and tongue, and turned his head to
spit out shining jets which sat there bright and bubbly on the
cobbles and hung on the seedheads. Brown was so brown that
brown was leaking out from him.

Klade edged forward. He touched the brown stuff and
sniffed and tasted. Harsh and warm and tart. More like the
paints he sometimes squiggled on bits of paper to try to make

Dogs and Cats and Cows than anything he could make come out of his own mouth. Brown was looking at him. Rubbing the top of his head.

'Well, I'll be . . .'

'Hello,' Klade said, feeling proud of himself for doing so. 'I am Klade.'

Brown's brown tongue licked his brown lips and moved something brown he was chewing from the side of one brown cheek to another. The song edged and swirled about him in joyous loops, but never quite went inside. He was like a rock in the middle of the Impassable Stream. 'By the sweet Elder,' he said in a flat, brown, songless voice. 'You're young to be that way, aren't you?'

'I am, and you're not Chosen.'

'Course you are—it's a *lad*, isn't it?' Without actually moving forward, Brown squinted more closely at Klade. 'But no one would know from the look of you. Mama got caught, eh? Poor little bastard . . .'

Then Ida came, and so did Silus, and then the Ironmasters and the Huntsman as well, and several of the Chosen from the Far Village who were capable of being a help. Brown opened the bigger wings at the back of his machine. Things came out: cabbages and bags of sugar and flour and sea-potatoes but mostly tins and sometimes even fresh books which Ida cuddled to her chest and the song brightened around her for a while like the eyes of the machine which were called headlights and were powered by something called electricity, which they didn't have in Einfell, but which was very important in the Outsiders' world.

Ida sat him down on his stool beside the fire in the Big Room and laid out sheets of newspaper around him on which the mice hadn't yet peed. She stroked his back, and the feel of her hands was like branches. The song, within Ida, was always happy and sad. It reminded him, in its highest reaches, of that part of the song which wafted from the Shadow Ones in the depths of the Wood; it was that lost and strong. When she took up the joined objects which were called scissors, Klade could tell she found them difficult to hold in her funny hands.

The song went *Snip*, *Snip* as the air whispered around

Klade's head and tickled his neck. There was something else
in the song, something from Ida's memory like a bit of summer stolen by the headlights of Brown's machine. Klade was
sitting there, and Ida was cutting not his hair—alive or dead,
remember the difference, although surely his hair was dead, or
else cutting it would have hurt—but the hair of someone else,
in a different room, and the hair had the colour of the memory
itself, which was sunlight, in shining, golden curls.

*I'm so sorry, Klade. Everything about you makes me
think—*

—*Not sad or sorry.* He remembered himself. 'Tell me, Ida.
I'm interested. What you're thinking is Outside, isn't it?' He
remembered one of the many labels of the tins he'd taken to
reading. 'Is it Floodgate Street, Deritend, where they make
the powder for Alfred's Custard, which is Every Housewife's
Best Dinnertime Friend?'

The scissors paused and he felt the tinkling rush which was
Ida's laughter, although the sadness beneath it didn't go away.
*No, Klade, it's not. It's in York. Not that it matters. It might as
well be Africa for all the difference it makes . . .*

So he sat there and the scissors *snip, snipped* and the walls
of Africa grew flowers which were like the flowers Blossom
formed in the air but yet were drawings on paper, and the shape
of the window and the smells and the sounds which came
through it were entirely changed. This was a quite different
part of the song to any Klade had experienced. The rainy growl
and rustle of something called *Traffic.* Many, many voices,
and Ida laughed with a different voice which was still hers and
stroked him with softer fingers as, one-handed now, she
snipped away the golden stuff of his curls. 'Careful, careful, or
I'll snip your ears . . .' The voice was and wasn't hers.

The *snip, snip* of the scissors, the feel of Ida both here and
now and in a far away place called York was sweet and dark to
him. *Snip, snip,* and the way she studied him when the scissors
had stopped and his hair lay fine and fallen about him was both
golden and dark. An ache came in his eyes and in his throat and
his belly, and Ida was all around him, warm as the sun and cold
as the moon and so big that for a moment she was like the
wildest of the Shadow Ones and there was nothing in her but
the song. But Klade longed for some reason to press himself

against her, to feel more than the branchy touch of her hands. He envied those books—the way she pressed them to her— and wished that she was softer, lighter, more giving. Lovely though Ida was, as beautiful as were all the Chosen, he wanted her to be something else.

The scissors dropped. *Well, I think that's finished.* She scooped up the papers, ran her clumpy fingers through their scatterings and then, in a sharp rush of smell and smoke, tossed them all on to the fire.

Winter came. Rain beat the windows. If he looked carefully, Klade could see the garden all the way to the shimmery dark of the woods held in every drop.

'That's an optical effect,' Silus told him. 'It's a bending of the light.'

'Like a mirror?'

A pause. The rain went *Drip, drip, drip*. 'Ah, but you haven't seen a mirror. We don't have those in Einfell.'

'But lots Outside, amid the Browns?'

The gutters chuckled. 'That's true, I suppose. But they're not Browns. I thought, Klade, we'd told you this already. Master Brown is just one particular man who does some of our deliveries. Brown is also a colour, but it just happens to be his name. We call the people who live outside Einfell in towns like Bristol or Taunton Outsiders. But that's just because they live outside Einfell and we live inside it. Do you understand?'

'Yes. York as well. And we are the Chosen.'

Drip, drip, drip. Chuckle, chuckle, chuckle. If Klade looked hard enough at the darkening glass, he could see Silus's face captured in it, rippled and stretched like a clouded moon. He could almost see his own. 'That's right. But you shouldn't spit as you talk, Klade—I thought we'd told you that, as well.'

The raining and the dripping continued, day after day, and Ida fed the fire in the Biggest Room with wet coal, which left everything hazed and smoked, and he helped her with the cooking. Sometimes, she would grow forgetful and just stand there in the smoggy light, her song drawn down and inwards like the swirls of the smoke. He had to remind her at these times when to do things, and how to do them. She cut his hair again, and this time her song was distracted and she did *snip* his ear. Klade was astonished. He was Red inside, not Brown, although he knew in reality he was Chosen, and he knew by now the difference between what you really thought in your head and what you could say with your tongue. *Drip, drip, drip* went the rain and the gutters couldn't stop from laughing and suddenly there was an almighty crash as the roof decided to come down the stairs and the whole place was fuller than ever with the song in creaks and moans.

Some roofers came to fix the roof. Klade, who'd read many adverts for *Building Services* in old copies of the *Bristol Morning Post* by now, was tremendously excited. He watched through the thistles on the far side of No Through Road as they lifted ladders from their van. Smoke came streaming from the things they had burning on their lips. When one was thrown away, Klade combed the wet grass. Short and wet and white and stubby—he gave it a sniff, and nodded knowledgeably to himself, for these guildsmen were definitely Browns.

He listened to their voices, that songless song.

'How bad can it be, eh? Triple time on a Fiveshiftday. Just a roof, innit? But did you see that one—Jesus Christ . . . What a dump this place is! You'd never ever believe anyone actually lived here. And them things in that fucking wood. Fucking wafting about like stray bits of fucking washing . . .'

'Excuse me.'

The roofers looked down at him from their ladders, grins frozen on their faces through teeth where were even brighter and sharper than the Huntsman's until one of them spat them out into his hand and Klade saw they were the metal things called nails.

'I was wondering if you might not be from Frandons of Frimley, who offer Services to all Kinds of Guilds and Reasonable Prices and Free No-Obligation Quotes,' Klade said, pleased with himself for remembering the exact advert, and for not spitting once.

'Come again?'

'I was—'

'Nah. You're one of them, aren't you? A little fucking troll. What d'you reckon, Eddie?'

Another roofer called Eddie peered down from a new

patch of slate on which he was spread-eagled with a hammer.
'Can't be, can he? I mean, look at him.'

'But—see, his wrist—he's got no Mark. Old enough for
Testing as well, I'd say.'

Klade looked down as well, studying the grubby off-white
stretches of flesh where the veins met his palms and then
holding them up for the two roofers to see as they balanced on
the dripping roof and the winter sky poured in around them.

'Or maybe it's true. You know—all them tales. The bastard
changelings really do steal our fucking babies. Just you wait
'till I tell our Shirl . . .'

The men, turning away from Klade, went back to their
work up amid the sky, and shouted at him soon after to get out
of the way, you fucking freak, because it's not safe down
there. But their left wrists, Klade had noticed, all had the same
small wound on their insides as if they'd all somehow caught
themselves when they were cutting their hair or hammering.
So, he noticed later on, did Brown and the other delivery men.
He experimented with the same effect himself, *Snip snip* and
some more of the fucking red came out of him, and Silus
found him and spat all over his face as he told him he should
never, ever, do that again, nor use that sort of language. He
sent him away, and then came looking for him later to say he
was sorry and that he sometimes forgot just how awkward
things were.

'The Outsiders,' he said, 'they have this Mark on their
wrist which shows they're not Chosen. It's something we
don't have—or that we lose. And they don't call us the Chosen, Klade. They have bad words for us. Words like the ones
you were using. Troll and monster and sometimes—although
this is not quite so bad; there are graduations even in these
things—changeling. They fear us, and that's why the roofers
talked to you in the way they did.'

'This Mark—where's it from?'

A long pause. The song was oddly quiet and was mostly
that new-roof smell, which was cut wood and raw stone. 'The
Mark comes from aether, Klade. It's the same thing which
makes us Chosen.'

'What's aether like? Is it like electricity?'

Silus considered this. The angles of his face were as

smooth as a plate. 'It's best if I show you all the things that aether isn't before I help you to understand what it is. After all, it's time you learnt a little more about the world . . .'

Silus showed him the things called maps, which Klade had seen before in the adverts in newspapers—*How To Find Our Showroom*—but had never really understood. The blue, here, was water, and there was so, so much of it, and the green—and, yes, Klade, the brown as well—that was land. Klade touched his finger to the place to which Silus's black nail had pointed, which was Einfell, then twisted his gaze out of the window and up past the tapping beech tree to see if he could see it coming down out of the clouds. Silus laughed at that. *Sometimes, Klade . . .*

Klade came to love maps. The blue water you couldn't drink because there was so much salt in it. He liked the ones best of all where the whole country they lived in, which was called England, was made tiny. He loved Africa, which was dark in its heart, yet hot and bright under a bigger sun. The people were mostly brown there as well—but here, Klade, you're getting confused. And remember when you asked about electricity, and I told you there wasn't any here in Einfell?

It was a warmer day, and the study window was open and the song was full of birds nesting and the moss which was growing over the new bit of roof. Silus gave a chuckling sigh. His eyes brightened.

'This, Klade, is the first thing I was shown when I was apprenticed as an electrician. Despite all that's since happened, I still remember it now.' He took out a rod of something he called amber, which was beautiful and heavy, and rubbed it whisperingly with a fabric he termed silk. 'Now. Watch what happens when I pass it over these scraps of paper . . .'

Klade gasped in wonder. They lifted and danced like snowflakes.

He tried walking the other way down No Through Road where thin trees grew up through slabs and there were fallen things called lampposts. He felt all the life and colour seeping from him until he saw in the downhill distance a fence fierce with firethorn and the hills of Outside rolling beyond in cloudy haze, and strung with marching poles and lines as if the world were sewn up and would otherwise fall apart. He stood there, breath-less. The song was scarcely in him, and he pitied these greys, these browns, these Outsiders, for having to live in this empty world which they had made. Pitied, but was also fascinated.

There was a Meeting Place which lay on the far side of the woods. It was a newsprint-before-the-mouse-pee-had-got-to-it sort of place, grey and flat and surrounded by a wide space of lawn which the Master Mower, who was generally best avoided, came out to cut on summer twilights, hands which weren't hands spinning like the webs of insects in the trembling dusk. The song here was like the passage of water in winter when ice grew across the Impassable Stream, and Klade was borne on its arms as he stepped inside and smelled the Meeting Place smell, which was overpowering, and yet no smell at all. Shivery with excitement, he clattered along the corridors.

Sometimes, people were brought to the Meeting Place—Chosen or Outsiders, Klade; these things don't always matter. But, always, they were in Some Bad Way. Once, there was a thing there called a baby, which was like the cats having kit-tens, which an Outsider had left at the gate. It spoiled the clean Meeting Place corridors with its songless mewing and off-sweet smell. Klade, looking at it, prodding when it stopped squawking until it started again, twisted it around by the wrist to see if it was Chosen. He still wasn't sure. But he didn't like the way so many of the Chosen crowded around it: how even the Huntsman brought lumps of meat which he laid red-blue and bleeding on the Meeting Place front step to be found there in the mornings, and which Ida told him to get rid of and wash away. He didn't like the way how even the song from the Shadow Ones in the deepest part of the wood changed.

The baby had a face which was drawn up with fleshy web-bing and only one eye through which it didn't seem able to see. That in itself, Klade, doesn't mean it's Chosen. Some things just didn't come out right, which was like the kittens again which Silus collected in a bag to drop into the Ironmas-ters' butts because that was a mercy. The baby didn't last long either, which was at least something, although Silus grew as cross with Klade when he said this as if he'd used words like cunt or witch or monster or you bastard fucking changeling.

Then came what Klade thought of as the Diving Man. From

what he'd glimpsed of him, he looked like a picture he'd seen in the *Bristol Morning Telegraph* of a guildsman dressed in a huge diving suit topped with a portholed brass helmet, although the outfit had become part of the Diving Man, so that he seemed to have been made from rubberised canvas and brass and glass and bloody flesh and loops of strappy leather. The Diving Man, Klade learned, was nothing to do with the sea and had in fact been some kind of aether worker. He'd come from a nearby place called Invercombe, where so much of the stuff had got into him that he was bright at night and dark in the day, which was called a *wyreglow*. Klade was warned on no account to go near him—*You most of all, Klade*—but he crept up to the Meeting Place anyway, and peered through a gap in the door into the shuddering gloom where the Diving Man lay on his bed dripping and gasping through his porthole face as Blossom tried to sing his pain away. Dark and light tendrils of gas like bits of the Shadow Ones floated around him.

Klade was happy when the Diving Man left them to lie under the earth and the Meeting Place went back to its old, empty ways. There was a sense of lost purpose along its corridors which reminded him of the announcements he found in newspapers for *Guild Open Days* which he now knew from the dates had taken place long ago. He came often to wander there when he was sure no one else was about, and brought with him the new tinned drinks of which he was growing especially fond and was always asking Master Brown to bring in his van. They were called Sweetness, which was exactly what they were, and they were *Made With Bittersweet* which was a *Product For A New Age*. There was *Ripe Raspberry* and there was *Honey Orange* and there was *Candy Apple* and there was *Mellow Tonic*, and the lists of their ingredients in tiny print were something Klade loved to read as he sat in the corridors with his back against the cold white walls. He wandered afterwards with their sweet secret bitterness still filling his mouth through rooms dedicated to the sad Ages when the Chosen were chained and imprisoned and marked with a cross and a big letter C. He found the mottled prints and photographs of the Chosen in all their marvellous variety both comforting and fascinating. He experimented, with a puzzled excitement which reminded him of the feeling he got when he looked at the adverts for *Hygienic Suspenders and Stays*, with closing the creaky manacles around his ankles and wrists, although they were mostly so big they simply fell off him.

Then more Outsiders were coming, for their own Outsider reasons, and in that sudden, inexplicable Outsider way. And no, Klade, they're not bringing any produce—least of all those blessed tins. And they're not in Some Bad Way, either. Sometimes, they're like us and they come here because they want to say hello just as you might go to visit the Ironmasters. These particular Outsiders were from York, which Klade had discovered wasn't in Africa at all, but nevertheless struck him as a coincidence which he wanted to share with Ida until he felt the sad turbulence of her song and smelled the charcoal wetness of her face.

'You should stay down at this end of the Meeting Place,' Silus told him. 'I want you well out of the way when they come.'

'Why's that—is it because they think we're goblins and steal their babies although in fact they simply leave them at our gates?'

Silus's breathing lisped and rasped. His eyes settled like a slow fog on Klade. *I can't get angry with you now. Please, just do as I say . . .*

By now, Klade knew the doorways to slip behind and the corridors to duck along. Windows, especially, to peer through. And here they came. Outsiders. Big ones and little ones, with big and little voices and not a trace of the song, and holding on to each other as if they could scarcely see or had lost their way.

'Come on, Stan. You said you would.'

'Some bloody way to spend a Noshiftday.'

And here was Silus and here was Ida as well, fully dressed up in their big green cloaks and their hoods up so you could scarcely see them as if they were ashamed of being Chosen.

The one called Stan let out a barking moan. He said, 'Jesus, Ida.' Klade had a rough idea who Jesus was—he was dead, and important—and he knew his name was not a word you should use in that way.

I don't know what to say. Were you my children—you're so grown! Were you ever really mine? Is that you, Terry—whatever happened to your golden curls . . .

'Christ, don't do that—talking in my head!'

It's all I can do. I have no—

Klade was surprised when Stan covered his ears with his hands against Ida's song. Doing that didn't even work very well with ordinary sounds, and it was obvious it wouldn't stop Ida talking to you. But the whole scene went on surprisingly long, with a large amount of sobbing and howling from the Outsiders who were worse than the Farmers at milking time in the sounds they made. Klade didn't particularly like these Outsiders—not with the way they were making Ida feel and behave. Silus's lisp was getting worse than ever as well as he tried to *Calm Things Down* and created nothing but hiss and spray.

The Outsider called Stan eventually stumbled out of the Meeting Place into the grey light of the Master Mower's fine lawn. Klade, curious, followed him through a side door and watched from around a corner as he wiped his face and looked across at the woods as if they were something terrible, although there would be no sign of the Shadow Ones or the Huntsman at this time of day. Then Stan made another barking sound and started laboriously coughing up lots of the stuff which was inside him, all of which struck Klade as surprisingly copious and colourful, considering little globs of brown were all Master Brown ever made.

Stan finished and wiped his mouth. He checked the thing on his wrist just below his Mark, which Klade knew was called a wristwatch, and his gaze trailed back towards the main door of the Meeting Place, then settled on Klade.

Klade just stood there. Stan just stood there for a while as well, his mouth going loose and tight and gulping like the fish in the Impassable Stream, and his face turning even more blotchy white.

'Sweet Elder—this place is even worse than I thought . . .' Stan coughed again, staggering away from Klade and spitting and hawking. Then he went back in through the shining doors of the Meeting Place, and Klade hid—properly this time—and then eventually he and the other Outsiders went away. This wasn't the first occasion Klade had had a bad experience with Outsiders. He already knew that whatever it was about the Chosen which made them react was something which he seemed to have strongest of all; stronger than the Master Mower, even, which was saying something. Normally, he wasn't bothered, not even by the things Master Brown said to him as long as he brought him his tins of Sweetness, but today he was upset in a way he couldn't explain. Ida came to him as he sat on the empty edge of the desk in the furthest of the Meeting Place's rooms, kicking the boomy metal of a filing cabinet. Her mood was wet and her mood was grey; the sadness leaking out of her like rain from the sky.

I'm so, so sorry. People can be so hurtful. In a sense, Einfell really is a haven—

'Why else would we live here?'

He gave the filing cabinet another booming kick.

We all start as Outsiders, Klade. Being Chosen—it's being caught in a spell.

Klade nodded. *Boom, Boom* went the filing cabinet with a hollowing of the song which was just how he felt. *Boom.* He knew all these things which Ida was trying to tell him. *Boom.* He stared at the wall. There were photographs there—but in this particular room they were not of the Chosen but of Einfell's so-called benefactors and friends. Men and women. Guildsmen and mistresses. Ladies and gentlemen. Stan and Eddie and Mum and Terry. All those names they gave themselves. Fuck the fucking bastard cunting lot of them.

When you came here, Klade. When we first brought you here, we thought—

'Don't tell me! I don't ever want to know.'

But—

'—NO!'

Even as the afternoon was deepening, it remained bright in this room, with the windows kept clean here and the glass sheets of the picture frames shining so strongly that they washed away the photographs which lay inside in the pureness of their light. Klade studied each one, and the face in the glass which blinked and flinched in surprise was that of an Outsider, and was always the same.

* * *

Klade was growing. Klade, in his own different way, was changing as well. He helped Master Brown unload each shifterm's produce mostly unaided, and stacked it himself in the so-called New Barn where the cats kept the rats away. Master Brown, whose first name was Abner, talked to him more easily now, and spat less often, even though he still chewed his wads of tobacco, which he told Klade was a filthy habit he should never acquire. Klade took a hand now in deciding what was ordered, especially the new promotions and the tins of Sweetness in all their surprising new flavours.

'It's all right,' he would say when he saw a new face climbing from a van or wagon as he crossed the Fold Yard, for he'd now learned how to distinguish one Outsider from another with almost complete accuracy, 'I'm really not what you think . . .' He'd practised and refined that phrase and the smile he put on with it in the glass of the Meeting Place's picture frames. He'd learned, in these moments of meeting and interaction, how to make the song fall quiet within him so as not to become distracted. For Klade understood now that he wasn't like the Diving Man, who had been poisoned by aether, but that he was like that baby which had mewed and stank. Not that he'd ever been in A Bad Way, but he'd been left by his mother in some Bristol institution, which struck him as pretty much the same as being dumped at Einfell's gates.

Sometimes, Silus or one of the other Chosen went Outside. After all, it was only a matter of climbing into the shining green wagon and hooking up the fine horses the Farmers tended. Still, it was a surprise to Klade when Silus came to him one morning, dressed in his best grey cloak, and announced that it was time that Klade also went.

'Why?'

Silus made a sound which approximated to laughter. 'After all the newspapers you read, Klade!' *I'd have thought you'd have been desperate . . .* 'You should wear this.' Silus was holding out in his white hands another cloak.

'But won't I . . . ? I mean—how will they . . . ?'

'The thing is, you're with *me*, Klade.' *You've seen how people react . . .*

The horses were already waiting in the Fold Yard, and Klade

was glad of his cloak as the carriage started moving and bits
of Einfell began sliding away. Past the edges of the wood,
which looked dark and homely and strange. Across the lawn,
with the Meeting Place afloat at its green centre. Silus talked
to the horses. His song was absorbed and strange.

'Will you get those gates for me, Klade. You just lift that
latch.'

Rusty metal complained. A wonder, really, that he'd never
thought to do this thing himself. Then he was back in the carriage, and they were Outside. The hedges were green, and the
road was long and flat. There were fields. Beyond, and sometimes closer, lay the neatly ridged backs of houses. A dog
came scrabbling beneath a wooden gate. It was the first dog,
out of the pages of books and Ida's thought imaginings, which
Klade had ever seen.

On that first and his other subsequent journeys Outside,
Klade was struck just how similar everything was. How one
field was square, and then so was the next. He wondered how
the Outsiders understood which house to go in at night when
they wanted to sleep, and how Silus knew which turn to take
along these daunting lanes. The song had drained, was almost
gone, and the silence was clamorous with the noise of the
horses and the rattle of the carriage. Breath and heartbeat, the
feel of his buttocks against the bench and his tongue lying
trapped and songless in his mouth, and the dim focus of Silus
as he steered. Other carriages now. Whole clusters of houses,
their chimneys straight, not beckoning, their gardens like tiny
fragments of field, and just as square. Windows as well, glass
eyes staring. Some Outsiders looked and some didn't, Klade
noticed, as their carriage went by. Some twisted their heads
and spat like Abner Brown and others pulled the little Outsiders to them and made shapes with their red mouths and
signs across their chests.

There were, Klade discovered, snatches of the song to be
heard Outside. One of the first came when they passed a forge,
which was recognisable from its smoke and banging, and then
from the salty singing of men—who were ironmasters, and yet
had fleshy Outsider faces and hands. Klade felt a homesick
ache. Then there came trills and cascades of other notes,
abrupt and surprising, from places called guildhalls, and from

the bustle of other workshops and mills and factories, and then
as their carriage passed under the black lines which looped
here and there on the long fingers of poles, where it was whispering and intense. Klade cocked his head and brightened as
he saw another line knitting the space between treetops and
sky. But the song here was different. Scarcely a song at all, but
nevertheless surging pale and familiar. The hairs on his hand
prickled. There were, he had learned, two types of pylon.
There were those of the Telegraphers which bore messages,
and those of the Electricians which bore electricity, and both
were the pride and the emblem of their separate guild.

They reached Bristol. The song here was in the buildings
as well, if buildings was what they were, for, torn out of the
newsprint, unflattened and daubed with dimension and colour,
they were extraordinary beyond Klade's imaginings. And it
was joined by shouting tumults of ordinary sound and guildhouse bells. Outsiders were teeming here like woodlice, up
and down the streets and in and out of the traffic, within which
their small carriage was indistinguishably lost.

Things to be done that first time Klade went Outside on what
Silus called Business, which, it transpired, involved settling the
many bills which Einfell's running of incurred and arranging
for the organisation of the funds which had been established at
the start of this Age. Klade learned how to brace himself as he
stepped from their carriage, and remembered to pull up his
hood. Cold shock of the pavement. Bodies, elbows and smells.
Words hawked to the pavement by his feet in shining gobs.
Troll. Bastard. Changeling. As he stood waiting for Silus to
arrange for the keeping of their horses, Klade leaned to look
above at the looping lines, both telephone and electric, at the
advertisements from his newspapers made elephantine. *Snow-
berry Sweetness. Mistress Bessie's Water-Apple Pie*. Then dark
offices, walls and ceilings laden with ornament, and the song
sometimes heavy and sometimes dim in the smoke-hung air as
Outsiders called accountants consulted machines which were
both far off and near and were called reckoning engines, which,
Klade surmised, were quite different to the engine which drove
Abner Brown's van. In time, there were many things in this
Outsider world which he came to understand. The gaze of the
men behind desks which lingered on him when he wasn't look-

ing, then scurried away when he did. Tremble in the hands as
they offered Silus a pen to sign. The breathing through the nose
as if there was something bad they couldn't resist smelling.
Words muttered more quietly as they were leaving than they
were spat on the street, but the same words nonetheless.

Fuck
Changeling
Witch
Jesus
The Lord Blood Elder
Troll

Silus took Klade to Clifton Dam. Here, the song was joined;
aether and electricity—and water as well. As they stood on
abutments high above the city, it arched out in streaming jets to
fall far into the distant gorge. For long moments as he stood
there, Klade didn't feel lonely. The song here was almost as
strong as in Einfell, but purer, sleeker, and the pylons marched
off across the hillsides and his mind journeyed with them and
his skin tingled in the charged, misty air. Silus was involved in
debate over crackling sheets of plans, and the guildsmen were
almost bowing close to him and had nearly lost the panic in
their eyes. Klade wandered off along the thrumming gantry. He
let his fingers stroke dewed loops of pipe above the marvellous
drop. He even let his hood slip a little from his face as he looked
down.
    'Hey, if it isn't the freak-face.'
    'Freakiest thing about him is, he looks normal.'
    'Wonder if he's got a dick, though.'
    'Did you see the other one. Face like a skull with the eyes
still in it.'
    'Old Manny's been of a tremble all morning.'
    Klade turned to the source of these comments. 'It's all
right. I'm not really what you—'
    'Can talk as well.'
    'Clattery pissings, I'd say.'
    'What sort of accent do you call that, mate?'
Two young Outsiders. Men—lads, really, for Klade could
now tell these things—with sleeves rolled and their bodies

slung with toolbelts. One had a cigarette behind his ear, and the other's face was somewhat disfigured by red eruptions—although he certainly wasn't Chosen. Klade could smell their flecky, meaty, Outsider breath on his face. He took a step back. The rail of the gantry nudged cold against him.

Fingers plucked his cloak. Klade was clothed underneath, but he felt naked.

'Maybe he *has* got a dick—'

'Wouldn't know how to use it.' The hand which had been tugging at his cloak made a downwards swoop. Its fingers tightened around a surprising part of Klade's anatomy and gave a testing squeeze. 'Poor bastard.'

'Maybe we should shock him. See how many volts . . .'

'Easier still. Let's just have him over the edge.'

'Upsadaisy.'

'Bloody heavy for something made of fairy wishes.'

The sense of being physically surrounded by Outsider flesh was so strange to Klade that he was slow to realise that his feet were no longer on the gantry and that its rail was slipping beneath him. Soon, he was nearly hanging in space, although the hand which was no longer holding his crotch had left such a strong impression there that he could still feel it. He glimpsed the whole side of the dam, its marvellous walls which were the song made concrete, that endlessly falling water, and the places far below were dimpled and spumed. The fact was, it all felt oddly pleasant, and it was with a sense of regret that he heard shouts, and was jarringly dropped against the gantry. The lads dusted him down. With grins, they straightened his cloak. Just a bit of fun and games. No need to get upset. But on the way back to Einfell, Klade thought that Silus really did look as fearsome as the Outsiders sometimes muttered he did. He cracked the reins, was angry with the horses.

Klade made sure now that he received the most up-to-date papers: the *Bristol Morning Post* and the *Evening Telegraph* or the *London Times*, or the plain old *Taunton Advertiser* if there was nothing else. He read them top to bottom, main headline to shipping news. In many ways, he came to feel he could understand the world of Outside far better through newsprint than he could when he was actually in it.

'You really shouldn't be buying that stuff,' Abner Brown told him one day out in the Fold Yard as a new generation of cats swirled around his legs and Klade carried off a two-dozen box of the latest flavour of Sweetness, which was *Blackcurrant Dream*, which he could almost taste already even though he had never tried it. 'Nothing but chemicals—it's doing good Bristolians and the sugar estates in the Fortunate Isles out of a job.'

By the time Klade had returned from the barn to pick up the next box, he'd already decided that it would be useless pointing out to Abner that he should simply cease selling the stuff if he objected to it. Outsiders were almost like the Chosen in their inability to see the obvious, and he knew what Abner and the other tradesmen's reaction was when he ventured an opinion which didn't support theirs. After all, he was just some changeling, and all the more freakish for looking like an Outsider—*Will you listen to the child fucking goblin*—even if he was Klade.

But still, it remained obvious to him. Even Silus had commented that the trust funds which had been set up on Einfell's founding were no longer producing the income they once had. Money, to Klade, was a simple concept, based on the logic of adding one pound to another—or not, as the case might be. He understood about falling share prices as well, and also that if there was less profit people would inevitably be paid less, and would thus have less to spend, which was what the editorials in the *Bristol Morning Post* called a vicious circle. He saw the way things were going in the fact that Abner's van had been crudely repainted to read *Foresters' Fine Supplies* and then sanded off shortly afterwards so it didn't say a thing. He saw it in Silus's hissing complaints about making ends meet.

Now, when Silus went off to Bristol, Klade made himself scarce. Klade was far happier, he told himself, sorting supplies and taking them—the necessary food and odder requests—to the places in Einfell where the more ghostly and solitary of the Chosen dwelt. Sunny days or wet, he was like the Huntsman with his prey, leaving things on stained window ledges to be snatched away by approximations of limbs and hands, or at the edges of the woods through which the Shadow Ones swept and moaned like plays of stormy sunlight. Klade whistled to himself, which was something none of the other

Chosen could do. Why, after all, would he need to go Outside, when he already knew so much more about it than the Outsiders did themselves? He was like the birds which looked down from those bird's-eye views in advertisements of *Our Factory* with engraved chimneys swirling; he was like God the Elder who was supposed to hover somewhere far above the world's maps. Klade whistled to himself, and walked on, entirely unafraid. And all the Chosen knew who was passing; even the wildest of the Shadow Ones changed their song. After all, he was unique. He was Klade.

Sometimes, a new one of the Chosen arrived. Some were so changed that they joined the Shadow Ones in the woods, or found a place in the Far Village. Others might stay in a Meeting Place room for a while to die there, just as the Diving Man had, whilst Blossom sang over them until they came to the end of their pain. But Fay was nothing like the Diving Man, nor particularly like any of the other Chosen, who were all as uniquely different as the spell which had caused them to become what they were. She wandered the landscape for some shifterms, dragging what remained of the ragged taffeta dress she'd been brought in until Silus sent Klade with something better.

'Here you are . . .'

She jumped at his presence as if startled, even though she'd been watching him come through the dusk across the thistle fields as she crouched at the woods' moss-hung edges.

'I was sent to bring you these.'

She snatched them, sniffed them, backed away into the gloom, then edged forward and seemed at last to properly regard him with her frantic trapped-bird eyes.

Klade was unused to judging the Chosen by how they looked, but nevertheless the appearance of Fay was of interest to him. What little she wore could have been from a rain-stained advert for *Ladies Particulars* even if her neck and shoulders and arms and what might have been her bosom were joined in one pyramidal and unbreaking slope which peaked into a ridged crest which poked through the remains of her hair. Her hands, in comparison, were tiny, and her skin swirled, changed, darkened, beneath its moss and mud stains. Like the twilight, it had no particular shade. Perhaps she was destined to soon join the Shadow Ones, living out here in the cold and the rain. Perhaps she would die. But he'd brought some food along, a sticky sea-potato tinned in Taman's Ketchup, *Best Of All Brands*. He held it out.

'You're to—'

Snatching, she scuttled off between the trees.

But she returned, next evening, to the same spot. And the next.

'Where is this place? Hades?'

'It's called Einfell. Surely you've heard of it?'

Fay chewed loosely at another sea-potato and picked the dropped bits off herself with her tiny, filthy hands. The clothes she'd put on, the old ones and the extra ones, scarcely covered her. Even by Chosen standards, he saw that she was different to how he was between the legs.

'Can you speak without talking?'

Full-mouthed, Fay shook her head. *I don't understand . . .* Some never did. Ida said remembering—or not remembering—was the hardest thing of all for the Chosen. Day by day, he brought things to the place by the edge of the woods which Fay seemed to have made her own. Bits of blanket from the charity wagon. Corrugated iron and fencepost to keep out some of the rain. Nails to fix them with. He whistled as he hammered once they were out of his teeth. The bluebells were coming up in the woods behind her. It would soon be summer.

'I used to live in Bristol,' she told him, wiser and more confident now as they squatted in the low and rattly space he had made.

'Can you show me?'

Fay reached a tiny hand over the mossy blanket. Her skin swirled. She touched him. He saw a house squashed between many others, filled with flames and pipesmoke and a sweet, talcumy smell. There were vases on a window ledge, and stairs covered in carpet, and no smell of rot. The evening after, she showed him again. Klade came to see, Fay helped him see, a Bristol which was brighter than the newspapers, and better than the place he'd seen on his journeys Outside with Silus. Yes, he much preferred this place. In the *Evening Telegraph* now, there was Unrest, there were Lock Outs, there were Trials, there were Marches. There were disputes in the

Editorials and the Letters Pages over the question of bonding, which some called slavery. But in the Bristol Fay took him to through the touch of her swirling fingers, there were no debates—there were only sunlit tram rides and cold drinks in the beer gardens of the Green Lattis. There were only the ships moored at Saint Mary's Quay in fluttering forests and there was only Goram Fair, and candyfloss, which filled Klade's mouth although it was something he had never tasted, and was almost better than Sweetness itself.

Yes . . .

Searching the barns and derelict houses for more things to make Fay's spot more habitable as the thistle fields browned, Klade came to the place at the end of No Through Road where he had once stood, and gazed Outside. Just hills and trees and a hint of what might have been sea in the distance. Nothing had changed but the season's light and the shapes of the clouds. Those telephone lines swooped so close to Einfell's firethorned fence that they might have been considering entering. Silus had told him that they once had, and did so still by some subterranean route to an abandoned booth in the woods. If he stood close enough, he could even feel and hear their characteristic wheeze, which was like a door's distant creaking. He laughed out loud, to think of the place the world might become, if Outside and Einfell were united, just as they were inside the dreams Fay brought him.

'Are you sure, Klade,' Silus asked him, 'that you're not bothering her?'

You must remember, Ida said, *that memories are difficult.*

And some greater doubt was also there, which they disguised from him even within the transparency of their song. But Klade was helping Fay relive her life, which was surely what she needed. He was her guide, and she was his. Picnics and the best Nailsea cider. Lanterns strung over the Green beneath the careering stars swaying with the brassy thump of the oompah band.

It was full summer and beyond. Whistling, a new piece of canvas sheeting tucked underarm as waterproofing for whenever it finally rained, Klade crossed the shimmering fields and rapped on the corrugations of Fay's shelter. Not that he needed to, for she always squatted in this dark place which he had made for her beside the summer woods. She didn't seem to notice the heat, any more than she noticed the smell.

'Silus says you should move with us into the Big House. There are plenty of spare rooms.'

I'm still not sure . . .

Fay shuffled and scratched. More than with any of the other Chosen, there was the Fay of the song to Klade now, and then there was the real Fay. The two in his mind were almost entirely separate. Yet at the same time, under this baking iron roof, he could still see almost the young Outsider woman she had once been. In the shape of those hands. In the shadow slope of her chest and thighs. Her flesh swirled, and she brought dreams when she touched him, but Klade was more and more conscious that Fay had once been, and partly still was, a woman.

You look . . .

She touched his face, leaning forwards.

Human . . .

She'd asked him before for a mirror, but there were no mirrors in Einfell apart from the polished glass picture frames in the Meeting Place, which Klade didn't need Silus to warn him that Fay was best kept away from.

'I used to think I was a Brown.'

Brown? No, Klade, you're pale, you're dark . . .

Her hot fingers traced his hair, his lips, his sweat-damp cheeks. Wonderingly, they shaped his ears. His heard himself give a low chuckle. 'Brown was just something I once thought. It's hard to explain . . .'

Still, the cloudy fingers explored. Grasshoppers chirruped outside and the tin heat bore down, but Klade felt cold and sad and warm. The feeling reminded him somewhat of the times when Ida had cut his hair. There was that same delicious sense of being the focus of the song, but there was something stronger as well. Sour honey taste of bittersweet in his mouth and a straining in his groin. He laughed again, his voice high. He had to pull away.

I'm sorry . . .

'No, Fay. Don't be. It's me.' *My voice—my body. I'm changing as well.*

But I have an idea.

'Oh?' A tremor in his voice. 'What?'

You can be my mirror, Klade.

And she reached out to him again, and Klade's eyes unsaw the toadish creature squatting before him in the noon-lit shadows of her fetid lair. Instead, framed in gilt, far brighter and more real than anything he had ever witnessed, sat a young Outsider—a woman, with long tresses of ebony hair which she was combing with a shining silver brush and humming as she did so through red lips which smiled a secret smile; amused as only such lips could be at all the happy foolishness of the world. Bare at the shoulders. A fire-lit shine to her breasts. Perhaps she was wearing something below the mirror's reach. Perhaps not. She would have been perfect, Klade decided, either way.

The hot stink and the shambles of the place beside the woods.

Fay had drawn back.

That was me.

Silus expressed surprise when Klade insisted that he wanted to visit Outside again. *I thought you'd lost interest . . .* Then Klade explained what it was that he wanted to see, and all Silus's surprise was gone. But he was still resistant to the idea.

'You read the papers, Klade. Don't you know Bristol isn't that safe nowadays?'

'Half a million people live there. How unsafe can it be?'

'I'm not even sure that the place we brought you from is still there, Klade. Nor that we'd be welcome.'

'Haven't you always told me that it's important for the Chosen to try to understand what they were?'

Silus inclined his head at that, but not with any particular acceptance. There was a wordless weariness, a resignation, to this part of the song. But still, he agreed. Ida's flesh had dried out and stiffened like pinecones in this heat, and Klade could feel her pain back in the Big House as the Farmers brought the horses and their meticulously polished wagon into the yard. The cloak he'd worn before was now too small for him, and this bigger one felt itchy and odd. Why should he have to hide himself, when he was Klade, and it was a warm day, too close for these thick clothes, and hard even to breathe?

The smell of leather and horses. The road's hot tar. The air was turbid even as they passed the songless fields, and swirled dark with the sourness of industry as they approached the city. Bristol, today, truly was the non-colour of newsprint. Silus's ongoing song of regret was part of this metropolis as well, unravelling like the gutters and the limp lines of washing. The sun dimmed with a smell like hair cast upon a fire. Shouting people swept by, and the sides of the carriage were rocked and banged. Then uniformed men were standing in the middle of the road where smoke uncurled.

'Whoa! What have we got here—fairies! You really should go back, mate. Can't be responsible for freaks.'

But Silus was insistent. With a songless glace towards Klade, they moved around the barricade as the horses tugged unevenly across fallen glass and banners. Down a side street, several buildings were in flame and someone was swinging by their neck from one of the lampposts. The song of the city today was darkly shapeless.

They climbed into quieter streets where, amazingly, the sun came out. There were gardens now and glimpses of Bristol below in a swoon of fumes.

'This is it, Klade.' Silus wiped his raw wet lips. 'This is the place you said you wanted to see.'

The horses were calmer now, but Silus's feelings were infectious even when he did his best to disguise them, and Klade could tell as they climbed down that he was afraid. But this was such a peaceful place. There was a long wall with spikes of rosebush showing over it, a rusted wrought-iron gate with the sign which spelled, in twists of metal and a few caught leaves, *St Alphage's Refuge for Distressed Guildswomen.*

'It's never been in the newspapers. It's not that sort of place, Klade.'

The path to the house was overgrown with spillages of sallow and lavender and the windows were shuttered. It had never struck him before that there were many different qualities to the songless silence of Outside, but this one spoke of long emptiness. And the gate was chained and sealed with the kind of device Klade knew would hurt him with a spell if he tried to open it. Whatever business this place had been engaged in had ceased many years before.

'You didn't know it had closed?'

'We never kept in touch. It was an arrangement, Klade—an agreement.'

'How convenient.'

'It wasn't like that. Girls used to go to Alfies—'

'Alfies?'

'That was what people used to call this place. Girls, women, used to come here if they were expecting a baby which they didn't feel they could raise. You can't imagine how difficult the Outsiders make life for someone who has a child outside marriage. Usually, the children were adopted by what is termed good families. Always, and as with you, their origins were kept rigorously secret. There was nothing disreputable about the place—at least not outwardly.'

'My mother came here to have me? What was her name?'

'I don't know, Klade. The whole point of Alfies is—was—that the child was given a new start.' *The slate wiped clean.* 'I think she was a maid working at a place called Invercombe. I'm not entirely sure. But your father was certainly much more highly guilded.'

'They abandoned me?'

'I don't know. It's quite possible they both imagine you're dead, if they know you exist at all . . .' *Alfies was a place of secrets, Klade.*

'And I'm one of them?'

I suppose you could say that . . .

Beyond the house, the grainy bowl of Bristol expanded and fell in shimmers of smog. This was so, so far from the city of Fay's dreams.

'Something happened long ago, Klade. Between me and a woman. A greatgrandmistress. I should never—should never have allowed myself to get involved with her. But I did. I did things, Klade, which were wrong. I betrayed the people who trusted and needed me most of all. Becoming Chosen changes many things, but it can't change regret. And when Alice Meynell came to me again, when she came to *us*, at Einfell, I found that I was still in her debt, despite all that she had done to me.'

Through Silus's gaze, this woman, Alice Meynell, smiled a knowing smile at Klade with eyes which were both bright blue and colourless.

'She asked that we adopt you, Klade. I think you were the child of her son, who was called Ralph and had been ill for some years. And we really had no choice. The Chosen aren't powerful, Klade, and the settlement she gave us was generous. The high-guilded are their own kind of Chosen, Klade. You can't possibly fight them . . .'

Klade nodded. The world he had come from was like this city which roiled and burned in his throat. It was browned newsprint and the burrowings of unwritten things which happened beneath the pages like the bad words he'd taught himself not to think. Unwanted offspring—bastard; and wasn't that the real meaning of the word? Stupid, really, to have expected anything else. The Chosen were as blind as the Outsiders.

I'm sorry, Klade. I should never . . .

They climbed back into the carriage and drove back through Bristol. One of the sugar factories had gone up in flames, and Klade's throat was dry, his eyes ached.

'I always thought it was a lie,' he said, 'when the Outsiders said you stole their babies. Now, what am I supposed to think?'

Back at Einfell, Klade slumped down in the hot haze of the barn. The smell of Bristol's burning was still on his cloak. He threw it off and stared at the boxes of stores. He read their comforting tales—addresses of factories and competition medals—as he experimented with varieties of ways of expressing his situation until he'd finally boiled it down to its essential dregs. *You're the unwanted child of some nameless maid, Klade. You're sired, Klade, by some guildsman who probably doesn't even know you were born.* All these years, he'd probably been wiser than he'd thought in accepting Silus's wariness. Lies weren't something which existed in Einfell, but then neither was the truth. The cats came prowling and purring around him. Stroking them absently, he felt the dig of their claws.

Reaching for the tin opener he kept in here, he levered triangular holes into the top of a tin of *Cherry Cheer*. The fluid was salt-warm as pebbles on the bed of a dry stream until the sweetness of it finally kicked in as it gushed over his teeth and tongue. He sucked a dribble from the corner of his mouth, and ran his finger around the rim of the tin and offered it to the

nearest malnourished tabby, which licked it all away with precise, tickly roughness. He tried to remember the names Silus
had used. Alice-something, he'd said. Meynell, wasn't it?
Which meant that she was his grandmother, although Silus
had danced lightly around the subject as if he'd feared that he
might fall through into something else entirely if he settled on
it for too long. But she was high-guilded; one of those faces
you saw in the Society Pages. Alice Meynell. It almost
sounded familiar. That smile, that face, and her son, whose
name was perhaps Ralph, and who'd possibly been staying in
a house called Invercombe, and who'd impregnated a nameless maid. Klade found another tin of *Ripe Raspberry* and the
kittens swarmed needily around it as he drank.

He'd noticed before that one of the pleasing contradictions
of drinking Sweetness was that it made you feel more thirsty.
Previously, he'd always been too frugal to succumb, but he was
in a reckless mood on this late, hot afternoon. The bright tops
of the tins flashed cool and enticing, and there was nothing he
could do now but puncture them and lift their warm metal lips
to this mouth. Klade's lips were gummed. He belched. The cats
crowded around him in their fur heat. Yes. He was Klade, and
he was the song. Finally, the tins emptied and his throat raging,
he stumbled from the barn. The sky was the colour of *Blackcurrant Dream*, with clouds of *Fizzing Lemon* stranded around
the sunset. He wandered on up No Through Road. He was the
song and the Sweetness and the light. He was bittersweet itself,
and he'd have whistled if his lips weren't so sticky. He crossed
the thistle fields where the air mazed with late insects and
swallows. He rapped, *tum-ti-tum*, on Fay's corrugated roof,
then squat-walked his way inside.

As always, a darkening concentration of the sheeny dusk,
she was there.

'I've been Outside, Fay. I tried to find out how I became.'

She scratched, stirred.

'I've been to the place Silus calls Bristol. Although I much
prefer the city you take me to.'

What are you, then, Klade?

'I'm a story no one seems to be bothered to know the
whole of—or is too ashamed. I came as a baby from somewhere called Alfies.'

Alfies . . .

'You've heard of it?'

It was the place our schoolmistresses said we might go to if we didn't behave. I didn't believe it was real, though. Any more than I really believed in Einfell, or Hades . . .

'And here we are.'

I'm sorry, Klade.

'No.' He shook his head. Bastard fucking changeling fairy. 'Please don't be sorry for me.'

And I've been thinking as well, Klade. I remember more and more of it now—the time before I was changed.

The roof had been basking in the sun all day. Now, it creaked and squealed as it cooled with a sound like that the house martins were making as they swooped the thistle fields.

Do you want me to show you?

Hungry for a better Bristol than the one he'd visited today, Klade let Fay touch him with the moist tips of her swirling fingers, and opened his mind to her song.

You feel different today, Klade. Not just the way you're thinking.

'I've been drinking Sweetness.'

Ah—I remember that as well.

Remembered also the flocky glitter of the room where she had slept and lived, where she had brushed and rebrushed her ebony hair. Fay's skin had gained an extra layer of sensitivity in those long hours as the shining handle pulled and swept. She could feel the sparks; crackling surges of lazy light which hung in the air. Fay loved her bedroom, which she'd made her own in many small ways. The pictures on the walls, which she'd collected whenever her fancy was taken as she wandered the markets. Egypt or Thule, other climes and Ages. The mirror's bevelled glass gleamed so highly in the light of the tasselled lampshade that it reminded Klade of the pictures up in the Meeting Place. But now all he saw was the red of Fay's lips and the shine of her bosom and hair.

'You're beautiful. Do you know that?'

Fay shook her dark and sparkly head, but not in negation. It was hotly dark now; as hot and dark as it would ever get, which was hottest and darkest of all inside Fay's hide here at the edge of the woods in Einfell. The vision in the mirror, the softly glowing hair and room, vanished as the hands of the changed creature who was with him withdrew.

I'm sorry, Klade, I don't remember anything more—not even what guild I belonged to. Stupid, really.

'What happened was just an accident, Fay. A misjudgement, at worst. That's the thing to remember about being Chosen. It could happen to anyone.'

But didn't, did it? It happened to me. You don't understand. How could you?

She was just a sense of breathing, and Klade was breathing hard as well, the airless heat pouring in and out of him. His mouth still tasted of Sweetness and the powdery softness of Fay's old room. The song was in him now. It was there as strongly as he had ever felt it. But changed. It turned and joined, a secret unfurled like an airless breeze across his bunched and sweating limbs. The song the need to feel, to know, to touch, to understand. It was glimpses of Fay as she turned and pouted. It was her red-lipped smile as she presented herself in the mirror.

Klade stirred. He felt as he had felt when Ida used to cut his hair. He felt as he had when the apprentices had tried to tip him over the Clifton Dam. He felt as he'd done when he'd lifted those heavy shackles in the Meeting Place's exhibition rooms and tried them around his wrists and arms. He felt, as well, like those long times of looking at the adverts for *Ladies Particulars* in the back pages of the *Evening Telegraph*, with *Fine-Stitched Fabric* stretched taut against secret flesh. He felt as he did when he rubbed himself and the stuff which came out seemed for a moment as if it might be purest aether, but then pooled salt-leaden and stickier than Sweetness in his palm.

'Fay.' This time he reached out. 'Please—I want you to show me . . .'

He moved. Fay skittered, and her hands scrabbled against him. He grabbed them.

No . . . !

'You don't understand.'

Pressing down, he gripped the trembling slopes of her flesh, imagining one Fay and finding another, and then another still, a tumbling arrangement of limbs and resistances which he was determined to unravel. He'd seen the animals that the Farmers kept. He'd seen the cats, the kittens, and he'd read what little there was to be found about the ways of the flesh in newspapers. He touched ridges, hollows.

Fay fought, bucked. Her song was an outraged scream in his head. Only the dulling of the Sweetness made it bearable. If it hadn't been for this heat, this darkness, perhaps he'd have stopped. But he couldn't. Couldn't. She drew away. The roof clattered in a raw rush of metal.

Stop!

There was Fay, crouching and mostly naked. Her flesh was like the moon's, cast over with cloud. She was the Chosen and he wasn't, and her eyes were trapped in pure fear. Klade gasped, his sight pulsed. Stickiness seeped across his belly.

'I'm so sorry Fay.' He moved towards her, wanting to atone, but her fear rent the air and bit through the last residue of the Sweetness. Uselessly blocking his ears, stumbling out, pushing through the litter of the den, Klade staggered away.

He spent the night crashing amid undergrowth. Stings and scratches flayed across his limbs, and at some point it began to rain. He tilted his head up and let the heavy drops fill his mouth, wishing there was more of it to wash everything away. Dimly, in the dark and on through the dawn, he could hear Silus's voice, and Ida's song, calling hopelessly for him.

The rain didn't last. As the morning ungreyed, Klade found himself standing once again at the edge of the thistle fields. Rain had pooled in twinkling furrows across the dents in the corrugated roof of the shelter he'd made for Fay. He peered inside. Nothing. Fay had gone to hide deep in the woods with the other Shadow Ones. Perhaps that was where she'd always belonged.

Careful to avoid the Big House and the Ironmasters' ringing, gleeful shouts, Klade lumbered back along the edge of No Through Road. He'd never felt so remote from the song. He reached the place in Einfell's fence where the landscape of Outside rolled away and the cables stitched the hillside close to the firethorned fence. Where did he belong? Outside—or here? More likely, he was the fence itself, harsh and heedless and destructive. He considered climbing it, blooding himself *snip fucking snip* on its thorns until his body was nothing but Marks. The hills shimmered, gold, yellow and green. Then something, a wave, a tremor, swept across the landscape. Quietly thunderous, it passed west to east, blazing in the telephone lines, roaring with power and aether and electricity, bowing the corn.

III

In the hot light of that same midday, the London air rose up from the pavings and warehouse roofs of Tidesmeet and pushed down from the sky to roil about the pinnacle of Dockland Exchange. A weatherman, somewhere, was calling a breeze, but all it brought was the sour breath of an oven. This was a Half-shiftday in the hundred and fourteenth year of this Age of Light, although people had long given up counting, and the telephone lines hung weary of messages, and it seemed as if time as well might hang this way for ever, with the sun unable to shift and the clock of the world finally unwound. Then something happened. It passed first across the Westerlies. In the zoo, dragons fluttered in their cages and elephants started dustily trumpeting. Across Hyde and along Wagstaffe Mall, loitering cabsmen extinguished cigarettes and looked up at the sky as if in expectation of rain. In Goldsmiths' Hall, the reckoning engines left to nurse England's ailing economy gave an odd surge in the breathless heat. Something massive was coming.

Whatever it was moved on towards Tidesmeet. Telephone lines thickened with darkness. Power cables sighed. Those who looked up at that moment saw them writhing as if caught in a windless storm as they surged upwards from the pinnacle of the Dockland Exchange. The ground shook, London dimmed, and a

huge pulse of lightning-veined darkness spewed out. A shuddering blast was followed by a grinding of unstuck masonry and
screaming steel as the intricate network which the exchange had
anchored flurried up into the sky. The snapped cables continued
to rise, shearing up from their pylons for miles across London.

Greatgrandmistress Alice Meynell had been hard at work
high up in her office at the moment the spell struck. She'd
conceded some of her usual elegance to the August heat and
was in a short-sleeved blouse and had taken off her shoes,
and was fanning herself with the file she should have been
reading. She'd spent the whole morning distracted by the
knowledge that she should act entirely normally, and that, as
always, there were papers in need of her perusal. Then, they
would need Ralph's signature, but in truth he'd made an uncertain greatgrandmaster these last nine years. She'd hoped
that induction would change him. Then marriage. Then children. But they hadn't, any more than had Invercombe, or
Highclare. He still looked to her to guide things along their
appointed path. In some ways that was disappointing, in that
he reminded her so much of poor Tom in his unnecessary concerns, although in many other ways it suited her well enough.

The doors to her balcony were open, letting in the smoke
and rumble of the docks. This, really, was a quite impossible
place for her to be, at this of all times. But in Alice's experience,
the eye of the storm was often the safest haven. Then it came. A
tremendous wave, and she was sure as pictures slipped from the
walls and her bones juddered that the entire exchange was actually taking off into the sky like some Christmastime rocket. The
balcony doors flapped, and then there were no doors at all, and
no balcony either. There was a tremendous sense of falling iron
and masonry. The spell she had summoned was aimed at the
keyplate which was embedded in the scant foundations of the
Dockland Exchange which had been laid in the slippery London mud two Ages before, but as it dissolved the entire great
building was coming to the shuddering realisation that the ordinary physical laws of friction, gravity and tensile strength were
all that now bound it, and that they weren't enough.

One half of the ceiling crashed in on Alice's office. Energised, hurrying to the floor below, she found her personal staff
battling storms of paperwork. Of course, they had no idea

what was happening—was it just this room, this floor, was it all of London?—but she knew from the building's blueprints that the main stairways would be blocked already, and shouted for everyone to follow her down the service stairs which spiralled tightly around the core of the exchange. The building groaned. A lift clattered by like an express train. The floors were falling in on each other now. Whatever she'd imagined, it certainly hadn't been this.

People were already being drawn from the Easterlies and across Northcentral to witness the spectacle of the expiring exchange. It blazed brighter than Hallam Tower, and, in the fevered atmosphere which had already seen bombs in wastepaper bins at Great Aldgate Station and several high-profile kidnappings, few doubted that the terrorist agitators of the West were to blame. Fire bells and sirens started clanging. Pumps started coughing jets of water which sprayed and glittered uselessly over the first few floors of the smoking exchange. It seemed by now that everyone who was ever likely to escape had done so—and thank the Elder this was a Halfshiftday—when Greatgrandmistress Alice Meynell and her ragged but surprisingly long line of followers began to emerge. The newspapermen were there already, and volleys of flashguns exploded through the murk.

Two hours later, the Dockland Exchange keeled over through the smoke-twilight, buckling midway, then circling like a flaming mace before finally falling towards the quays, crumpling warehouses, ships, then cascading beautifully into the Thames in white explosions of steam.

Alice didn't witness that last chapter of what people were already calling the Falling. After a few interviews and a brief wandering amid the crowds, she had managed to retreat to her townhouse, and then to hobble to her bed. It was true what they said about the heat of the moment; it was only afterwards that you felt pain. She could scarcely stand, and the skin of both her arms ached and felt oddly stiff as she splashed herself with iced water. By that evening, when Ralph and Helen and the children came, she was a little feverish, and a top layer of skin had risen slightly up from the flesh almost from her shoulders to her palms. Her feet were the same. And her head was pounding. Inside though, she felt essentially happy.

'You should see a doctor, mother,' Ralph said as he kissed her cheek. Helen, a pale breath of lavender water, did likewise. Then came little Flora, who leaned so firmly against her left arm that Alice had to tell herself not to scream.

'I'm fine . . . Just a little shocked, I suppose. Do we yet have an idea of how many people have died?'

Ralph gave a troubled shrug. Helen had picked up Gussie from the hands of the maid who'd carried him in and was holding him up from a sprawl of blankets so Alice could see, whilst Flora was stomping around the fringes of her bedroom, boredly inspecting things. Alice had made sure they'd all been safely at home when the spell struck, in that intricate little house Helen had insisted they bought because it was midway between the shops of Oxford Row and the cafes of Hyde.

'Everyone says'—Helen smiled into the eyes of baby Gussie—'that the sick bastards in the West did this.'

'We mustn't jump to conclusions,' said Ralph, who never jumped to conclusions about anything. In this pale room, he looked more than ever like the ghost of her husband Tom. Thinner at the shoulder, and possibly more handsome. But still, Alice sighed. Her flesh tingled and itched.

'They haven't traced the spell?'

'The general direction seems to have been through Reading, Newbury. From the West, although I doubt they'll be able to narrow it down. I can't believe how people can do these things. To callously . . .' Ralph waved a hand. But his agitation, she realised, wasn't entirely due to the horror of what had happened. He was probably acutely aware that how he dealt with this catastrophe would be the judging of him, especially with his mother abed. He still came back from work each evening and set himself an hour to study some obscure plant. Helen didn't seem to mind; Alice doubted if they had that much to say to each other by now in any case, marriage being the lonely institution it was. *Does the world really want to deprive me of the one thing that interests and excites me?* he'd said to her with surprising vehemence when she'd raised the issue. But the truth was, yes—it did.

Alice was genuinely tired. It was past time to say goodbye to her son and grandchildren.

'Things can't rest like this, can they?' he said, looking

down at her after Helen and Gussie and Flora had trooped out. 'And I don't mean that we just need a new guildhouse. *Nothing* will be the same . . .'

He kissed her, and left. Alice lay back, feeling pain and weariness wash over her. But some part of Ralph, more than merely the surprisingly brisk pressure of his lips on her cheek, seemed to linger with her. What *was* it? Something genuinely different about his mood . . . Alice smiled when she realised. It wasn't just agitation her son had brought with him tonight; it was excitement. After all, he'd complained often enough about the mundanity of his day-to-day duties. But today, to-night, tomorrow and the day after, the significance of his role was no longer in doubt. London was in chaos as a result of the Falling. Yes, and almost for first time since he'd defeated the illness which had dogged his childhood, Ralph had found a battle he wanted to fight. Perhaps, forced into a corner, he'd be more her son than she sometimes gave him credit for.

Throughout that night and on into the lurid dawn and through the pain of the second day, Alice mulled the things which had brought her to this time, this place. Rather like the old saying, she'd have started somewhere entirely different if she'd ever felt she'd had the choice. But here she was. Between occasional near-feverish musings about the site and architecture of the new Great Guildhall of the Telegraphers—which would span a good portion of Wagstaffe Mall, preferably on the east-facing side where its glossy pediments would catch the sun in the morning—she marvelled at just how far things had gone.

Quite where, she wondered, had it all begun? Perhaps it was those pompous forms in Bristol's post office, or having to wait in cake shops as if she was just anybody. Or perhaps it really was as the moralists claimed, and down to that ugly and continued Western colonial practice of bonding. Not that she hated the West, but part of her had long seen it, in its tangled mendacity and malpractice, as the most significant obstacle to-wards the progress of her own essentially Eastern-based guild. It all went back, she supposed, and just as it often seemed did so many other things, to Invercombe. Arriving there on that grey dawn, and Ralph sitting beside her in the car as the pulse of his breath grew and faded across the glass. The sense that the place had been waiting for them; for *her*. Then that glimpse of her sagging jowls in the mirror so soon after they'd arrived, and with it the first terrible realisation that she was ageing. And meeting the shoregirl, and all that had followed. Yes, Invercombe had lain at the core of things long before she had recently begun wondering where she might find a hidden source of aether of sufficient power to generate a spell to destroy the Dockland Exchange. So she'd returned, at first not physically, and had explored the turbulent gardens which lay beyond the barrings and warning signs she herself had ordered to have erected. After all, the place belonged to her guild, and the men she'd had sent there were doing no more than their duty in attempting to recover and refine the spoiled aether which had washed into Invercombe's foundations, even if several had suffered in what was admittedly dangerous work. Raw aether—as if the place needed more magic!—but of course she'd fought legally and by all other means to ensure that the salvage rights fell entirely to the Telegraphers. Nevertheless, and like many of Alice's small projects, it had been something she'd been almost mindlessly tending, an option retained but unexplored, until she'd come to ponder how best she might bring to a head the country's frustratingly slow drift towards a conflict which she was certain would be of enormous benefit to her guild.

She'd ordered that the work of clearing the aethered wreckage from Invercombe's sea foundations be abandoned, and the last of the skeleton staff dismissed. When she arrived there alone by car several shifterms after, the place should have felt entirely deserted. Of course, it didn't, but that came as no more of a surprise to her than the leakings of its roofs and the abandonments of its furniture. She knew all these things already. She felt them as her own. Even beyond the prickly presence of its slumbering weathertop, or the whispers she seemed to hear standing amid the surging wildness of its gardens, and just like the shamans who had once danced around Durnock Head's bloodied stones, she understood that this place had power. And what was power for, if it was not to be used?

In the aftermath of that London noon, she permitted herself a cold herb-infused bath, and ate half a bread roll and a little watercress soup. Outside, there were lynchings; anyone with a Western-sounding accent or name—Spaniards, too.

There should also have been arrests, but the so-called Western authorities were still bleating about due process and the absence of proper evidence. Their attitude could not have been more inflammatory, and London-registered ships had been set aflame in Bristol's docks.

In her room, with the doors locked and the maids sent away, Alice applied herself more avidly to the process of her healing. She consulted her portmanteau, and the fingers of her right hand picked unthinkingly at the loosening scab on her left wrist as she turned the pages of her notebooks. Her skin needed emollients now as it had never done ten or fifteen years before, and there would doubtless be a further price to be paid by her complexion for the Falling of the Dockland Exchange. Normally, she'd have put her gramophone on to soothe her ears, but the song was here already, and once again she was back at Invercombe, with the push of water over rock, the salt rush of air across sand, and the power which had called to her in her time of need . . . Her mind was a blunter knife these days, no denying. It wandered more easily, and she had to reconsult the spread pages of her notebooks to complete the cadences of her spell. The baby— yes, there had been a baby. An odd arrangement, really, but the creature had been half her son's seed and—mere squeamishness when seen from this distance—she hadn't found it in herself to organise its destruction, or even that of the girl. Marion Price— *that* had been her name, and she could tell from the lost expression which sometimes stole across Ralph's face that he still remembered her with something less than hate.

There. Her face was done. She blinked. Frowned. She looked older. Stupid not to—for what would people say if she never changed? With slow, sad gestures, she stroked the infused wads of cotton wool across her poor arms. She dipped and dabbed, wincing, then tossed the wads into the bin. Her hands, at least, seemed to have survived the fire unscathed. So graceful. So elegant. Yes, yes. Alice. Alice Meynell. The things those fingers had touched, done, perfected. She studied them in the pale light as she sat before her mirror, smiling at first until the edges of her eyes began to web with the beginnings of surprise. It was surely quite impossible, but she could see the shining edge of the dressing table straight through her palm . . .

IV

With autumn, Marion decided it was finally time to leave Bewdley and take the cabin boat downriver. Noll was easy about that as he was about most things, and stood the following morning on the jetty, hands stuffed into his white coat as he watched her disappear, not bothering to wave. With a little help from Nurse Withers, he was quite capable of coping on his own. After all, as he'd said to her so many times that she'd often thought he meant something else, he'd managed the infirmary well enough before she came. She even wondered now, as the bridge tollhouse took the last view of the infirmary roof, which still dimly proclaimed *Merrow's Feedstuffs*, if he really expected her to return.

The last of the town slipped away and the banks rose higher in clusters of forest, green turning effortlessly to amber and bronze. Working and travelling the Severn, she'd come to love this season above all others. Autumn hadn't existed on the shore as it did here, where smoke twirled above the next scatter of woodsmen's houses to join with the sky's overarching grey. And it was possible to think of the river herself— although admittedly sometimes dangerous and capricious, a stealer of fortunes and a taker of lives—as a friend in a way which you could never think of the Bristol Channel and the open sea. Yes, she decided, this was what she'd wanted to do. This, for as long as it lasted, was where she had wanted to be.

She reached Stourport by mid-morning. Here the Severn met the Stour, and linked with the canals of Dudley and Deritend, then north towards the Trent and Preston, and south and west to the Thames and London. If ever there was a town which looked both east and west, this was it, and instead of the NO TO THE BONDING STATUTE and EQUAL RIGHTS FOR THE WEST posters which fluttered elsewhere across England, the walls merely advertised picture houses and dances; the ordinary pursuits of a life she was sure would soon disappear. Swirled out and on from the locks, she reached a flatter landscape of fields and small towns. In Worcestershire now. She moored at Worcester at lunchtime, with the cathedral looking down from its cliff, and headed for food, and regretted not saying more to Noll.

'We've had a letter from the Church Board,' she'd said to him last night as they sat outside on the jetty. 'They're handing responsibility for our entire infirmary over to some emergency committee.'

'We can't refuse?'

She'd shaken her head, and Noll had continued smoking his cigarette. He managed to keep himself as aloof from all the recent bad news as he did from the practical business of running the infirmary.

'But I think,' she'd said eventually as they both stared out at the darkly purling river, 'that I'd like to go and see my family for a few days.'

Leaving Gloucester somewhat the warmer for a pie and a light ale, with flyboats and stageboats and joeys and tugs pulling the ubiquitous double-ended trows, Marion remembered how she had first met Noll. She'd cut her right hand on the metal of a capstan, and she'd known, as she spilled an astonishing amount of blood through an oiled rag as she stumbled up the river path towards the infirmary where he worked, that she'd been lucky he was there. She remembered his pinched, intent features as he tightened a tourniquet and sewed the brimming folds of the cut. Perhaps mainly to distract her, he'd asked her as he did so about her work, and what she'd been doing before that. It was a surprisingly long list. With her hand temporarily being of no particular use, she'd been happy to repay him by helping sort through the infirmary's paperwork, which mostly meant throwing it all away, and then to keep an eye on the other patients.

She came to like the work, and had taken more and more command. Noll was useless at managing people, or money, or most other things apart from being a physician, for which he had a peculiar brilliance. Marion had organised the cleaning of the wards, she'd thrown away old mattresses, and made sure the food was appropriate and didn't go to waste. The infirmary was an adjunct to one of the church missions, founded on the pious belief that anyone who worked England's waterways was in dire need of salvation, although Noll freely admitted that he didn't believe in anything, and took his comforts in the dispensary from the medicine chest. Marion, somewhat curious, had tried them as well. They'd produced little more than nausea, although one night when Noll suggested that they might as well do what he called the obvious thing and sleep together, she pretended to be dazed enough to accept. She enjoyed their physical intimacy—in many ways, their lonelinesses matched—and the infirmary had prospered; in fact, it was probably more Marion's now than it was his, and scarcely recognisable from the place of old.

The longer run towards Tewkesbury took her through the afternoon. Bridges echoed. Drays heaved the other way. She sang softly to keep the trim of the boat's engine, and lit the lanterns at prow and stern. In the quickening dusk, beneath King John's bridge and the meet of the Avon, the river was as great as she became, and the taint of the air changed. This was as far as the wash of the tides ever reached, and seagulls bobbed in the marina as she poled in through the near-dark. The town seemed festive tonight, and Marion expected to find hurdy-gurdies and rides in the main square, but men in baggy uniforms were parading before the eyes of an admiring crowd instead. Some hefted axes, or the handles of brooms, bristles still attached, to sweep away the unwanted influence of London in the affairs of the West. A very few had guns.

She cast off early next morning. The day was greyer than ever, the trees redder. Once she'd reached the bigger wharves of

Gloucester, there was no doubting the influence of the sea. Ships sailed up these channels from as far away as Thule, although it had seemed such an inland place to her when she'd first arrived. Being a shoregirl, she'd thought that she knew about water, and about boats, but the Severn's tides were capricious and delayed. Riverfolk, though, were a friendly enough sort, especially if they had to peer at you under your cap when you asked for work to tell if you were male or female.

She'd worked day boats. She'd sailed iron and wooden trows. She'd toiled with lock-minders and tunnel-haulers, and with families and alone. She'd become—still was, for all her time at the infirmary—a rivergirl. Her cabin boat was dwarfed along the deep cut from Gloucester to Sharpness by stageboats and stationboats, and keeping out of their way was no one's lookout but her own. Then the waters spread, the horizon unfurled. Now, there were banks to be avoided and buoys to run. The clouds brought scatters of rain as she passed close beneath the cliffs of Chepstow, and noted how much improved the castle had become. Guns, now, of the modern sort—fat, wyre-black barrels like nostrilled beasts—guarded this entry to the West. Then came the Severn Bridge, which grew and grew to a scale beyond belief as the outswing of the tide pushed her beneath. A train swept heedlessly towards Wales, and she tasted its smoke on the downpour. Then, in the clattery silence which followed, she glimpsed the gargoyles which tended the bridge worming along the buttresses like caterpillars on a cauliflower.

She was cold and wet as she turned hard towards Avonmouth, but also exhilarated by the feat of navigation which had brought her little cabin boat this far. Then the rain even stopped, and the sun blazed through turrets of cloud and across the estuary steam rose from the piers. This, she decided, was where river and sea truly met. Here, low, flat butty-boats which had travelled downstream from Shrewsbury were moored close to the spars of ships which had rounded the Cape.

When she'd first come to Avonmouth, walking up the Avon Cut from Bristol after leaving Alfies, she'd studied the chalked signs offering work to the non-guilded at cheap rates. From here, and if you weren't fussy, you could either head seawards or upriver. Part of her had longed to journey to the Fortunate Isles. But the thought of heading upstream into a country she realised she scarcely understood had finally drawn her. All things considered, she'd rarely regretted her decision since. She didn't now, although she lingered on the quays, where the *Devon Lass* was heading out on the night tide for Arawak, and looking for deckhands. She could pull her old trick of wearing a cap—they might still even take her for a lad—and lose herself and this war-gloating country entirely. Eventually, though, she lit the lanterns of her cabin boat and set off past the gloaming into the heart of Bristol.

Once she'd paid the huge rental amount for her mooring, she wandered over the bridges. This city always took her by surprise. Suddenly, it was no longer late at night but the turn of another promising evening, and Bristol was teeming, and she was flotsam on its rivers, pushed this and that way by the hawkers and the hoi polloi on Boreal Avenue. She headed past the castle, which was webbed in scaffolding, and on up the hill past the houses of the middle and lesser guilds. Western enlistment posters lolled from many of the walls, but little else had changed. Apart, that was, from Alfies. She stopped at its gate, and felt the ponderous chain. Just as she'd heard in a letter from Denise, it was closed.

After Clyst and Invercombe, Alfies' rooms had seemed small, and its rules impossibly small-minded. Pregnancy was treated like an illness, and a sense of homesick guilt hung heavy in the air. The other girls had made decent enough companions, Marion supposed, but none of them had been at their best: they came; their babies were born in a separate wing; without goodbyes, they away went again. Their few trips down into the city were closely chaperoned, as if they might escape—but where could you possibly escape *to*? The question had begun to obsess Marion as her time grew near, and she became mistrustful of the late-night tea, and was pleased to find that she was sleeping far less well, and grinding her teeth through prayers, once she'd starting watering it into an aspidistra. She'd stuck so far with the deal she'd made with Alice Meynell, but had decided that she couldn't possibly relinquish her baby.

Marion had had no real idea what to expect from her confinement. The girls were full of stories, but they were best discounted, and Mam had been no help on the one tearful occasion she'd visited, and neither had Denise. Marion had never felt more alone, nor more determined, and she'd hidden a bundle of old clothing to cover Alfies' ridiculous uniform and to wrap her baby, and followed Master Pattison, and listened carefully to the spells he muttered at locked doorways. Then her time came, and thoughts of any kind beyond getting through the next wave of pain were an impossibility. But still she was fighting not just for the life of her baby but against everything that had brought her here, and she batted away the sponge-soaked potions Mistress Pattison tried to squeeze past her lips. Finally, there was an end to it, and in her exhaustion she'd been sure she heard a baby crying. Even as the weariness surged into her, she calculated how she might conserve her non-existent strength. The room swarmed—and here came Mistress Pattison, bearing her baby back to her after the washing and weighing. But she could tell that something was wrong.

Marion laid her hands on Alfies' gate as that white room swarmed around her with the vividity of hallucination. She saw the dead, blue-white thing she was offered, and heard Mistress Pattison's words. *Never took a breath. Some of them, the Sweet Good Elder wants to have back right away . . .* Her world had collapsed at that moment in a way it hadn't through all the things which had happened before. The cold, dead child had been prised from her, and she'd fallen into feverish sleep. Three days later, and without seeing any of the other girls again, Marion had left Alfies and had walked into the city and along the Avon Cut.

Turning back towards the city now, she headed down around the edges of the empty markets she'd once wandered with Ralph and then on towards the dreamhouse where Denise worked. It was still too early for the evening's trade, and there was a long delay before the door opened. Marion was conscious as she stood inside that the earlier rain was still drying out of her clothes, and of the riverish smell they gave off as she and Denise hugged.

'Owen's in Bristol,' Denise said. 'Although it would have been a lot better if you'd *told* me you were coming. Don't they have telegrams up in that hospital place?'

You could never say, Marion thought as they set out along Silver Street towards the Halls of the Mariners' Guild, that

Denise was unchanged. Her sister had never settled on merely being pretty—the ruffed and puffed red extravagances of this particular season's western fashions were extraordinary—but beneath all of that, she was starting to look just a little aged. She grew breathless from the mere business of walking, and, between gales of perfume, gave off the characteristic sour-dust smell of dreamhouse smoke. Marion reminded herself that her sister was now passing thirty, just as she would soon be doing herself.

They rung at the Mariners' gates and waited as Owen emerged from a many-windowed annexe. Of course, it wasn't the old Owen, and Marion wondered if she might have walked by this figure, fatter now in his uniform, with his scalp gleaming through his hair, if she'd passed him in the street. And then there was the question of where a mariner, a dream-mistress and a rivergirl might choose to eat, and they settled on an artificial-looking inn on the rise of Park Street. The place was thinly busy, threaded with tinny music and smoke. Nailed on the walls for purposes which Marion presumed were decorative were many implements she recognised. There were shrimp nets, whelkers' hoes, a half-rotted rudder, and it struck her that something shorefolk and riverfolk had in common was that their ways of life were now regarded as quaint.

'So, Marion,' Denise said, 'I'm still to say you're a *nurse*, am I?'

'I've been at the infirmary for four years, Denise.'

Undaunted, Denise gave Marion a We-all-know-why-that-is look. 'Don't know why you keep hopping about so. I'm sure you'd be good at something if you kept to it. And don't think we dream-mistresses have it all easy,' she added.

Owen pushed and picked at his plate. The silver-buttoned greyness of his helmsman's uniform rather stood out here in Bristol, where belonging to one of the Great Guilds was no longer the sure statement of identity it had once been.

'Why people can't just get along with each other?' Denise said philosophically. 'The number of times I've had to help some Master Accountant or Senior Tailor dream they're fighting for victory in the West, I feel as if I've won it all already . . .'

'What I can't believe,' Owen said, 'is how anyone can take pride in slaving.'

'We don't use *that* word here,' Denise hissed.

'You haven't seen what it's like, sis. They still transport people in ships over from Africa. Oh, I know they say it doesn't happen, but it does. Just board one once, and you'd never touch sugar again.'

'Well, I doubt if that's . . .' Denise trailed off.

'So,' Owen said. 'What about you, Marion? What's your position?'

'I don't agree with bonding, if that's what you mean. But I can't see how the guilds in London can simply pass a law to remove it.'

'The thing is,' Owen said, laying his fork and knife around his unfinished dinner. 'I've got another ship. I'll have to travel east to London tomorrow. She's just been refitted as what's termed a protection vessel. She'll be carrying guns . . .'

There was a long pause. Denise clicked her teeth. 'Isn't there something else you could do?'

'It's a choice I've had to take. If I stay here in Bristol I'll either end up crewing something similar, or I'll be put in gaol. It's not . . .' He chuckled grimly. 'It's not as if I've become an Enforcer.'

When they left the inn, it had started raining again and Denise, in a quandary about ruining her clothes, was in a haste to get away. Still, she offered to put Marion up for the night on one of the dreamhouse sofas, and Marion declined as she had many times before, and she and Owen watched their sister scurry off down the wet street, then walked back together towards the Mariners' Halls. They chuckled. Always, with Denise, it was hard not to smile.

'You could stay here as well, you know, Marion . . .'

She shook her head. They were standing outside the guild-house gates. 'I have a cabin in my boat.'

'Of course—we Mariners forget that there are other kinds of craft.'

'Don't forget, Owen.'

'No.' He gazed back at her. 'I won't.' He attempted a smile. 'You'll be seeing Mam?'

'I thought I'd look in tomorrow.'

'Send her my love . . .' He made to turn. 'I'd better be away.'

Marion laid a hand on his wet epaulettes. 'What you were saying, Owen—I mean, about the slaver ships. You crewed one, didn't you?'

Owen blinked. 'The pay was so good, sis.' She felt him shrug. 'So I have to do *something* now, sis. I have to find some kind of recompense.'

'Even if it means joining the East?'

'Even that. I know it doesn't sound right, but it's the best I can manage.'

'Good luck, then.'

'Good luck yourself . . .'

The sugar factories—Bolts, Kirtlings—smelled of desertion and the wet leavings of fires. Much of Bristol had declined from the sunlit pomp of a few years before, but people still needed cheap places to stay, and it was no surprise to find that Sunshine Lodge was still in business. There was even the same smell of damp carpets in the hall. Could it even be the same old woman in the same hairnet? Marion asked for room 12A, and ascended the narrow stairs. The bed had been turned the other way, and the night's rain was seeping a fresh contribution to the ceiling's stains. Voices sounded through the walls. She considered rearranging the bed. It would be like the ritual elements of a spell; get them exactly right and she'd become Eliza Turner again—but Ralph would still be Ralph, and they'd still probably have that same tiff. The bed admitted her in sour creaks, and the room unspan through the stages of her weariness.

Their departure from Invercombe certainly hadn't been the joyful thing she'd imagined. Ralph had changed in those last shifterms—or become more like his true self—although she'd imagined things between them would return to what she'd naïvely thought of as their natural state once they got properly away. But more and more, he'd been talking about their journey to the Fortunate Isles as some excursion from which he could return after a year or so and simply pick up his guilded life. Where would that leave her, she'd often wondered? And where would that leave her baby? The time had surely arrived for her to tell him, but she'd started to wonder if she wasn't putting it off not because she didn't want to make him feel tied, but be-

cause she feared he'd simply walk away. Then they'd gone to
that guildhall where the pillars glittered like insects. It was the
sweet arrogance of youth, Marion now supposed, which had
made them think they were the first to discover—what had
they used to call it, *Habitual Adaptation*? Clumsy phrase. Yes,
she'd understood Ralph's disappointment as he paced this
room, but then he'd started talking as if proving his theory
was all that mattered. Questions had tumbled in her mind, and
she'd felt, it had to be admitted, nauseous. She'd needed to be
alone for a while, although she'd imagined as she stumbled
down the stairs that she'd return a few minutes later. After all,
they still had a ship to catch.

Then she was out in the street, and not exactly breathless or
tearful or running, but in a state which lay close to all of these
things. The ships had been sounding, the air stirring in excited
flurries, the bright posters flapping, and hawkers were selling
chapbooks about the best wagon routes to take across the al-
kali deserts of Western Thule. The sugar factories had still
been at full production in those days, and their characteristic
sweetshop-and-burning smell thickened the air. It was a smell
Marion would never be able to catch again without sensing a
light tap on her shoulder, and hearing a well-spoken female
voice.

Excuse me. It is Marion Price, isn't it?

She'd turned unhesitatingly. Greatgrandmistress Alice Meynell had been dressed in a long coat and skirt and tight boots,
all of them black, which Marion had previously thought to be
one colour, but which she now realised to be something of
many sheens and textures and shades.

'I'm so glad I found you, Marion. Yes, yes, I know you're
worried about time and about Ralph—but you really needn't
be. Perhaps if we could just find somewhere to talk for a few
minutes?'

She supposed she could have turned and run, but the idea
that she and Ralph might escape undetected to the Fortunate
Isles was gone, and she sensed as she had before that this
woman was not to be resisted.

'You're looking pale, Marion,' she said as they sat down in
a small café. 'I mean, I understand as a mother how wearying
it is to be in your condition.'

Alice Meynell had smiled at her. She seemed to know everything. Then she moved the condiments aside and placed a copy of today's *Bristol Morning Post* before her. Marion had been dimly aware of phrases to do with *Arrests* and *Seizures* as she and Ralph passed the placards of newsvendors, but she hadn't understood what they meant until she saw the front page.

'I'm sorry to say that Invercombe—and my trust in that place—has been sorely misused . . .'

Marion had known that some sort of delivery had been due last night, although it had hardly been uppermost in her mind, but a whole ship filled with aether was a prize beyond anything she'd ever heard talk of, and it represented an enormous betrayal that the Enforcers should discover it in the process of unloading in the weathertop fog of Clarence Cove.

'I'm afraid, Marion, that your father is amongst the men who've been arrested. Weatherman Ayres did not survive. The whole business is a most sorry instance of what I believe you Westerners like to call the small trade. Perhaps I'd have been able to discourage such foolhardiness if I'd have been there at Invercombe and kept a better eye on things . . .'

'My father. You said—'

'He's been arrested, and I also hear that he's injured, but I honestly can't tell you how badly. Invercombe, so I gather, is no longer safe. Such waste—all those lovely gardens—and so many arrests. Not just your father, but staff at Invercombe, and shorepeople, and then all the way up through the guilds to the Merchant Venturers who apparently financed the whole project. And there, really, lies the crux.'

Despite what she'd already heard, Marion felt herself grow cold. But Alice Meynell looked more composed and beautiful than ever, and her gaze, which was always attentive, had grown almost hypnotic. No one, Marion thought, as the greatgrand-mistress of the Telegraphers' Guild explained what she thought should now happen—not her mother, nor Ralph, nor anyone—had ever looked into her eyes quite this attentively before.

Cissy Dunning was already under arrest. So was Wilkins and so was Wyatt and so were many of Invercombe's maids. Even if the prosecutors were persuaded that they had no involvement in the use of the house for smuggling, they would have a difficult time getting further employment in their guilds. The situation was worse for the shorefolk of Clyst. After all, they had lit the bonfires and crewed the boats. Unfortunate though it was, even those not directly involved were likely to be tainted by this affair. Why, Alice understood that Marion's brother had only just recently been inducted into the Mariners' Guild, which was notoriously strict on such matters. Even her sister, and her plans to become—what, a seamstress?—might well become compromised . . .

'What are you saying?'

'What I'm saying, Marion, is that things are at a most unfortunate stage. Of course, I'll use all my influence to see that matters are dealt with as compassionately as possible. Then there's Ralph to consider. One way or another, he's been drawn far too closely into this. I certainly don't advocate the practice of smuggling, Marion, but my feeling is that the blame should rest unequivocally with the senior guildsmen of Bristol who funded this and many another escapade, and not with the men and women who were simply trying to make the best living they could.'

Slowly, colder than ever, still falling, Marion nodded. 'You're saying you'll help?'

'Of course I will. But I expect a little from you in return. And before you say anything else, I should perhaps remind you why you're here in Bristol, and the deceit you were carrying out. Fraud. Impersonation. And you knew about this delivery as well, didn't you? None of us are quite innocent in this, I'm afraid, but it's vital that Ralph should be able to go to Highclare without further delay or interruption, and it's important, therefore, that you accept that you should have nothing further to do with him.'

'If I don't?'

The blue eyes hazed. 'I believe you're just *saying* that, Marion. I mean—do you really imagine you could carry on your relationship? I do realise that this is a lot for you to absorb, my dear, but, if it's any comfort to you, such daydreams of escape as you and Ralph toyed with are to be expected from young people. Of course, it couldn't possibly happen, any more than my poor husband Tom probably ever imagined when he made that amusing bequest. Although I'm sure it was fun while it lasted.' She smiled. 'I'm not some monster. I do understand how a woman feels about her child. I also realize that the baby is partly of Meynell blood, and the last thing I'd want is for any harm to come to it.'

'How did you know?'

Alice smiled. 'Call it intuition. But in all frankness, my dear, I don't think you could guarantee you could give this child the life it deserves. I want you to have it adopted.'

'You're asking me to give up the one thing I have left.'

'What I'm asking you to do is to be *practical*. There's a place just up the hill not so far from here. It's called Saint Alphage's, or Alfies colloquially. Ah—I see you've heard of it. I've already arranged funding, and I can assure you that you'll be well treated. And once the child is born, it will be given a good home, and you'll be free to get on with your life as you wish. So, I should add, will your brother and sister, and also, as far as I can manage, will the people of Clyst and the workers of Invercombe. The arrests and the enquiries would be kept to a minimum. Your injured father will be released on compassionate grounds. I give you my word that I will do everything which lies within my powers to ensure that the only people who suffer are the Merchant Venturers and greatgrandmasters of Bristol. And I somehow doubt that you have any great concern for *them* . . .'

Marion considered. That was the strangest thing: this woman had reshuffled her life like a pack of cards and had laid it out in this horrible new way, and yet she found herself meeting her coldly compassionate gaze and debating what was to be lost or gained. 'If I refuse?'

'Please don't put me in that position, Marion.'

She tried to remind herself of what she knew about Ralph's mother. She remembered the first time that she'd seen her wandering the shore, looking for a specific but quite useless variety of pearl, although she had no doubt that Alice Meynell had her reasons. The woman was nothing if not considered. Would she really refuse to help the people of Invercombe and Clyst simply for the sake of Marion not giving up her child? That, at the end of the day, and looking into those falling eyes, which were blue into endless dark beyond all the colours of blackness, was the one thing she couldn't afford to doubt.

'I'm glad you're seeing things sensibly, Marion.'

Had she really said yes? Then Alice Meynell had settled the bill for whatever it was they had drunk and they were standing outside the café in blustery sunlight, and, for the sake of all the people she loved and knew, her whole life taken from her and twisted around and returned to her in this impossible new shape, Marion had started walking up the hill towards Saint Alphage's, and nothing was ever the same.

She settled the bill at Sunshine Lodge early and was out in the ungreying morning, taking short cuts through the quarters of the city where the Jews primarily dwelt, and then the men of Cathay, and then the famine-fleeing Irish, and then the free bondsmen. She was glad, after these sorry hovels, to be piloting in her cabin boat back along Avon Cut, and let the craft submit to the currents which bore her out from the sea-locks and further down the Bristol Channel.

She'd never visited Portishead by boat before, and navigating the channels towards its little-used harbour was a task she used to keep other thoughts at bay. It was too late in the season for holidaymakers, and there were many Vacancies signs in front windows as she walked the rows of sand-swept terraces until she came to the particular house where her mother now lodged.

'She's in her room . . .' Cousin Penelope, hands gloved in soap, gestured up the stairs. After testing several identical doors, Marion found Mam sitting at a window in a front bedroom.

'*Marion*, isn't it?' Mam was wearing a holed shawl, and working something round and round with the fingers of her right hand.

'I'm up from Bewdley. I saw Denise and Owen up in Bristol yesterday evening. They're both doing fine.'

'Owen off on some ship, then, is he?'

'I believe it's this very morning.'

'So he won't be visiting me.'

'Didn't he look in last Fourshiftday?'

'Denise, now *she's* a good girl. Sends me these scarves she says she's made. Course, I can't wear them—what use are they to me? And her downstairs has always got her eye on my things . . .'

Mam's gaze wandered towards the window beside which,

from the wear of the linoleum, it seemed she spent most of her time sitting. Beyond back yards filled with neglected washing and gables of houses lay a small triangle of sea. Marion sat with Mam for a while as they both stared out. She'd have held her mother's hands, but the worrying fingers were too busy.

Afterwards, in the dull afternoon, Marion took her mother down towards the sea.

'I'm not in a bloody handcart yet...' Mam batted her offered arm away.

They walked round the stone jetty where a domed emporium, its paint peeled and seemingly abandoned, promised *Serpents of the Deep*. 'Taken them all away, they have,' Mam informed her. 'Something to do with the war effort.'

Out in the channel, a white plume rose and fell. A *boom*, another plume. 'Get that all the time here.' Mam chuckled. Her fingers were turning something blue and glittery. 'There's a new emplacement up by the toy boating lake. Getting their range, they are.' *Boom*. The sound rolled back and forth across the channel as they sat on a bench and ate fish and chips, which Mam ate one-handed as her fingers still turned and turned that shard of glass. As Marion peeled her last grey chip away from the newspaper, she found the face of Greatgrandmistress Alice Meynell smiling up at her from the greasy society pages. Balling it up, she stuffed it into an over-brimming litter bin.

Back at the house, standing in the hall and refusing cousin Penelope's less than overwhelming insistence that she stay for tea, Marion decided that she could still tell herself that her mother, if not quite happy, wasn't entirely sad. As they kissed, she took her hands, and saw that the whole of Mam's palm was scabbed by the endless turning of a shard of blue Bristol glass.

Marion found her own fingers were working around the tiller after she'd cast off from Portishead as she thought of Mam's hands, that blue piece of glass. Dad's injuries from the *Proserpine*'s blast, if you excluded the considerable one of being arrested by the Enforcers, had seemed slight at first. He'd been placed in Luttrell's small infirmary to recover from his burns and a few embedded splinters of hull, and it seemed that Alice

Meynell really had kept her promise when it was announced that charges would not be preferred. Marion, although she'd given up expecting Ralph Meynell to ever return to her, was beginning to feel something like genuine hope when she was first permitted to make the trip from Alfies to see her father. Dad certainly didn't blame Weatherman Ayres for blowing up the *Proserpine*. He'd have done the same. Only a matter of shifterms, he kept saying, and he'd be out sailing the channel again. But the odd darkening transparency of his hands was beginning to get worse.

Marion only saw her father alive once more, and by then his skin had been blued and brittled. Blood pulsed through bottle-depths of glass, and he couldn't speak, and all the fingers of one of his hands had already been snapped off by a careless nurse. She'd doubted, in fact, if the man who'd been her father was still there at all. There had been some talk of taking him to Einfell, but that was a place of guilds and madness; even in this state, Dad would never have wanted to go there. He died a day or so afterwards in any case—of, quite literally, a shattered heart.

Despite the changed currents, there were still a few fishing smacks at Luttrell, and the foreshore was strung with nets, although they looked as if they'd been hanging there for a long time, and a rapidly filling creek now somehow encircled the walls of what had once been the Mariners' academy. Luttrell itself, Marion knew, had suffered in the wake of Invercombe's decline, although she noticed as she walked up from the rough new jetty in the fading afternoon that the old lighthouse was now another gun emplacement; perhaps this war would bring it better fortune.

The shore road, which had never been a particularly fine thoroughfare, now diminished after the church, which itself looked unkempt and unvisited. How quickly things changed! Yet the sound, the smell, of windy marram grass, was entirely familiar to her. As the first buildings of Clyst unhunched themselves from the general outlines of the shore, she came to the first warning sign, although it was rusted and pockmarked. Then to a whistling stretch of fence. Another warning sign. Red lettered DANGER. But she walked on.

The wind fell back, and the rockpools ceased rippling. Night was settling, and the fences were more persistent now;

near invisible barbed-wire clutched at her hands and clothes. Then there was a wooden bridge across a trench which might once have admitted vessels. This was Clyst, and yet it wasn't, for new shapes of rock, quite unrecognisable in their uncovered strangeness, prodded from the dark where there had once been dunes. Of course, things never stayed the same for long here, but this was something more. Her memories, her old life, had been scrubbed out by the changing currents which had surged from the chaos of Clarence Cove. Here, beyond a rill, was what was left of the cottage where she'd been born, but it was a mere straggle of foundations, tumbled by waves which had only ever sprayed the windows in the worst of storms when she was a child. Nothing was the same.

But Durnock Head was a little clearer now, and she was standing, she was sure, on the stretch of shore where she'd once collected cockles for three shillings a bucket. Here, as capriciously as they had obliterated so much else, the tides had left the shapes of some of the smaller rocks by which she had unconsciously navigated entirely unchanged. The air hung blue and heavy, piled ahead into the dark. Her skin prickled. The weather here changed as quickly as it ever had, and she could taste the salt-lightning edges of a storm. There was a pulse of sound, light laddered, and for a moment she could see Invercombe as clearly as she had ever seen it, and its weathertop gleamed and the physic garden shone green and the specimen trees scrolled towards the vinery, then on and up, fizzing against her eyes, towards Durnock Head and the Temple of Winds. Then the light disintegrated, and Invercombe retreated into agitated gloom.

The rising wind pushed at Marion as she turned away. She passed the signs, the wires, the ruined houses, and then the overcrowded graveyard of Luttrell's church. It was entirely dark, but, making swift and simple calculations of time, fuel and money as she kindled her cabin boat's lights and edged out from harbour, she reckoned she'd be able to navigate her way back out to the channel if she stuck to the main passage. Lit water gleamed about her. She was at that point where the tide and the outrush of the Severn were held in near-equilibrium, and it was not so very hard to imagine that this boat, which had served her so well in her journey here, might just as easily take her further—out across the Boreal Ocean, far away from England and this coming war. But it would be a difficult enough journey, she finally decided, just to get herself back up the Severn to Bewdley and Noll's infirmary and face whatever lay ahead, and that was the way she turned into the stinging rain.

V

Seasons had passed. Tides had shifted. Creatures in bizarre outfits with windows around their faces had shuffled within Invercombe's deepest caves. For some of them, the song the land had nurtured became a scream. Wagons came and went. Then, of all of these things except the tides themselves, there had been less and less. Were it capable of loneliness, Invercombe would almost have felt lonely, with the little attention it received, although the memories of past hopes and presences still stirred and muttered along its corridors and across its gardens, and the house was stronger than ever in its slow dreams, which now sometimes encompassed ships and far horizons, and the clouded white shoulders of mountains, and the blood-threaded cries of extraordinary spells. Sometimes, as well, a ghost amid other ghosts, it sensed the reaching presence of the same creature which had dwelt there with her one offspring in the summer of its brightest warmth. No, it was not alone.

'Hello, you,' Greatgrandmistress Alice Meynell had said as she worked open the main door when she returned to Invercombe in her physical self.

Invercombe had not replied, but it listened and watched as she brushed aside cobwebs and straightened the occasional plate or picture frame on its rail as she moved, lightly but not as lightly as she had once done, through its rooms. Then she entered the telephone booth, and sat there as she had so often sat before. Inasmuch as it welcomed anything, the house welcomed her, and its stones and draughts and hangs of light and shadow were ready to receive her amongst the drift of all its other memories, but instead the spell which she incanted unspilled with a complexity which gripped even Invercombe in a strange kind of awe. The land saw its history. The sun and the moon seemed to hang trembling in the skies. The tides, as well, were an aching breath, held and held and held, and joined with them was the power of aether, although the distant act of the Falling was a puny release in comparison to the strength which remained within the land.

And how the telephones sang, even as destruction rang out! In London and the East, slavery was the issue. In the West, it was self-determination and free trade. That, and money, and who really governed the colonies, and all the intricate meshing of the interests of companies and guilds. In France and Spain and Saxony and the Lowlands, the same or similar conflicts were at play—fruits of a long Age of growth and extravagance which were now beginning to shrivel—and for them, just as in Ages before, England made a convenient cockpit where matters might be resolved. Trade in sugar from the Fortunate Isles had weakened on the back of several years of poor crops and a new parasitic beetle, and also with the burgeoning of a product called bittersweet, which was blisteringly sweet but strangely moreish once you had overcome your initial distaste, and grew like a weed on the poorest eastern soil. There were mutinies and riots and lock-outs and lock-ins in Bristol and Gloucester. There was piracy on the high seas. The real slaves, the impoverished Westerners came to feel in the waves of arrests and shootings and curfews which followed, were themselves. Bondsmen, after all, had guaranteed employment, guaranteed housing; a warm and simple life. The protests escalated. Families were divided. There was arson and bombings.

Like the conflict which had taken place many centuries before, this English Civil War began with seemingly unplanned skirmishes. Forces called from the East to retake Swindon from so-called looters mutinied and further fortified the town's defences. The predominantly Western navy blockaded Hastings until the prisoners in its jail, sugar refiners who'd sacked and razed a bittersweet processing plant, were released. The older, greyer Eastern heads urged caution, but in London, and despite warnings from Bristol that it would precipitate a final breach, a law was passed outlawing what the West termed bonding and the East called slavery. Even that might have been accepted, but—through machinations which perhaps only Alice Meynell herself could ever explain—the statute also stipulated that all products made using such labour should be impounded by the Great Guilds. Effectively, it was a demand for the West's unconditional surrender, and the West refused. Its armies, no longer mutinous, but well-motivated, and swelled by the ranks of the unemployed and disaffected, as well as those who still imagined that the whole exercise would be an afternoon picnic, set out towards London in what was termed at first an Armed Demonstration. The plan was merely to occupy the Halls of the Great Guilds and tear up the infamous Bonding Statute; to give the East a bloody nose. London, more surprised by this sudden aggression than it should have been, met the West at Oxford with rapidly organised forces which were easily routed. With further defeats for the East at Watford and also at Peterborough as Yorkshire, siding with the West out of what some said was pure opportunism, marched south, all of England slid into protracted and bloody Civil War.

If the leaders of the East still remained shadowy—a mere expression, as they still somehow managed to see themselves of the forces of order, reason and continuance—the West became known for Greatmaster Cheney, a red-faced grandee of the old school, who had suffered years of imprisonment for the so-called crime of being involved in the smuggling of aether, which no proper Westerner saw as a crime at all. Wheezy and tweedy and gouty, white-whiskered and silver-haired, he made a good poster, and a good figurehead, whilst the brothers Pike, whose father had committed suicide in the aftermath of a ruinous dispute with the Telegraphers over a construction contract, were energetic and well organised and eloquent. The West, it seemed, had the better songs and even the better soldiers. It even claimed, and not without considerable justification, to have the more beautiful landscapes. God the Elder, of course, fought on both sides.

Invercombe, for all that it had long been fortified, was soon dismissed from the maps of Western strategists as being far too vulnerable to modern shelling to be of any practical use. In any case, wasn't it abandoned and ruined? Once again, it found itself forgotten, and the remaining locals kept their distance from the place. The house and the land fell back into its long-established dreams. But still, it could listen. As the telephone lines which had once drawn all of England together were riven and unpicked to become the lifeblood of Western military communication, it experienced the carnage in much the same way that it had all the other deaths which had fertilised its soil. Not that it felt pain, and not that it cared. But perhaps, at last, it came to feel that it understood. For these busy creatures killed each other as willingly as they killed other species, and that was just as it had always been, as far back as the times when they had offered blood on Durnock Head.

The war was death. The war was a song—a savage drumbeat. The war came and went like the pulse of some capricious tide. The war took things in, flesh and wood and metal, and spat them out again in mangled bits. In the festering camps of the wounded, the unprepared and disorganised guildsmen and women of the healing guilds were presented with the hacked and blistered meat of battle. The minds of many were soon secondary casualties, whilst the rest retreated into dithering or sleepless cynicism, and learned to wear facemasks, and to weep and vomit quietly at the end of their shifts.

This seemed the most unlikely place for a symbol of hope to emerge, but, for the West, it did. The wounded soldiers who survived, or those who raved to others in their death throes, spoke of a particular creature, so kind and wise and caring and beautiful that she scarcely seemed like a woman, let alone a mere nurse. The guilds as well, those of the First and Second order of Pharmacists and those of the Greater and Lesser and, also, the Intermediate Chemists, along with all the dizzying varieties of Apothecaries and Sisters and Medics and Matrons and Nursemaids who made up their professions of healing, found one persistent voice calling for integration and organisation towards which, much though they would have wished it otherwise, it was hard to remain deaf. Greatmaster Cheney himself, on a ponderous tour of the Gloucester infirmaries, was accosted by her. So, on other occasions, were both of the brothers Pike. But by then, her name was already a subject for public regard and myth and speculation, and that name was Marion Price.

With the conscious blessing of the Merchant Venturers, who'd had more than their fill of the stultifying influence the guilds' restrictive practices were having on their campaigns, she emerged from the mutterings of the delirious on to Western front pages. Songs were written about her. Pamphlets were published. As the hospital facilities continued in their failure to cope with the flood of disease and casualties which war proved effortlessly capable of producing, Marion Price was given a free hand. It was sometimes hard, as those who opposed her found to their dismay, to separate the woman from the haze of adoration and myth which came to surround her. That was part of her strength. There were Marion Price medallions and Marion Price figurines. Other hardworking nurses, gripped by the spasming hands of men falling towards death, would assure them that, yes, yes, they were her. Even as she banged her fist in fury on the cedarstone tables of meeting rooms in Bristol guildhalls, Marion's spirit drifted on a healing breeze above the stinking, moaning beds. The very sound of her name became a reassurance, and then a battle-cry. Mari-on. It sustained the march of weary boots, and shaped the cough of guns. It filled the telephone wires as well, and tumbled on old posters blown up-channel towards Invercombe to snag in the laburnum walk, and Invercombe listened. As other creatures filled with twisted murmurings crept towards Invercombe's boundaries from nearby Einfell, the surface of its seapool gleamed in grey remembrance of summers gone.

PART THREE

I

All day long the guns had spoken, but with evening came a kind of quiet. The wind sighed over the marshes which had lain between the battalions of the opposing armies and were now polluted with blood and wood and spent iron as Ralph wandered amid the dying beasts and the great dead engines. The crows which had followed his army these recent shifterms settled in black flocks. He breathed the reek of death and burnt rubber and spent cordite. His boots sucked out of the oil-rainbowed effluent and mud. He wondered if this was how victory felt.

'Sir?'

The four elite guards who followed him, hanging back in understanding of their general's mood, yet wary still of the unextinguished jaws of a hookmine or the last bullet of a dying sniper, spun to the sound. They raised their guns. But it was only some squaddie from one of the new regiments which the East had created for this summer's campaign. His boots flapped around his naked ankles as he hobbled along the blasted remains of the tracks for command of which this battle had been fought. He looked ridiculously young.

'Found?' Ralph knew instantly who the lad meant, but it was necessary for him to consider his every reaction at this time and place. God the Elder might not be watching—indeed, Ralph had come to believe that the old fellow had probably averted his gaze some years before—but his men certainly were.

'Yes, yes! Marion Price . . .'

He grew conscious of the pressure of a long-delayed headache crawling around his skull. Calmly amid his orders for the rounding up of casualties and the interrogation of officers and the setting up of camp, he had repeated the long-standing order that she should be looked out for. But it had been a mere matter of housekeeping. Or so he had thought, although the feeling which was strengthening in his head now whispered otherwise. He made a downward gesture to his men with their guns and stepped towards the squaddie. 'You mean she's been captured . . . ?' She could, the thought came quicker than his words, already be dead.

The squaddie nodded, then gave a belated salute. He had a bandoleer slung across his shoulders, but that was empty, and he seemed to possess no weapon. Ralph, who himself was unarmoured and bareheaded, had cause to envy his guards their armoured casing of blue-grey liveiron, which, even now that it was battered and rusted and bloodstained, somewhat masked their weary stance. *How is sh*— His head swam. Hold back the thought. No show of frailty or weakness. Never be hasty, least of all at moments when haste is required. Random instinct is the animal luxury of the common soldier—or these damnable birds. The next unthinking step is where your gravestone lies. 'What measures have been taken to secure her?' he asked.

'I don't know . . . Sir.'

'Show me where she is.' He gestured to his guards. 'The rest of you, get some food and rest.'

'Sir? Are you . . . ?'

But the squaddie was already hobbling off down the rails, and Ralph followed him.

'Where are you from?' Ralph asked.

The boy gestured towards the fire-gleaming smog. 'Place called Shenstone, although no one I tell's ever heard of it and they always say it wrong.'

'Where's it near?'

The boy shrugged. 'My dad once went to Stafford. But that was years ago . . .'

Some anonymous Midlands village, Ralph supposed. The sort of place where people lived their lives without travelling much further than the nearest church and pub. At least, they had until this war began. He wondered if Shenstone would still be there, if and when the lad got back to it. And whether his family would be alive, his home standing.

'Why have you come to fight?'

'Same as all of us, s'pose.' From the pale angles of the lad's face, Ralph sensed surprise that he of all people should ask such an obvious question. 'Freedom and decency.'

Back at the main camp, which had been brought forwards from nearby Droitwich once the West's main guns had been silenced, barrels of cider had been found hidden in a farm attic, and songs and curses of the kind of Lor-Bless-You-Guv familiarity which would have been unthinkable before the battle briefly reigned. The victory had been an undoubted one, which often wasn't the case, and Eastern casualties had been far lighter than anyone had expected. The railhead for the Midland line had fallen surprisingly easily. What was left of the West's Third Army, a paper tiger in any case, which had been trapped between the twin fists of their advance, was seemingly in disordered retreat with its morale, infrastructure and main armaments destroyed.

The clean sizzle and smoke of cooking brushed Ralph's senses as he strode the edges of the main camp. Fire-lit faces, rifles stacked, breastplates piled like tortoises copulating, the corporal singing arm in arm with the private those rowdy old songs which had spread from the music halls and the picture palaces. Whispers and nudges as the meat spat and the sparks spiralled and their general went past. *Make yourselves* . . . But already he had gone. Not the evening for the spit and polish, for the weary salute which he would then have to return. Not the time for looking ahead or for remembering. For them, dawn could take care of itself.

'Must be careful, Sir,' murmured the squaddie. 'You know what they say—'

'And what *do* they say?'

'Well, that she's a witch.'

'Then they're wrong. She's just a guildswoman—and scarcely even that. That's why the men of the West so . . .' He didn't want to use the word *revere*. 'Feel as they do about her.' *Ma-ri-on. Ma-ri-on*. The three syllables of that name turned into a foot-stomping yell, a battle cry. Yet still, to Ralph's ears, such a soft sound.

Here, hunched in the dark, lay their main armaments. Cannon raised sleepy snouts from under awnings like huge steel moles. A dim mist had permeated the ground from all the day's smoke and the spells. Like lovers, the artillery masters who tended the pitch-black wyreglow of these charnel-house mouths had special names for each of their charges; sounds whispered in the roar and the dark of battle which, even under torture, they would never reveal. But it was as quiet here now as it could be anywhere in a military camp, as if all the daytime thunder of the guns had blasted a crater-like silence through the substance of the evening.

'Do you think she should be put on trial for treason when this has all finished,' the squaddie asked, 'with the rest of her lot . . . ?'

Ralph didn't bother to answer. Even now, and after what he supposed would be called the Battle of Droitwich, when it looked as if peace might truly be there for the winning, he disliked speculations about the end of the war. Beyond some shell-wrecked buildings lay the cages and the chains of the raveners; a bizarre circus of huge claws and impossibly jointed limbs. Tonight, amid the sounds of much ripping and tearing and slobbering, they were feasting on more of their own. To the victor, the spoils. One, part reptile but horned like a bull and twice the height of a man, eyed Ralph with its red gaze, its mouth strung with the innards of the gargoyle which lay before it in its cage, as if wary that he might want some of its feast.

Then past the hospital tents, where, but for the silence of the guns, all the sounds and the stench of battle seemingly continued. A miasma hung here, too dense to be dispelled by the winds which had touched the lower marshes, beating back all the usual odours of mud and cordite and poor latrines with the sweat of pain and the first edgy smell of meat on the rot, which would strengthen over the next few days into a presence which no spells could disperse. The flies came from nowhere, just like the crows. And here were the bodies of the already dead, heaped out in loose rows where they would wait until morning for the priests and a final checking. It seemed to Ralph that he was being led past every horror of his campaign.

The edge of the Salwarpe Valley had risen to meet them. Here, above a cratered moonscape of mud where some of the worst shelling had been, the rails which they'd fought over gleamed almost intact in a bloody sunset. An awninged station platform which had somehow survived the destruction announced itself as DROITWICH JUNCTION, although the chocolate vending machine was bullet-riddled and pillaged. Beyond slumped the corrugated bulk of an engine shed.

'This is it . . .' The squaddie gestured towards its entrance. 'She's in here . . .' But the lad didn't sound that certain about it. Somewhat warily, they entered the warm, dim interior, which still retained the sweetly purposeful smells of oil and iron.

'Ten-hut . . .' Eastern soldiers reshouldered their guns. They seemed alert, edgy, afraid.

Ralph cleared his throat. 'Everything as it should be?'

Their corporal, a small man with a dead eye and a stain of blood—presumably not his own—across his tunic, gave a grinning salute. ' 'Bout as good as things could be, sir.'

'This private came with a message. I know this sounds ridiculous . . .' Ralph chuckled. Now, suddenly, it really did. 'He said you'd captured Marion Price.'

'She's down in the pit.'

'Pit?'

A pause. The dangling chains. 'S'pose it was the place the ironmasters used to get at the undersides of their engines. I mean, it seemed the best spot for her. And we thought—'

'No, no. I'm sure you chose the best possible situation.'

Ralph no longer had the faintest idea of what to expect. This, after all, was exactly how the long-anticipated might arrive. In the last place you might think, and in the wrongest possible way. But what would Marion be doing here—when the West always kept her well away from the front? They were standing almost at the edge of it now; a pit between two rails. It was twelve foot deep if it was anything, and oiled water glinted at one end of the concrete floor. For a moment, it seemed as if there was no one down there, and the claws of Ralph's headache pincered his eyes. Was this some joke? Always, behind the kind words and the bluster, his steady insights and his moments of unpredictable rage, he was expecting his authority to be snatched away. It was that old dream-like feeling. He was a child, naked, or in his pyjamas. *Think you should go to bed now, dear*. The whole world was laughing at him and his men thought him a fool. But—

There in the corner, what could have been a bundle of sacking suddenly raised its face. Her eyes were hollow, then fever-bright. Hair in snakes, and the broken split of a black-toothed smile. Slowly, in a slurred Western accent and looking right up at him, she began to sing. The cracked voice, which didn't belong to that tiny body and thin face, echoed up from that well of concrete, shivering the dead machinery and chains. She was looking right up at him, uncoiling herself to stand with arms outstretched on pipe-cleaner legs. Her attire was extraordinary. She was clad in ribbons of threaded and eviscerated insect. And she was thin and ragged, and her wrecked voice was somehow strong, filled with the word of God the Elder and the endless certainty of victory.

The voice became cawing, taunting, as Ralph turned away. Then it softened, grew—as a faint wind picked up and blew through the engine house and tinkled the winches and chains—into a cooing, wordless lullaby. He saw the soldiers making secret signs. He felt the hairs of his neck prickle as he shook his head.

'It's certainly not her . . . She's just—well, like all the rest, the followers. Injured in the head. Perhaps there was a sweetheart, or a son who died. Perhaps she's just drunk too much hymnal wine.' He shrugged. Chill sweat came across his body.

'So what,' asked the corporal with the blood across his tunic and the one good eye, 'do we do with her?'

'Release her in the morning. Put her on the back of a wagon and take her somewhere far enough away from here that she won't trouble us again. Meanwhile, I don't want *anything* done to her. You understand?'

The corporal's grin was impenetrable. *Ma-ri-on. Ma-ri-on.* Ralph's head pounded. He glanced back down to the creature in the pit. She looked like some corporeal expression of all the madness of this war. It was quite impossible to imagine that she could have existed before it all began, but at the same time, he had the odd sense that there was *something* about her . . . Perhaps his expression changed, or something in his already weakened stance, for she changed the pitch of her mutterings, and raised a spidery hand towards him.

'You . . .' The sound was half-whisper, half-screech. 'You were *there*. Look, look, that summer at Invercombe. You *knew* her . . . You're *him*. You're the—'

A lobbed chunk of iron bounced against the creature's side, and she squealed and hunched down, rocking and moaning on the concrete as another of the squaddies chuckled and prepared to take aim.

'That's *enough*. I said she wasn't to be harmed.'

Ralph turned away, his skin crawling, no longer sure of what he'd seen or heard. War, after all, was drenched in fear and superstition, and it was his job to rise above all of that and provide clarity, logic and leadership. Go the other way and the fall was too long and far to be contemplated. But had she really said *Invercombe*? Surely not. No, it was all just another sign of his inexpressible weariness. Certain he'd made a poor impression on men he'd probably never see again until he sent them to their deaths, and telling the squaddie who'd brought him here to get some rest, he headed out of the shed.

The stench still hung, even if the smoke had cleared somewhat. The smell of war was of shit and of burning, with a salt edge of cordite. That, and of rotting meat, and an all-pervasive damp which never seemed to dissipate even on days as warm as this. Needing to refocus his mind on the tasks in hand, he called in at the command tents on his way back to his quarters. A telephone pinged, and its mirror brightened, then darkened apologetically and was ignored as faces looked up from tables of maps. The questions and options which would be put to their general at dawn tomorrow were being refined by his staff officers. Courses of action which, in the cause of a larger good and a greater victory, would inevitably lead to many deaths, although he knew that they needed to push their advantage as hard as his weary troops and stretched supply lines could sustain.

Here, pinned out for the first time beyond the maps on which this battle had been planned, and warm and intricate and green, lay the way ahead, which now stretched all the way west across England. The black mandibles of Ralph's headache scrambled again behind his eyes, huge and real as the earwig he'd once glimpsed magnified within the card tube of a kaleidoscope as a child. He'd known death as a close friend then, always hovering in the shadows, pooled in each day's inky remains. That small, innocent insect—the way it dragged and wavered across the blaze of colours from his sickroom window—had become part of his deliriums, which were touching him again tonight with the trailing visions of that insect-apparelled woman. He reeled and gripped the rickety edge of the map table.

'Sir? Are you all right?'

He coughed and swallowed and nodded, and looked down again at the map. The swirl of roads and contours and rivers. The twisting curl of the River Wye, the Avon and the wider Severn; a sweet and intensely English landscape which this war and foreign powers of ignorance and greed and bigotry had grabbed and would destroy. The rivers met, grew great, and there, at some indefinable point like the taint of a woman's scent after she has left a bed, the water grew brackish and ebbed and flowed to the moods of the moon, and the land widened its arms to greet the salt ocean. Ralph let his gaze soothe itself on a landscape which he so often thought of, but which he had scarcely dared to envision as conquerable—and yes, he knew the correct word was *reclaim*—even though this was the way in which all the strategies led. But perhaps, after today's victory, he really could allow himself to imagine that the job could be done efficiently, with such a great show of skill and force that the West would admit defeat and end this dreadful war. Yes, that would be a nice thought to think.

He allowed his fingers to touch the map's new print. Bristol. The Severn Bridge. Those distant hills of Wales, which he had gazed at through the misted window of a car long ago on a morning journey towards what proved to be the happiest and saddest summer of his life. He remembered the prickle of the blankets and the churn of the engine and the driver's grubby neck. Of all the many places across Europe he and his mother had travelled in search of a cure for him, England's West had somehow seemed the most distant of all to him. It still did. And Invercombe. There it was, named on the map just any other place.

Ralph straightened up and nodded to silence the officer who was telling him about the need for more coal. To wary stares, he headed outside and wandered on through the gloom. There was scarcely room inside his own small tent for his trunk and bunk bed. That was the intention; this was his last place of retreat where others couldn't come in. Carried on the wind, he could still hear the voices of his men. They'd gone beyond bawdiness, and were softly singing. In his weariness, their cadences sounded much the same as those that madwoman with her cloak of dead insects had sung. Was it a hymn? Perhaps some new patriotic song? Ralph thought how nice it would be, to be taken away in a cart tomorrow and left in a field somewhere, far away from this mud and chaos. Then he remembered the blood-stained corporal's grin.

Hunching around, he lifted his trunk's lid and pushed clothes and letters aside. Musty in here. Musty everywhere. But here was his old canvas bag. He unpicked the laces from rusty eyeholes. Inside lay a loose sprawl of notebooks and reckoning engine punchcards, the elastic which had once bound them into neat blocks snapped into brittle worms. *Ma-ri-on. Ma-ri-on.* Wild, waving figures still fluttered inside his skull. Why on earth had anyone ever mistaken that bizarre creature in the engine pit for Marion Price? And had she really said *Invercombe*? But faintly, beyond all the echoing odours of military life, there rose a lingering smell of salt. Sand still glittered in the seams of an old notebook's bindings between the words and sketches within which he'd once tried to capture and explain the world. His fingers trapped and rolled a few precious grains. Sealight washed over him. He thought of lost days. Lost love. A lost child. Despite everything, he smiled.

II

What *was* the song? How did it go? Klade loved the mingled voices, the tramp-drag of feet and the thunder-rumble of wheels before the silence which came over everything was broken by the voices of the big guns, but some fragment of the song always seemed to escape him. Soldiers' voices joined afterwards in unison around the campfires when the ash drifted and trembled, with the battle lost or won, and their voices grew and were joined on the wind by the moans of the raveners in their cages and the wounded in their long tents and by followers like Klade himself. They were happy and sad. They were brave and they were afraid.

> *The trees they are growing high,*
> *And the woods grass is growing green*
> *And many's the cold winter night*
> *My love and I have seen.*
> *Oh, my Bonny Boy is young, but he's growing . . .*

Klade knew that verse perfectly, and it always filled him with a delicious sadness which made him forget about his own lost aches and hungers. But the other verses always escaped him. He knew that they grew sadder still, and he felt and shared that sadness, but he still didn't understand quite why it was the saddest thing of all that the Bonny Boy was young and that he was growing, when surely that was a happy thing. But the song was about war—this war; wars in general—and Klade knew that such songs were often sad of their nature, when they weren't about Marion Price, or angry or bawdy or just plain mad.

The First Western Army was a huge beast. It sprawled along miles of hedge and roadside in the quiet dark of pre-dawn near a place in Worcestershire called Droitwich. It breathed and clanged and stank. Klade entertained no illusions about the significance to the First Western Army of followers such as himself; they were the ticks on the beast's back, and would be squashed with the same grim relish with which he dealt with the creatures in his own clothes and hair. And the beast was especially agitated at this point in the weary cycle of moving and waiting as it ploughed across the English countryside. Clambering towards it, slow and fast, invisible as smoke yet huge as a city, was another, Eastern, army. It seemed ordained that the two great beasts were to meet here, amid these patches of stone and field and the bright, precious tracks of the rails which linked Portsmouth with Preston, although Klade couldn't imagine that that was a particular journey many trains took these days.

Klade stirred, feeling dew on his face. It was still dark, but he could just make out the shufflings of the other followers who had clustered around this spot. A gun somewhere went *bang*, but it was an overture to nothing, and Klade was still filled with weariness. A battle was coming, and he would have loved to sleep. He would have loved, as well, to remember how the Bonny Boy really grew ... He remembered the shudder which, years ago now, had passed down the pylons over the hot cornfields as he stood by the fence at Einfell on the day he had lost Fay to the Shadow Ones. He remembered the pictures he'd seen soon afterwards in newspapers of that London building toppling aflame. He remembered, too, how the very texture of the paper had cheapened in what was called *the current emergency*, as, like the creased pages of his disintegrating maps, the landscape of England began separating. But he knew he was a Westerner, because that was where Einfell lay, and Silus had warned him that it would be unwise to say anything else.

First hint of grey was seeping now into the sky. What came with it was the memory of the hazy spring day at Einfell when the trucks had come. Klade, now that supplies had grown scarce and hunger gnawed at his head and belly, had leapt along the rutted road, expecting some bounteous delivery of *Cherry Cheer* or *Blackcurrant Dream*, and he'd been disappointed to see that the men who stepped out of them were carrying guns, and dressed as soldiers, although they looked, as far as Klade could then judge the ways and feelings of Outsiders, as edgy and afraid as the tradesmen like Abner Brown who no longer came.

'It's all right,' he said, approaching them. 'I'm not really what you . . .'

But already they were turning to Silus, their guns raised, and the soldier whose uniform was stuck with the most bits of brightness was shouting in a loud voice. The song grew agitated, and the woods rang with the lost voices of the Shadow Ones, and the Ironmasters howled at their forge, and the birds cluttered up in a dense cloud from Mr Crow. Even Silus, Klade could feel and tell, was filled with a dense, buzzy agitation.

'That's quite impossible!' The words coming loose and slow around his bright grey lips. 'I can't allow . . .'

But the soldier shook his head, for it seemed that all the Chosen were to step into the warm and metal-smelling back of one of the vans.

'What about that one?' another soldier asked, sniffing the barrel of his gun towards Klade. 'What the hell's he supposed to be?'

Silus came to stand by Klade. 'He's nothing. He just happens to be here. He can be left alone . . .'

'See your wrist, son.'

Hesitating, Klade felt himself grabbed.

'Nah. He's coming as well.'

'*But*—'

But it seemed there were to be buts today. Nudged towards the van by the point of a gun, Klade saw that its greens and browns had been crudely painted over a sign. Perhaps it had once been Abner's, and that made him feel almost happy. Then Ida was pulled, dragged, almost carried, from the Big House. And Mr Crow lost some of this feathers. Apart from their hands, the Ironmasters had to leave behind their tools. Blossom came last, gently shedding petals and weeping.

'That them all?'

Soon it was, apart from the Shadow Ones, and they were in a wild fury. Some of the soldiers were sent towards the woods, although the song was so piercing he was sure that even the soldiers standing in the yard heard it as well. The others came back with their guns lowered, shaking their heads.

'No use to anyone, sir—barely nothing but rags of ghosts. Give you the bloody creeps even worse than this lot . . .'

The rest of the Chosen were stuffed into the van and two soldiers, after some dispute, squatted with them, tenderly nursing the metal aches of their guns. Klade sat close. He breathed their fear-smell, and wanted to ask them about the war. He'd followed it himself as closely as he could through the odd newspaper he'd discovered clinging around Einfell's firethorn fences. He'd rejoiced in the victories at Bicester and Swindon, and then again when the forces of Yorkshire met with them at Grantham. Even Klade, with his admittedly limited military knowledge, could see on what remained of his precious maps that the East stood no chance now that London and Preston were split apart. Western cannons were nearly within reach of the so-called capital. It would all be done and dusted by Christmas, and Klade had been looking forward to normality and Sweetness' return. But that had been the Christmas before the one before last.

'Westerner, are you?' the soldier in the van had asked, looking Klade up and down.

Klade said yes enthusiastically, but the solider spat between his legs. The van, crammed with sickness and song, took them to a puddled yard where they were unloaded and told to stop all the damn howling and gibbering and just form a line. There came an odd jingling, and Klade thought for a moment that the soldiers had brought with them the contents of the old displays in the Meeting Place, but these chains were new and bright, and there was some difficulty as Outsiders in brown coats tried to fit them around the limbs of the Chosen, many of whom were too oddly shaped.

Unlike the ones he'd once played with in the Meeting House, these shackles now fitted Klade easily enough, although

Silus, who was bleeding from a mis-hit steel rivet, was slurring again about how he should be let free. Still shouting and spitting and bleeding, he was taken away. Soon, only Klade and Ida were left in the yard. Although she was beautiful to him, Klade knew that there was something about the fissured arrangements of her face and the way she talked without using her mouth which made Outsiders more afraid of her than they were of most of the Chosen. And they'd dragged her here without her usual hooded cloak.

He's with me, was all she said as she offered the black boughs of her wrists to be shackled, and although there were many other moments when they might have been separated, Klade and Ida's togetherness came to be accepted over the shifterms which followed as they were moved from place to place in the backs of cars and carriages and trains and wagons and vans.

We should have known this would happen—these chains . . . She'd raise her thinning, trembling hands, although in fact the chains had long come off. *This is the way our kind have always been treated. They'll be branding us next with a cross and a C . . .* Klade had seen such implements in the old displays, and knew what she meant, but that never happened either, and he told Ida through the long journeys and the cramped nights and the endless hours in factories that things weren't so very bad, and would probably soon get better, just as soon as Christmas came and the West won the war and they got back to Einfell.

With dismay, he followed news of the Battle of Royston, which even the *Bristol Morning Post* termed A Significant Setback, and then the Second Siege of Oxford, and the long forwards and backwards skirmishing of that crucial front between Leeds and York. Maps were precious now—something which, if any of his minders had happened to see him with such a thing, would have been instantly snatched away from him for the *nosy little changeling freak* that he was. But Klade still retained an image of the way this country looked. He knew that the Western forces which had met with those of Yorkshire at Grantham were now separate, and that London was much too far away to be reached by their avenging guns.

The war, their journeys, settled into an uneasy rhythm. Never quite stopping, never quite starting. Never quite total defeat, nor

entire victory. Always busy, always waiting. The jibes. The cold
slops. The absence of Sweetness, which he knew from bruising
experience his minders grew angry at the mere mention of. They
often had to half-carry Ida, in her weary soundless sighs and the
grind of her bones and the bleeding of her breaking flesh,
through the doors of whatever office or factory she was being
taken to. More and more, since she moaned and resisted him the
least, this became Klade's job. *Upsadaisy ... There we go ...*
Then concrete floors. Offered cups of water in old tins. This was
the Western War Effort, for Ida and Klade.

   He'd never known that Ida had worked in sugar mills before
her flesh had changed, and it was usually to such industries that
they were taken. The huge silos with their peeling names. Bolts
and Kirtlings in Bristol. Fripp & Eddington elsewhere. Not
that sugar was processed any more in such places, but its sticky
smell lingered in the air; a lesser sweetness mingling with the
salt-bitterness of the new chemical processes in ways which
were achingly reminiscent of Sweetness for Klade. The sugar
cane which now got through the French blockades was too precious to waste on mere food, just as cotton, which was equally
scarce, would never be put to the trivial use of making cloth.
They, and the pulp of trees and the grindings of mines and the
efflorescence of stable walls, had all become part of the crucial
business of making explosive. It was Ida's job to sing to the
vats as they churned and spewed and boiled, to place her ruined hands on hot rims and dodge swirling pulleys and listen to
their mindless song and teach them and their masters how they
might work more productively. These factories with their broken wheels and blocked chutes were so messily unlike the neat
views Klade had once studied in newspaper adverts. Sometimes, filled as these places now were with explosive—and
these were the worst visits of all—they'd simply blown up, and
he and Ida had to wander through their ruins searching for precious amulets and boilerplates amid the bits of bodies.

   Ida was getting no better, and her minders often grew infu-
riated with her slowness and the slippery bleedings of her
burnt-toffee skin. She told Klade that she'd always hated her
work in the Confectioners' Guild, and had only gone back to
it when her Terry went to school because she and Stan
had needed the money. Not that it mattered, not that anything

mattered, and her song, even when she applied herself to the machines, grew weak and was threaded with pain. One morning, in a dim shed against the door of which their current minders had leaned the weight of a lawn roller to prevent their escape, Klade awoke. Yet another Christmas had gone, and it was spring again, and the West was as far away as ever from victory, which was infuriating, considering all the efforts he and Ida and everyone else had made. He listened to the birdsong, and enjoyed the absence of the ghosts of Ida's pain which usually echoed in his limbs. He hoped there'd be windows in whatever car, wagon or carriage they were taken in today, and seats for them to sit on. He hoped they'd give them food as well as water for breakfast, and he hoped that lunch wouldn't be just stale slops. But the song really did seem different today. It was faint—but it was filled nevertheless with an invigorating sense of release. He shuffled himself around the broken pot shards towards Ida to share this news. She was lumped against an uncomfortable collection of rakes, and Klade prodded and shook her for some time, puzzled by her songless stiffness, until he finally realised that she was dead.

Klade knew that he had an hour before their minders came to shove and shout at them to get going. There'd be trouble, then; the minders always grew angry and unhappy if anything got broken—so how would they feel when they found Ida like this? His mind, as he shuffled around a spill of old deckchairs and Ida's ruined face stared back at him, was filled by urgent, practical considerations and he began to push against the door. A crack slowly edged into light and birdsong. Klade kept pushing. Then, in a rush, the door was open and Klade was out. Klade was running. Klade was away.

The sun was up now, there were spiderwebs of noise and light in this place called Droitwich, and Klade scrambled beneath a hedge just as a Western soldier came down the narrow decline, kicking aside sundry followers, telling them to get the hell out of this place. But the man's heart wasn't in it and the guns were already calling to each other. There were whistlings overhead, drifts of smoke, and the smell of new earth. Klade soon found himself alone, and the war-song was all about him now, in smells and spells and smoke. Hot, steaming air rose nearby from a

crater which glowed about its edges with the festering brightness of residual heat and aether, and Klade wondered why he
was ever drawn to such scenes after he'd escaped from that
shed and what remained of Ida. Partly, he supposed, it was the
song of battle. Partly, as well, it was the bittersweet smell of
high explosive. He'd been drawn to its backwash, where there
were near-deserted towns with larders and shops which still
had the odd tin of Sweetness for him to hack open with shards
of shell or stone. He'd come across his first followers romping
in a graveyard and drinking hymnal wine. They hadn't minded
his lisping voice and odd accent. They'd laughed when he said
he was from Einfell and one of the Chosen, even when he
showed his unmarked left wrist. They'd offered him the brimming red chalice they'd been passing between them, and Klade's
head filled with visions and song. Even in the aching, retching
aftermath, he'd been happy to join the followers; to share their
belonging of not belonging.

The followers didn't really feast on the bodies of the fallen
after the battle as some people claimed. Neither did they mu-
tilate them—or at least very few did. They pilfered, it was
true, and some claimed they were the son of the Elder flown
back down to Earth, or that they were Marion Price and could
heal with their touch. Others, perhaps the commonest of all,
were wives or mothers looking endlessly for husbands and
sons. Some, even, were Chosen: Klade recognised the signs,
although, and as was usually the way, most seemed not to notice themselves, and died or disappeared before the process
of changing was properly done.

Boom Boom.

Klade ducked and turned. Things whistled around him.
There was smoke everywhere. Men lay sprawled in the mud
of battle. Maybe there would be ghostgas. For all that the
soldiers feared it, Klade quite liked the changed visions it
brought. A beast lumbered by; a ravener, twice man-height,
tusked and bellowing. There was a smoky belch—a mine—
and then there was only meat and no ravener at all.

'Look look look look look . . .'

Klade did the obvious thing, and looked. One of the other
followers, her clothes tinkly bright, was scuttling up. He
dimly recognised her, and submitted to the pull of her arms.

'Look—you'll get yourself killed.'

She drew him along a ditch into a more covered place. Klade peered out through the half-buried gap in a low wall. Something whistled over them, and a tree flew up, boiling and fizzing with sap. Its branches ignited.

'Just wait here, shall we? Be nice and safe . . .'

Klade wasn't so sure, but he couldn't be bothered to disagree. This not-botheringness was part of the song of battle. It was like the Bonny Boy; one of those verses he forgot when he wasn't actually hearing it. His fellow follower settled herself down. In the stark light of the flaming tree, her attire looked particularly impressive, for she had adorned the greyish rags of her clothes with a large variety of insects. Anything from the tiny husks of the bugs Klade found stirring on his own body to the huge, clanky, colourful carapaces of dragonlice which infested the munitions camps. Some, indeed, Klade thought from their continued stirring as the flaming tree began to fade, might still be alive.

'Quite some battle, this eh? Biggest we've yet seen.' The woman—the Beetle Lady, he remembered she called herself—blinked at him through eyes kohled with weariness and smoke. 'Who d'you think'll win?'

Klade shrugged.

'I think we've had it, personally—I mean, the West . . .'

Klade nodded. Disloyal though he knew it sounded, he was easily bored now by such military talk, and another ravener was bellowing too close by for comfort.

The Beetle Lady leaned forward. Rummaging through insect veils, her fingers snagged at the torn edges of a newspaper clipping. It was of a familiar head and shoulders, and just at that moment the guns roared her name. *MA-RI-ON.* 'Knew her, I did,' she breathed as another shell shook the ground. 'Long ago, when she was a girl . . .'

The ravener had passed by, but Klade still felt a sense of something imminent as the words poured from the Beetle Lady's mouth like a tumble of stones. Over the battle's roar, she told him how she'd once lived in a place called Luttrell, doing the necessary social rounds with her doctor husband until one summer had been brightened by the arrival of a senior greatgrandmistress and her ailing son at a fine nearby house.

The house was called Invercombe, and the place had been so perfectly beautiful that the Beetle Lady much regretted that she hadn't visited more often when she could, especially as it was now ruined.

The battle-song had fallen quiet immediately around them, but was raging everywhere else. They were at its quiet unbeating heart, and now, creeping around them in pale tendrils, furrowing the mud and brightening his visions, came tendrils of ghostgas.

'Look, listen—the thing I keep forgetting, the thing I haven't told you, is that Marion Price had this *theory*. It was a way of looking at the world which made absolute sense of it. Even this battle, here and now, and these . . .' The Beetle Lady clattered her insect cloak, which seemed to Klade now to be chirruping and crawling with the ghostgas. 'If I could just *remember*. How *did* it go?' She cocked her head. 'It was all about life and about death as well, and how they both mattered as much as each other and they fitted together in a perfect tapestry . . .'

Both Klade and the Beetle Lady grew less and less coherent as the ghostgas glowed and day and the battle drew on. She told him how she and her husband had been posted to tend the wounded at the start of the war, which should have been fine and interesting work, for her hobby was insects, and she'd never encountered so many of every conceivable shade and variety—the maggots, worms, flies, lice, scorpions, wasps, fleas, dragonlice and beetles which thrived on war in a way which humans seemingly didn't.

By now, the big guns around them had mostly quietened, and all that was left was the rattle of small arms, the occasional light *bang* of a grenade, the screams of the wounded. All signs that the battle was ending, and that the remaining enemy positions were being tidied up. The only question, Klade thought as this woman continued to mutter and ramble about her old, lost life, was, who'd won?

Bang. Screams, and soldiers' voices. Klade peeked over what was left of their wall. The ghostgas had faded, but it was hard to tell how much of the rearranged world he now saw out there was real and how much was some terrible vision. A head lay nearby, and a scorpion-thing was plucking at the frayed flesh of its neck. Flies, the great black swarms which somehow

appeared at the end of every battle, were shading out what was
left of the light.

Bang.

The Beetle Lady chuckled. 'Told you the Easties would
win, didn't I? Don't think they'll be that impressed by the
likes of us, though. Look—perhaps I should show them
this . . .' Again, she produced that ragged newsprint photo-
graph. 'I could tell them that I knew Marion Price . . .'

'Everyone says that.'

'Ah, but I *did*. You haven't been *listening*, have you?
Knew her at that lovely place called Invercombe. Surely
you've heard of it. It's on the channel down from Bristol,
and not so very far from Einfell. Ah, so you *have* heard of
there—all those stories, eh, of changeling sprites and grem-
lins? Marion Price wasn't anything special then, just a maid,
but pretty enough, to be sure. And she was with that poor ill
lad—did I mention him. Now what *was* his name? Something posh and big-guilded anyway, an Easterner for sure.
Not that he was a bad sort, and they became what you might
call an item. Even heard that she might have got in the family way with him.'

'*Family* way?'

'You know.' The Beetle Lady mimed an outwards curve
over her moth-winged belly. 'Although everything was going
wrong by then already, just as it seems to have done ever
since. Doubt if the poor thing ever survived. Now, what *was*
that boy's name? And then there was his *mother* . . .'

But Klade was hunched back and scarcely listening, suddenly shivering inside what remained of their brick and earth
shelter. Followers were unreliable witnesses to their own daily
existence, let alone what had happened years ago but still, even
as the footfalls and gunshots of the victorious Eastern soldiers
grew close, he felt that here—in the Beetle Lady, and her stories and her buzzing, stirring clothes—was some essential
truth. A maid—some high-born lad—and a place not far off
from Einfell. Even the name, Inver-something. Hadn't Silus
said that to him as well?

'Tell me again,' he whispered. 'Was it really . . .'

But the soldiers were blocking the holes in the bricks with
their boots and guns.

'Up you get.' The Eastie with the highest rank, who had one eye which roved and blood shining down his front to which many flies were clinging, smiled down at them. 'Turned out quite nice in the end, didn't it?' The other soldiers chuckled, and one of them cocked his gun, but then the Beetle Lady flapped herself up and waved her clattering arms.

'Look, listen, look . . .'

She muttered something more, and the flies swarmed about her. For a moment, their cloud grew so dense that Klade couldn't breathe or see. 'Don't know who I am, do you?' she shouted in the buzzing roar as the soldiers stumbled back from her. 'Look—I'm Marion Price, you fools! Can't you see?' Then, still beaded by bluebottles, she started singing in a voice which was so keen and beautiful that even Klade for a moment believed.

As she pirouetted covered in gleaming insects, the Beetle Lady looked oddly beautiful. She could have been anyone— saviour or nemesis—in the hot evening light, which gleamed towards the clustered roofs and junctions of a nearby station. The soldiers glanced at each other uneasily.

'Lying, ain't she?'

' 'Course she is . . .'

But their guns were lowered. The soldiers turned to their corporal as, swaying, arms upraised, the Beetle Lady still sang.

'Guess we *could* keep her. Put her up there in that engine shed for a spot of interrogation. Least until morning.'

'You don't reckon?'

'Bit old for that . . .'

'We'll see how cold it gets, eh?'

'And him?'

A gun, once again, was cocked, and Klade gazed into the hole in the world which it made.

'Run!' called the Beetle Lady. His back flayed by the hot expectancy of bullets, Klade scrambled up the slope. But none came.

Then he was out.

The Bonny Boy was away.

III

The month which had followed the victory at Droitwich was one of steady advance. It really seemed, at least to Ralph's officers, and sometimes even to Ralph himself in his brighter moods as they followed the quietly unwinding roads and occupied the undefended and often near-empty towns, that the West was in abject withdrawal. But then came Hereford. Even the weather, previously mild and dry and warm, had betrayed them as it broke into torrenting rain just as they were establishing their forward positions, and with it and the crackle of thunder had come the boom and whistle of Western shells.

Vital weeks had now been wasted in ugly stalemate, and many lives and precious ordnance and stores had been lost in the muddy roads and damaged tracks which snaked from the supposedly safe Midlands towards this new front line. Ralph had argued from the start that they lacked the necessary numbers to properly support their supply lines, but London had repeatedly assured him that the counties of Worcestershire and Salop were entirely tamed until the first sabotages had begun. Not regulars in proper uniforms with clear lines of command and appropriate ranks, but shabby groups subsisting on pillage and stolen weapons, many of them women and children. Ralph had to admire the skill with which the West had responded to

their summer of defeat: retreat and retreat until the lines of
your advancing enemy were overstretched, then use your own
starving citizenry to attack from behind. Hereford itself no
longer seemed like a prize worth the fighting, but a symbol of
Eastern vanity and Western cunning shaped from rubble. And
still its citizens refused to submit to his offers of sanctuary and
free passage.

At least the weather was finally improving, and the last of
the mist which had cloaked Ralph's morning departure from
Advance HQ was replaced by innocent autumn sunlight as the
repatched rails bore him in fits and starts back towards London across the innocent-seeming countryside. Choppy seas of
hills, and the old stone crowns of abandoned aether mills
which mimicked the sarsens that had surely stood there before. Wary trackside guards, waiting for the next explosion or
wrecking spell, made yet more edgy by the latest story of poisoned apples left ripening in orchards for them to pick. Ralph
had no idea whether that was true or not, but it often seemed
that things had got to the point where such distinctions scarcely
mattered. The heavily armoured train finally picked up speed
after it had passed the freshly fortified castle at Warwick.
Pricked by guilt to be staring aimlessly out of the window, he
returned to studying the papers and maps he'd spread across the
seats of the carriage.

A neatly typed report attempted to make sense of the essentially unknowable situation of Western morale. On the one
hand, there could be no denying that there was a general sense
of pessimism. But capitulation was another matter, and there remained a feeling that London and the Great Guilds would still
concede most of the West's territorial, legislative and trading
demands if they could just hold on, and a near-religious faith
was being placed in their much-vaunted new weapons. Essentially, Ralph thought, these people had lost too much to admit
that it had all been pointless, which meant that the thrusts by his
companion armies towards encircling Bristol and cutting off
Bath and Gloucester and Swindon, which he'd previously
thought of as exercises in planning and logistics, would have to
take place. But first, he would have to capture Hereford.

He slanted the fluttering angles of light across a type-
written final addendum, which dealt with what it termed *the*

alarming fondness which many lower ratings of his own side were now displaying towards Marion Price. Of course, the report meant the myth, not the real person who, as the report went on to confirm, was rarely reported on these days in the Western press in any case. Most likely, any real deeds by a single person would have got in the way of all the stories and songs and medallions, although there was some suggestion that she was no longer in accord with the main policy-makers within the Merchant Venturers. She might even have fallen ill from one of the many diseases which were said to be rife in the over-brimming Western hospitals, or possibly have been killed or captured in one of her famous forays to the front, although no verifiable trace had been found of her despite many disproved reports.

Ralph sat back, remembering that evening after the victory in Droitwich, and the small madness which must have seized him to ever put credence on that ragged lad's report. The train rocked on, and tiredness crept over him in a painless grey wave. The papers fell loose from his fingers. The clouds, the hills, the sheep, the fields, the whole onrush of the journey, crept by him, then suddenly, as his eyes jerked open and his senses jarred with all the things he'd planned and failed to do, the train was huffing into London's Great Aldgate Station. He got up and snatched his falling papers just as his ADC poked his head around the door and the train gave a final jolt. Then he was climbing out into sunlight and pigeons and steam, his throat raw and his face stiff and his left arm numb with pins and needles, and there were the kids and there was Helen, and everything was much too blurred and quick.

'You really must learn to unwind,' Helen said to him through the bathroom door as they prepared for bed that night. 'It's not as if we don't have our own difficulties and privations. But we just laugh and get on with it . . .'

Moving within the strange, soft weight of his dressing gown in the tiled expanse of their bathroom, Ralph opened his shaving kit and stropped up the razor with its soap-encrusted diamond stud, lathered his face, and drew the new blade across the roughness of his cheeks. Then he washed his face, and enjoyed the warm oblivion of the water, although the huge white towel he dried himself with came away streaked with pink. He sighed, and the gaunt-looking man in the mirror sighed back at him. He'd never been much good at this.

'People are still talking about Droitwich. You should take more credit.' Helen's voice slowed as she neared the open crack of the bathroom door. 'Everyone says I'm married to a military genius. But I suppose that's all shop to you, isn't it? Even here in London, it's so hard to think about anything but the war . . .'

Her voice trailed off, although Ralph, as he stood at the mirror watching two thin rivers of blood make their way down his neck, could tell that she hadn't moved away.

He cleared his throat. 'I'll be out in a minute.' He dabbed himself, clicked off the lights and crossed the long space of the room. The sheets felt coolly enormous as he climbed into bed. The air was hissingly quiet.

'Darling, I can't wait for this to end.'

'Neither can I.'

'And I've so, so missed you.'

She leaned over him on her elbow. It was never truly dark here in this city. Despite the room's velvet curtains, the end-less electric wash of London filtered in, glowing silver on her cheek and shoulder and the fine, sharp cut of her fashionably short bob of hair. He could hear the rustle of flesh against silk as she breathed. Beyond that, the sound of traffic.

'My hero.' Her fingers touched his jaw not far from where it had scabbed, played with a top pyjama button, moved down. 'And the children are so, so proud, although I know they're not always good at showing it.'

'I know it's difficult for them. I should spend more time . . .' Ralph swallowed. Bat-wings of night flickered be-fore him. There was this new kind of creature the West had long been rumoured to be developing. He'd doubted their true existence, but reports he'd read today on the train before sleep had ambushed him suggested they'd been encountered by a re-connoitring party near Slough. Like bats—moths—nocturnes were suicidally drawn to heat. Their acid wings filled engine vents and cooling systems to cause irreparable breakdowns. They were also drawn to human faces.

Helen's eyes were shining a little too brightly. Moving slightly up the pillow so that he could only see the pale edges of her cheek, she slid the strap of her night-gown from her shoulder and offered her breast to him. He drew himself to her, filled with sudden need.

There was blood on his pillow in the morning—a surprising amount of the stuff considering it was only a cut from shaving, as if in evidence of some crime—although Helen, who had primped and primed her already obvious beauty, was simply amused. Perhaps, Ralph thought as he pulled on his uniform in preparation for the morning ahead, women have a different attitude towards the stuff. After all, they have to shed it every month. He paused in mid-trouser leg, struck by a regret, a memory. Women bled, but Marion never had—not in the near-three summer months in which they'd been lovers. All their talk of science, love, nature, and he'd thought himself obsessed with her body, yet he'd never known or noticed that she was pregnant. Not until he was in the heart and heat of this damnable war, when it was all too late.

Outside, traffic was muffled in fog and the city's great structures seemed, in their dimness and size, to drift with him as he followed the ribboning pavements. He had to think hard about the route he was taking, then backtrack and dodge a ferocious tram. He was breathless and nearly late by the time he reached the base of the greyly robed triumphal arch of the Halls of the Great Guilds, and regretting he hadn't called for the car and saved his energies.

Greeted in the chilly mosaics by staff officers even younger than those who served with him at the front, Ralph was led up ascensions of stairs. Tea ladies steamed past. From the balcony of a large auditorium, he looked down on a vast map of England. The land was green and flat as a weed-scummed pond. The cities were numbered dots. Across this placid surface, pushed by long poles wielded by beautiful acolytes, sailed the flagged armies and fleets of the East and West. Their movements were dictated by the ribbons of paper which streamed from a far wall. Beyond, through enormous doors, lay the sea-on-shingle rush of the reckoning engines where all the messages of war surged and were resolved.

The meeting room was predictably enormous, although it would have been bested in almost every aspect by the halls of the specific guilds which lay around it along Wagstaffe Mall. The guilds, for all that they had worked together here on the difficult business of running the nation for several Ages, were always more willing to outshine each other than they were to co-operate. Ralph, as he raked back his chair and sat down at the furthest end of the table and golden doors which would have admitted a medium-sized ocean liner boomed shut behind him, thought he detected a shoddiness to the stonework of the pillars, a murkiness amid the great paintings. None of them were quite of the best. Otherwise, they wouldn't be here. Perhaps, he thought, clearing a sandy dryness in his throat, I'm getting the hang of being back in London, to notice such things.

The men, their faces and decorations hovering reflected in the table, received his words with nods and blinks and a faint shifting of fingers. What Ralph wanted was to push on. The weather had admittedly been poor recently, but mobility shouldn't be a problem for divisions experienced in fighting through the often pretty awful weather of your typical English summer. The transport infrastructure was in place since the taking of the railhead at Droitwich, when it had briefly seemed that they might have captured Marion Price. They were *ready*. They were *fresh*. They were *chomping at the bit*. Although he also knew that these phrases were intrinsically laughable, Ralph used them not because he believed, but because he knew they were the sort of thing that High Command liked to hear. Then he paused, his head ringing. Had he really mentioned Marion Price? Foolish if he had. He fought his way to the end of his presentation, and then through the few questions which the greatgrandmasters of High Command seemed to think were worth asking. He collected himself, his plans, his papers. He left the hall, and was surprised, when he finally emerged outside, to find that the fog had cleared and that he was standing in warm sunlight.

He, Helen and the children went to Great Westminster Park that afternoon. The blue sky, monumental against the city's stonework, darkened through amber leaves in the giddy wing-beats of Hallam Tower as they walked the elegant streets of Hyde. This, Ralph told himself, was exactly what he was fighting for. His men as well—or for the privilege of living in the Easterlies, from where they could rise before dawn to deliver at the tradesmen's doors to the rear.

Tall railings surrounded the green mountain of the park. There had been several explosions and atrocities in the difficult years before the war, and visitors were being searched before entering by a couple of squaddies from the Essex Regiment. Ralph expected a salute as they clacked through the turnstiles, then remembered he'd changed into civvies. The steep paths wound upwards through incredible frondage, and Flora and Augustus scampered ahead. Despite the crowds, the gardens were so big that he and Helen soon found themselves walking alone. There were views across the Embankment and towards the grey toil of World's End as tugs came and went on the wide, oily river and chimneys flew their long flags. Ralph couldn't help thinking about the arcs of throw these positions would give to artillery. Capture Great Westminster Park in a surprise assault from the Thames. These endless turns and grottoes would be ideal for the killing sweep of machine-gun fire.

Helen still looked, Ralph decided, stealing glances as they pretended to inspect some particularly extraordinary flower, almost entirely like the tall, coolly beautiful blonde to whom he had once been so impossibly drawn. The fact that it had suited both their guilds—and that they made, as everyone agreed, such a handsome couple—had seemed like mere bonuses. Back then, she'd even been prepared to share his passion for the natural world, although now she only smiled with barely concealed boredom when he pointed out the peculiarity or wondrousness of a particular plant.

They headed upwards. No need for a weathertop here; the whole point of this edifice was that, no matter what the season was, the flowers never ceased blooming. The graceful white bark of Cathay. The huge red trunks of Thule. The vines and lianas of Africa. Ralph, for all his botanical instincts, found that it was like wandering inside a huge glass case, even down to the breathless sense of trapped air. But then they came to the sunny pathways dedicated to the Fortunate Isles, and here it was harder for him not to believe. They were too high and too sheltered in this jungle landscape to catch the grumble of traffic, and the air smelled verdant. There were palms and gingers and peppers and myrtles. Walking beside him, even, could have been the presence of a different woman—here, Ralph forced his mind shut. He was thinking about the past far too much these days. Moments amid his family were far too precious to waste.

They reached the summit, where Flora and Augustus were already waiting, and the upturned bowl of the sky pulsed down on him, and the light had a rawness, and all of London was small beneath. Everything, the waste paper bins and the groups of families and the lads who were kicking a football, seemed unmoored and adrift.

Ralph remembered his father as he said goodnight to his children that evening. He'd promised himself that he'd be different to Tom Meynell in such situations, but the very act of thinking that promise, and then of acting it out by going into the extravagant toy-grottoes of their bedrooms, chapels of childhood where Flora was sitting up reading and Gussie was already lying with the light switched off, somehow negated the possibility of it ever being fulfilled. It all came back to him. A big man, weary from his day, looming uncomfortably from the landing to squat at the edge of your bed as you lay there wishing him and his entire world away. Questions he'd rehearsed and now, and knowing that they could tell, wished he hadn't. That purely sweet childhood smell. The worst thing of it was that part of him, the largest part of him, thirsted for the reports which a military courier was waiting for him to sign for in the hall.

'Not long to Christmas now, eh?' Pincer movements and possibilities of assault clawed red arrows through his head. 'What are you expecting from the Lord of Misrule?' Darkness heaped up from the corners, smothering his breath. Misjudging the distance—wishing he'd shaved again, but that would probably have meant more blood—he kissed a cheek, hitting bone against bone.

Hurrying downstairs, he bore the buff folders off to his little-used study. The desk had been his father's—the one he'd been sitting at when he, much to his own private anguish, had sometimes been sent to wish the man goodnight or good morning or goodbye when he was a little older than Flora was now.

Much of the other furniture was also the same. He'd intended this appropriation when his mother sold off their house as a kind of tribute to the man. Instead, by recreating the room he'd so disliked entering, he realised he'd been taunting himself. Sighing, he untied the reports and set to work, but thoughts of the Fortunate Isles, white or black beaches, the sheer blue clarity of the sea, kept returning. He'd rarely doubted the truth of Habitual Adaptation, but he'd come to think of it differently over the years. What had once been entirely beautiful, a parade of the life teeming and dividing into ever more extraordinary adaptation and complexity, now seemed too much like a commentary on events in this late Age. What, after all, was war but humanity's more organised way of the strong eliminating the weak? And what kind of being might prosper when everything was geared towards self-interest? We should all be monsters, he sometimes thought. If, that is, we're not monsters already.

The bat things, the nocturnes, couldn't be regarded as a serious military threat, but they made another lurid story—another thing for his soldiers to fear, another dent in morale. Then there were reports of a rapid-growing and hitherto unheard of creeper blocking many of the roads along which the advance convoys were attempting to progress. It seemed as if the West, in the moment of its cornering, was uncoiling itself like some dangerous snake. He scanned communiqués from the northern sea-front where things seemed to be going far better than they were close to home. Maritime matters had never been of much concern to him, but tonight, as he unfurled the printouts under the fan of the desklight, he was reminded of how close this war truly was to winning. The North Sea had been a cauldron of skirmishes and sinkings a year or so before. Now, it was a matter of tidying up mines and killing the odd rogue dolphin.

His gaze caught on a name. The coastal vessel *Hell's Bliss*, Owen Price, Helmsman-captain, was currently moored in London for minor repairs. He wondered, in fact, if that wasn't why he'd been looking at these papers in the first place. After all, there was nothing like a wound unlanced, a scab unpicked. But perhaps this was simply something he needed to do back here in London to clear his head and recover some kind of purpose when he returned to the gaping pit of Hereford with whatever new orders and support and finance he could prise

out of High Command. He put away the folders, clicked off
the study lights, locked the door, descended the stairs.

'Is everything all right?'

He jumped at the sound Helen's voice from the middle
landing. 'Something's come up,' he called up to her, hand already on the front door. 'I shouldn't be too long, if you're
planning—'

'Oh? And I was thinking . . .'

'Yes?'

'Oh, nothing, darling.' Beautiful in diamonds and a blue
dress, she'd obviously had something—perhaps a small dinner, surprise gathering, or a trip to the cinematograph to see
some ghastly patriotic film—planned.

'I shouldn't be long. I could . . .'

'No.' She waved him away. 'You go and do whatever it is
that you need to do.' The thing was, he thought as he stared up
her, that she seemed relieved.

Outside, London was evening-dim. Winter, and all the logis-
tical complications it entailed, was already gathering. He could
feel it in his bones. Still, the city seemed more itself by street-
light, and he was able to find his way unthinkingly east and
north towards the docks. Along Wagstaffe Mall and past the
Great Guildhalls and the theatres along the Strand. Goldsmiths'
Hall was a starry bridge of windows; Great Westminster Park
a pyramid of light at his back. People swept past him. Women
in stoles and luminous jewellery, the men sleek as newly processed photographs, glossy white and black. Ralph had to
glance down at himself to check what he was wearing, which
seemed to be this afternoon's shirt and jacket, which felt thinly
cold by the time he reached Tidesmeet, and, having forgotten
any proof of his identity, had to endure several minutes questioning by the guards at Collis Gate before he was admitted.

In war, the docklands seemed to be thriving. Weathertops
were stirring. Ships moaned along wharves. Still, the skyline
struck Ralph as odd until he remembered his own guild's tower
which had collapsed in the Falling. Reaching the quays, he
found the Helmsman's quarters, and gave his rank and name to
a sentry, and waited until a broad figure emerged from a doorway. Ralph found that he was shivering as he walked over to
meet Owen Price.

'Oh. It's you.'

'I saw you were in port, Owen. I thought we might have time for a drink. Of course, if you don't . . .'

The Owen Price which all these years of peace and war had made shrugged his bulk inside a uniform which might once have fitted some other man, and they fell into step and headed between the warehouses in near silence. There had never been any real pretence of friendship, but at the same time, it had often struck Ralph on their occasional meetings that they both felt that they deserved each other's company, with its inherent reminders of lives unlived and misunderstood betrayals. He'd first come across Owen's name by chance amid a roster of others near the start of the war. His eye had alighted on the name Price. Not that he'd known Owen Price well back in that lost summer at Invercombe, but he was sure he'd been studying to be a helmsman—from what Marion had said, he'd struggled somewhat—and that same profession and forename would have been too much of a coincidence. This was before the East had alighted on Owen's kinship with Marion—in fact, it was before Marion's true fame, although Ralph still felt somewhat responsible for all the subsequent publicity, which, along with the arrest and accusations of spying which had preceded it, had hardly contributed to what now passed for warmth between them. But Owen Price seemed to have been as ill-equipped as Ralph was himself for photo-shoots and empty speeches, and had sunk back into the anonymity of routine maritime service.

They reached an inn beside an old ropeworks, a mariners' haunt, which was filled with big men with sun-lined faces, their muscled arms blued with tattoos and marks of the haft. It was plain that Ralph didn't belong here, although he did his best to take the lead by ordering two beers from the sullen barman, and then was grateful to retreat to a small alcove with Owen.

They talked, as seemed inevitable, about the progress of the war, and both men pretended an optimism which they plainly didn't feel. Owen had already finished his beer, and the next drinks he signalled for came with chasers as well. Ralph watched Marion Price's brother as he downed the cheap spirit which passed for brandy nowadays, at least this

side of England's divide. Another drink, and the slight tremor
he'd noticed in Owen's hand had almost gone. Of course, drinking was as common as cursing and breathing amongst these sort
of men, but it was plain from the red threading of Owen's
cheeks and eyes and the bloated puffiness of his features that he
consumed more than most, or was poorer at taking it.

Ralph couldn't bring himself to keep up, and the glasses
piled around him until Owen settled for just ordering for himself. Still, he felt drunk and dizzy enough when, and as always, the conversation turned towards the past, and Marion.

'Come as a shock, eh?' Owen muttered, hotly belligerent
now. 'All these years, and you could have been a daddy if that
baby hadn't died at birth.'

Ralph moved the damp circle of the glass he was pretending to drink and nodded. Here, at least, was something they
could entirely agree on. He had to admit that the shock of discovering from Owen that Marion had been pregnant had been
immense. Still was. Probably always would be. 'She never
said anything.'

'That's how Marion is. And you don't still really think she
took your father's money?'

Ralph shook his head. 'Of course I don't.'

'Four and a half thousand pounds.' Owen whistled. 'Maybe
she should have taken it. Maybe we could have buggered off
to the Fortunate Isles and Dad need never have bothered trying to honour his part in that small trade delivery. Maybe then
we wouldn't be sitting here like the fools we are and wishing
everything different.'

'I'm truly sorry, Owen . . .'

'Sorry doesn't crack it.' Owen's still essentially happy face
contorted in a spasm of anger. 'My father died thanks to your
bloody Excise Men.'

This was always the time, Ralph remembered, when he
wondered why he bothered to torment himself with these
meetings. But the wound remained fresh and raw. 'Don't suppose you've heard anything from her?' he asked—always did;
he couldn't help it.

'What? As if *she* could write me a letter, and it would
get through to me? They'd think it was some kind of code or

spell—the whole bloody East's undoing. They don't even trust me to write to *her*, for Elder's sake!'

But Owen Price wasn't essentially a belligerent man, Ralph thought, only a deeply aggrieved one. And here he was, general of the East, unwitting impregnator of Marion, fleer of Invercombe, the closest thing Owen was ever likely to encounter to the cause of his grievances. But perhaps that was something; a favour of sorts. Long ago, in the first wake of his returning to that room in Sunshine Lodge, Ralph had allowed himself to believe that Marion and the Price family were fleeing to the Fortunate Isles with his father's money. But the truth was, he'd have taken whatever excuses his mother had offered him in his precarious state as protection for his continuing need to be Ralph Meynell, Greatgrandmaster-elect of the Telegraphers' Guild. Then, too quickly for him to think otherwise, had come life at Highclare, which he'd coped with as well as she had predicted, and yet hated even more than he'd imagined. That had been followed by wave after wave of challenge. Becoming Greatgrandmaster, and then a husband, and a father. And then this damnable conflict. War twisted time and identity, and to find Marion Price re-emerging through its mottled prism, her face changed in Western newsprint but still endlessly recognisable, had been far less surprising to him than it should have been. Even discovering the truth of her pregnancy and still-birth from Owen had made a sad kind of sense. In fact, the condition of surprise itself seemed to have been put on hold for the duration of hostilities.

Smoke bloomed through what was left of the inn's air, which was turning rowdily breezy as boozy mariners sang their party-trick zephyrs. Ralph felt distant from the scene, and from himself. For want of anything better, and to clear a sudden constriction of his throat, he took a long gulp of beer. It didn't help. The stuff came gargling back. He spluttered and coughed and wiped his mouth.

'Wouldn't touch that now, if I were you . . .' Owen nodded towards the brightly dancing contents in one of Ralph's several glasses. 'It's got blood in it.'

Then they were standing outside in the alarming cold, and Owen was talking of his duties aboard the *Hell's Bliss*, a cheaply converted trawler which hunted for the few remaining renegade Western dolphins, their bodies rusted with bloody rivets and failing armour plate. Always more of a propaganda weapon than a true threat to shipping, their explosives had generally spoiled. It was easy enough work, as long as you didn't allow yourself to think of these rotting creatures as sentient beasts.

'Why did you choose'—Ralph had to ask before they parted—'to fight for the East?'

Owen Price studied him with almost the same look of contempt he'd borne when they first met. 'If you need to ask that,' he said, 'then why the hell are you fighting for the East yourself?'

Ralph took breakfast next morning with Helen after the children had been whisked away.

'Did it go well?' he asked.

'What?' She put down her lemon juice.

'Your do—the thing you went to last night.'

'Oh . . . It was nothing. And you look *so* tired, darling. You know, the world can get on without you. What time did you get in?'

'I'm not sure. I thought I might catch some sleep on the train back to the front this afternoon.'

'Is *that* when you're going? This afternoon?'

'Didn't I say?'

Taking an uncharacteristically large mouthful of toast, Helen waved the question away.

'I really think we're near the end of it,' he said to her a few minutes later as they stood in the hallway.

'Of *what*?' Her voice was edgy.

'Of this war. All the signs are there.'

Helen studied him, beautiful as ever even with her hair still sleep-untidy and her face unmade. *More* beautiful, indeed. Did women ever imagine that by all that painting and decorating they made themselves more attractive to men? She was only wearing a light morning gown, with seemingly little underneath. Oddly, she gave off a slight smell of cigarettes, although neither of them smoked, but he longed to bury himself against her, part that silky material and rid himself of everything but the simple fact of being as near as physically possible to another human being. But her lips felt cold when she kissed his cheek, and she tightened the gown's sash and drew quickly away.

Now that the big townhouse had gone back into the possession of their guild, his mother lived in an elegant terrace set in a discreet cul-de-sac within convenient reach of the main thoroughfares of Hyde. She'd always promised Ralph that she'd retire to such a place, although of course she hadn't actually retired from anything.

As she greeted him in the tiled hallway and let him through a series of rooms, Ralph noted the sparse but intricate furniture, the contrasts of colour and the sense of purpose and control. As well as the very latest model of telephone booth, she had her own reckoning engine outlet as well; a model so new that Ralph would have had no idea how to use it.

'I'm surprised you ever need to leave here to get work done . . .'

She smiled. 'I have to set an example. We might as well sit outside . . .'

'It's hydraulic,' she explained as they settled in peacock-backed rattan chairs. Looking up, he saw that the entire space was enclosed in glass. 'I have the roof fanned back in the summer, but it's been so much chillier these last few days and none of these flowers would withstand the frost. After all, this isn't Great Westminster Park.'

'Helen and I went there yesterday. With the chil—with Flora and Gussie.'

She leaned across the glass-topped table and raised a silver pot. 'Coffee?'

'Only if it's not got bittersweet in it.'

'Darling, you are such an old stick-in-the-mud! How else do you think we should make the ersatz stuff palatable?'

She poured a cup and slid it towards him, although he noticed she didn't take one herself. He dutifully sipped, and felt the sour heat spread into the aches of his bones. He noticed she had on the fine silk gloves she often wore these days, and there was a smoothness of her face, a near-sculpted perfection of her hair. That polished edge was so much part of what she was that she could never let down her guard. Not even here, and for her own son. For a moment, he felt sorry for her.

'So how did your meeting with High Command go yesterday?'

'Why don't *you* tell me?' He put down his cup. 'After all, I'm sure you've heard far more than I have.'

'Oh . . .' Almost, although for barely a moment, she looked surprised. 'Well, I suppose I *have* had my ear to the ground. Basically, darling, there are the go-aheads and the waverers. Half of High Command's coming to the view that the war's ending so swiftly that there's little need for more effort or investment—and, by the way, that Hereford's a sideshow and doesn't matter. The other half, although quite frankly many of them are that way out of dumb inertia, favour plodding on.'

'You'll be telling me next that they might give up just when we've got our best chance of outright victory . . . ?'

'But things *have* dissipated since all the flag-waving of a couple of years ago. After you did so well at Droitwich, this summer campaign's ended up as a bit of a disappointment.' She gazed at him for a moment with what Ralph couldn't help feeling was a look of mild reproach. He felt a ridiculous flush of guilt: not for the conduct of the war, but that he wasn't more than merely competent and hard-working—something large and legendary; the figure which the West had and the East so conspicuously lacked. 'Then there's the hike in taxes, the loss of vital staff, the grade shift, the guild intermingling—it's all cost a lot more than the poor dears really expected.'

'So it's about money?'

'You know,' she sighed, 'how the Great Guilds always vacillate.'

He felt uncomfortably hot. He suppressed a cough. 'It's simply a matter of what's necessary to bring the war to a swift conclusion.'

'Of course . . . But you look so drawn, so tired, darling. I'm worried—'

'I went out to see Owen Price yesterday evening. He's still helmsman in the North Sea.'

'Well, I'm glad that *someone* in that family is still making a decent effort to liberate the slaves—'

'That really isn't the point. But you're right that he's a decent sort—not that he thinks the same of me.'

'Well . . .' He watched her study her fingers, smoothing

their spotless silk, before she cast her eyes back towards him. 'This is an odd time to start raking over such old coals again, darling. Although I'm of course not surprised that they still retain some heat for you. Does he have any idea of where she might be now, the shoregirl, this brother of hers?'

Ralph shook his head. 'If there are any letters or attempts at communication, the censors get at them long before he does. And I wish you wouldn't keep calling her that. She's part of our lives. That can't be ignored.'

'She could be dead, you know. That would explain the . . .' She sought the word. 'Diffuse nature of the current reports. And then all these ridiculous rumours that she's been captured! But my feeling is that her death—and, of course, it would become a martyrdom—would be much more to the West's advantage than it would be to ours. So I think that it's better for the conduct of our war that she stays alive and makes whatever feeble difference she probably really makes in the Eastern hospitals.'

'Why are you steering the conversation back towards the war?'

'Isn't the war what counts?'

'Not at this moment, no.'

'What do you want me to say?' She sat there as if frozen. So still, in fact, that he assumed for a moment that it was some glitch in the telephone link before he remembered that he really was here with her.

'I want you to tell me again what you knew.'

'I *did* know,' she sighed finally, 'that Marion had become pregnant. In fact, I helped place her in a hostel for such girls. As best I could, in fact, I tried to help her entire family. The father never was arrested. The fact that he died was as a result of the aether ship's wilful destruction by Weatherman Ayres— well, we can hardly blame ourselves for *that*. But I've told you all this before.'

'But not until I found out.' Because, Ralph now understood, he'd spent half his life fleeing the truth about Marion and Invercombe as if his mother had put him under some kind of spell.

'And you never *would* have known even now, Ralph, if you hadn't met that damnable brother of hers. And do you think you're the better for it now? Do you think I'd have been doing you some great favour if I'd have given you that extra burden to carry with you through Highclare and all the rest of your young adult life. And you weren't *well*, Ralph, you forget that. Or at least never as well as I wished you might be. I was trying to protect you.'

He nodded. 'And what happened to that money?'

'I have no better idea than you do. And how would you have preferred matters to have been dealt with? A criminal investigation, perhaps? Your father was in a strange state before he died. Who knows why he gave that money to you, or just how badly botched was the giving. And glitches, losses and corruptions of data do happen—you of all people scarcely need me to remind you of that.'

'And that hotel—how did you find me there?'

'Ralph, Ralph, how many times do I have to explain? You were missing, and I went searching for you. With the s—with Marion missing as well, it seemed likely that you'd fled somewhere, and Bristol was the obvious choice. Then Doctress Foot—remember *her*?—well, she told me that she'd met you both in the city. I'm sorry to disappoint you, Ralph, but finding you wasn't so very hard. I tried the guildhouse libraries— the ones with all those insects where you'd used that false name, and they told me where you were staying, and that you were planning to leave for the Fortunate Isles. People *noticed* you, Ralph. Whatever else you were, you and Marion Price made a striking, handsome couple . . .'

He could have asked more, but his mother was right; they'd been over all of this before, and he didn't doubt that she would have reasoned explanations which would bring the unstitched elements of his past back together into some seamless whole. She always did. And it *was* a long time ago, just as she said, and the entire truth was probably past resurrecting. But the fact was, he no longer trusted her word.

'All of that sad affair is far better left behind, darling. I can see that it hurt you. I can understand that. But that's why you need to let it go. Imagine, if it came out now that someone in your position had been in a relationship with Marion Price, no matter how young you were, and no matter how long it was ago. And then there's poor Helen to consider, and then the children. Imagine how *they* would feel . . .'

Was this some kind of hint or threat, or merely a sensible

warning? As with so many other things to do with his mother—odd events and deaths and coincidences—Ralph didn't know.

'You look quite ill,' she said eventually, in the face of his continued silence. 'I'm not at all happy to think of you going back to the front like this, especially with all the new work that's going to be involved.'

Blood. Something about blood. Cutting himself shaving yesterday. Blood on the pillow, and in that beer glass last night. And this war. Blood everywhere.

'Ralph? Are you hearing me? I really can't let you go like this, darling. You should see a doctor. You're truly not well.'

IV

Autumn was tumbling in now, swirling the trees, scurrying the slates on the houses. Klade was trying to flee the war, but the respite of previous years when the urgency of the summer campaigns subsided into the longer nights was hard to find. Once, he and Ida had been allowed time off, were scarcely chained as their minders went off picking things in the abandoned fields or drinking, but now she was dead and he was running and this year was different in every kind of way. *Boom boom boom*, Ma-ri-on, went the guns and the tramp of armies as they chased him through his dreams and on into the days beyond as he stumbled in the face of the wind in what he hoped was a south and a westerly direction.

He'd learned long before to keep his head down, his face away, to avoid the shouts and nudges of curious Outsiders, but this was a lesson he had to relearn again and again. The farmers, those who still tended their crops and beasts but never sang to them as the real Farmers had once done, had guns just like the soldiers, and so did many of the people in the houses you were drawn to by the smells wafting from their windows when you were desperate and hungry. That, or they threw stones like the little Outsiders, who ran wild as rabbits. Klade picked the stones up after they'd bounced off him, then crammed them in his mouth to suck off the raw taste of the earth. Somehow, that seemed to send the little Outsiders away far better than throwing their stones back at them.

The berries, this being autumn, were the best thing. They hung from the bushes bright as the drops of blood he'd often seen beading their charred cousins on the battlefield. He fought with the birds for them. He squeezed out the maggots and ate them as a second course, although he knew that strictly that was the wrong way around and that meat came before sweetness. But it didn't do to think of Sweetness, although nevertheless he thought of it often. Sweetness was like Home. Sweetness was the lights of the windows in the houses he now always avoided. It was pure and yellow and unwavering. Sweetness was Einfell and Inver-something.

Back when he'd been with the followers, Home had been a place that many of them had often talked about—or cried or moaned over, which was almost the same. If they'd ever bothered to ask, he would have told them that he didn't have a Home himself, and that he couldn't really see the point of having one either, seeing as all it seemed to do to you was to make you upset. It was the same with having Loved Ones, although that was a phrase which still left Klade puzzled. But he understood about Home now. He even understood what made Outsiders so sad about the place—or places, seeing that there was plainly more than one—because he felt sad himself when he thought about it, although sad wasn't quite the word, because there was happiness wrapped up inside it like water in a frozen river or a secret in a box, just waiting to be let out. His Home, of course, was Einfell, which was obvious now he knew it, and there were so many reasons for him to head back towards it and Inver-something that he grew lost in their counting as he slept in abandoned barns and avoided towns and followed what he hoped were the right roads on the far sides of hedgerows in a direction that was south and west.

Home was the place, after all, of the thing known as childhood, and all the unfrozen, unboxed happiness which that mostly meant. Home was where Ida was still alive, and where he could be with the Farmers again, and the Ironmasters, and Silus and even Fay. The logical part of Klade's brain knew that they were still likely to be working just as he'd worked as part of the War Effort if they were alive at all, but the rest of him, the part which grew larger with weariness and starvation, wasn't so sure. Klade discovered that memories weren't just memories when you were in this kind of state. He could talk to Ida almost as often as he liked, and the lightness of her presence and the loss of her pains made her companionship all the easier for him, especially now she didn't have to be carried.

So Klade was heading Home, and people made signs to themselves when he risked asking directions and often cursed him, which he took as an encouraging sign. Home was Home, but Home was more than that. Home, whilst he was away from it, had grown bigger, and not just with memories. For Home, unless the maps had moved, which often seemed entirely likely on days when the rains beat through him and the sun was lost and the cold winds swirled too capriciously to guide, was close to another place called Inver-something, and at Inver-something there had once been a maid who had once had a baby. Here, and like the worsening weather itself, Klade's thoughts often grew confused and contradictory. Perhaps he'd eaten too many maggots. Perhaps he was turning into that woman—the Beetle Lady. But here was the story which Silus had also told him, or a version of it, which was like the song of the Bonny Boy, which was always essentially the same, although it came in many styles and verses. And wasn't that song about Home as well, and the sad and happy thing about the Boy returning there was that he was lying under a tree instead of a roof? But Klade's thoughts were drifting, and he knew that that was bad for him and for them.

Yes. *No*. Look. *Listen*. He was almost sure of it. At a place called Inver-something, a girl or a woman who'd once been a maid had had a baby just like the cats had once done back at Home in the New Barn and that baby had been him. Wasn't that exactly what Silus had told him as well as they stood outside that place in Bristol before the War Effort even began? But, here in the cling and swoop of Klade's thoughts, came the biggest thing of all, for that girl or woman who'd once been a maid had a face in the tattered newspaper which the Beetle Lady had shown him before the soldiers had taken her off to do whatever it was that soldiers did to women, and that face had belonged to Marion Price. There, Klade sometimes

thought, he had it. Plain, if you squinted to look, as the nose on
your face. And then the wind boomed out at him and the
hedgerows fluttered their drops of blood and maggot and the
distant, looming guns and the scrawls on the walls of abandoned houses also screamed out her name. Ma-ri-on. Sometimes, in those moments, he had the thing all so nearly arranged
he was sure he'd never lose it. And then, like water dribbled
through his fingers over the wild face which peered up at him
from the shattering surface of the puddles from which he drank,
he lost it all. But still he pressed on.

Closer and closer. Souther and wester. The sun at sunset was a
red berry he longed to pluck in his maggoty hands. Sometimes on
the roadsigns, or what remained of them, he caught echoes of the
places he was sure he and Silus had passed through as they went
about their ways in the wagon. Not Bristol, no. What with the
War Effort and the Damn You Bastard Changelings, Bristol was a
place best avoided. But Luttrell, perhaps, and Hockton, as well,
and the air and the light which breezed ahead of him now had
changed in taste and scent. Not that Klade knew about seas or
channels, but he understood that Einfell had always been close
enough for the seagulls to be a nuisance, and there they were
again, sailing around and ahead of him with that fresh drop of
blood which was always on their beaks as if they'd been pecking
at the sun. Then there was no doubt about it. The very turns in the
roads sang out to him, even if the hedges had gone mad. A station, even, although abandoned, empty, bore Einfell's name.
Then fences, firethorn hedges, as if he was an Outsider and not
some Troll Changeling Bastard and the wild and lovely place he
was sure he could see beyond their rust and ivy was trying to keep
him away. The rise, the puzzle, the harsh metal thorns which as-
saulted him, proved near impossible to surmount, but Klade was
Klade, and this was Home. And Home was Sweetness, and he
was crashing, falling, bruised and grazed, and Home was Everything. And Home was here.

Something was wrong. The quietness and the wildness were
both more and less here than in his memories, and the memories
themselves had sunk back down inside him now that he needed
them the most. He stumbled along No Through Road in the
quietness of a blustery evening. All that twirled around him
were leaves. Not one single shadow or ghost. He fought open the

door of the Big House. His voice shouted back at him, empty and dulled. He tore at the damp-rotted space in a pillow where Silus's face should have laid, he smashed his fist through the songless glass which kept him from the Garden and the Woods. The Big House creaked and whispered complainingly against the storm of his anger, but only with dust and air and mushroomy wood. Even outside, where he'd lived and laughed in the Garden, the Impassable Stream had betrayed him and coiled itself up into mud. Even the stones tasted different, and he drank instead his own blood as it oozed through shards of glass.

Still, there were always the Shadow Ones, even if he only caught the trace of a whisper of their once-vibrant song. Arms outstretched, catching the ragged darkness, Klade entered their thorny wood. He didn't fear the Huntsman now, or the Master Mower, for they were like the Loved Ones over whom the followers had often sobbed, and Klade sobbed as well. He didn't fear them. He didn't hate; he loved. In truth, what Klade feared and hated that night as he raged through the empty darkness and howled at the taunting moon, was Klade. Fay—where was Fay, and the forgiveness he craved from her for the terrible crime of being Klade? Klade was trapped within himself. Trapped within his rage. Time, nevertheless, passed just as it always did, even if it offered no escape. Night left its reluctant threads between the weirdly ornamented trees, and with it a few strands of mist, but even they wouldn't stay for him as he plucked at them with desperate fingers. This was just another morning, and Einfell wasn't Home; it was just another place. Klade rocked himself and listened to the wintery birdsong taunting the near-songless silence. Songless, but not quite. Oddly, what called out to him most strongly was a brick shed-like thing he'd never attended to before. For a delirious moment, he even thought he'd found the Huntsman cowering inside, but it turned out to be some version of his own reflection fluttering in a mirror. *We don't have mirrors here in Einfell*, Silus's old voice reminded him, and Klade staggered out before the horrid thing or things could get to him.

He wandered through the trees into the morning as the cold sun peered down at him. So much for Home. So much for Einfell. So much for the War Effort. So much for Ida and Silus and Marion Price and the Beetle Lady. But then the sense remained that the song wasn't entirely lost. For hadn't the

Beetle Lady said to him, at least in his wilder imaginings and her ghostgas ramblings, that Einfell was so close to Inversomething that you could almost see the place and taste the air, and hadn't that Inver-something been part of Home as well? Klade wandered down the road which crossed the rough grey meadow which now surrounded the meetingless Meeting Place. Glaring at the empty woods in reproach, he passed through the iron yawn of the open front gate. Once again, and seemingly just as always, he was Outside.

Which way from here? That was the question. He let his feet lead him down the quiet, empty lanes. The sky had clouded over and the wind had settled. He could hear the ragged pant of his own breath. It was like being indoors. It was warmer, as well. This was more like it. Whatever *this* was. He was the Bonny Boy returning, and he would have lain down under any of these trees, which still clung to earlier autumn days than the many which he had passed. Once more, there were berries, and then there were signs to tell him that there was Danger and No Admittance, but when had he ever heeded those? He would happily have laid himself to rest here amid any of their roots. But now he was running, being carried by his feet. He let out a yelp, and the sound came back to him as a song. He tilted his head, almost stopped, suspicious even at the moment when he seemed closest to the brink of everything, for how can you find Home in a place you have never been?

Unfolding hills like the splayed pages of a book. A larger hill at the spine of them, warted by some sort of church or temple. The sky unhazed. It was genuinely warmer here, and the trees were scarcely red. Further moments of doubt as Klade wondered whether he wasn't somehow falling backwards through all his recent days. That larger headland still rose as if he really was approaching it, and there, off to the left, was a tiny castle, all spires and turrets—the sort of place fairies might live in, if fairies had ever existed in the first place. Now a gatehouse, and now a grass-tufted drive curling down towards a valley, and Klade's hands and feet still had a mind of their own as they climbed the fences and chains and the slope led them down and on. The glow of something like a bald giant's brass head, and the glint of windows, and the faces of flowers, barely withered, hovering armfuls of astonishing green. All of Klade's previous thoughts on the subject of Home were confirmed and yet confounded, for he'd come to believe that Home was many different places, yet here, surely, was a Home for all. Its song called out to him in incredible range and power. And it was light and it was Sweetness—for, surely, here was that very scent . . .

Klade's feet veered from the path and tumbled, half-fell down some steps. The sun pushed down at him. Moist grass untwined beneath his splaying hands and tickled his cheek. He was in some sort of grove, wherein it seemed that all the warmth he'd been craving these long last days had been preserved. A cluster of trees zigzagged their shadows at him, and the berries which hung from them were larger than apples, and they were green and they were orange and they were the brightest, brightest yellow, and their shades roared a blissful song into his head. Standing up, stretching, Klade reached for the nearest fruit. He'd never seen such a thing before—but then he realised that he had. Egg-shaped, and with a little knobble at each end, he'd seen it, oh, a million times, on the sides of cans of *Fizzing Lemon*. He even recognised, as his nails scrabbled at the waxy outer coating, that same bittersweet scent. He bit down and through hardness and pithy softness, and the juice at the heart was such sharp delicious agony on his fissured lips that he gave a choking, happy scream as it flooded into him.

Klade gorged himself until finally he was sated and lying in sticky amazement as he dug his hands into the towering earth. But the light still played, and he ungummed his eyes and felt a shifting of the song which was more than the sway of these boughs, much though that was. There, in the shadows which were not shadows, were jigsaws of movement. Klade belched an acid belch, and sat up, and felt a smile crack his face. The song had never been closer. For here were the Shadow Ones he'd so missed at Einfell, and yet even the Chosen were changed here. They were scarcely there to his sight, and yet their song was overwhelming. Here was the Master Mower, who no longer needed to mow. Here were the Farmers, who didn't need to farm. Here was the Huntsman, unhunted. And he was the Bonny Boy, and he was Home at last.

V

Through a cauldron rattle of wind and rain and small-arms fire, Ralph breathed the necessary spell as he trained his binoculars along the pockmarked outer walls of Hereford, and the cheap lenses cleared to an impression of finely ground glass, and the city swam back into view through the hazing rain. The shifterm since his return had been a sleepless blur of endless problems and decisions, and meanwhile a large portion of the yards, workshops and dwellings which comprised this city had been reduced to rubble. Yet still it resisted, and he dared not risk a full assault with all the extra slaughter which that would entail.

He passed a sense of movement. Helmetless, ducking along the breached battlements, the man paused as if to admire the view. Smiling, and in need of shaving, he returned Ralph's gaze. A Western soldier. Deep, narrow-set eyes. It was like one of those childhood games: who'd look away first? Then, in a spray of flesh and bone, the top of his head was blown away.

Unslinging his binoculars, Ralph handed them to the duty-captain, then descended the slippery duckboards which furrowed around to the slope of the hill facing away from the city. What had been fields two months before was now a settlement sprawling on trampled, ruined grain. Still, in many ways, it represented the pinnacle of what could be achieved at this particular moment in this late, technological Age. Last night, he'd watched as the last volleys of siege-dragons were prepared for launch. Not dragons at all, in the sense of the beasts used for pursuit by the wealthy in the hunt, although these ones did at least have something approximating the gift of breathing fire. Red-eyed, quivering and wheezing at their tethers, they drank from waiting drums of paraffin. A torch was lowered to ignite them, then they were released in a whoosh of wings and oily smoke, heading up towards the city like giant paper lanterns where, belching flame as their innards exploded in flaring gouts, they sought the targets which had been imprinted on their tiny minds. The moment was beautiful, even in the horror and terror it contained. ◂

Coughing, refolding his big handkerchief so the blood-stains wouldn't show, he crossed the shining sea of mud to reach the old farmhouse where main command was established for his evening briefing. Salutes were returned.

'Sir? There are some things we'd like to show you. Captured ordnance . . .'

The rain, Ralph realised as it stung his face as they crossed the ruined yards, was becoming sleet. It twirled prettily through the arc-lights which had been erected around some kind of display as he leaned forward, thinking of that faraway morning when he and Helen had wandered Great Westminster Park, pausing to admire this or that display of guild ingenuity.

'Wouldn't get too close. It can still spit.'

Basically a distorted species of bat, the nocturne had a rot-and-sulphur reek, and looked to be dying as it clung to the stained titanium bars and the acids which had been somehow contained within its body leaked out. It was more spell than any man-made creature Ralph had ever encountered.

'How come they don't attack Western machinery and combatants?'

'We think they probably do. It's just that they're left to eat their way out of thin wire cages as the army retreats.'

Clever, to think of a weapon which would work best in defeat. Clever as the ironblight which blistered and corroded any type of metal it came into contact with, or the mines which clicked to a numbered passage of feet or the tug of specific spells before exploding, or as the slobbering monstrosities of claws and teeth they'd found buried in basements. Even when their assault began—and were it to be successful—Hereford would be a nightmare to claim. Ralph coughed. His hands, he saw, were crimson.

'Sir? Are you all right?' He sensed his staff officers' faces, glistening and hooded against the sleet, gathering round. 'We're a little concerned—'

'Save your concern for the enemy,' he snapped.

He threw his jerkin down on a chair in his farmhouse bedroom when the briefing was finally completed. That damn nocturne; this fluttering blackness behind his eyes. He shivered and ached, but couldn't bring himself to think about sleep, and there were things he needed to study. Of course, there were files, printouts, numberbeads—all the endless detritus of raw military intelligence—but they had ceased to the main subject of his attention in the wretched stalemate of Hereford. Since his return from London, his researches had focused with a horrid compulsiveness on discovering more of the true history of Greatgrandmistress Alice Meynell. He knew by now that his mother's high-guilded lineage wasn't all that she claimed it to be; knew as well that a freakish series of serendipities and misfortunes seemed to surround those who opposed her. She was lucky, certainly. And manipulative. And she didn't always tell the entire truth. In many ways, he, personally, had always been in her thrall. But, just as when he was on the edge of discovering Habitual Adaptation, he sensed that he was on the brink of a far bigger realisation.

A stray numberbead rolled playfully towards the hollow in the mattress as he sat there. He trapped it between fingernails still reddened with blood. A compendium of interrogations of Western captives; shellac recordings transcribed into aethered stone. As his weary consciousness slipped from the bedroom, his attention was drawn to a particular extract, which was unusual for the prisoner being a changeling. This one, its name recorded as Silus Bellingson, had apparently had access to much potentially useful information about the Western power grid—or so its interrogators claimed . . .

After the denials, there were inhuman howls, then strange crackling laughter as the buzzing decreased. Ralph couldn't imagine what the creature must be suffering, nor what it looked like.

'There's a weak contact in that rotator . . .' it hissed. 'You should have it resoldered. I *told* you this was the work to which the West put me. The same work I did before I was . . . Before she . . . You think *I* don't know about electricity . . .'

The hum increased. The howling returned.

'And what other punishment should I expect?' A sound of spitting. 'But let me tell you this. Let me tell you *some*thing. About your precious greatgrandmistress. *Please* keep your hand away from that dial. It's not what you think. I loved her once, you see . . .'

The recording, at a point where it had surely lost any military relevance, crackled on.

'She came to London, and she was the most beautiful creation I had ever seen. Things between my wife and I had— no, I don't need to offer excuses. Alice was mocking, radiant, flirtatious, and she needed me and I had power then, gentlemen. Power in your precious East, and we were lovers, me and Alice Smart, as she was then. Oh, I *knew* that she was dangerous. But at the same time I didn't. Or perhaps it was the danger that I liked. She has that effect on you, you see, gentlemen. She blurs what you know and . . . The fact is, she moved her attentions towards a young telegrapher, a great-guildsman who would have been the catch of this or any other season. After all, she'd got what she wanted from me. I was no longer needed. And there I was, gentlemen. Alice took my old life and left me as you see me. It's a sort of trademark of hers, I think, that the person she wishes to destroy seems to have brought it upon themselves—and it's probably the truth. After all, we're human and polluted—yes, even us changelings—and Alice, Alice, Alice Meynell—she rides above it all. Yes, it's entirely my fault, gentlemen, and not hers that I'm here and as you see me, and for that I deserve to be punished . . .'

With a buzzing howl, the recording hazed into the interrogatee's screams.

In the morning, Ralph wiped the crusted blood from his face, pulled on his jerkin and, quite unable to face breakfast, went

straight out to inspect his troops. Walking a captured outer
street, he was as much struck by the destruction his own armaments had wrought as by the traps and dangers left by the enemy. The charred trail of a dying siege-dragon ended in a
blackened mass of feathery flesh. A dusty *boom* rolled across
what remained of the rooftops. Could be another mine going
off, but it was more likely by now to be his own engineers
dealing with one of the many Eastern shells which—either
through poor manufacture or some resisting spell the West had
developed—had failed to explode on impact. It seemed as if
the West and the East were unknowingly joined in the same
busy task, the meaning and eventual purpose of which was ob-
scured in all the blood and smoke and rubble and rhetoric.

The frosty air drifted as he called for a halftrack to take him
south along the front. One of his deputies cleared his throat.

'There's been a little concern, sir, about the state of your
health. We've been given authority—'

But here came the halftrack, and Ralph climbed in, and the
wrecked city vanished behind him amid humped brown hills of
mud. This early thrust around the city had failed to achieve anything resembling encirclement, and the majority of the wreckage along its route was civilian; wheelbarrows and wardrobes
cast aside in the act of fleeing. Then, as lingering drays and
cows were also discarded, it became bony and bloody. Any
wandering cattle were shot on sight by the Eastern troops for
fear that their malnourished bellies contained bombs. There
were no flies—it was, and this was one small blessing, getting
too late in the year for that—although the crows were feasting;
more flutters of black to confuse his eyes.

There was blackness behind this blue sky, and clouds—
look how quickly they formed—were unrolling like smoke
from the south-west. Ahead now, the landscape grew yet more
ragged. Vehicles were sprawled. Drays neighed. Men stood
around or guarded their backs, made yet more edgy by the silence as they awaited some fresh assault. Ralph climbed out
from the halftrack where the road stopped at a huge, loose
hedge. The officer in charge saluted and welcomed him.

'Is this it, then? Nightlock?'

'Stalled us all shifterm, sir. It's like untangling a huge ball
of barbed wire . . .'

The men who were cutting through the spring-like tension of the purplish double-thorned stems wore full armourplate and wielded heavy wire-cutters.

'You've tried burning it?'

'Only makes it stronger, sir. We'll get through, but it'll take an age.'

'No trouble from the rear?'

'None at all, sir. But it just makes you wonder what they've got cooking . . .'

Off to the right, and surrounded by red mine clearance flags, lay a small telephone relay station where two sappers, telegraphers in their civilian days, were unloading as they prepared to reconnect the wires back towards London. Ralph inspected their workings as a few first flakes of snow, large and light as goose feathers, hung in the air, and then told them that he'd keep an eye on their equipment if they took a tea break. Somewhat bemused, they saluted and headed towards a brazier tent.

They'd left a testing box open on the bare earth floor inside the squat brick hut. Beside, freshly tamped and refitted, lay the arm-thick bundle of aethered steel and copper which would soon bear messages East. Studying the testing box, Ralph realised that it lacked the handcrank of similar devices he'd used back at Highclare. Otherwise, it was a simple enough device from a mechanical viewpoint, although in a magical sense it was enormously complex. This, after all, was the boundary of all communication. This was where East no longer met West. He lifted the discarded Western end of the cable which the telegraphers had been about to destroy and tightened it to the binding posts. His lungs cleared and his frosted breath uncurled as he incanted the activation spell. Since the Falling, massive failsafe gateways had been placed throughout the Eastern grid to stop any such Westerly connection, but a carrier signal remained necessary to keep the entire system alive. He touched the twin binding posts on top of the testing box. The world rippled. Working telegraphers often disdained mirrors, and sang like their forefathers who'd stood at the haft, although Ralph was aware that he was taking this technique a little far. Still, the process was alarmingly easy, and it was a relief to leave the aches of his body and push as close to a state of pure information as any sane telegrapher would ever dare. In the swish and

sigh of information, he was soon recognisably within the network of the city of Bristol, and sought the heaviest, busiest cluster of data, a veritable maelstrom, an erupting volcano. This,
surely, was the High Command of the Merchant Venturers.

A telephone pinged, and he was able to watch the Western
soldier, who was dressed in uniform not dissimilar to his own,
get up from his desk and reseat himself before the mirror. His
expression changed as soon as he saw Ralph. He was quick—
not some superannuated dotard—which was good. There was
even a dim sense that he and Ralph had probably met at some
party or meeting in London or Bristol or Dudley, long before
the war . . .

'I'm Greatgrandmaster Ralph Meynell. I'm in command
of the Second Eastern Battalion of the Loyal Forces.'

The man's gaze flickered. 'Why are you calling me?'

'I want to talk about peace.'

To his credit, the Western general remained composed. He
pursed his lips. Then there was a wrenching lurch. Ralph found
that he was sprawled back on the cold earth of the transmission
house when his consciousness returned, and Eastern soldiers in
full body armour were blocking the door's light.

He was steered back to a halftrack, where his second-in-
command, a bluff, gruff, ginger-moustached ex-Savant named
Arundel, was already waiting. In convoy, another halftrack
ahead and behind, they moved off down the slushy road back
towards Hereford. It was snowing more strongly now, the winter's first whiteness coming down so heavily that the dark
ground seemed to rise to meet it.

'Have some of this.' Arundel offered him a shot of spirit
from a flask, which Ralph did his best to hold in his unruly
hands as the halftrack jumped and juddered, and then work
down his burning throat. 'You look as though you need it.
We'll probably be able to get you on a train back to London
later on, if this bloody snow doesn't really set in.'

'I'm a traitor. I don't deserve this kind of treatment.'

'You're ill, Meynell.' Arundel took back the flask, thought
about taking a slug himself, then glanced at Ralph and capped
it and lit a cigar. 'What did you say to the Westies?'

Ralph, who had no reason to dislike the man, did his best
to describe the circumstances of his call to the West.

'That was *all* you said?' Arundel spat over the side of the halftrack and wiped his moustache. 'That you wanted peace—and your name and rank?'

'I was interrupted.'

'You're hardly in a position to deliver peace, man. None of us are.'

'But I'm sick of delivering war.'

'Look, Meynell—you're plainly unwell and under stress. What you did back there today was so hopelessly stupid that people will laugh it off. Tell them what you've told me when you get back to London, and all they'll give you is a few shifterms' rest. You'll be back here in God-forsaken Hereford before we ever take the place.'

'In that case, I'd better tell them something different.'

They both chuckled. Sometimes, in this war, it was hard not to laugh. The snow drifted. The treacherous landscape was softening and receding. It looked beautiful as sleep. Then the halftrack ahead of them tilted. It puffed and churned impotently as it lodged in a deeper rut, forcing them to a halt as well.

Arundel cursed and ground out his cigar. 'Why can't you lot—' He began to stand up. Then, at the same moment as something out in the blurring white went *snap*, he gave a grunt and slumped back down, half-covering Ralph with his considerable weight. Heat seemed to be flooding out of the man although, even with all he'd seen and experienced, it was a long, shocked moment before Ralph realised that it was the hotness of blood and urine. He tried to lever him away. Arundel, with what was left of his fading life and consciousness, groaned and pushed and struggled back.

The soldiers in the other halftracks were tumbling out as the white air grew suddenly loud with the sound of shouts and guns. Finally, Ralph extricated his limbs from Arundel, and scrambled down as well. Bullets whanged and whined against armour plating. The snow swirled with smoke and orange flashes. He had no idea what was happening, although it was as likely that this attack was from some Eastern soldiers spooked by this poor visibility as that it was anything to do with the West. He rolled away from the halftracks and fell into a ditch at the edge of the road and coughed and vomited before he regained his senses, and began to crawl through the filthy water.

The ditch tunnelled on. Behind him, the shouts and the gunfire continued. Ahead was only whiteness and dark. The stupid thought—he couldn't help it—turned in his mind that this early onset of winter would play hell with supplies. Then, for all that he was now plainly a traitor, he wondered if he might be able to reach the next checkpoint and raise the alarm. On hands and knees, pausing now and then to cough and retch thin, bright sprays of blood, he scrambled through thickening scums of ice and mud. The sound of the guns had almost faded. Then there was a shape ahead, and with it came a voice, and that voice was humming.

Friend or foe? East or West? But all the usual questions seemed irrelevant. After all, what was he, now? But still, he should stop, take stock. For the next step—crawl in this case—the next unconsidered move, is where your gravestone lies. But bizarre though the creature seemed, and weirdly wavering though the voice was, Ralph scrambled on. The odd thing, the oddest thing of all, really, was that he recognised that sound, that figure, that song.

'Ah, listen, listen. Here *he* comes . . .'

The figure paused in its humming, and straddled the ditch to welcome him with her ragged, insect arms.

VI

Each morning as she awoke, Marion allowed herself the lingering luxury of not knowing where she was. The fact that she always knew it *was* a luxury, and that there were certainly things, important things, things which, done or not done, would lead to outcomes good or dreadful, all added to its loveliness. She thought firstly of water, cool, glittering expanses of it bubbling and racing towards her. It drowned her legs and swarmed over her senses in the salt cry of gulls. And then, in another rush, came the chuckle of waves. She was lifted through marvellous warmth amid brilliant gardens, up into a high room with a single slant window and a narrow yet coolly expansive bed. And it was early, yes, for the sun was just creeping over the lintel and across these whitewashed walls, and the air smelled faintly of bleach and was inordinately, purposefully, importantly and beautifully clean. Yes, there was so, so very much to be done.

Thinking of brasses in need of polish and ash-dusted grates, Marion opened her eyes. Even though she knew this wasn't really Invercombe, this dim room wasn't so very different to the place where she had once slept. Sighing, she climbed up from her bed and got dressed. Half past five, and freezing cold. She took the long central stairs and headed on past dark offices to receive Chief Matron's report. It had been a quiet night. Few deaths or new arrivals. No emergencies had necessitated her awakening.

'That's all?'

The matron nodded in a way which didn't seem to mean entirely yes.

'Something else?'

'It's just I was wondering if you'd heard what people are saying?'

'What is it now?' Marion felt tired already. 'I'm sorry, Matron. What I mean is—'

'No. That's quite all right. It's just that word's getting back from the front that Hereford's fallen . . .'

She headed down the next set of stairs, then along the main wards. Considering that Cirencester College had been a school for the Joint Guilds of Engineers three years before, it had adapted extraordinarily well to its role as a military hospital. The dorms, each partitioned alcove of four beds easily visible to the nurses, had scarcely needed changing. The perpetual cold, the echoing footsteps and voices—even the sense of suppressed loss and loneliness—had all been here long before she'd requisitioned the place. There had been probably even the same secret drinking amongst the teachers as there was now amongst the nurses.

The wounded grew used to her presence but still, as she entered the dim wards, there were cries and groans. *Thump, thump, thump*; that dreadful chant they took from her name and beat out with bedpans. Individual patients quietened as she approached them, but still, ringing back and forth along the hospital, there were those damn three beats. *Ma-ri-on*. It wasn't her—it wasn't anything—but she was nevertheless its cause, and it was useless to shout and rage at the sisters and nurses. The only answer was for her not to make these inspections. Then, what would she be worth?

Ruined heads turned on pillows in the burns wards. Hands which weren't hands reached for her supposedly healing touch. Who was she, she wondered, as she heard their gagging whispers; the tired and irritable woman who was trying hard not to notice the cooked-meat smell, or the ministering angel they imagined? And word of this supposed defeat at Hereford was everywhere. Depending upon who you listened to, the West was said to be retreating, regrouping, retrenching . . . More work, another sleepless night, was being yawningly anticipated by the staff, but few new casualties had yet arrived apart from the usual dribs and drabs from accidents, shell shock, syphilis and food poisoning. Coldly worried, she headed out along the corridors.

Years before, in the time before the bodyguards and amulets, Marion would now have set straight out towards Hereford herself. Or at the very least, she'd have spent the day here in triage, helping deal with the carts and carriages as they arrived. Now, she was conscious that the systems she'd imposed on this and most other Western hospitals worked better without her presence. Fingers grew flustered when she was near. Kidney bowls were dropped. Soldiers tried to unstick themselves from blood-soaked stretchers so they could touch her. *Ma-ri-on, Ma-ri-on.* It was the last thing anyone would have wanted. And she'd never possessed sufficient vanity to imagine that things wouldn't happen without her watching over them. Still, she couldn't sit here idly, so she entered the main office and announced that she was going to Bristol, and would someone please find out the times of the trains?

There was chaos at the station, with relatives of soldiers crowding for non-existent news, to which Marion, by her very presence, made her own contribution as she fought her way past the pleading hands and faces into the carriage which had been set aside for her. There were, she thought, as the train pulled off, some advantages to being Marion Price. At least she had a compartment to herself, and sweet freedom to study the morning newspapers, interrupted only by the stammering requests from the guards that she sign something for their daughters, wives, mothers . . .

Hereford was certainly in the papers, but it was only all the usual rubbish about *Brave Western resistance* and *The turning of the tide*, and the front pages were dominated by the sinking of a French ship, which supposedly signalled a loosening of their blockade. Marion slid the papers aside. She tried to remember the heady feeling of those early advances, the times when London had seemed within reach, and she'd probably wanted to see the East cowed and defeated as much as the next Westerner, although her reasons had probably been entirely selfish. And then, with all the setbacks, it had still always seemed as if some new weapon or alliance or incarnation of peace or victory lay around the corner. Now, war had raged for three years, and even Hereford was supposedly falling. Marion's eyes travelled back from the flashing countryside to a short column of reportage. *Forces apparently led by General Meynell . . .* War was like a fever—a nightmare gripped by its own internal logic where flashes of lost memories entwined.

She'd never sought to follow Ralph's progress, but, just like his mother, he'd always been there, and every newspaper she'd ever picked up over the years had seemed to include his or her name somewhere in a long list of Guild Occasions. Often as not, it was so small that no one else would have noticed it, but she invariably did. But her old anger, the sense of betrayal which she had nursed through Alfies and the loss of her child and then on through her years along the river and with Noll, was gone, or had at least remanifested itself in all the energies she'd poured into her battles against stupidity, inefficiency and prejudice. More of which she would be prosecuting here in Bristol today.

She'd grown used to this city over the years, but every arrival was still tinged with the memory of taking that clattery train from Luttrell with Ralph, and the swarm and noise of a summer-hot Templemeads Station—the glorious escape of being someone called Eliza Turner. Today, though, as her train slowed and the tracks gathered in silver skeins under thickening grey skies, she could only be Marion Price, and she thought of the nearness of the Eastern army, and the route that they would take down the Wye Valley from Hereford, cutting off what was left of the West's lifeblood. From here, and barring miracles in which she no longer believed, all that lay ahead for the West was defeat.

Marion spent her day warring amid the guildhalls of Bristol. She'd long known Greatmaster Cheney as a man rather than a poster, and one who had aged far beyond the point where he was capable of bearing the pressure of the day-to-day decisions about the conduct of the war; all he could offer her now was sympathy and a shaky cup of tea. Even one of the brothers Pike, although this was something she was one of the few to know, had suffered a nervous breakdown. Those who survived and prospered in the command hierarchy were, she was coming to think, those who were blessed with the thinnest grip on reality. But how could it be otherwise, with reality as it was now?

The greatmasters she confronted were as evasive as the newspapers about Hereford. Perhaps, indeed, what was in the papers was all that they knew. But for Marion everything was becoming clear. Not that she argued for capitulation, but it was vital that several hospitals around Ross and Monmouth were evacuated now in an orderly fashion. The alternative would be a log-jam of patients dying on jolting wagons amid the retreating soldiers and civilians, and the final collapse of the medical infrastructure which she had worked so hard to build. She was listened to with quiet sympathy in a series of impossibly grand rooms, and offered coffee, with cream, and fine moist sugar— the kind you couldn't get anywhere these days, which she was too tired and hungry to refuse. Outside, great flakes of snow touched the windows with silent fingers. An early fall, the first of the year, and the signal that winter was here, and that this terrible war would continue through it unabated. These very halls had been the places where she had won her most significant victories as she had fought to overcome the ridiculous over-specialisation of the medical guilds, but now she felt powerless, lost . . .

'Thing is, Mistress Price, if we start emptying the hospitals behind Hereford, which, by the way, is still being held as bravely as ever, it would be interpreted as defeat. Bad for our lads, to know that Marion Price is shutting up shop behind them just when they need her most. Although we do understand and admire your grasp of practicalities. Would you care for another biscuit?'

'And if I issue orders for the hospitals to be moved anyway?'

'This is war, Mistress Price. Even being who you are, that would be treason.'

There was to be a big dance in Bristol tonight. If not quite in her honour—for Marion got the impression that there were still big dances here most nights—it was certainly expected that she show her face, and there were no trains to take her back to Cirencester. She felt trapped, but at least she could see Noll, and there was the dim chance that she might achieve more here than by flustering the medics back at the hospital.

Marion was saluted and stared at by the guards as she entered the halls of the doctors' guilds beneath their stone scrolls of occult dogma in a square just off the Horsefair. She descended the stairs into white-tiled catacombs where the smell always reminded her of butchers' shops. Not that she of all people could afford to be squeamish, but, unlike Noll in his stained white coat, his off-white smile, his pale face, she preferred to work among the living.

'Heard you were here today, stirring up the old ants' nest.' He gave her a formaldehyde hug. 'You're looking . . .' He peeled off his rubber gloves. 'Tired, I have to say.'

'Have you heard about Hereford?'

He leaned against a marble slab and lit a cigarette and shrugged. 'More cadavers.'

'You're not that cynical.'

'It's what I have to be.'

'We're losing the war.'

He blew smoke and shrugged again.

'But there's no point in fighting battles we can't win. We should have sued for peace this summer. Enough people have died—'

'You've said that before, Marion. Look—' He smiled, gestured. 'I've things to show you.'

Blued hands and feet lolled with the easy repose of the dead. As Noll showed Marion the progress he was making in refining his guild's knowledge of the workings of the human heart, she remembered how he'd suffered and complained about all the restrictions when they'd worked together in Bewdley. Now, in this coldly important place, she was in the presence of a calmer, better Noll who could act as he pleased. He'd had a good war. So, he'd undoubtedly tell her, had Marion Price. But she'd only ever done what any other reasonable person would have done in her situation. Healing, as she'd always seen it, was essentially a matter of common sense. If you had clean sheets, mopped floors, sufficient bandages and blankets and all the regular habits of hygiene, much of the rest took care of itself. She'd never intended to give speeches, or to harangue the grandmasters when they came in their long, exquisite cars to inspect the dead and the dying. Still, no one had forced her to give those first interviews to the papers, nor to pose for the photographs, and then that first portrait, or to write those homilies on Aspects Of Care which were now in their eighth reprint.

Noll had always remained in the shadows. Even this place, for all its scientific rigour, was palely secret, subterranean—a retreat. He showed her jars filled with the glowingly viscous varieties of parasite he was extracting from the cadavers and preserving, monitoring how they grew and adapted generation on generation, the weaker falling by the wayside and the stronger passing on their heritage.

'War's a changed environment,' he explained, replacing a jar within which something large and white and many-horned rocked as if it were still swimming. 'So you're bound to get the emergence of new varieties.'

'You'll be telling me next that war's a good thing.'

'I think it's probably an inevitable and necessary state; a catastrophe we humans strive to create now that we mostly avoid the natural ones.' He laughed. He sounded genuinely happy. 'Think of the advances just in these few short years which the guilds would probably never have otherwise made . . .'

Noll took her to his apartment, which was neatly stylish, in the wintry and abstract modern way. He undressed, still talking about the ways his thoughts and ideas were taking him. Perhaps he was expecting her to do the same, but she smiled as he laid a hand on her shoulder and suppressed a shudder as she shook her head.

'It's just . . .'

'That's all right.' He gave her a peck on the cheek, then, whistling lightly and puffing on a cigarette, began putting on sleek evening clothes. Noll had always had such a glum view of the world, but now that his every worst expectation was happening, he seemed as bright as the waistcoat he was buttoning.

She looked down at her own clothes, which were a deliberate mix of the daily working attire of the various guilds involved in attending the invalid; a dowdy statement of equality. 'I can't go anywhere like this.'

'People would be disappointed if you turned up looking anything other than as you are, Marion. Isn't this how you like it, anyway—standing out?' Smelling now of nicotine and ambergris, Noll kissed her cheek. 'I think you're quite marvellous, Marion. We all do.'

She'd misjudged Noll, whose appearance seemed understated compared with the rich and fortunate of Bristol who came gliding out from their carriages along Boreal Avenue in the continuing flurries of snow, but she couldn't imagine what was essentially wrong with being well-dressed, even if the women's make-up, as if in mute tribute to Noll's cadavers, was bluish-pale. Or perhaps that was just the cold. And—ah, yes, it's just as the late-edition headlines promised—Marion Price is back in Bristol to put things right! Whispery lines of fans and faces gathered beneath the lanterns in the glittering air. She was granted curtsies. There were frosty clatters of spontaneous applause.

Marble balconies and screes frothed overhead in the main hall's suffocating brightness. Soon, at least if it stopped snowing, there would be fireworks. Definitely, there would be drinks. Soon as well, and even if Hereford hadn't yet fallen, the cannons of the East would come within range of this beautiful palace, and Marion Price would be arrested by one or other side in this bloated conflict for things the real woman who lived within her shadow had probably never done or said. But already, there was dancing. Always, at least in this realm of the privileged, there was copious food. Look how the waiters and waitresses have blackened their faces in tribute to the bondsmen of the Fortunate Isles, who are fighting as avidly as the Bristolians for a freedom they'd never possessed!

'*Entre nous*, what you were saying just lately about losing the war,' Noll muttered as he guided her in, 'probably isn't best repeated here.'

The ballroom seemed to slope and sway, rolling the dancers to and fro to the swell of the music. The bottles, Marion noticed, were without labels. Someone laughed and tapped their nose. It seemed that all of Bristol was rejoicing in the illicit

thrill of the small trade and running the blockades, but a more
sombre tide was flowing for all the surface jollity and the ridiculously complex dances, and the strange wailing of the band.
Amid the medals which the men wore, and the women affected
as brooches in mimicry, were pinned the diamond-set faces of
sons and brothers and husbands lost to some recent campaign or
epidemic. Brush against them as you tried to extricate yourself
from a chattering group, and treasured memories and voices
breathed out at you.

Buffeted on these currents, fielding smiling or desperate
faces, Marion encountered a finely made woman in silver and
red striped dress with a lace ruff collar.

'Marion . . .' Denise swallowed back the last morsel of the
sugared fancy she was eating. 'You're looking well.'

'So are you . . .'

Denise licked her fingertips. 'I only come to these dos because of business. Dreams of victory, dreams of defeat, the
beloved returning in something other than a wooden box—
you can imagine. Dream-mistresses have never been more
popular . . .'

'People were saying this morning that Hereford had
fallen.'

'Oh, I wouldn't have thought so. It's the West's last redoubt
and all of that, isn't it? But I *did* hear someone over there saying that the Eastern commander's been killed in an ambush,
which is obviously good news.'

'Who?'

'He's that one dressed in gold and blue beside the fat
woman with the—Oh, you mean the *Eastie*! I really haven't
got the foggiest idea, Marion. They're all the same, aren't they,
anyway? Only in it for the pillage and the blood and the vir-
gins . . .'

It seemed that speeches were about to be made; Marion
recognised the signs. Most likely, she'd be called upon to say
a few words which she'd never prepared but which always
came out anyway. And now, an amplified voice from the mez-
zanine was drawing the people across the floor's shining slope
as some newly created monstrosities were unfurled in their
cage. Some kind of bat, but black as night, they fluttered and
screeched and bared their acid fangs.

'Why don't we pop off to the loo, eh . . . ?' Denise murmured.

In the toilets, which were cool and bright and blissfully, empty, she beckoned Marion inside a cubicle which was bigger than their entire old cottage and rustled down on the toilet lid.

'*That's* more like it.'

Marion had to agree that it was.

'Heard anything from Owen lately?' Denise asked as she poked about inside her handbag.

She shook her head.

'Well, you know what post from the East's like. He's probably still mine-sweeping and killing our poor dolphins off in the North Sea. Somehow, I don't worry too much about him. There's something *bouncy* about our Owen, isn't there, even if he's gone with the East? But I can't believe he's involved in any of those atrocities.'

'Have you seen Mam?'

'Not lately.' Denise was laying out on her lap a glass and silver syringe which was so much better made than the blunt devices Marion's nurses had to deal with that it was a moment before she recognised it. 'Although she is doing pretty well,' she continued. 'Portishead's never been so lively—although I know that's not saying much. And cousin Penelope's really raking it in, what with all the gunnery officers and being kin to Marion Price and having her very own mother there on permanent exhibit . . .' She gave the needle a brisk squeeze and tap to check for bubbles. 'She probably dreads peace. Oh, don't mind *me*, by the way . . .'

One-handed, Denise unclasped the silver bracelet around her left wrist and jabbed the needle into her Mark. This would have been a disastrous choice of point of insertion from a strictly medical viewpoint, as the scar's residual aether contaminated any ordinary drug, but the spell Denise was injecting was strong enough for the fluid to shine dark against the white tiles and pool inside her eyes. As she slid the needle out, her gaze had already thickened. 'Help yourself if you'd like some, by the way. I'm sure you of all people can manage the necessary.'

Marion, who'd watched Noll in not dissimilar situations, shook her head.

Settling back against the cistern, Denise smiled dreamily. *'That's* the ticket. And as I was saying, most of us seem to be doing pretty nicely out of the war. And even if we lose, people will still want dreams. How bad can it be?'

The upper plate of Denise's false teeth clicked lightly against the bottom as she spoke. Her smile, as it broadened, grew more and more lopsided. 'We all have our places, don't we? And even dream-mistresses need their dreams. Me, I like to go back to that Midsummer—*you* remember the one. I was Queen and bedecked in flowers at that lovely house where you used to work. And the perfect weather, and the lads all wanting me. And me saying no, no, no . . . I was going to Bristol, see, to be a seamstress. You must have somewhere as well, Marion. Everyone does. But things always work out. Look at Mam. Our Owen. Poor, poor Dad . . . And Sally. And you, Marion Price. Look at you . . .' She chuckled, her eyes far away. 'Never any need to be sad. Even that baby . . .'

'What baby?'

She chuckled again. *'Your* baby, silly. It's like I say. Always the happy ending and never the sad.'

'My baby died, Denise.'

'Did it? You'd be surprised, the stories you learn from inside dreamers' dreams. Alfies wasn't such a bad place—you always said that, didn't you? Gave away the babies of course, but always to good homes. Had a guildslady not so long ago. Done well for herself. Thought her baby had died like yours. But then . . .'

Marion crouched beside Denise, gripping her arm. 'Then *what*, Denise?'

'Lots less trouble if the girls *think* their baby's died, innit? Keeps them quiet. Specially the bothersome ones—which was probably you, eh, sis? Then you never go searching around and messing things up. Everyone just gets on with their lives.'

'But I *saw*.'

'Ha! But did you, eh? All tired and drugged up and not in a fit state for anything. They had this thing at Alfies, was what I heard. Like a dummy you might use to pin up clothes, only this one was shaped like a wee babbie. A few minutes, a small spell . . . You *do* understand what I mean, Marion, don't you . . . ?'

Denise, in the bliss of her needle, had slid further against Marion. Hunching against the tiles, Marion settled her into some sort of balance, then debated if it wouldn't be safer to lay her flat down on the cubical floor. But that was hardly Denise's style. She looked into her eyes. 'I'm going to leave you for a while now, sis. Do you understand?'

Denise nodded and exhaled. Her eyes rolled. The lids fluttered over.

Marion looked about her. The cubicle, the entire washroom, was quiet, although people would rush in here as soon as the speeches had finished. Hitching her skirts, she clambered around a gently snoring Denise on to the top of the cistern. It was some way up from there to the window, but there was a shelf-like scroll of tiles—a tangle of waves and shells—at a level to which she could just about hitch herself. She did so, straining and scrabbling, and battling the ridiculous image of the great Marion Price being found sprawled beside her drugged sister in a toilet. Even the Western papers, she thought as she worked the window's hinges, would have a hard time making something mythical and positive out of *that*.

The space was scarcely big enough for her to squeeze through, and then only headlong. Perhaps thankfully, perhaps not, a rubbish-heaped skip lay directly beneath her in the darkness outside, and the only thing for her to do was to squirm through the aperture. Pushing herself through, she tumbled, crashed, into foul slippery waves, and swim-clambered quickly out and over to land jarringly on the paving of a dark alley.

Catching her breath, picking away the bigger lumps of rotting vegetable, she headed towards the sound of traffic. Tramlights and wires flickered and sprayed through the down-drifting snow, but there were few people about and, after her climb through the window and her encounter with the rubbish skip, she doubted if anything but the closest scrutiny would single her out. Beyond the whitening walls of the refurbished castle, she reached the houses of Greyshot Street where late-glowing night blooms glinted through the snowflakes beyond the softly piling railings. Alfies' gate was still chained and the wall, for all its roughness, proved much harder climbing than the toilet. She tumbled into the beds of sallow and lavender which Mistress Pattison had made her girls tend, and brushed the snow from herself and studied the house.

There were no broken windows, and just a few fallen slates. It was ridiculous that this place had been abandoned when it would have provided much-needed bed-space. The front door was locked, but she remembered the spell she'd secretly learned from Master Pattison's mutterings. With a damp shudder, it opened. It was dark inside, but she knew the way across the hall, and studied the forbidden door which led to the birthing rooms. Only once were the girls allowed through here, and even now it felt odd to breathe the spell which opened it, and then enter a corridor where trays and implements, even the sheets, had been left as they were. Cobwebs stirred across framed photographs of babies and benefactors in the soft light of the snow. This, even more than she'd expected, was a difficult place to be.

She reached a kind of storeroom or scullery. Shelves of medicine jars glinted with engine ice as their potencies faded. There was nothing here other than that which might be expected, and soon all that was left for her to inspect was the curtained space beneath a sink. Anything secret, anything troublesome, would surely be kept better hidden than this. So why, as she reached towards those tired flaps of cotton, did her fingers tingle? Why did her heart race?

There was an old scrubbing brush with most of its bristles missing, and lumped and stiffening packets of Scott's Universal Scouring Powder, but there was also a mannequin—a doll; the crudely made shape of a baby. Marion lifted it out. Its eyes were mere lumps of glass and its body and limbs were nothing but winds of cloth and stuffing, but her fingers, tracing its back as she cradled it, found the spiny lumps and hieroglyphs of some magic inner core. A faint glow came out of the eyes as she breathed and rocked over it, although she had no idea of the spell which would make it come sufficiently alive to seem dead.

She returned to the hall, and entered the parlour, which had also been out of bounds. She hadn't thought before to try the lights, and blinked as their yellowish flood touched the drifts of white beyond the windows. This room, with its broad, grey-black fireplace and neatly arranged armchairs, was where the guildswomen came to collect their babies, and it was impossible not to feel a lingering sense of loss and need. Taking a poker from the fireplace, she splintered the locked bureau in the room's corner. Its slide-out drawers were filled with forms which had been abandoned along with all the rest of the house. Proof, Marion thought grimly as she riffled through alphabetised names, that, here or in Western hospitals, no one ever read these things . . . Yes, she remembered some of these names. *Marion Price*. Lifting the form out, she recognised Nell Pattison's scrawl, but the rest of the document was filled out in a more flowing hand. The box was ticked for Boy. He would be seventeen now. Almost a man. What street? Marion wondered. What house? What school? What life? What loves? What fears? What comforts? What hopes? What guild? The hand looked masculine. Silus something. She retraced the flowing signature. Bellingham? Bellington? Hellingson? Then, more neatly printed in a separate box, the address. Still, and for a long moment, Marion thought she must have misread.

Einfell.

VII

In the firelight, rings around the cold, they gathered. Faces and not faces, eyes and not eyes. The wounded and the variously whole. Those who had ears listened with their ears, and those who hadn't listened in any way they could to the song. The Beetle Lady rocked and sang. The Beetle Lady cried and beat her fists.

'Can't you hear it?' she said, and the air made shapes before her. 'Can't you feel it in the air . . . ?'

It's coming! agreed the others, and the acclamation passed mouth to mouth, and the dead trees beyond in the darkness and the gathering nightlock sighed and thrashed in celebration.

In the requiem dark, they came. In the winding-sheet light, they stayed or hid or burrowed. Day by day and moment by moment, on and on through the unending, ever-changing winter. Crawling limb by limb through mud and snow, the followers followed.

'Listen—can't you hear the song of the trees? Listen! The most beautiful place, and it's calling to us. No, not Einfell even, but the place beyond. Imagine this—imagine the summer of your dreams. Forget life. No, no—listen, *listen. Dreams.* Imagine . . .' As the wind rose and the snow resettled and gusted, rising white from the black ground and twinkling in flakes of flame towards the black, black sky. 'Imagine the scent of grass and the red shine of fruit. Wind and water, and light and air, sweet sunlight strewn like bedstraw along cool corridors amid the shadows. Listen. Imagine . . .'

Here the words grew past saying, and the heat of the fire at their faces and the cold at their backs and the shapings of the one beside her, the one who had a face of potpourri, petals dried beyond their season and scent, ignited and became the full glory of the song. Oh, how the snow danced, how it laughed and pranced! Through garden archways, onward and onward in the tunnelling dark towards the place they had always known. Ralph, rousing himself, chuckled as the warm light laughed over him and sweet breezes stirred within the snow. Yes, yes, *listen*! In cracked tones, between gasps and shudderings, he raised his head and joined in with the song.

The followers had gathered around Hereford and the scents of battle just as they always did, even as it was made beautiful with snow. No, not terrorists or guerrillas, nor freedom fighters or Easties or Westies, the Beetle Lady had muttered to him as she half-dragged and half-pushed him past the snow-drowned flags of mine-clearance work to the ruined walls where others almost as madly attired as her were waiting. Not mad or sane or sensible or deluded, for such distinctions were silly and stupid. Not all or any of those things, for they were the followers, fruit of the battle, and, as they murmured and wailed to the urging of this essentially quite small and shrewish woman, the followers were being led.

Ralph had gauged from the first sunset as they trudged away from of what he supposed he could no longer call his army that they were heading approximately south and west. The snow had settled and deepened, and he lost all feeling from his face and limbs. Gasping, near-drowning in the next tidal wave of white, he'd sensed the Beetle Lady's roughly impatient hands hauling him out and on.

'Listen, listen, Master Meynell. You of all people can't give up . . .'

The singing, the chanting, was dying now with the fire. A chorus of snores and grunts—an extraordinarily ordinary sound after all the evening's shrieking and moaning—arose from the dark. How many days had it been now? Almost wilfully, an act of forgetting, Ralph had lost count. He'd lost touch, as well, with any proper sense of whether he was hostage, captive, deserter, prisoner of war. After all, as the Beetle Lady had often muttered amid all the many other things she told this ragged gang, such distinctions had become foolish. They were all simply followers. And, day by day, night by night, mile by mile, their numbers were growing. Not just the disaffected Western and Eastern soldiers whom the Beetle Lady had somehow persuaded to organise that ambush, but many civilians, if civilians could be said to truly exist in war, men and women and children—and other things as well. A ravener squatted nearby, anteater claws hooked over hairy haunches, its mastiff maw droolingly composed. Beside it slept a balehound, one side of its flanks shiny-roasted by the heat of some explosion, but calm as a puppy and seemingly oblivious to all pain. Both, Ralph supposed, had either been created with the instruction to kill faultily inserted, or lost during exposure to battle. And then there was that creature of petals . . . Ralph coughed and wiped his mouth. His fevers and hallucinations were becoming so much more convincing than the actual realities which surrounded him—if realities was what they truly were.

'*There* you are . . .' the Beetle Lady said conversationally as she squatted down beside him. Ralph had no idea where she'd got glow-worms from at this time of year, but she certainly had a glow about her, unless she'd simply ornamented herself with the embers of the fire. 'Not so far now, eh?'

'Do you really expect us to get to Invercombe?'

'Ahh—but I've been there many times. Just as you have, Master Meynell. Why, otherwise, do you think we're so alike?'

If he strained his eyes—or if he closed them, which was far easier—Ralph could sometimes imagine he could see the prim woman with whom he'd once shared a dinner at Invercombe, and then met with Marion at Hotwells. But it was like most things; it came and went. No wonder, he thought as something small and black-backed crawled from the edge of the Beetle Lady's mouth and she picked it from her cheek and cupped it and set it flying into the dark, that he hadn't recognised Doctress Foot when he'd seen her captured in the pit in that Droitwich engine house. But then, he almost *had*, hadn't he? Once again, the uncertainties began. And from there, if the story she told and ornamented and amended and expanded according to her and the other followers' moods was to be believed, she'd been released in some abandoned village and had reached Invercombe just as summer was fading. Whatever it was she'd seen there had given her madness this greater focus—that, or this war, or what his own soldiers had done to her—but she was certainly possessed of an appealingly delirious certainty. No wonder the followers were drawn.

'Why did you claim you were Marion Price, when my men arrested you?'

'How else would you have come to me, eh? And Marion is here—she's with us all. Listen!' The Beetle Lady cocked her head. 'Can't you hear it in the guns?'

Not that there were any guns firing within their hearing at that moment, but Ralph knew what she meant, just as he now found he generally understood whatever the Beetle Lady was driving at; he'd even ceased to find it worrying. For Ma-ri-on was everywhere, even in these mutters and snores. And so was the place of lost rest and summer and repose which was Invercombe. It was true that he'd been there many times in his mingled memories and dreams, just as the Beetle Lady said. He coughed and inspected his hands, but they were so filthy that he couldn't tell if there was any fresh blood. Not that it mattered. Not that anything mattered so very much now. They were heading towards Invercombe. Whatever it was that was waiting there, he couldn't think of a better place to die.

VIII

The new halls of the Great Guild of Telegraphers could be said to face both East and West, for the light of dawn and sunset shone entirely through them. Set midway along Wagstaffe Mall, the structure appeared to hang on wires, and played tricks with the refracted images of London which were captured in its many huge planes of angled glass. Hallam Tower often hung there; a dancing needle. So, frail and refracted, did the massive pyramid of Great Westminster Park. It was on the itinerary of every recently published guidebook of London. Birds flew into it, imagining it part of the sky.

To Alice, it had come to represent much of her guild's ambition. It was resolutely modern, uplifting, transparent, and yet solidly well engineered. The onrush of the war, though, had caught the building at a precarious moment, and many contracts for the final fittings and decorations were left unfulfilled. The building was a monument, in the botched interior construction and misuse of intended spaces, to the demands of this conflict.

Up in her office a shifterm after news of Ralph's bizarre arrest and yet more bizarre disappearance had reached her, and in no mood to exchange her usual pleasantries with the staff, she stood out on her balcony. The structure was glass, moulded entire with spells and filaments of crystal. Alice, as she stood there, seemed to hang in nothing but space and air. London was blue and grey and gold beneath her. The tiny traffic moved along Wagstaffe Mall. The trees were flames of phoenix feather. She'd dreamed of moments such as this long ago back in her aunt's house by the waterfall when she'd merely been Alice Bowdly-Smart, but in truth the day-to-day business of being Greatgrandmistress Alice Meynell often left her wearied.

Alice sighed a cloudy breath. She'd have leaned against the cold rail for support were the glass not so sharp. She had a meeting at eleven with High Command, and their eyes, she knew, would be looking questioningly at her. Life was so grimly unfair. Even the maternal anguish she felt to think of her only son roving ill and unprotected across the war-ravaged landscape—for she was sure that he was still living—seemed a poor shadow of her old feelings. Like this sunlight, like this beautiful city, nothing now touched her with the strength it once had. Her bones ached. Her mind swarmed with half-grasped thoughts and feelings. Her beauty was fading. Of course, she was still referred to as *striking*, as *graceful*, as *elegant*, as—and this was the most hateful phrase of all—*exquisitely well preserved*. But they were comparing her to the harpies and bloated sea-beasts who wrongly imagined they shared their age with her, and not with laughing and youthful debutantes.

Feeling discomfort in her hands, raising them from the crystal rail, she saw that she had been gripping it so hard that they were smeared with blood. Mere scratches, but the potions and foundations which she now so carefully applied over her entire flesh had smudged and run. She turned the revealed flesh in this brighter light. No longer quite flesh at all; it reminded her more of part-thawed ice, and this late autumn sun was so bright that she could see her bones as well, which looked fine enough, considering the pain they nowadays caused her, although they, too, were edged with a sort of translucency . . .

This was nothing like the near-instant changing she had once inflicted at Battersea on poor Silus—now *what* had been his second name?—but cumulative aether poisoning, according to most of the many books she'd now studied on the subject, was at least as common as a single catastrophic event.

She put her state mostly down to all the years of spells she had cast from her portmanteau, and perhaps to Invercombe as well, and the wilder experiments of disembodiment she'd risked that summer there, and to the backwash of the Falling which had so nearly killed her.

She had wondered over the older texts which portrayed the changed as monsters, witches, goblins and demons. They had been burned then, or ostracised. Later, they had been branded and chained and put to use for the unusual proficiency they sometimes possessed in the mastery of spells. The same was apparently happening during this war, especially in the West, which of course had the benefit of a ready supply from Einfell. More interesting still were the gaudier tales and myths which flourished about the lives of some changelings. Goldenwhite, for example, who was said to have led the poor and the dispossessed to the very gates of London in the Wars of Reunification before she was betrayed and burned at the stake.

The time of her meeting with High Command was growing closer, and Alice knew that she would have to go back inside and remake-up herself for it. But it would be amusing, really, to come lolloping in to see them one day as whatever it was that she was becoming. Of course, she'd never imagined herself receding into bland dotage. And how much worse, she sometimes wondered as she studied the Mark which was now nearly entirely faded on her wrist, would her life become if she was Chosen, changed? And she was sure that she was beginning to experience some of what might possibly be the benefits of this new state. Just as her ears were growing weaker, she sometimes found herself hearing things which, from the surprise with which people responded to them, she realised they had merely thought. Of course, it all added to her reputation for perspicacity. And then there was the extra pull of spells. Aether, this city and all the people in it and the westward-threading telephone lines of her own guild, seemed to be calling to her in inexpressible song.

It was a far more composed and energetic and, indeed, happy greatgrandmistress who faced High Command on that unseasonably bright November morning than any of its members might have expected. If there had been a slight loss of faith in her, a feeling that she was no longer quite the acutely able and maturely beautiful woman whom they all admired and secretly coveted, it was soon dissipated by the challenging gaze of her blue eyes and the smile with which she swept the room. Even the sad business of her son—the sheer *grace* with which she'd accepted it!—enhanced rather than diminished her. Still, and even then, there would normally have been queries and murmurs at what she was proposing. Not that any of them would have ever doubted her ability—individually, they all knew and owed her too much—but there were, or at least should have been, practical considerations of security and chains of command to be addressed.

But light shone through the windows, and Alice Meynell shone with it. Even the cynics, and that included most who sat around this long table, were inexpressibly moved. For they were sick of this war and its death and mayhem, and had privately come to wonder whether questions of free trade and taxation and slavery and local influence had ever been worth the sacrifices which were now being made. They feared, as well, that the general population would challenge the prosecution of this war if it didn't end far better and more quickly than now seemed likely, and that they would be challenged with it. And here was Greatgrandmistress Alice Meynell offering to go west herself, and either take or destroy the continuing open sore which was Hereford. This, as she raised her arms and her hair fell sheer and silver as the light and her whole body and everything else about her seemed to float on nothing but sheer hope and aspiration like the building she'd engendered, was the essential truth they'd lost in these years of attrition.

IX

Dawn was coming, blurring the night's certainties in slow shades of grey. It was incredibly cold, and the fire was waning. Ralph shuffled himself deeper into a rotting blanket. He wasn't sure whether it was he or this moisture-laden air which was trembling, but the scene which quivered at its edges in the fire's fading smoke and light was certainly feverish enough. He shivered, and coughed again. The air shook with him. Then, as the wind rose and the snow resettled and gusted, rising white from the black ground and twinkling in flakes of flame towards the black, black sky, the Beetle Lady rose herself to her feet and started shouting.

'No, listen, No—join in . . .' She stood wavering as the light and the carapaces crawled over her. 'She's coming, can't you hear it? She's coming . . .'

Heads which were heads nodded. Ears which were ears listened and heard. The wind gave a balehound moan.

'Marion Price, yes, yes, I once knew her. Knew her for what she was and what she will be. Knew then that she would lead us all into this final battle. No longer Clerkenwell, no. No longer Boadicea or Goldenwhite. No longer London or Bristol. No longer East or West. She's back in the past but here as well before us in the future present. Leading us on into the realms beyond cold and thirst. Yes, yes, I was there at the place beyond Einfell which is called Invercombe. I saw it all and believed. And listen, listen, can't you hear the guns . . . ?'

Boom-ba-booom.

Ma-ri-on . . .

Another morning was arriving at the camp of the followers, and a man who was a priest, or who at least had assumed something resembling the raiment of one, was moving amid the bizarre throng. In his bare hands, he was carrying a shell case which had been heated on the campfire's ashes. It took a serious effort of will for Ralph to take it when it was offered to him, but the brass was so beautifully magicked that its metal was cool. Either that, he supposed, staring into its steaming, spinning contents, or the flesh on the palms of his hands was now entirely dead. The dark swirl of hymnal wine within was threaded with twilit agitations of ghostgas. Tipping the shell case up, he swallowed and handed it back to the priest, who bore it on to the next penitent.

By now, Ralph was almost used to such rituals, and knew what would come next. First the blood, and now came the body. A huge haunch of meat which, for all the fat-dripping weight of it, he couldn't remember seeing cooking on the fire. Some kind of ham, far bigger and richer than even the massive joints he'd found ambered in honey amid the breakfast collations at Walcote, was passed to him. Delicious strips of tendon ran eagerly through his loose teeth. Juices slipped over his chin. Part of him thought that he never tasted meat this sweetly delicious, and part of him gagged and fought to swallow, and saw that the stuff which the other followers held looked more like some unlikely jerky blackened by frost and age. But then came more of the hymnal wine, wherein most prayers are answered, and Ralph ate and drank and believed.

He was reminded of other breakfasts—of the confections of coffee and chocolate of which Helen was fond before she'd decided that she should only drink lemon juice or hot water for the sake of her thin frame. He remembered frothily swirled spirals of steam and scent filling the cool morning silence as they both studied their separate daily papers. He heard the tink of spoons against monogrammed porcelain. Glancing at her across battlefields of white cloth set with crystal emplacements of condiment, he saw that the children were also with them today for breakfast. He struck his spoon more loudly in the hope that it might catch their attention. He was dimly aware that he was dying, and felt that he owed them some sort of apology before he did.

The Beetle Lady shook him. 'No, no. Not *death*—not *sleep*. Now listen, listen . . . I've been to the place which is called Invercombe, where the thunder beckoned. Yes, there is darkness, but beyond that . . . Ah, beyond that . . .' Her eyes whitened. 'Beyond that . . . She will lead . . . Listen . . .'

Ralph listened. Was that thunder? Was it wind? Was it guns?

Ma-ri-on.

Soon, although he'd as happily have stayed here as any- where, it would be time to move on. He made the effort to hitch himself up from beside the dying fire. He swayed with hunger, weariness, illness and loss of sleep. He believed the Beetle Lady when she talked of Marion Price in the same way that she talked of the lost days of myth, and of a different Einfell, and of Goldenwhite's ragged army.

He hobbled around dead trees and the fallen bodies of the still sleeping. The followers had become a sort of procession, a safety of mixed numbers and madnesses. Day by day they grew. An increasing number of soldiers had joined their company, and there were familiar morning rituals and ablutions: gun-and-harness jingle; the scrape of shovels; the scratch of heads; the curse-and-hawk-and-spit. These deserters from the East and West fitted together so easily they might never have been separated, and Ralph wondered if any of them recognised him, although, un-uniformed and hollowed-out and bearded as he now was, he doubted it.

'Ralph Meynell?'

He stopped, turned. Someone neither quite civilian nor military was squatting on the ground. They wore a cap and a loose grey coat, and their boots, or what remained of them, lay beside their bare feet. Somewhat ruefully, they had been kneading their blistered and frostbitten toes. Oddly enough, it was those toes, and in particular their upward turn rather than anything else about her appearance, which made Ralph Meynell recognise the person he seemed to be seeing. But then, it was just as the Beetle Lady had long been saying. For where else but here, amid these followers and in this place, would you expect to find Marion Price?

X

The power was down and had been that way since long before dawn, and the fine house, a mixture of styles and Ages, which had been requisitioned as Headquarters for the First and Second Eastern Armies over which Alice, in the matter of a few shifterms and by divers means, had assumed almost total control, was seepingly cold. The spells which had once been cast to keep up the plaster which frothed across the extravagant ceilings were failing. You could hear the crashes like cannonfire each night as more of it collapsed. What furniture remained in the desolate rooms was crooked and unstable. The plumbing had failed, to be replaced by hosepipes, buckets and standpipes. The carpets squelched. The silk wallpapers were sloughing from the walls. In her previous visits to the front, she had always been aware of grey, grim military utility, but living amongst it was something else entirely.

Climbing out from her fold-up bed which lay in the clotted gloom cast by the huge red four-poster which was too damp to be inhabited, she winced, and waited for her head to stop spinning. The air swished about her. Jungle fronds of damp climbed the walls, greyly exploring the interstices of stone and wood and plaster. A shadow, a madly haired extension of the grainy light, she crept across the loosely carpeted floor. With a

sag and a stagger, her portmanteau opened. Many of the jars
were stuffed in places where they didn't quite fit, or had
crusted and jauntily angled lids. Pages and cuttings from her
notebook had loosened to line the dim bottom like the fallen
leaves of her own personal autumn. One day, Alice told herself, she would give the whole thing a proper clear-out. But in
truth she had come to like the loose, powdery and jangling
sense of disorder it now gave off. It was all hers, an entire spinning world, and here, at the heart of it, the star which they all
orbited: a small, bright chalice of aether, which brightened still
further as she lifted it out. The hissing in her head grew much
stronger as well. The sense, the song, of the aether infused her.
Almost regretfully, she laid it down on the nearby dressing
table, then rummaged for the other preparations and powders
she required to feed her small retort. She struck a match, lit the
flame of the spirit, which fluttered, a rag of dark, against the
aether's continuing flare. Opening the lid of her gramophone's
silent, lacquered box, she laid the needle in mid-track. She slid
the turntable forward with the tips of her fingers. A faint roar.
Slid it back. A dim clamour of voices, more of the song . . .

An hour later Greatgrandmistress-Commander Alice Meynell emerged along the dank corridors. There were some advantages, she thought as she entered the briefing room, to
living in this military way. The frank nearness of death, for
example; the unflinching acknowledgement that it was a sacri-
fice which it sometimes became necessary for certain people
to make. Killing people here was almost easier than keeping
them alive. She listened to the wearying reports of divisional
commanders or their deputies, and read the printouts and studied the arid insides of numberbeads. She touched her lips to
the disastrous coffee.

She's wearing odd earrings . . .

Her hair's astray . . .

*Why is she asking all this again, when we told her yester-
day . . . ?*

See, how her hands tremble in those gloves . . .

Mere wafts of thought from these sour-smelling men, kept
well in check as they unrolled the maps and talked of the details of emplacements, and why should she care as long as
they feared her? Outside in her car, doubly gloved and hatted

and blanketed, she acknowledged the troops as she was jolted painfully around potholes and the craters of mines. A pity, really, that the title greatgrandmistress didn't convert into a chant as easily as the name of that shoregirl, who had recently taken the clever step of disappearing, and had thus removed herself entirely from the awkward businesses of being real. And this certainly wasn't yet the world of blissfully glowing telephone lines and endless fields of bittersweet she'd always imagined she was creating. But England, for her, was a work in progress. Soon, everything would change.

After the desultory queues along the muddy, half-frozen roads and the confusions of engineering work, she found herself elated as she drew closer to the very westernmost edge of the East's defence. Here, where the big guns waited, and the raveners were fed and the ammunition pointed its steel tips and the very earth remained unsafe, lay a refreshing sense of discovery and danger. Purpose, even—or the closest one got to it in wartime, and as she was led along duckboards to tents and temporary shelters, as she spoke to the gatherings of men, Alice could feel the rain-bowed spells of all this aethered machinery fountaining around her. They called and crooned.

The power was still down back at the damp house that evening, and the shadows stalked her as she hunched to her room, and opened her portmanteau, and undressed in the starlight cast by her aether chalice. After she had removed her unmatching earrings, and Jackie Brumby's teardrop chain, and Cheryl Kettlethorpe's thin silver bracelet, and the silver-threaded button from the shirt Tom had been wearing on the night of his death, she unstoppered the chalice and dabbed a little aether on her wrist where her Mark had been. Then, to the other wrist, and on her palms and neck, and the tip of her tongue and behind each ear, she dabbed some more, and felt it roar into her blood. The huge, red shadow of the four-poster bed leapt in the wyrelight. Smiling, humming, glowing, she returned to her portmanteau and lifted out the black, wyre-bright pages of her greatest spell, and danced with them as they shone and slipped and slid. Then the light changed. At last, the electricity had come on, although the single bulb was more wan than today's sunlight, and equally unwanted. She extinguished it with an easy glance, as, in a long, slow roar, her gramophone returned to life. Its song possessed nothing of the beauty of that which she was already singing, but she let the record play until the needle crackled and swished into the run-out groove. Yes, that was more like it. The music, the swish and sigh. Tides of light. Something vast breathing. Oceans and caverns. Lost summers reclaimed. Yes, Invercombe; or whatever lay beyond it. Alice Meynell laid herself down amid the sheets of her spell and the shadows of her presence, and fell smilingly towards sleep.

XI

The procession, the gathering, the snake of hunched backs and hats and heads to which now had been added varieties of wagon and handcart, along with drays and ponies in various states of malnutrition, now snaked back across the horizons of the West. Steaming and stinking, it broke into knots of arguments, surprised clusters of greeting. Flags and banners, and sheets and poles, umbrellas, even, danced aloft. There were spontaneous outbursts of sobbing and song. Most often, the Beetle Lady scampered at its front, calling and beckoning with increasing excitement that yes, this, listen, this really was the way. Some part of her, or the person she had once been, truly did recognise these roads.

The snow had vanished, but the cold had deepened. Every footstep on the sharded mud was loud, and every wheel rumble and drag of possessions rang taut over the hedgerows. If the procession moved most obviously through any element in this serely greyed winter landscape, it moved through the element of sound.

Boom-ba-boom . . .

Ma-ri-on . . .

Along its way, the followers had gathered musicians, or at least those who imagined themselves capable of making music,

and each of the endlessly circling syllables was given a toot
and a shriek of emphasis, and the rattle-bang of drums. The
effect was hypnotic, especially now that the procession had
grown so long that its rhythm staggered along the lines in
echoes and decays. More than the Beetle Lady's shrill shrieks,
more than the many individual sounds which mingled into
frosty distance with a chilly rumble, like a shudder of the very
earth across which they were travelling, it predominated.

The woman who shared her name with this sound had
hacked off her hair, and wore a thick felt cap, loose trousers
bagged at the waist, collapsing boots which hurt her feet, and
a split overcoat. None of it was quite enough to keep her warm
even in the stumbling midst of the procession, and she would
have given much she didn't have for a decent pair of gloves,
but it did mean that she was most often thought of as a man—
or, when anyone made the effort to speak to her and she actually replied, as a lad. In that she radiated anything at all, it was
a desire to be left alone.

Ralph Meynell, or the scraggily bearded invalid Ralph
Meynell had seemingly become, was walking with her now,
and she supposed it was part of the madness of the war and this
procession, or perhaps merely an expression of their weariness, that neither of them had seemed that surprised to find
each other. After all, this procession of followers resounded
day and night to losses, reunions, loves and animosities for-
saken or renewed . . .

'I've seen so many things since I fled Bristol,' she told him.
'Before that, I could still pretend that there was order. I could
pretend that there was some purpose and the hope of saving
lives.'

'This war . . .' Ralph spluttered and put his hand to his
mouth, and the grumbling, tooting, thumping crowd elbowed
around them as he spasmed into a fit of coughing and Marion
waited beside him for it to stop. She had seen this hot brightness, this thin and cheery sense of purpose, many times with
tubercular patients, and knew that it normally presaged the final crisis. 'It's like a drug, an addiction,' he said eventually. 'It
led me *so* far. I even thought I could end it all by Christmas—
I mean, the war. Take Hereford, at least. But all I've done was
cause more and more death . . .'

The coughing subsided. He still wore, Marion noticed, the remains of a senior Eastern officer's uniform, but no one here took that as any indication of who he really was any more than it might have occurred to them that the figure, possibly male or female, who hunched beside him was the physical incarnation of Marion Price.

'Is that why you left Hereford?' she asked as they moved on. 'Deserted—whatever it was that you did?'

'I was arrested. I'd tried to make contact with the West by relinking a telephone connection. I thought I could talk to them about peace.'

Marion almost smiled. Perhaps some part of the invalid who limped beside her really was the old Ralph Meynell. Still ridiculously idealistic—still imagining there was reason and logic in the world.

'And then?'

He coughed again. 'There was an ambush. I think the Beetle Lady wanted me as much as she still wants you.'

'What for?'

'I do think she really remembers us from Invercombe, or imagines that she does. In another life, she was a guildslady called Doctress Foot. We met at her Hotwells. Do you remember, that time we went to Bristol?'

Marion nodded. Previously, it would have been hard to imagine that anyone could change that much. But now, confronted by the evidence of what had happened to Ralph, and to herself . . .

'It all goes back to Invercombe,' he sighed. 'Everything does.'

'But why? Why *us*?'

'We're nothing. It's all of this'—he gestured around him at the followers—'that counts.'

'But this is madness.'

'And you're walking with us, Marion.' He lowered his voice slightly at the mention of her name, although she doubted if anyone else would ever have heard his wheeze in this stomping, yelling herd. 'So you must be mad as well.'

The countryside through which they were passing had been saved from the destruction of battle. Those residents who had stayed on watched warily from upstairs windows or from

around doors, whilst the few soldiers and police had made the
obvious calculation of numbers and vanished when they heard
of the procession's approach. Still, as they thumped and
steamed and the pipes piped and the earth trembled, there was
none of the pillage which Marion might have expected. And
still the Beetle Lady shouted and beckoned and waved in her
mad raiment, *No, no, this was not the place—Listen! You must
move on* . . . as they passed farm gates and post boxes and
waymarks. It was bizarre, to witness the followers passing
through this ordinary Western winter landscape; the untouch-
ing of two realities. In their wake they drew the curious, barking dogs, children, the mad. Some hung back or vanished.
Many, many others joined with the shuddering march.
  Ma-ri-on . . .
  Boom-ba-boom . . .
  Marion wondered just how long this blurred sense of order
would last. When would hunger and frustration break out—in
the next town, at the next farmhouse, the next village? And
once that line had been crossed, what of sanity would remain?
She was worried as well because of the gathering ranks of deserters who had been drawn to this procession. Word of their
passage would certainly have swept along the telephone lines
which hung dark across these fields. It could surely only be a
matter of time before a regular army was mustered to see they
were bloodily dispersed. The whole situation was hopeless,
and yet she was marching towards Einfell and Invercombe to
the rhythm of her stolen name in the hope of finding her lost
son. She supposed that Ralph was right; she probably had
grown a little mad herself . . .

The landscape dimmed. Earlier and earlier now as the year
turned towards its close, it was growing dark. Flares were lit,
the flaming crowns of dead branches. As sparks drifted and the
chanting grew ever louder, it seemed that they could see further
and further ahead over the unrolling hills. What *was* that light at
the edge of the horizon? A signpost flickered in the passing
flames, and Marion was sure she recognised the name. Not that
she'd been to Edingale, but hadn't Dad once bought a pig from
a man who'd lived there? It was all so impossibly strange . . .
  The followers spread out from the road to rest amid a mix-

ture of copse and pasture. Fires were started. The stranger creatures which had been part of the procession, those which hid from daylight, emerged shyly to crouch before the singing heat. Food was thin, and there was scarcely any water. For all the Beetle Lady's encouraging words, there were mumbles of disappointment. Where, indeed, was the manna? Where were the pillars of smoke and fire? Where was this happy place called Invercombe, Avalon, Paradise, Eden, Einfell—whatever *was* its name? But the songs were a help, and the bodies and fires provided some shelter in the closeness of their gathering.

She found Ralph some dirtied hunks of bread and a few capfuls of watery milk. What he proved incapable of eating, she gave to the old man who was hugging himself beside them. She even allowed a little for herself, for she, as well, was some ailing creature, and since leaving Bristol she'd come to treat this husk of Marion Price with something resembling her old beside manner. She'd been kindly, but remote. The begging, the cutting of her hair, the swapping of clothes, the asking of favours, the sleeping and eating as winter set in, the shedding of what seemed to be left of her identity, had all been accomplished by looking down on herself with distant, clinical sympathy. After all, she came to realise, Marion Price had never belonged in only one time or one place. She had always borrowed identities and purposes. Shoregirl, maid, penitent mother-to-be, riverperson, nurse, administrator, figurehead, lover; none of them had ever really been her.

And this war. The guns, the madness, the gleefully organised brutality. How could wrong and right matter so much that bones poked from the mud and skin hung from the trees? What exactly were these armies defending? Ways of living? Preferences in food or religion? She didn't believe in bonding, but now it seemed to her that, one way or another, most of the population of England was enslaved. Since fleeing Bristol and trying to find her way towards Einfell in the teeth of a fresh enemy advance, she'd witnessed a war which even the insanitary chaos of her hospitals had kept at bay. *Boom-ba-boom* . . . *Ma-ri-on* . . . As if the Marion Price she'd discarded had grown into the spirit of all the destruction she saw around her as some final conflict gathered and the guns of both sides came to taunt her in their distant rage. Her name shook the air. It was

scrawled on walls. She found it carved in the grinning ribs of a
corpse. And then she had encountered other followers who had
grown in number and had joined in turn with this vast procession which now bickered and coughed and sang and
dreamed. And then she had met Ralph Meynell—or whatever
he'd become.

'I was wrong, you know,' he said as he shivered inside the
blanket she'd found for him. 'When you walked out—what I
said to you that day in Sunshine Lodge.'

'What *did* you say?'

He gave a wheezy laugh. 'I can't remember. And we never
did get to the Fortunate Isles, did we? Either of us? Or find
a better name for Habitual Adaptation. And I've seen Owen.
Did I tell you that, Marion?'

'How is he? Is he still . . . ?'

'He's fine—or as well as anyone can be in this war. The
work he's doing isn't particularly dangerous, although it
hasn't been easy for him, being the brother of Marion Price.'
Dim redness and light pooled and went from Ralph's eyes.
'But he told me the truth, Marion. Before that, I never knew.
He told me about the baby that died . . .'

As instantly as the striking of a match, she felt her old
angers and disbeliefs flare inside her. 'Your *mother* knew—
your so-called Greatgrandmistress. It was she who persuaded
me to go to Saint Alphage's. *She* was the one who stopped me
coming back to you that day in Bristol.'

'I know about that now, Marion . . . But the money had
vanished from that account my father created for me. Did you
know that? All of it?'

'And you thought that I . . . ?'

Ralph nodded, coughed. 'I didn't know what to think. Forgetting was like falling, and there are other things as well.
Things I can't . . . It suited my mother to keep me in the dark.'

'All these years, and you call it the *dark*! What do *you*
know about darkness?'

But Ralph said nothing as he shuffled on, and she sensed
that, for all his chains of command and his fine houses and his
stupid Eastern ignorance and everything that his war had
brought down on him, he had perhaps glimpsed some deeper

kind of darkness in the life he'd been living, even if it was something he could still scarcely barely bring himself to face. He'd stopped shivering, but his breath remained an agitated wheeze. It occurred to Marion that, like many of the patients she'd sat with as they began to sense the nearness of death, he was asking her for absolution. But she couldn't give that to him. The girl, or the young woman, who could had long gone from this earth, and so had the arrogant young man. Instead, perhaps, she owed this new Ralph the truth. But that was the hardest thing; the truth always was. Einfell, for all her wanderings against the teeth of this winter war, had been the one direction towards which she'd found it hardest to draw her own thoughts. Cradle memories, creased limbs, the downy scent of hair—all the things she'd striven to forget in the years since she'd walked from Bristol along the Avon Cut and decided to head up the river—had returned to her that night as she gazed at the records in Saint Alphage's. Her baby hadn't died. But with that knowledge had come all the old stories of aether-twisted monsters. And then there was Dad, the blue glass, Mam's scarred fingers . . .

With something akin to her old bedside manner, Marion wondered whether Ralph's mind and body were capable of coping with what she'd discovered about their son. In a way, it was like the decision whether to move someone for better treatment when the journey itself might kill them, or whether to tell a solider that all his mates were dead, or that the letter he'd sent to his fiancée had come back *not known at this address*. But this pain, if pain was what it was, was at least at much hers as it was his. Wasn't there still hope and purpose? And if it turned out that there wasn't, perhaps she and Ralph would be better off leaving this world.

'Look, Ralph . . .' she began. She'd thought, inasmuch as she'd ever thought of a moment such as this, that these events and feelings would be difficult, if not impossible, to express. Instead, the words rushed out. And not just about the baby she'd lost so many times and in so many ways that the truth about his seeming survival was just another form of separation, but about her family and the river and the lost village of Clyst and the dreams of the shore, and yes, goddamit, about Ralph and Invercombe and what had been done to her by his

own bloody mother and all the broken certainties and happi-
nesses of that summer that some part of her mind was still stupidly trying to reconstruct.

When she'd have expected expressions of doubt or surprise, Ralph merely lay beside her and listened. He pressed
closer to her, and she felt the breathy fever-heat of his bones,
as, much to her frustration, she began to sob.

'Who knows what's good or bad, Marion.'

'It's like this war.' She wiped her face, then balled her fingers into the earth. 'It's like *everything*.'

'No—that isn't what I mean. Listen, can't you hear her?' The
Beetle Lady, her feverish energy far stronger than Ralph's, was
still stuttering and screeching as she wandered amid the followers and the quickening winter wind whipped and moaned.
'We'll be close to Einfell tomorrow. We'll soon find out . . .'

The air was windily damp in the morning. Even as she and
Ralph huddled at the heart of the followers, Marion felt as
cold as she had ever felt as they marched on. After yesterday
and the day before's strange normalities, the few houses they
now encountered were abandoned. The world, as the wind
chanted through the hedges, seemed unmade and raw. But
there was no mistaking the lie of this landscape, these signs
and the mileposts, the shapes of the trees, the colours and textures of the earth. She could even sense the near-presence
of the sea. Here a wooden finger pointed to Einfell, just as
it might to any other place, and the procession followed, although there were murmurs of unease amid the chanting,
which grew louder as a long, dark fence began to loom. For all
the stories of Goldenwhite's ragged army and palaces of
dreams, this was a place few would have cared to visit even
now in the uncertainties of war.

Then the road gave out entirely in the giant spreading of
barbed fences, but the Beetle Lady was not deterred, nor apparently entirely irrational, for she drove them around and on,
to the south and west, until they met an open gate.

Emboldened, the followers flooded through it, their fears suppressed by their numbers and the Beetle Lady's urgings, and by
the surprising ordinariness of what they found inside. Einfell's

roads were wild tangles of upturned concrete. Winter abandonment lay across its fields and woods. Why, they exclaimed as they fanned out through the deserted spaces where a few tired buildings sagged and leaned, this was just like every other place the war had left in its wake! But Marion, as she left Ralph behind and ran ahead of the laughing wave, realised that Einfell's abandonment was far deeper. Had anyone ever lived here, in this recent Age? But a larger house showed a brighter patch of roof, and there were small signs, as she waded its dead nettles, that its garden had been tended. The front door, indeed, looked as if it had been recently broken in by angry hands. Breathless, she glanced behind her, but the shouts and cries of the nearest followers were still some distance away. She went inside.

Was this the moment, she wondered, was this the place? She could have shouted out hello, but the creaking silence seemed oppressive, and who or what would answer her here, in Einfell? She moved across the slate hallway, which was dimly lit by filthy windows. A coat—a cloak of some kind—grey with mould but heavy and large, and with a hood as if its owner might once have sought to cover their identity, hung from a peg. She lifted it, almost thought of wearing it. But that would have seemed like some sort of trespass or theft. There was no doubt that people—or something resembling them—had lived in this place. Knives in the kitchen. Plates on the table. Rusty scissors. Food left in a pan. But whoever had been here had left, to judge by the coating of dust and fallen plaster, some years ago. Beyond another window in which a cleaner space had once been made, woods crawled into deeper shadows beyond the bank of a small stream.

Upstairs, there were more signs of habitation, and of sudden abandonment. Beds. Heaps of old, old newspapers which nevertheless, in the piling and folding, looked as if they had once been carefully read. What, in any case, had she been expecting? A child tended by monstrosities, or a monstrosity itself? She'd encountered the effects of over-exposure to aether since this war began—limbs turning to steel plate, new antlered shapes of bone peaking from bleeding flesh—but such patients were invariably dying, and always rare. The worst cases were shot long before they got close to a treatment tent, especially if their comrades thought they might survive. Or so it was said.

A last rise of the stairs, and she could hear the wind rattling the loose slates, and the cries of the other followers, and the crunch and crash of things being broken as more and more of Einfell was explored. An upper bedroom, lit by mullioned glass. A table and another bed. Scattered and piled magazines and newspapers. Something rolled from her foot, and she picked up an empty tin which had contained a sugar-free product called Sweetness, which she recalled had been briefly popular in the East before the war began. There was no sign of any toys. But there *was* a children's book, which opened easily at the first page, and the word *dog*. Marion sat down on the bed. She raised the grey sheets to her face, but all she could smell was Einfell's abandonment. This was the place; she was sure of it. But she was even more certain that Einfell and all of its inhabitants had long left, or more likely been taken for the War Effort, just as the war had taken everything.

Time passed. The house still stirred and creaked. Faintly, the wind still whispered and sang. Ridiculous though the thought would have been to the woman who was once Marion Price, it almost seemed as if the place was trying to comfort her. This, after all, wasn't such a terrible life to have lived. Hadn't she spent her own childhood sleeping on hay amid the smell of smoke and fish? She stood up and walked slowly down the stairs and out of the house, with its patch of somewhat newer slating looking comically out of place.

Despite all Einfell's apparent neglect, the followers had discovered a cornucopia of pre-war supplies, mostly well preserved, inside one of its barns. Fires were being lit, and people were shouting, drinking, eating. They called and beckoned for Marion to join them, not because they knew or even cared who she was, but because here was a bounty to share after these shifterms of denial. She wandered on. A white building lay amid a spread of wintry pasture beyond a thinner arm of trees. It was a near-modern structure, and all the followers who weren't ransacking the barn seemed to be seething around it. Office chairs and furniture were being tipped through broken windows for no better reason than the fun of it. Inside, there was an even greater bustle of destruction. Old paperwork spewed everywhere. Beyond a reception, and offices, in a kind of museum, followers were cheerily rattling manacles and oohing over old books and pictures of varieties of the changed. In another room, the wastage was of greater concern. For here, in beds and screens, was the skeleton of a decently equipped treatment room, and Marion's nostrils twitched at the chemical scents which had been spilled recklessly from cupboards. Her instincts were roused. After all that she had and hadn't found here today, she felt she had to do *something*.

Soon, she had sort of a roster going. Any potentially useful medicines were to be stacked in boxes and wadded with the papers from old files. To treat the many minor injuries—for, by definition, the followers were walking wounded—she doled out responsibilities amongst those willing to assist her. She shed her coat and rolled up her sleeves. She even took off her cap. But the occasional references to her as *Marion* were no more than any competent medic in this day and Age would have received. The real Marion Price, after all, would never elicit these screams as she dug thorns from people's skin, and neither would she have looked so weary. But it was reassuring work; these were no longer people, but conditions, complaints, and there was picric acid for burns and hydrogen peroxide for cuts, and surgical spirit and iodine and the faint, hopeful glow of new stitching. By mid-afternoon, she had treated all of those who needed it, and anything of medical value had been carried outside to a wagon.

She found Ralph at the back of the building, sitting on an old office chair and staring into the greying trees.

'There's nothing here,' she said, righting another chair beside him. 'Nobody.'

'You're sure it's true—what your sister told you, what you saw at that place in Bristol?'

She shivered. She really should have taken that cloak. But someone else would have found it by now anyway, and their need was probably greater than hers. That house with the patched roof would be being ransacked like all the others, and what, in any case, had she really found?

'People get lost in wartime, Marion. You hardly need me to tell you that. But nothing's lost for ever. Not yet. I still feel as if we're going somewhere.'

'Invercombe?'

'Everything's just as the Beetle Lady said. Einfell's a staging post. What you did in there, helping those people, that's all part of it as well, of why we're here and what's happening.'

She shrugged. Ralph looked and talked just like all the other followers; in fact, he was a lot worse than some. It was all stuff and nonsense. 'No one recognises me as Marion Price.'

'Isn't that what you want?'

She took a breath. Suddenly, she felt angry. Angry with this place, and with this man, and all these ridiculous dreams and chants.

'What I want is to know what *happened* to my son, Ralph! Is that so bloody much to ask?'

She left him and walked off towards the twilit trees. There were plays of brightness where the woods grew thinner. There were more signs of habitation as well. Trees strung with twirls of bark, odd arrangements of tin, fabric and kitchenware. A patch of earth paved with stepping stones of dinner plates. Everything was rotting and rusted, but frozen ribbons and bottletops tinkled like windchimes. Ice-adorned trees glinted like chandeliers.

Bang bang bang.

Shots and shouts rang ahead where the followers had gathered in a wider clearing. Marion watched them from the edge of the trees. Had something been found here? Some*one*? But no—there were just more odd conjunctions of everyday things. Flower-patterns of cog, trellis and piano key. An old fishing net strung with the rubber teats of babies' bottles had been hooked between the trees, and a fire was being kindled from a loose wigwam of old timber, and other followers pranced and fired their guns as the Beetle Lady flapped her iridescent wings.

A small, squat brick building lay on the far side of the clearing. It was some kind of transmission house; Marion recognised the sigils of the Telegraphers Guild moulded into the bricks. She ducked through the broken doorway as the wildness of the chanting increased. The place was damp, but had been left surprisingly intact, and the telephone's mirror gleamed, and there was even a chair. The firelight flowed through the doorway to play shiftingly across the reflected image of her face. Expression, glints of meaning, came and went from the mirror's scummed surface with the pulse of the flames. How long had it been since she'd seen herself? Perhaps as far back as Noll's flat; perhaps further still. Her hair was growing again, even if it stuck out in random hanks. She didn't look anything like as bad as Ralph, but still . . .

Bang bang bang.

Ma-ri-on.

Outside, louder than ever, the chanting continued. The features of Marion Price, or some woman who resembled her, flickered redly. For all it was a relic of its kind, and plainly disconnected, this device still seemed to exert a kind of pull. But then, she'd never liked mirrors of even the simplest kind. What she'd seen, what she saw now, had never been the real Marion Price. Now, flakes of greater blackness seemed to be separating themselves from the mirror, and Marion wondered for a moment if the telephone was still live and making some random connection. But the blackness spread, and with it came a fluttering sound. Another moment, and it exploded about her in screeching waves.

Flailing, she stumbled outside amid black flurries of wings. Scraps of darkness swirled about her in the firelight, and followers were running, and screaming and rolling in unaccountable pain. Feeling something prickling at her shoulder, Marion saw a stubbed, ugly snout crawling towards her face. She dragged and batted it away. Shrieking, one wing loosely broken, it still attempted to cling to her until, finally, she stamped it dead. Blisters were already raising where the nocturne's spittle had touched her skin.

The ravener, at last discovering some instinct to fight, howled and battered the air with its great claws, whilst the deserters drew back and began firing their guns.

'Here! Look! Listen, listen . . . !'

Shoving a handful of branches into the flames then waving them over her head, the Beetle Lady circled, shouted, beckoned, and the nocturnes swarmed about her like billows of smoke. Some settled on her. Others flew away. But still she called to them as she twirled her sparking branches, and still she danced around the flames. It was horrible to watch as more and more of the wings spread over her. Then, stumbling backwards towards the fire, she was engulfed as the remaining nocturnes ascended in flame.

'Get back! Give her space . . .' Marion crouched over what was left of the Beetle Lady after she'd been dragged away from the fire. Smoke and sparks wormed over her clothes. Only one eye shone, for the other was a black pit, but somehow she smiled.

'You're *her*,' the Beetle Lady whispered.

Marion tilted her head closer to be sure of what she'd heard. But the voice came louder.

'You're her—you're Marion Price!'

Marion looked around. Almost all the followers who had reached Einfell seemingly stood watching in a wide circle around the spilling flames. Whispers and signs were made at the mention of her name.

'I remember you now.' Charred skin crinkled around Marion's hand. '*Tell* me . . .'

Marion met the woman's dimming gaze. 'Yes,' she said, 'I'm Marion Price.' A gathering murmur swept back through the crowd.

'Ahh . . .' Once more, and yet more impossibly, the Beetle Lady smiled. 'I *knew* you'd come. Now . . .' She breathed. 'Now listen, listen, listen . . .'

Marion leaned closer, but the Beetle Lady said nothing more.

They buried the remains of the woman who had once been Doctress Foot in the same clearing in which she had died, beneath a rough cairn over which were laid objects which the followers had collected from around Einfell to commemorate her. Shortly after, the clouds darkened and it began to rain.

People might look strangely at Marion now, but didn't question her commands as the wagons were stocked and piled and they moved off into the gathering downpour towards Einfell's gates. After all, she was Marion Price, and she had come to the followers in their time of greatest need, just as the Beetle Lady had prophesied. Still, it was plain they resented this rain. And how far was it to this place called Invercombe? Marion would have guessed less than five miles, and she was unavoidably near the front of the procession now; she had no choice but to lead. *It's her . . . Look, those hands. That face . . .* Dripping fingers reaching to touch. Eyes seeking and then avoiding her gaze. The ridiculous hope. Ma-ri-on. It was like the burns wards. It was like that ball in Bristol. It was everything she'd fled to escape. But, as the wild hedgerows dripped and the drums rattled and the voices chanted and rusted chains and signs of prohibition swung and creaked, it sometimes seemed to Marion as she trudged at the head of this steaming, shining procession that even the boom and hiss of the wind and the rain spoke the same three syllables of her name.

XII

Ralph had watched Marion all morning. She was all the followers had left now that the Beetle Lady had died, and their numbers had swelled remarkably. Not that he was up to doing a precise job of counting, but even now, struggling across muddied fields pushing prams and dragging sacks laden with their possessions, more were arriving. A large enough group, certainly, to attract attention, but nothing like enough, for all its guns and drums, to do a satisfactory job of defending itself against the forces of the East or West.

Inky clouds roiled, growing, changing. It seemed as if they could walk for ever across this teeming landscape. Then suddenly ahead, shining local slate topknotted with wildly waving weeds, the walls and the gatehouse of Invercombe's estate emerged from the rain. As if by huge hands, the gates had been unhinged and twisted aside. The followers hung back, for this, surely, was the place of which the Beetle Lady had spoken. A gateway into summer—the place beyond Einfell—beautiful beyond all describing—where the light of truth blazed. But the wind shrieked more loudly, and the followers moaned and cowered as hats and umbrellas wafted towards the churning sky.

'It's plainly ridiculous,' Marion said, hunching over to Ralph as the crowds shivered and circled. 'Shelter, at Invercombe! The

place is dangerous. My father *died* from what happened there.
There's probably raw aether—'

'No one knows what Invercombe's like now, Marion—unless
the Beetle Lady really did get here, and who knows what she did
or didn't see . . .'

Ralph lost track of Marion as the followers shouldered by him
and began to push impatiently on through Invercombe's gates.
It was mid-afternoon. Wet darkness would soon be falling.
Perhaps they really would find better shelter within the valley,
he reasoned as he trudged with them, frozen and drenched.
But it seemed unlikely. The willows along the estate road ges-
ticulated wildly. Sodden flocks of leaves surged. Squinting, he
tried to catch sight of the weathertop, but all he saw beneath
his dripping eyebrows were more swirls of mottled grey. He'd
been too feverish to notice this road into Invercombe when
he'd first come in that car from Bristol with his mother, and afterwards he'd been too preoccupied. A thundercrack boomed,
bringing, impossible though it seemed, an even stronger surge
of rain.

He stared at his blued hands, then down at his muddied
clothes. It was still incredibly cold, although the wind was
coming less regularly now, playfully ambushing him, then
dancing away with laughing whoops. Several times, he almost
fell. Crawling through these puddles would have been easier.
Lying down in them would have been easier still. But he knew
that he'd be trampled in the followers' wake if he did. It was
all that kept him walking. And at least the thunder was fading,
and with it the wind and the rain. He laughed out loud, to think
that the hope of shelter might actually be true. As always, the
Doctress Foot had been right. The trees swayed and glittered.
Here was the very last hook of the road which wound down
into the valley of Invercombe, and there ahead, shining against
a clearing patch of sunset, was the weathertop.

This was the south plantation. There were the orchards and
the citrus grove. Not that it wasn't winter here as well. Not
that darkness wasn't falling. Not that things hadn't changed.
But still, this *was* the place. The house was unlit, but somehow
waiting as the followers ahead of him waded the slopes of undergrowth towards the bowl of the valley in a fanning grey

wave. Ralph stumbled and fell with them. More warning signs and prohibitions against trespass had been erected around the main courtyard beside the stables, and its gravelled space was occupied by several sheds and the rusty arms of an aether engine. People were milling, pointing, exclaiming in the thinning evening. He heard Marion's voice. She was blocking the chained front entrance, telling people that Invercombe wasn't safe, that they must go no further, that beneath the foundations of this house and out into the cove beyond there had been a huge spillage of aether. For now at least, and although there was much grumbling, they were doing as she said. Perhaps, but only for tonight, they might sleep in these grim old sheds. But the atmosphere was uncertain. For why had they come so far, if it wasn't for this place which the Beetle Lady had promised? And how could this woman who claimed to be Marion Price now be telling them they couldn't enter this fine and beautiful house if she really was who she said? A gun sounded in the falling darkness. The rumour was passing that there were strange creatures out in the gardens. Monsters, even. There were gasps, hand-clutchings. Ralph had seen such situations when hope and disappointment collided in the times of unrest which had preceded this war. Things could easily grow dangerous.

'We can't just let them go in there, Ralph,' Marion shouted to him as he forced his way through to her. 'These signs are your own guild's. *You* tell them . . . !'

'They'd take no notice of me, Marion.'

She nodded her head, but it was in frustration rather than in agreement. Fires were being lit from stuff plundered from the courtyard. Figures and flames leaped across the high walls of Invercombe. '*I'll* go inside, Ralph. If I tell them what it's like, they might just believe me. After all, wasn't all this work done to make the house habitable again?'

'No one cared about the house—it was done to reclaim the raw aether. And who knows how much is left.' The door, Ralph noticed, was already ajar beneath its antique lintel. There was even a suggestion of the scuff of footsteps amid the grit and dust. 'Marion, you *can't* go in there. Haven't you just been telling these people that it could be dangerous?'

'Then who does?'

Ralph took a slow breath. 'The house belongs to my guild, Marion. And look at me, what have I got to lose?'

A torch, its bulb and batteries still working, was found in one of the sheds. There were contoured plans which showed Invercombe's familiar outlines overlain with dense swirls of magics, although, as other followers clustered helpfully around him bearing useless logbooks and tea rosters and pre-war calendars, he had little idea of how to make sense of any of them. Still, he felt an affinity for these departed guildsmen. Just how much aether was left? Enough, certainly, he thought grimly as something black and figure-like danced towards him from a clustering, excited group, for the men to need to wear rubberised suits whilst they worked in there. The outfit stank as if it had been worn through many shifts, but he supposed that he had little choice but to pull the thing on, if only for the sake of show, and then to submit to the added weight of its fishtank helmet. The supporting brass collar dug across the bones of his shoulders. Its angled glass presented a fractured version of the world. The filters were old, as well. Each breath was a musty weight. Someone, perhaps a guildsworker who had once used such things, then found an aethometer amid the ransacked equipment. Rectangular, knurled, glass-faced, about twice the size of a cigarette packet, its pointer gave a lazy twitch in its bath of mercury—still low, still safe—as Ralph studied it in his gloved hands. This was hardly how he'd imagined re-entering Invercombe, but it certainly felt like some kind of dream.

Fumbling with the torch, he unhooked the last chain with his insensible fingertips and pushed open the door into Invercombe's great hall. The hazily penetrating beam glinted across dusty parquet. The ceiling had held, although there were some signs of damp. He clumped forward. As his beam lingered on the paintings, he saw that many of them were hung upside down, and then that pickling jars and razor shells had been placed along the marble dressers where fine Cathay vases had once stood. Guildsmen's humour, he supposed. Shivering, alternately hot and cold inside the clammy embrace of his suit, he laboured on.

Everywhere, these slight rearrangements. Flashing the

torch back towards the ceiling, he saw that the lightbulbs had all been neatly removed. But perhaps that was also the aether workers—and it was better, certainly, to concentrate on practical considerations than to worry about ghosts and uncertainties. That way, the library, although, as if the sea itself had somehow risen this impossibly far, the carpet was strewn with rotting weed. This way, the west parlour and the peacock room. All surprisingly intact. He checked the aethometer. Still barely registering. Perhaps this place really might provide a haven for the followers.

He flickered the torch into each of the main ground-floor rooms, saw fine chairs he'd once sat on and longed to sit on again, although there were more pebbles and other bits of shore. He had a choice now of going up or down. He debated routes and possibilities. The sensation, as his head throbbed and he took the quick needy breaths which were all his lungs or the suit's filters seemed capable of achieving, was entirely familiar . . . He had no particular desire to investigate Invercombe's damp lower reaches, but if there was danger left in the place, that was surely where it would lie. And he could check the generators as well. It made every kind of sense.

A green service door lay to the left of the lavender room. A red warning triangle had been nailed to it. The oval of his torch dancing below him, he took the spiral stairs, then leaned to catch his breath against the long, arched corridor which led one way towards Steward Dunning's old office (*what chances*, part of him which he didn't want to listen to was muttering, *that she's still there?*) and the other various storerooms and to the next set of stairs. Narrower, these. Then gleams of damp, or possibly engine ice, although still not enough to cause concern. Funny, when by logic he should be hoping that it remained safely dark, that he should be wishing for light. He inspected the torch. Was it fading? He tumbled the last steps and landed in a sprawl.

This was the service level. He could tell, even in the cocoon of his helmet as he crawled himself back upright, that the generators were still turning. Their hum reached through his bones and the torch, as if encouraged by their presence, shone more brightly over their beetle cables and red flanks. *Yes yes yes yes* . . . He could even hear their song over the gasp of his own

breath. Then there came a clicking. Imagining footsteps, he
froze, held his breath. But the sound was familiar to him as
well. There, beyond the last fading needlepoint injunctions—
There's No Work Like Early Work—lay the reckoning engine,
still working on some seep of residual purpose and current. He
studied it in amazement. It, far less amazed, seemed to study
him. He picked his way on. More red triangles. Ralph had
never gone lower than this into Invercombe's catacombs, but
the barred metal gate which led towards Invercombe's sea caverns had been broken open, and the downturning tunnel beyond seemed to swallow the light of his torch, and yet gave off
a definite glow, which grew as he descended. He glanced at the
aethometer's needle. Still safe here, but considerably less so.
His feet skidded. He steadied himself. The roof, as he descended, gripping the ropes hung from rusty iron hoops in the
walls, rose and fell, dripping and glinting, then ascended into a
larger space. Unmistakably now, these were caverns carved by
the sea. A shifting mist shone in the beam of his torch. Still, the
meter was climbing. Who knew what tides and ravages had
been summoned to Clarence Cove? This—for the steps were
scummed and luminously green—was surely as far as he
needed to go. But Ralph's weariness was lost to curiosity in
this strange, sea-breathing place.

He entered the full breadth of a natural cavern which
opened to Clarence Cove. There was no need to check the
aethometer here. The tides pulsed with brilliant darkness. The
salt air glowed. He turned off the torch, which now only produced a useless fan of black. The aethered sea, darkly gleaming, booming, beating, rose and fell, and Ralph breathed with
it, and it breathed with him. Its froth was densely braided with
a wrack of weed and timber and many other leavings. Jewelled with chains and the bones and bodies of strange fish and
a scuttled ship's wreckage and fragments of terracotta, it rose
and broke. In a shuddering heave, the sea washed closer.
Against the dimmer glow of the night beyond, climbing in
scaffolding, riding on buoys and pontoons, bobbing on chains,
scrambling out across rocks on concrete and rail as if attempting to escape, were the structures with which the aether workers had attempted to tame this place. But they had failed, and
the remains of their work now sprouted mocking ornaments of

cuckoo-growth. The sea laughed with the jagged purple mouths of giant mussels, it streamed with glowing fronds of bladderwrack. Glad at last for the discomforts of his suit, Ralph turned back to the steps, but then something seemed to move far up in the cave. Were those eyes, or pebbles in a jellyfish? Was that phosphorous hair, or merely rotting weed? And what exactly had the followers claimed they'd seen out in Invercombe's gardens? But the panes of his helmet were misting, and this place was simply starting to play on his mind.

Angling down the torch until its light finally brightened, he felt his way back up through the bowels of the house. This climb seemed far longer than the descent. He coughed, hacked. Part of him longed to rip this damn helmet off and *breathe*, but at the same time it seemed ridiculous to risk exposure now when so little of the house was left to be seen. The impossible purpose of the generators and the reckoning engine ticked and clicked and lingered with that half-seen face as he climbed the service stairs, and then leaned through a final green door, and shuffled towards the best stairs, which soared above him, a veritable waterfall of carpet. He coughed. A spray of blood coated the inside of his visor.

This was just like old times, and worse. At last, crawling on all fours, his consciousness floating on the dimming beam of his torch, he gained the landing. He thought of checking his aethometer, but realised he'd left it far away at the foot of the stairs, which he doubted if he would ever have the strength to return to. But all that was left, all he owed himself and the rest of the followers, was to prove that Invercombe was safe. Then, he could rest. Ralph's helmet clanged a wall as he stumbled along the main landing. He hesitated, swaying beneath its weight. All the forgotten horrors of his old fevers, their bland unreasoning logic, the hot sense of conflicts which he alone could resolve, were returning. Then, but certain this time as the ache of his breathing, something moved ahead.

This same corridor with these same pictures. Dustier, yes. And distorted through the blood-mottled panes of his helmet. But still these same gilt-framed pictures of flowers on the walls, even if they were strung with scraps of weed now and ornamented with old bits of lemon rind, of all things, and then hung upside down. Yes, this was the place it had always been and something, quite beyond doubt, had moved ahead of him. A shape, which, in its departing, had turned the same corner which he must turn, which he knew would lead to his own room just as it always had, and still did in his dreams. Nothing had changed. Not even him. He moved forward. His torch had paled, and there was no aether here, but the night sky outside had cleared to admit a rising moon which danced and shifted amid the mullions. A dresser shone. His shadow moved across the walls and the house seemed to move with him. This was like that moment before that meal, when he'd been wandering the gardens. The thing about ghosts, he'd realised then, was that you only saw them afterwards. What you saw at the time was simply reality.

Ralph, as he moved on towards his old room, wondered why he'd clung to logic for so long. After all the things which had unravelled, why should he have ever expected this house to make any sense to him? It wasn't about danger or not danger. It wasn't about the crowds or the Beetle Lady or this war or even Marion Price . . . The door to his room swung shut ahead of him. This was far too much, but then again, it was all to be expected. Time was running backwards, and many spells had been cast, and many seas had risen, and he fully expected, as he gripped the handle in his gauntlet hand and twisted it, to discover his younger self lying there in the bed in the grip of a fever through which the rest of his life had been lived. The fleeting sense of meaning, the heavy heat, the restless purpose, all seemed entirely right. Perhaps logic did exist within a final core of meaninglessness. And perhaps this was it.

His old bedroom, in the moonlight, was more than ever an expression of all the life of the sea which, he smiled to realise, he'd been the first person to bring to it. But the rocks and the leavings of the strand had multiplied, and been loosely strewn and returned to their natural randomness in the process. Even through his helmet, he could smell the rot of weed. His throat whistled and groaned. He dropped the useless torch. There, before him, dimly illuminated, blue-lipped and ghastly pale, floated a face.

'What *are* you?' he heard himself ask.

The face tilted. It smiled queerly. Even more odd was the way the look of it reminded him of Marion, or his own features in a mirror. Not, at least, a face of pebbles and fishscales, but then he saw that many other things, seemingly naked yet made partly of old leaf or rusted metal or naked bone, were moving at the far corners of his lost room and the far, dim edges of his helmet.

'I know who you are.' *Know who you are . . . who you . . . are . . .* Echoes of the words rode on Ralph's thoughts. He coughed and shook his head. The room twirled dizzily. The creatures which now stirred in the strands of moonlit darkness were one thing, but, for all his sea-filth and ragged attire, the one who spoke lispingly to him was unmistakably human. It reached out. Dimly, Ralph felt a finger indent the rubberised fabric which covered his chest. 'You're one of *us*. You're the Diving Man.' The spitting voice and the rustles of meaning which tumbled afterwards gave every word an extra emphasis. 'And these are the Shadow Folk. This is our home.'

It seemed pointless to disagree, and it had begun to strike Ralph that, for all this lad's wild manner and the bizarre other things which filled the room's shadows—changelings, he was beginning to guess—his own appearance, suited, and with bloodstained glass fracturing what they could see of his face, was probably at least as strange, and as frightening. He tore at his gloves and thumbed the clasps to release his helmet. Ripe, rancid, blessed air broke over him. 'And who are you?' he asked with what was left of his voice.

'I'm Klade,' the lad replied. 'I'm the Bonny Boy. I'm what Marion Price made. I went to Einfell until it grew empty and then I came here. I'm part of the War Effort.'

XIII

Some of the braver or more foolhardy followers had already entered Invercombe's halls that night despite all Marion's attempts at prohibition, and it was one of them, a buttoneer from Penzance, who found Ralph Meynell, and the wild lad called Klade who was with him. Ragged and wet and proud and exhausted, the rest of the followers took Ralph's survival as a signal that this house was entirely safe. After all, why had they come this far otherwise? And wasn't this, they exclaimed as they wandered, amazed, amid the halls and state rooms and the waiting bedrooms and bounteous kitchens, exactly what the Beetle Lady had promised? Candles were found and lanterns were lit and fires were set in grates. Boots were taken off and feet were ruefully inspected and massaged amid the spreading light and heat. The changed, the monsters, whatever threat there ever had been which might have existed here, had certainly fled. And good riddance. And who cared? Everywhere that night and on into the coming dawn, as the followers filled out through the house and faces were washed and fresh linen was found and instantly dirtied and people milled and talked and laughed in all the ways which their long journey had precluded and Invercombe's chimneys smoked for the first time in almost two decades, there were expressions of surprised recognition.

'Just like home.'

'*You* never lived in a place like this!'

'You know our *son* up in Nottingham?'

'Nottingham ain't where we used to live.'

'Where *is* this, anyway?'

'Look at the size of them chairs . . . !'

'Me, I could murder a fag.'

'Heard there's a box in that room with all the books. Nah, I think it's that way . . .'

'Place is a bloody maze.'

'Great, innit.'

'Just like home.'

'You know, I'm sure I've dreamed about this place.'

'I'm dreaming still . . .'

Everywhere, this constant happy babble of voices. There were families from Tipton and couples from Bracebridge and lonely men and absent lovers and the hunched, arthritic elderly, all reunited and re-joined, and Marion could almost feel that she was just another part of this as she settled the hunched creature who called himself Klade in Steward Dunning's old office at the far end of an unpromising low white corridor with its lines of framed injunctions, where she imagined they were unlikely to be disturbed. The lad was wild and itchy and wary. He stank, and she could tell right away from the way he looked about him and shifted his elbows in the creaking swivel chair that he was uncomfortable in small, enclosed spaces. And the layout of the room meant that she had no choice but to sit like some figure of authority on the opposite side of the desk whilst all around her in the lanternlight, in that kidney bean paperweight and the old diary still open on the page for that last day of her and Ralph's planned escape, her own lost past screamed out to her. In every way, she had made a bad choice of place.

'Ralph, the man who found you here, says you might be—'

'Who *are* you?' he hissed back through bared teeth in an accent she'd never previously heard.

The question, simple though it sounded, made Marion pause. She certainly wasn't the creature whose name the people were still shouting and banging out on pots as they ransacked— and this was something she would have to take in hand, it was certain no one else would—this house. But still, she had to say it. 'I'm Marion Price. I think I might be your—'

'You're not! You can't be . . . !'

He looked a little like the younger Ralph, she had to admit, but perhaps it was no more than the resemblance she saw etched in the pain of many other faces.

'I'm sorry, but I am. It's just that people have . . . the wrong impression of me.'

He leaned further back from her, still blackly tensed as steel. His chair creaked. But at least he hadn't attempted to escape. Or attack her.

'Were you really raised at Einfell?'

He nodded, or at least gave his chin a jerk. *He doesn't look old or young*, she thought. *He doesn't look anything—he's like the soldiers you can heal in the flesh but who still remain wounded. He's something only this war could have made* . . .

'Do you know where you were born, Klade?'

'It was . . .' He licked his lips. He tended to spit as he spoke, and dampness flecked her face. 'A place called Saint Alphage's. That was what Silus took me to in Bristol away from the song and showed me.'

'Silus?' *Song?*

'He was . . .' The lad gestured vaguely. Like everything else he did, the movement was slightly off key. As if he'd learned to be human at one remove. Which she supposed would be the case . . .

'Was?'

'He and Ida raised me.'

Signatures on the papers she'd seen back in Saint Alphage's, although she couldn't remember the names. But, with a falling sense of horror, Marion realised that Klade must have stared through those same iron gates.

'Ida's dead,' he muttered. 'I don't know about Silus and that man who said he was my father won't say . . .'

Which father? When? Did he mean Ralph, or the changelings? 'I'm sorry.' How many more times was she going to have to say that? Klade, with his reddened eyes and spiked dirty hair and murmuring hands and impossible voice and name, was more like a grown version of that thing she had

discovered under the sink at Saint Alfies than the child she'd
once dreamed she might have had.

'What I mean is, I never *knew* about you, Klade. When I
did . . . When I did, I'd have come this way sooner. But I'd
learned then that you might have been sent to Einfell. And part
of me feared that—'

'*What*?' His hands skittered on bright black metal. The bolt
clicked back in an aethered glow. His eyes suddenly blazed.
'That I'd be one of the chosen, a changeling?'

'I didn't know, Klade.'

'Well, I am. Look.' His fingers scrabbled ferociously at his
sleeves. Rotting threads ripped. He shoved out his left wrist
across Steward Dunning's desk towards her. 'Go on! Look!
Feel!'

Touching her son's flesh for the first time, conscious of its
smoothness and warmth, the indentations of skin and bone,
Marion could tell that he bore no Mark. 'All that means is—'

'What it means is that I'm like bastard Blossom. I'm like
that fucking ravener out there. I'm the bloody moon in the sky
over Inver-something. Now fuck off and leave me alone . . .'

Marion had dealt with too many suffering patients not to
know when to comply with this simplest of human requests.
Standing up slowly, moving as unthreateningly as she could
around the desk, and leaving the door half open, she walked
and then ran along the corridor and up into Invercombe's
main rooms. She didn't know what to think. She didn't know
how she felt. After all, Klade and the few changelings which
had now seemingly fled Invercombe had used as this place a
haven. And look at it now.

In the beginnings of grey daylight, the noisy chaos stilled
as she moved through it. Eyes followed her. Prayers and whispers were made, and in many ways the situation of being in
this place wasn't so unfamiliar. A house requisitioned and in
need of order; in need, above all, of someone to take the lead.
For all that she had seen and experienced, the sense of being
here, of being back at Invercombe, suddenly broke over her.
For she was alive, and so was her son, and she could sense the
power of this house which had delivered him to her stretching
out towards her in lazy welcome like the paw of a yawning
lion. After all, there was so much that needed *doing* here.

Grime on the windows. Leaking pipes. Tiles in need of reset-
ting. Statues fallen from their pedestals. Blocked sluices and
perished valves. The gardens gone entirely wild. And dust
everywhere. And half the sheets and towels filthy already. And
this ridiculous shore-detritus. And beds unhygenically unmade. And mess. And grime. All to be fought against. What
would Cissy Dunning have said? Work to be organised and
prioritised. Order to be found and then maintained. After all,
these people believed she was Marion Price, even if Klade
didn't, and it was time, Marion decided, as she rang the dinner
gong in the hall and climbed on a chair and the people gathered around to listen, to prove to him and the world who she
really was.

XIV

In the days and nights which followed, guildsmen and women returned to their old labours. There was enough work in Invercombe for a battalion of lost trades. From electricians to stonemasons to chefs to the common washers, there were few who couldn't apply their skills. Disputes about guild demarcation arose which only Marion Price could settle, and she couldn't be everywhere, hard though she tried. But still the work went on, and still, and more certainly now, they sang her name.

Flues were cleaned. Fires were lit. Boilers filled and leaked. The house rang and creaked and steamed, and lightbulbs were found and set wildly ablaze against the dull midday as the generators were reapplied to the business of powering the house. Clothes were washed, bleached and hung up in dripping fronds. And everywhere, in this bustling frenzy, people were singing as they washed and wiped and dusted until the windows steamed grey-white. Klade sought solace in the wild gardens and the sharp taste of strewn windfall apples and rotting lemons amid the passing sweeps of rain. The lush and noisy house which shone out at the centre of it all, where Outsiders ate, and talked, and bustled, and walked arm in arm, mouth to mouth, hand in hand, was no longer the place of refuge which had once welcomed him. The Shadow Ones had fled with the followers' arrival to Inver-something's furthest caves and caverns which even he couldn't reach. Amid all this touching, shouting, feeding, dancing, cleaning, shining, breaking, bothering, eating which went on day and night, he was entirely alone. Klade would have blocked his ears, but there was no escaping this song of the Outsiders.

There was to be a Dance on the third night. Dance was what they called it, although as far as Klade could tell these Outsiders had never stopped jigging and dancing and singing to the orders of the woman who called herself Marion Price since they'd got here. It was too much for him, and once more he had to go outside into the welcoming dark through the big main door where the balehound which now stood guard growled at him. Klade snarled back. Inver-something had been everything he'd hoped for, a haven of Sweetness and Home, but now nothing, nothing, nothing was the same . . .

Voices. Faces in the sharp glow from the windows. Succumbing to old instincts, Klade cowered and hid.

'Breathe that air.'

'So *mild* here. Could almost be spring coming again.'

'Finest drop of cider I ever tasted.'

'You'd drink your grandma's piss to get yourself tipsy.'

'I would, that.'

'Know what they say—well, it ain't exactly *her* that used to live here, but her sister.'

'Makes sense that she did as well, then, dunnit?'

'Nah, nah. Marion Price was brought up in Einfell by the goblins, see. That's why they're here, hiding in the walls . . .'

A long pause.

'They say it'll all be over by Christmas.'

'Can't be long then, can it?' A woman's laughter. Low and liquid.

Klade watched the Outsiders entwine. And the Singing and the Dancing went on, and there seemed to be no escape from it, not even outside, for here was the ravener, being coaxed to roll a barrel up from the cellars by two young Outsiders who briefly stopped laughing when they saw Klade. He wandered further afield. He found a quieter place as it began to rain, and squatted there, listening to its ticking dripping as the singing house glowed out at him through the flashing, waving leaves.

But at least, if he hummed to himself, or if he opened his mouth and screamed as he drank the acrid, chilly rain which rattled over his skull and let the truer, deeper song flow over him in chilly rivulets, he couldn't hear it.

Chill and hunger drove Klade back to the house when the night was ending. He'd expected mess and stink, but those Outsiders who hadn't been up late Dancing had arisen early and were cheerily and noisily cleaning and washing and sweeping and polishing and putting things away as the first cloud-churned light threaded through the rooms. Klade's skin tingled. His nose itched in an inside place he couldn't reach. At least the Outsiders quietened a little when they saw him. But the pause was only brief, and Inver-something shone and bustled like a tune you hated but couldn't shake, and the gleam of all the corridors and surfaces hurt his head and eyes.

'Pass us that rag.'

'Right and proper homely, eh?'

But Klade had never come across anywhere more unHomely than Inver-something was now as, still dripping from the rain, and getting what he knew were called *black looks* from other Outsider faces even as they sang out his supposed mother's name, he shuffled over sneezily soft carpets which had lost their comforting scree of shell and weed. More and more of this place was being lost to him even as it was reclaimed. Did Outsiders ever really live in places such as this? How tall would anyone have to be to need ceilings this high? And all these rooms for talking, eating, sleeping. Studies for Studying in. Drawing rooms for Drawing. And now, charging and humming towards him, trailing its wire like the tail of a kingrat and piloted by a woman in a scarf and a pinny who was hummingly joining in its song, came a machine which sucked up what little there was left of the floor's precious dust. Klade fled.

An enormous table gloomed and gleamed like a lake on a windless day in an otherwise empty room. Had he been in here before? It was hard to tell, with everything so changed, but Klade saw something resembling himself shifting within the shine of the wood. More of him, or at least some darkly ragged creature which moved when he moved, was tilted in the endless glass picture frames. Even the windows, which had been wiped

of their mist, blazed back at him. He sneezed. He took a knife
from a rack where it lay blazing amid many others like so many
netted fish and used its point to dig a trail of non-shiningness
across the table. There. He loved the grating sound it made—
then, as if summoned by the noise, a portion of the room's
gleam extracted itself from behind a baroque chair and moved
towards him on elements of its legs. Part flesh, yes. Part real,
too. Part not, as well, although, as Fay grew close to him, Klade
noticed that she still had that lovely rocky, watery, foggy scent.
He had to smile, although he knew she wouldn't understand.

'I wasn't sure if you were still here,' he told her.

You haven't come looking for us, Klade.

He shrugged. Finding the Shadow Ones unless they wanted
to be found was like catching leaves in a gale. His eyes trailed
over Fay—what Fay had become. She was watery gleams, she
was spills of grey. Look hard enough, and you might perhaps
imagine the freshly changed creature he'd encountered in that
hot summer at the edge of the woods back in Einfell, but he'd
known from the first moment he'd encountered her here that
those moments, the good and the bad, were gone as if they had
never existed. That was the thing about the Shadow Ones. Each
second was an endless escape. Nothing ever lasted, or remained. Of course, they still had the changed remains of what
passed for their bodies, but they cared nothing for sustenance or
pain, and were happy to fade. Sometimes, when he first ran with
them in the last of autumn which had then still clung to Inver-
something, stuffing his mouth with fizzing windfalls of fruit
which at first made him happy and then made his head ache,
he'd felt the same. For he was Klade, and the song was like the
song of Einfell which he'd heard from the very first moment he
remembered opening his eyes. But it was bitter here as well, and
it was sweeter, and the Shadow Ones always slipped from him
no matter how hard he chased. Only at night, as the darknesses
grew colder and he sought shelter within this house which had
garlanded itself with signs and chains, did they come closer so
that they might feed on his dreams. The sea, still strange to him
in its scents and sighs, washed in on their singing tide, and the
room and the bed which he most frequented grew embroidered
with gorgeous decay. This, he knew now, was why Silus had
always warned him against the company of the Shadow Ones.

Not because of what they were, but because of what they made
you become. And the house had whispered with them in the
dark driftwood silences and the stirring of limbs which only
came close when his own grew languid and could no longer re-
spond. Sometimes, he saw this land not as a thing of days and
nights or shifterms or even seasons, but of a perpetual *something* which was too slow to be time at all, across which he and
the changed and the unchanged all crawled like the ants he'd
once crushed or popped into his mouth, just to feel their momentary tingle on his tongue, and were just as soon gone.

The Shadow Ones could, he knew, let you see in them what
they thought you wanted to see. For there was clothing or not
clothing on Fay, a mere mist if that was what you wanted, and
she seemed storm-wet. Still, the image of the Fay he'd once
thought he'd known, and beyond that the young girl from Bristol whom he'd longed for her to be, was stronger to him than all
these Outsiders who had come to destroy Inver-something with
all their neatness and noise. He watched as her hand, cauled in
grey-white netting, silvered as the fishy moon, moved towards
the table and the long scar which he had made. Whispering the
sweetest inward part of the song, she made it go away.

There.

'I'm sorry, Fay.'

Sorry for what? She tilted her head in the swishing light,
watchful and listening, although it didn't seem to be to him.
It doesn't count. It's just a table.

'For that day. When I tried to—'

'Aaahhh.' A real sound, or a stormbeat of wind against
glass. *I forgot . . .*

'I was young then. I didn't know . . .' He paused, licking
his lips, wondering what it was he hadn't known.

*It doesn't matter, Klade. Nothing matters in the way you think
it does. I'm surprised that's something you've never learned*.

'This place is full of Outsiders now, you know,' Klade informed her, as if she cared about such news.

*That day you were saying, Klade. That hot day. Yes, now I
remember. The thing is, Klade, I always was who I am now. I
didn't realise that Bristol was just a beautiful dream*.

He'd had these conversations before. They went round and
round in his head like the feeling which came after eating

wormed and mushy apples. But still, and just like the apples, it was hard to desist. 'I *told* you! I've been to Bristol—the munitions factories. It's not the place you showed me!'

Fay's laughter rang like glass. *But it doesn't mean it isn't real, Klade! The further I've got from Bristol, the more real it becomes. This house helps me—it listens. And I love the song of its windy seas.*

Outside, the vacuum cleaner was still snoring at the carpets as the small, loose sea-smelling and faintly reptilian shape which Fay had become reached the pearly approximation of her arm towards him.

Remember, Klade, how we used to touch . . .

Even though he was sure that Fay remembered nothing, he saw her ebony hair shining in that bedroom back in the dream of Bristol amid the pictures of Egypt and the night sounds of traffic. And brushing, brushing. Sparks and flickers of light. But the lantern shade by her mirror was threaded with gulls' feathers and the jars before her were fish eggs' empty purses, and the light swarmed and waved as the vacuum cleaner still gave its foggy moan.

I could be your undersea-lover, Klade. I could be your mermaid . . .

Klade, drawing back, gave a wild, room-spinning shake of his head.

Fay, more calmly now, more of what she was, simply regarded him.

You're fainter, Klade. I can hardly hear you. You really have changed since these Outsiders arrived. We thought you were one of us when we had the house to ourselves. I'm sorry, but now you've lost your song . . .

The Chosen, those who were *this* Chosen, were, Klade knew, long past disappointment or regret. But still, he sensed a sadness; perhaps it was his own.

'Don't say you're sorry, Fay.'

I'm never sad.

'Sad and sorry don't mean the same thing.'

Just words. You're using too many . . .

'I'm not . . .' But it was too late to correct her, for she was drawing away across the lush, shining room, and back behind that chair and on into the panelling. What did it matter, anyway, what Fay or anyone else thought he was? Chosen or not Chosen; Outsider—above all, he was simply Klade.

The busyness of the house went on. Even the gardens were being tidied, and bonfires swirled cheery red as Inversomething's wildness was put to flame.

'Sweet Elder! Nobody told me *you* were here.'

'Thought we'd lost you back at Cleeve . . .'

People kept touching each other. Hands and arms and lips.

'Klade?'

Klade jerked, expecting another of the Shadow Ones. But it was the man who said he was his father who came limp-staggering towards him across the terrace's clean wet paving.

'Ah *this*.' Briefly, he waved his walking stick. 'I'm old before my time. Fact is, Klade, I've got something I'd like to show you. Well, a couple of things, actually . . .'

The house gleamed. Its inside light drummed at Klade's eyes. 'We don't really need *that* in here, do we?' One hand still wheezing on his stick, the man reached with his other—which was nearly as translucent as Fay's—towards the knife Klade realised he still held in his hand. He felt a snarl in his throat as he drew back.

'The thing is, Klade . . .' Without the beard, the man's face was sterner and thinner and greyer. 'We've made a few rules. And one of them is, no guns or knives inside the house. Makes sense, Klade, if you think about it . . . ?' Klade relented to the cold, unprising fingers and let go of the knife. After all, what did he know?

The man was a slow mover. Not that this was a problem to Klade, who'd long been used to travelling with poor Ida. Down and down the stairs. In the falling tunnels, hollows, with their strung lights and the happy smell of damp into which he was being led, the man, between waiting and wheezing, his stick tapping, told Klade about things which were being done to, as he put it, *bring the old place back to life* . . .

A big machine lurked in an alcove near where the generators ground. The man said that it was called a reckoning engine, which was the pride of his own and many other guilds—which is perhaps the sort of thing, Klade, that you should know. This one was an early version, but still immensely clever. Could think a thousand things quicker than a mere human could think one, although of course it couldn't think for itself, which sounded to Klade, as the machine grinned its ceramic wheels at him, like the sort of nonsense only an Outsider or a Shadow One would say. Anyway, he knew what reckoning engines were. Hadn't he read enough newspapers? And he wondered as he watched the man haul himself around the whirring device in weary gasps if he really was his father, and if telling you things you already knew was what fathers were for.

'*This* is the spinet, a type of keyboard where we input data. And here we insert the punchcards. Maybe it's something you can try, Klade. I spent hours down here when I was even younger than you are. Marion and I had this theory about the way the world worked. And I hoped this machine could store and process all the data . . .'

'The Beetle Lady told me.'

'The *Beetle* Lady? But you don't know her, Klade. That must have been something you heard since we got here . . .'

They moved on. After the sound of the generators, it grew both quieter and louder.

'Hear that? Goes right down to the sea . . . This was the way I went . . .' The man waved his stick. '. . . when I first returned to the house. You've seen the ones—the ones who came here from Einfell? They seem to be hiding now, although they're still somewhere in the house. They seem to be using spaces behind the panelling and down in these caverns. Perhaps there are passages as well. But the funny thing is, no one's afraid of them. They're just *accepted*. Like the balehound and the ravener, I suppose. Although I know that's entirely different. Don't you think that's the most marvellous thing, Klade? The way people have learned to accept?'

Klade nodded. He'd avoided these depths, and had little experience of the sea, but great frothy breaths of it now came pouring into boomy spaces.

'Down there is Clarence Cove. But we really can't go much further without one of those suits I had on.' Leaning against the wet rock, the man hawked in breath. 'Beyond here, the aethometer readings are still much too high for safety.'

'A thumb eater?'

'Never mind—it's just a device. See where this stone goes under . . .' The man shuffled onwards, and the tunnel dropped close to their heads and darkened. Then, it brightened. They were inside a small cave lit by an opening into the sky. Two shining bottles were set in a rough alcove like the shrines Klade had seen plundered in churches.

'Now *these* . . .' His breath whistling like the air, the man picked one up. 'Are chalices of distilled aether. They must have been left here by the aetherworkers once they'd been extracted and refined from the mess below—forgotten, I suppose, although they're worth a great deal . . . What do you know about money, Klade?'

Klade shook his head. He'd liked the taste of the few pennies he'd found, but he knew that wasn't what the man who claimed he was his father meant. And he'd seen aether before— more than enough of it in the factories he and Ida had visited where they made her sing to machines when the bombs went wrong. There was song in the glowing thing he called a chalice, but it was hard and harsh. Wire across slate. A single steely note. Both purposeful and uncontrolled.

'Well, it's worth *a lot*.' Its light was in the man's eyes, and his chest was fluttering like a bird's. 'Surprising, really, that they left it here. See how it glows. Now. Watch . . .' He held it towards the cave's opening. For a moment, he looked like a Shadow One in its strange backwash. Then the light changed and ceased to be light at all. Darkness spilled around them. 'It's called wyrelight. By the way, you should never, *ever*, try to open one of these chalices, or ever approach anything which contains raw aether. That's what all those warning signs you must have seen are for. If it gets on or in you, too much of it, well—it can . . . What I mean is, it's *dangerous*, Klade. Even more dangerous than a knife or a gun. You understand that? But what I wanted to say . . .' Klade watched as the man reverently returned the chalice in its alcove of wet stone. 'What I *really* wanted to say, Klade, is that when you get out of here—when this war ends as it finally must—there's a place for you. When I say a *place*, I mean good proper work with decent pay. No matter what happens to me, Klade, you don't have to live the way that you have up until now.'

'As an Outsider, a follower?'

'Before that as well. Neither Marion nor I would ever have abandoned you if we'd known.'

'I had a better song.'

In the aether's wyrelight, something like the Outsider feeling which was called *exasperation* crossed the man's face. '*That* doesn't matter, Klade. What matters is that you no longer need feel alone. People matter to each other, Klade, and you matter to me.'

Klade listened. Klade nodded. Klade wondered why people always said 'Klade' more often when they were cross or annoyed. Even Silus had done that, back in the times of the Big House when he'd never felt alone. Still, he felt sorry for this man, who plainly wasn't well. So he decided to do the thing he had seen many of the other Outsiders doing, and opened his arms and moved towards him so that they could Hug-Sing-Dance.

'No, no, no, no . . .' The man almost dropped his stick in his scrabbling hurry to be away. 'I'm sorry Klade,' he said, half on his knees. 'I have this disease. You should never get too close to me . . .' Then he leaned to cough and retch, and wyrelight shone across the reddish spittle.

Klade found his way alone back up through the house. As always, there were shouts and singing. Food smells from the kitchens. Steam smells from the laundry. It was scarcely mid-day, but people were already singing-dancing-hugging-working fit to bust. He'd never realised just how restlessly active Outsiders were. Then another smell caught his nostrils, and he was drawn to it.

'Touched me. Did she touch you?'

''Course she did. How else d'you think she could do it?'

'Passed the time of day, she did, just like anyone else . . .'

'Could do with a wee trim yourself, mate . . .' A hand slapped Klade's shoulder as he shuffled down the corridor. He gave a snarl and backed away.

Marion Price was sweeping the floor of a small room with a single chair and a large, bright fire. She had a slow, absorbed expression on her face as she swished the broom back and forth. She didn't notice Klade for a long while as he stood there watching, and when she finally did, he saw the way she tried to make her shocked expression change.

'*There* you are . . .'

'I've been with the man.'

'The man—ah, Ralph. I'm glad he found you. Is he busy?'

'Everyone's busy.'

'I suppose they are.' Marion Price rested her chin over her hands on top of the broom and looked back at Klade with her dark, blue eyes. Whispering black and silver around her on the floor like wyrelit snow were great drifts of hair, and the smell of its burning was in the air. Her own hair had changed, certainly, for it hung straight and close, yet was long and clean enough now to sheen with light and sway towards her cheeks as she picked up a dustpan. He thought of Fay. There were crackles and flares as she tossed more of the hair she'd been gathering into the flames. 'And what else have you been doing?'

He shrugged, still looking at her.

'Well—you can sit down in this chair. You need your hair cut at least as much as anyone else I've seen.'

In a dream, Klade did as she said. She seemed to like to have him sitting in chairs. Not that he found them particularly comfortable, but he really didn't mind that much. And sitting here as she moved behind him, he didn't even feel quite so afraid. Perhaps he was beginning to understand better now why the Outsiders looked and talked as they did around Marion Price.

'I know our lives have been very different, Klade. But that's gone—it's in the past.'

'Ida used to sing to me.' He opened and shut his fingers in a vee. 'She cut my hair.'

'The song was how Ida spoke to you? She was the c—the one who looked after you at Einfell, wasn't she, Klade? The one you said you were with in the war, and who died. I'm so *sorry*, Klade—'

not sorry never sorry or sad

'—You must miss her.'

'I miss Blackcurrant Dream. I miss Cherry Cheer.'

'But they're just drinks, aren't they, Klade?' He jumped at a buzzing sound. 'Don't worry. It's a just a hair trimmer, so *do* sit still . . .' The buzzing grew louder, and he glimpsed the small, black and angry-looking machine before it burrowed shiveringly close to his ear. 'People have been coming back for the second time. Can you believe that, as if hair needs cutting twice!'

'They think you're Marion Price.'

She chuckled. 'You know what, Klade—I really don't mind that so much now. At least I'm doing something useful, or pretending I am, so why should I care?'

The buzzing came and went like a huge summer insect, and Marion Price came and went as well. He saw her arms, bared to the elbow where she'd rolled up her sleeves, where the skin was differently white, with pale blue veins which ran smooth on one wrist and whorled on the other around the scab of the thing which all Outsiders had which was called her Mark.

'You know, Klade, so I'm happy that you and Ralph have been able to get to know each other. All these years, he and I never knew . . .'

'That's what he says as well.'

The buzzing paused. Then, but to a subtly changed rhythm, it came again as Marion Price leaned close and then back from him, and he caught the sweetly bitter scent which came from beneath her arms. 'He's not well, Klade. Things . . . Well things between us were made complicated even before you were born. It's hard to explain, but I want you to know that we meant a great deal to each other.'

'And now?'

'We're different people, Klade.' Closer, busier than ever, the cutter buzzed around the back of his skull. 'We can't undo what's happened. But it's a miracle that we're all here together, don't you think?'

Always, Klade thought, that pause when the man called Ralph and the woman called Marion Price mentioned each other. And they didn't Love-Dance-Hug like many of the other Outsiders did, no matter what she said about how they had felt in some remote time before they'd abandoned him. But the cutter still hummed and his hair fell towards his shoulders and drifted down to touch his hands. Here, indeed, was so much of what he'd been missing. For the song was in this machine and the song was Marion Price as well, as she and her cutter hummed. The sound was clear and faint, held somewhere deep within yet spilling out as he watched the slight changes which came and went around the edges of her mouth. As she leaned close, bits of her were often all he could see. An arm, the side of her face, a quick sweep of her cutterless hand as she pushed her own hair back around an ear. The soft white push of her blouse as she leaned the shape of her body against him. Klade remembered Ida snip snipping in the Big House, the golden curls she'd remembered falling in a different life. He felt light-headed. He really didn't want this to end.

'There.' Marion Price stepped back and tilted her head, and he saw her full face in the firelight, and the lovely fall of her hair. There were, he now noticed, tiny Shadow One slivers of grey in it. 'We haven't finished yet.' She laid her hands on his shoulders as he moved to get up. 'What about this . . . ?' Her fingers stroked his face. 'I guess you've never shaved, eh?'

Klade listened to a tinkling rush as something was filled with water, and he felt the weight of a towel, cool and clean-scented, across his shoulders. Then she was before him again, bearing a steaming, blue-rimmed enamel bowl.

'Hold this for me. Try not to shiver.' Scraping over a stool, sitting before him, she swirled up white billows of lather with a big brush and began to paint them over his face. The stuff smelled of new paint and flowers. It tingled, and corners of it crept into his vision like the edges of clouds. 'Tilt your head.' Her fingers touched his chin, and the brush went up and down. 'Now you need to sit *extra* still . . .'

Klade felt that he was beginning to understand this newly discovered Outsider obsession with tidiness. After all, what Marion Price was doing to him was similar to what had been done to the entire house, with all the shining cleaning brushing singing humming touching. No wonder the house felt so alive. No wonder he felt so alive himself. Then, alarmingly, she produced a long, sharp knife.

'You can't do that. The man called Ralph says—'

'Even stiller now . . .'

The knife hovered, glinting with the image of his own mouth and nose.

'Not so tense. Just let out a *long* breath . . .'

A soft pull-tug. Enamel tinged. Then the knife came again, and the air felt cooler against his face, but edged with flickers of firelight and the touch of Marion Price's breath.

'I always think it's like carving a statue. *These* are the kind of jobs I used to enjoy doing . . .' Her tongue prodded itself from her lips. The blade gave a final flourish. '. . . when people would just let me get on with simply being a nurse. These times are precious, Klade. Here and now. The war hasn't ended. Nothing's really changed. And I'm not the person these people think I am, much though I sometimes wish I was . . .'

Klade could tell from the extraordinary new feeling which had spread across his face that the job was finished, but he sensed in the long breathing moment in which he and Marion Price regarded each other that they both wished it would go on. Then, raising and dropping her shoulders, she took a breath. 'Now . . .' It was a brisker voice. 'Just give your face a good rinse and wipe.'

Klade splashed himself with scummy water, then towelled what felt like someone else's face.

'You really need to take a proper wash next, Klade. There are plenty of bathrooms you can use. After that, I want you to burn every single bit of those old clothes. They're past washing, and there's plenty of better stuff. And I want you to use this on yourself.' She pressed a squeezy rubber bottle between his fingers. 'Use this powder everywhere, especially in the other places where you have hair.' She was leaning before him again, but her eyes were as stern and far away as the man's had been when he'd told him about not having a knife or a gun. 'Do you understand what I'm saying, Klade? Powder yourself *everywhere*. Otherwise, you'll never get rid of those infestations and scabs.' Then, her hand rested once more upon his shoulder. 'One last thing . . .'

She lifted something up. It was a picture frame, no, a proper mirror, which was something Klade usually avoided, although for a moment he thought he was a Shadow One, for the image which she held before him was extraordinarily faint.

'This steam . . .'

The mirror brightened as Marion Price squealed her fingers across the glass. Clear and sharp, and shocked and thin, a borrowed Outsider face, partly the man's and partly Marion Price's, stared back at Klade.

XV

Everything seemed so ordinary; it was entirely bizarre. Marion supposed she was like all the rest; taking refuge in old habits, returning to type—whatever type that really was. This was the third day since they had arrived at Invercombe, and the dream hadn't yet broken, although every second seemed blurred. The clocks had all been wound, and set to a stagger of hours which meant that the place rang and pinged and rattled whilst the wind of this perpetual storm whistled over the chimneys.

The hair cutting, the tending of minor wounds, had been her refuge, just as others had found comfort in coaxing the boilers or polishing the china, but she had spent the entire war telling people to do things, and she was Marion Price, and people obeyed her. This identity was something she had come to accept the inevitability of. *Someone* had to be in charge. And because the followers now somehow imagined that she and not the Beetle Lady had led them here, she was also regarded as the lady of the house. They might permit her to give them purgatives to free their innards of parasites, but it was also a necessary part of this strange formal dance which they were all performing that Marion Price slept alone in the best bedroom in the house, and was served food on silver service in the west parlour according to a menu which she was required to approve. After all, she supposed, resigning herself to having her shoes polished and her clothes laid out for her, the house had been designed for this kind of work, and these people would have it no other way, as they reverted to their old guilded hierarchies. But it couldn't last.

Ralph, too, was accorded a kind of status. In a way, he deserved it, and rumours of their past life together here had slipped into the mythology of the place. Poor Klade, though, hard to find and fleeing often as not when you did find him, was never thought of as their child. He certainly didn't go around claiming it, and the space of his presence seemed to lie between them as she and Ralph sat for dinner that evening at opposite ends of the long dining table. Tureens were borne to them by women dressed as maids and men attired as footmen. There were clumsinesses and spillages which cook and Cissy Dunning would have rolled their eyes at, but the job was done with a breathy attentiveness which Marion found touching, and the food, just as it had always been at Invercombe, was entirely delicious.

Far off in the candlelight, Ralph picked and fussed at his food. It was hard to be certain whether he was eating. When he did raise a forkful of food towards his mouth, his hands trembled so much that most of it tumbled back to the plate. Then he'd put down his cutlery with a clatter as if to disguise the sound he then made as he coughed into one of a succession of handkerchiefs he kept balled in his pockets. Marion's instincts were to cross the ridiculous space of white linen which separated them and spoon-feed him, but she held herself back. There was little that she or anyone else could really do for Ralph other than to allow him the dignity and sense of purpose he seemed to have found here. His face had thinned and sunken over the bones of his skull. The greyed and mottled hands which gripped and dropped the cutlery were those of a geriatric. And yet his eyes were bright, and he smiled and responded to the things she said with a quickness with sometimes reminded her of the Ralph of old. He was entirely rational, even if he was spending too much time either fiddling with that reckoning engine or studying the books in the library.

One course was removed. Another came in its place. There was wine as well from Invercombe's fine cellars. That, at

least, Ralph did seem to be ingesting—although the redness
around his lips might possibly be blood from his suppurating
lungs.

'I showed Klade what little's left of the aether today,' he
said, after dabbing his lips again. 'We talked about the life he
might eventually lead, or at least, I did. He seemed . . .'
He gave a rheumy chuckle. 'I think he was humouring me.
But at least I got the knife he was carrying around off him. I'm
really not sure he was safe with it.'

'I saw him as well. For the first time, he actually came to
me, which I suppose is something. He let me shave him and
cut his hair.'

'He must look very different.'

'He looks rather like you.'

Ralph pushed at the food. 'Amazing, isn't it,' he said eventually, 'how well everything is preserved? Part of me still
wonders if the readings are wrong, and we're all poisoning
ourselves with aether.' He coughed. Tinned asparagus dropped
from his fork. 'Klade worries me, Marion.'

'He worries me as well. The way he looks at you—
everything he says—it's never quite what you expect. But
who knows what he's been through? He certainly doesn't
talk about it. Or, if he does, we fail to understand . . .'

'Perhaps we'd be having this conversation anyway.'

'Anyway?'

'If you and I had . . .' Ralph fumbled again for his handkerchief, and Marion waited for him to subside. 'If you and I . . .
If we had . . .' Still, he couldn't finish.

'I think I know what you mean,' she said eventually.
'Klade's not at an age when parents are supposed to think that
their children are behaving in any proper way.'

'So—our children are always a disappointment to us?'

'You have other children, Ralph. You should know.' She
was being hard on him, she supposed, as she pushed aside her
plate. 'What I mean is—'

'No, Marion.' Ralph raised a thin nugatory hand. 'You're
almost right. But it's the other way around. Parents are certainly a disappointment to their children, but they're an even
bigger disappointment to themselves. That's the thing . . .'

Working back another cough, he took another hurried sip of the wine. 'The thing that's hardest to bear.'

More food came and went. More wine, as well. With it, Ralph brightened. Even across this long space of linen, she could almost feel the heat he gave off.

'The state of balance this house had managed to maintain is quite extraordinary,' he was saying. 'It really is as if the Beetle Lady was entirely right and it had been waiting for us. And Habitual Adaptation. You know, all the information we put in is still stored in that reckoning engine. You and me, even. And Klade as well. All of the scattered pieces of our lives have come back together here. Don't you think it's our duty to make the most of this chance?'

Marion nodded, although she wondered what particular chance it was that he meant.

'I do truly regret the things I turned my back on when I left here, Marion. I made wrong decisions. I know that now. Always did, I suppose. But the one thing that's left to me is this theory. The data was always there. We were far more thorough than we realised. We just lacked the skill to collate it properly. But thanks to all my training—which, by the way, I mostly hated—I have that now as well. Nothing's entirely wasted. You know, I'd given up believing in destiny. But I do now. And I want you to promise me something.'

'Promise?' She imagined he meant something to do with Klade. Ralph had odd ideas about his son becoming some ordinary guildsman—or more than ordinary, she supposed, seeing as Klade was of the Meynell clan, at least in his eyes.

'Oh . . .' Ralph, sensing her wariness, bared his loosening teeth and receding gums in an understanding smile. 'I simply mean that I'd like you to take whatever you can of my—our—work on Habitual Adaptation with you when you leave Invercombe. I'm not asking you to move mountains, Marion. My feeling is that the world will be more ready and receptive once this war has ended.'

'I'll do what I can.' No point in her protesting that he'd be able to do the job himself; telling lies wasn't how you helped the dying. 'But I really don't know what we'll be facing out there. Or how long any of this can last.'

The candleflames leaned. Even beneath the shelter of Invercombe's weathertop, was she the only person to feel the imminence of a gathering storm? But Ralph, like these half-maids and part-footmen who clumsily tinked glasses and chipped the edges of plates as they lumbered about in their ill-fitting uniforms, was borne along by this sham normality.

'I really do wish I had the energy to explore the gardens and get down to the shore, but the data's all here. There's the library, and there are climate records which have been automatically transcribed all these years, and those of the workmen who came to this place. The seasons here have certainly been most odd. These last few shifterms, it's actually been getting *warmer*.'

'The seasons can't turn backwards though, can they?'

'You can't have summer after autumn, if that's what you mean.'

Somewhere in the house, a clock shivered silvery bells. 'All this power,' Marion said, 'all this aether. What *is* in control?'

Ralph shrugged his coathanger shoulders. 'I don't know. Although . . .'

'Although what?'

'I've looked at some of the records. It's there in the reckoning engine as well, as a sort of shadow. This place wasn't abandoned by the aether workers because of the war. They left before that. And then there was a huge surge. Most of the aether they'd re-purified and was seemingly left unaccounted was exhausted in one single rush.' He fell quiet.

'So? What happened?'

'It was . . .' Ralph didn't cough, but his hands closed around his latest handkerchief. 'It was on the day of the Falling. The day of the destruction of the Dockland Exchange.'

'And no one has ever traced it to here?'

Ralph shook his head. 'Invercombe was the private property of my guild. And by then, everyone had left. So there were no witnesses. Attempts to reclaim the remaining aether had already been deemed too costly and dangerous to be practical.'

'Deemed by whom?'

'My mother has always taken responsibility for major de-

cisions about the running of the estates of the Telegraphers'
Guild.' His fingers balled and unballed the handkerchief. 'Her
authorisation's the last thing on the files . . .'

After the meal had ended, Ralph made noises that he would
follow Marion as she headed up the best stairs, then hung
back as if gaining his energies as he leaned beside the curling
balustrade. She knew that he would probably spend the night
working and sleeping down by the reckoning engine. That
was, if he slept at all. The bedroom in which he had spent that
lost summer was still nominally his, but it was a place he
avoided even now that it had been cleaned and aired of all the
stench and sea-wreckage.

A fire shone warmly over the wide, tautly made bed in her
own room. The curtains had been drawn, although their fall was
less than perfect, and Marion felt compelled to cross the carpets
to straighten them, and they stirred towards her as she did so in
chill fingers of the wind which passed across Clarence Cove.
Looking down from here at night, you could still see a faint
glow. Like that ormolu clock frothed with golden birds, which
ticked although its hands never moved, Invercombe seemed
caught in some perpetual moment. She'd have been far happier
back in the servants' quarters where she'd once slept, but they
had been occupied by the people who had assumed her old
roles. And this was, indeed, a fine room.

So many of England's great houses had been ransacked by
the war. Marion herself, with a busy glee which she now understood better, had strode along their corridors demanding
that unhygienic tapestries, flurries of pointless furniture, be
instantly removed. But here she felt at home. She opened the
lacquered lid of the gramophone. She'd never possessed such
a device herself, although she could see how it would be a comfort to turn it on at the end of a difficult day. Marion smiled as
she watched the arm rise and fall towards the turntable with the
glide of good engineering. She was already humming to herself, although she had no idea of the record's tune, but the needle skidded, and what came out was a crackling howl. For some
reason, the machine was playing backwards. She turned it
quickly off.

She undressed, guarded the fire, lay down. The curtains

stirred. The sound of the gramophone still turned in her head, but when the ormolu clock finally chimed, it joined seamlessly with her dreams.

Next morning, she was roused by breakfast on a tray. The curtains were drawn for her, and sea-driven rain swept at the windows as sunlight came and went. It was already nine o'clock. Marion had rarely slept this late, although, as she poured herself a third cup of tea and pondered another slice of toast, she couldn't help wondering why.

Invercombe could run itself, and the minor dilemmas which were put to her as she toured the house were just part of the ritual. She approved lunch from the menu which had been prepared by a guildsman who had previously run a tearoom in Bath. She congratulated a master-launderer from Saint Austell on the whiteness of his sheets. She told herself that she should be accounting supplies and organising something more practical than this vapid role-playing. But she didn't. *Ma-ri-on*. Softer now, a murmur on lips rather than a full throated cry, the sound surged and whispered along the hurrying corridors where the threads of cook's framed mottoes had faded so irregularly beneath their glass panes that their dimmed shapes were more reminiscent of some obscure spell.

Finding herself at a loose end now that she had cut everyone's hair, the *bang bang bang* of a wind-thrown window drew her on into the peacock room. After she'd closed it, Marion noticed that one of the patterns in a row of Cathay plates was off true. As she straightened it, a plate further along the rail turned the opposite way. She tried again. Another plate, invisibly interlinked, turned. Shaking her head, but far less puzzled than she should have been, she headed back into the inner hall where the telephone booth gloomed beneath the best stairs, and found herself gazing at its bell. It seemed that it was the only one at Invercombe which hadn't yet rung.

Pulling on her old frayed coat, Marion went outside. It *was* getting warmer. Although the clouds still turned, flutters of greater brightness surged across the top terrace where the statues stood caught in mid-gesture as if they had just hopped on to their plinths. Huge seedheads rattled. Dry sweeps of sallow and lavender flailed. She thought of poor Ralph; the boy

who'd once craved logic was now a man talking of his destiny
to prove a theory which disproved destiny's existence. Thunder crackled. A blue flicker, a wave of sunlight, then a rolling
boom. Orchards on one side and the walled and parterre gardens on the other. She'd hoped that by wandering and not consciously looking for her son, she might bump into Klade; but
she remained alone, and the pools lay momentarily flat, filling
themselves with the sky then feathering in a fresh gust. There
were brighter colours in the more shaded hollows as evergreen
bushes shyly produced new leaves and fruit.

More and more of the gardens spread like a stormy rockpool below her as she climbed past the specimen trees and ascended Durnock Head. Was it possible that Alice Meynell
really had used Invercombe's unreclaimed aether to cast the
spell which had destroyed her own guildhall? Hadn't she been
there herself at the time of the Falling, and only narrowly survived? But she *had* survived, her guild had grown—and this
entire war could almost be traced to the Falling's aftermath.
For all the rumours, Marion thought as she climbed the temple
steps, no one would ever believe that the guild which had suffered most could have engineered it . . .

The wind boomed in the temple's domed white roof. It
thrummed the pillars like harpstrings, then swirled back in a
sudden clarity which revealed the Bristol Channel. Wales unrolled its mountains. A few ships were moving. There as ever,
crossing the water in proud, sun-dazzled leaps, was the Severn
Bridge. Little though she cared for feats of guild engineering,
Marion's heart ached to think that this graceful structure
would almost certainly be destroyed by one side or the other
in their final advance.

Boom boom boom. The wind, low and shrill, high and loud,
quiet and slow, called to her as she climbed from the temple.
Unavoidably, and although she knew that lunch would soon be
arriving in the west parlour, she was drawn towards the shore.
The waters of the seapool lapped and gurgled as she headed
through the gate, then out across the bare wet sand where the
tide teemed across great silver stretches of sheer, unrippled
light. She had come this way before the war began, and, then as
now, the ever-changing shore mocked her by seeming almost
the same. These rocks, these scents, these flaps of bladder-

wrack. Even before she had thought about it, she'd taken off
her shoes. Chill sand burrowed between her toes as she walked
amid the casts of lugworms and empty razor shells. Shrimps
darted for cover in rockpools as she stooped, and something in
her lower back tautened, but it was pleasant to dig her fingers
into the sand and find a cockle's ridged shell. Strewn oysters,
as well. Her fingers split one apart, and the creature inside
gulped and breathed. She felt saddened by her unthinking act,
but noticed something red under the glinting tongue, and
prised it out. For this was *Cardium glycymeris,* the beady oyster, and here was a blood pearl. She'd once pretended these
were money or jewels—sweets, when Denise was around.

Habitual Adaptation was, indeed, a clumsy name for something as harsh and beautiful as the process which Ralph sought
to define. It was founded on death and cared for nothing but re-
production and survival, yet could produce this shore, this
house, this world. No word, no phrase, could ever match something so wild and all-encompassing. Marion looked about her
and squeezed her toes through the tide's thickening rush. Then,
suddenly, there was a figure. Her skin chilled. For hadn't she
been re-enacting the very moment when Alice Meynell had
come to her? But this shape was smaller, and it was quick and
it was light. Laughing, too. Marion ran towards it before, in a
swirl of shade and sunlight, the mirage of her lost sister Sally
vanished.

This day had passed as inexplicably as days always did at Invercombe, and the sun was already setting as she re-entered
the valley. Up in the house, a fine teatime array would soon be
cooling itself, and she hadn't even seen Klade. Still, she turned
away from the house's lit windows and took the path which
wound up between the sighing fir trees towards the weathertop.
The building had a fragile glow, then turned ashy grey as the
light fell away.

Twisting the door's iron handle, she felt for lights. The great
energised pillar at the device's core rose up through the gantried
levels as they flooded on. There was a purposeful humming,
a sound like that of generators and reckoning engines, and
the sigh of telephone lines and the buzz of lightbulbs, but
differently tuned and refined; the song of this Age, or perhaps

of the one to come. The dials twitched, calibrations revolved, and the temptation was too great as she climbed the weather-top's levels not to try tweaking some of the controls. Imagine: to possess such power, to turn its winds against the stupidities of this war . . .

She glanced around. What was *that*? Probably nothing but her own presence caught in an angled display. Or perhaps it was one of the Shadow Ones. She curled her hands around the machine warmth of a delicately knurled knob, but the thing wouldn't budge. Neither would the next. They were all locked, frozen, but then she saw one of the big levers which she knew controlled barometric pressure slide upwards in a smooth glide. Another, in a slow reciprocal ballet, moved down. The weathertop hummed. Light slid on brass. More warily, but still fascinated, she climbed inside the whispering brass seashell.

It took a moment for her sight to adjust when she stepped out on to the weathertop's outer gantry, but it wasn't entirely dark. The Bristol Channel still shone. The Western landscape, in and beyond the valley, unrolled. It was hard to believe that it was near midwinter, for the wind which poured about her and sang across the railings was damply warm. The sky flick-ered. Perhaps a bigger storm was brewing, although hadn't Weatherman Ayres once told her that this was the safest place of all to be? She gazed across the landscape, amazed at how far she could see. That way lay the remains of Clyst, the lights of Luttrell, then Hockton beyond. She could almost be flying. And there was Einfell. But surely not, for the place was alight, alive. Blinking, looking north and east in the hope that her sight would adjust, Marion saw more movement there as well. There were campfires, the tiny jewelled necklaces of trains, the pale lanterns of tents. These, unmistakably, were the lights and shapes of two gathering armies. And there were sounds as well. Drums and flickering cannon, which the thunder glee-fully echoed.

She fled back through the weathertop and towards the house. Whatever would happen in this coming encirclement, she was certain the people here would look to her to guide them. But she had no idea what to do—not the faintest. Con-sulting Ralph with his illness and confused allegiances seemed laughable, but nevertheless she was heading in search of him across the inner hall when the bell above the telephone booth beneath the best stairs suddenly began to ring.

Breathless, disbelieving, still trailing the grubby threads of her old coat, Marion stopped and turned. Much as she disliked these devices, she knew it was her responsibility to answer whoever was calling Invercombe. She opened the door of the booth and sat down.

'Marion. I thought I might find you here.'

Unmistakably beautiful, entirely unchanged, Alice Meynell smiled at her from the mirror's far side.

XVI

The centre of the eye was an infinite falling, but it was a journey Alice no longer feared. There were stars inside that swirling blackness. There were empires of light.

To get to this place of final understanding had been the work of a lifetime. She saw that now as well. Her parents aboard that yacht had been sailing towards it even as they drowned. So had her aunt as she squirmed beneath the grey waters beside the falls of that ghastly house. The journey had continued in Lichfield, and walking Stow Pool with Cheryl Kettlethorpe, and in the smell of gas and damp and cats in the hovel they'd lived in, and the many guildsmen their thighs had enclosed. Then Dudley and pianos and the boredoms of parasoled Noshiftday afternoons in the castle grounds. And on to London, and the dream still unfinished, and Silus a staging post, just as Tom had finally turned out to be. Yes, even when she'd arrived as a greatgrandmistress, she'd still been travelling, and life and time had streamed past her, eroding flesh and bone—hope, even—yet leaving the vital truth, which was the journey itself, untouched. It had continued with Ralph, as well, in railway carriages which rocked endlessly into the feverish night, and his drowning gaze which she had always feared to meet, yet now she saw was just another part of the tunnel down which lay all knowledge.

And now she had reached the place which was known as Einfell, and nothing was behind her now, and everything waited ahead in Invercombe's falling dark. The matter of turning this winter campaign to her own will had been, even by the standards of her own machinations, an extraordinary task. She had called in debts, threats, liaisons which had lain dormant for so long that their holders had perhaps imagined they would never be brought to account. She had cajoled and argued for a fresh advance across the shining map which High Command in London tended, and then for it to be performed with a swiftness which went against all the rules of planning which they so worshipped. But that was the whole *point*, that was the whole *purpose*. This war would otherwise become an endless deathly dance. *That* was what she had had to make them see.

Alice knew she had only been partially successful. Yes, there had been consent to a diversionary advance. Indeed, she had been congratulated on the swiftness of her battalion's movements, which, just as she'd predicted, had taken the West entirely by surprise. But her orders and authorisations had been somewhat at variance to the actions she had finally performed, and that variance had expanded to a point where it could no longer be ignored. Alice had diverted far more of the East's resources towards this manoeuvre than had ever been approved, and had then failed to report back or secure supply lines to such an extent that even the grudging support she had once received from London was retracted. Of course, if she succeeded in reaching the channel and turning upstream towards Bristol she would be acclaimed as the Angel of the East. But Alice knew as well as the greatgrandmasters back in London that important practicalities had been neglected, and dubious deaths had occurred, and that her time, as the armies of the West finally wheeled themselves to face her in far greater numbers, was running out. But a military assault was the last thing she planned.

Everything had come together in these last few shifterms. Recently, she had submitted herself to the pull of the telephone's mirror with a recklessness which she had long denied herself. Even as her forces surged madly south and west, she had poured through the blackness at the core of her own eyes and ridden with the aether, soared on the light and the dark.

She saw, just as a hawk must see the landscape of its hunting ground, how all the conflicts and confusions of Europe and Thule had tightened into the particularities of English hopes and prejudices, and then knotted into war. Threads of it coiled like angry veins across the whole country, but ahead was the core, a heart, an ever-widening pupil, a nexus, waiting for her within Invercombe's stormy pillars of cloud.

She knew that the men who still executed her orders were close to mutiny. Only the fact that they were bound irresistibly to her by the wild onrush of this advance had led them this far. That, and the dumb respect for title and hierarchy which even now infused everything about the guilds. Alice, in recent shifterms, had insisted on conducting all serious business through the telephone so as to avoid the bother of meeting face to face. What, after all, was vision, but a random play of assumptions, lies and light? Only *she* saw the real truth, and that lay far inside the mirror, beyond the falling depths of her eyes.

Admittedly, Einfell's desertion had come as a slight disappointment, for she'd looked forward to re-encountering those pale lost shapes which Silus had once called the Shadow Ones, and with whom she now felt she shared some kind of identity. But, on second consideration, it all made sense, for her forces had recently been moving in the wake of some ragged procession, and the evidence of their passing lay here in smell of smoke and ordure, in the burned and ransacked buildings, and in MARION scrawled upon the walls. They, too, had moved on. For them, just as for her, this pale ruin of Einfell had only ever been a staging post. Invercombe always was the goal.

Dressed in the hooded cape she now affected, dragging the ageing bones which she soon planned to depart, Alice reached a clearing in the woods where many arrangements and orderings already seemed entirely satisfactory to her, although the wary men who followed her with their guns affected puzzlement and shock. Here, even, was a mound of new earth, which she had had dug up. Something in the slippery remains within their shroud of seething insects—a trace of identity or memory—had nagged at her. But no matter, for, having brought her own personal portable telephone booth with her this far—having, indeed, insisted on the protection and maintenance of a maximum bandwidth line back towards the East whilst arrangements for mere food and munitions lay in disorder—she now had a far more satisfactory alternative.

She remembered this small brick building from her previous visit to these woods in Einfell, and she had her tent and quarters erected over and beside it, and some dinner plates which she'd discovered nearby laid decoratively across the bare earth. Once finally established and alone and freed of the bother of acting the greatgrandmistress, she set her gramophone playing in the lovely swish of an out-groove. Dancing to the lit air's movements, inspecting and rearranging the burnt and bird-like corpses which scattered her enclave, she then set about the relatively simple business of re-energising the booth. The connection of this ancient station ran only to one place, but as the sappers and telegraphers unwound and restrung cables back towards the East, that would soon be corrected. And Invercombe, to begin with, was more than enough.

All Alice felt as the mirror finally cleared was a wondering sadness that she had ever troubled about how she appeared. Shrugging off her hood, wiping off what remained of her make-up with the balled-up fabric of her gloves, she regarded herself more closely. Haggard. Lividly pale. More like the dead, earthy thing they had recently dug up than the Alice Meynell of old. With a slight relaxing of some inner nerve, which was something she now could will and unwill with near total control, she could now actually see entirely through herself. She glanced towards her battered portmanteau and smiled. Too long, indeed, she had toyed with creams and potions and worries about the line of her chin. A mere effort of her undying will, and she could remake herself without all the bothersome practicalities of her notebook. Even as she studied herself, the strung, translucent flesh she saw in the mirror grew creamily smooth. Her near-lipless mouth plumped, softened, reddened, then parted in a slight smile over perfect teeth and a wetly playful hint of tongue. Cheekbones to die for. Jawline like the wings of a swan. Hair neither gold nor silver but that endlessly refined metal which the alchemists had long sought. She lowered the cloak further. She smiled as her hands touched the shining divide between her perfect breasts. Yes, she was Alice, Alice Meynell, even if all beauty was an illusion. She was the crackle of a gramophone and she was the song of a dying lover's sigh, and her eyes, in their dark core at the heart of her beauty, had never, ever changed. She fell through them. On into the blackness, and beyond.

Ah, Invercombe. Yes, Invercombe. Amazing, indeed, how beautifully perfect everything remained. The chimneys, the trees, the windows, the grounds. This place, in its power and mystery, had always called to her, but she, foolish Ulysses tied to the mast of her greatgrandmistress's duties, had for too long ignored its siren song. She had summoned the Falling from here, certainly, but she had remained far away for too long, over-fearful of the dullards who surrounded her.

She followed. She watched and waited. She made discoveries of things she had long known. With a flurry of sadness and relief, she saw, working amid the whispering pages of the library, the hunched and haggard creature her poor son had become. Just as she'd suspected, Ralph had been amongst the ragged band who had headed towards Invercombe before her. She sensed, as well, in stray flickers of light and song, the whispering passage of the Shadow Ones, who had been drawn to Invercombe for reasons far closer to her own. Outside as the sun flared and sank, a bonfire hung tremulous. The figures which murmured around it were far wilder and more dangerous-looking than those which cleaned and cooked inside. Some, indeed, were not human at all. But one especially caught Alice's eye as she swirled amid the uncoiling smoke. Something about his face . . . Something of way he held himself . . . It was—could only be. Alice, an angel of flame towards whom several of those gathered and chanting around the fire were now gazing, smiled. For here was the child Ralph had sired with that shoregirl. Then the wind surged through the fire, and she blew away in a laugh of leaves. Hovering higher, she saw another figure moving through the waving pines towards the weathertop in the light's last glow with a stooped and purposeful gait.

Odd, really, how the shoregirl she'd always imagined as some greater or lesser rival would soon become her most vital ally in the work ahead. But not so very odd. There were a million ways in which Alice could have destroyed Marion Price. But she had always held back. Call it instinct, destiny. Whatever and however, Alice watched her now as she stood on the weathertop's gantry. Even with that badly cut, grey-threaded hair and that filthy coat, there was *something* about her—the way she looked, moved. Some females, Alice had often thought, observed, attained a second and far higher level of beauty after the first easy victories of youth when character and the demands of life had imprinted themselves. It was far more than mere good looks, and Marion Price possessed it now. Forget about advances in the administration of medicine—*that* was why people followed and so adored her. And she didn't even realise, or care. Yet that was part of her loveliness as well . . .

It was some trick, Alice conceded with grudging admiration, to have played upon the world. Look at me, but don't look. Follow, but don't follow. A tightrope walk, indeed, high above the ordinary concerns of life. Yet Alice could tell that Marion was wavering over some greater precipice here at Invercombe, and drawn more and more strongly towards the intoxication of what she really was, or could become. It was especially apparent as she stood and surveyed—princess, empress, rival—the darkening world. Yes, Alice could sympathise with how Marion Price felt. She could will, even, a little strengthening of Marion's vision so that she could see out more easily across this Western landscape. Ah! These were moments which Alice treasured. Such power. Such control. The first gorgeous breezes of the opening gateway to a new Age. Then, confused, the tightrope suddenly wavering—nothing more, for all her vaunted powers, than an anxious bundle of unresolved hopes and fears—Marion Price ran, fled, back towards the house.

Alice followed. Causing the bell of Invercombe's telephone booth to ring, she regathered herself back on the far surface of the mirror, and waited for Marion Price to sit down.

XVII

'I have a request.'

'I suppose you expect surrender.'

'No, no—far from it. Marion Price, I need your help.'

Marion glanced down from the extraordinarily beautiful woman in the mirror. Instead of the dialling handle of a leather-clad booth, she half expected to see the gingham tablecloth of that Bristol tearoom where they had last met. She had that same immediate sense that Alice Meynell had long been silently reshaping the world around her into some vast and subtle trap which was now about to close.

'You don't need to listen to me now, my dear,' she said in her sweetly musical voice. 'You still have that choice. But, before you end this call, I think you should know, if you don't already, that two opposing armies both lie within ten miles of Invercombe. If you simply sit tight, it won't be long before one or other starts shelling you. That, or they may try to take Invercombe by storm, or possibly stealth. Or all of those things might happen at once . . .' She shrugged inside the misty fabric of whatever clothes she was wearing. Behind her, Marion could see, smell, a recognisable space of earth and wall. Alice Meynell seemed to be at Einfell, inside that old brick booth from which the nocturnes had emerged. Indeed, judging from the splayed shapes which hung at the edges of the light, the burned and wasted bodies of the creatures were still there, and peculiarly arranged amid other odd bits of hanging. 'You know as well as I do, Marion, not to expect logic and order at the precipice of battle. When a chance comes in these circumstances, you have to seize it in the instant, or leave it behind and watch as it is trampled underfoot.'

Marion's heart was pounding. 'You can't expect me to support the East.' She could still scarcely believe that she and Alice Meynell were talking to each other.

'What I want to suggest isn't about battle or bloodshed. It's about a way to put such things to an end. Or shall we just wait until my gunners or those of the West a few fields away grow trigger happy? I'm sure you don't need me to tell you that Invercombe is potentially of great strategic importance. Especially once people realise it isn't the wrecked wasteland everyone seems to suppose. So . . . Do you want to listen, or shall we end it here?'

'Go on.'

'Really, Marion, most of what I need to tell you are things you already know. So please bear with me if I seem to be at risk of insulting your intelligence . . .' Within the subtly shifting plays of her enigmatic expression, Alice Meynell smiled. Was this woman trying to flatter her, after all the terrible things she had done? But no, Marion decided. This was a mutual recognition which, even as her gaze flickered away from the mirror to the solid world beyond, she found hard to shake off. More strongly than she had ever felt the presence of anyone inside a telephone booth, it was as if Alice Meynell were actually *here*. It was she, Marion, who was floating, caught as she endlessly seemed to be in the journey between one state of being and another.

'Invercombe,' Alice said, 'may have exuded its raw aether, but a considerable amount obviously remains trapped within the energies of the house. Hence the weathertop. In my opinion, Marion, the place has always been charmed. Perhaps some untapped source of aether, or even an intelligence, resides within the very rock. But I digress. You will be aware, as you see me here, that there is an existing link to this place nearby, which is Einfell. That link, as my engineers work on

it, will soon be extended back through my admittedly somewhat fragile lines all the way to the main networks of the East.
Another link, meanwhile, lies from the transmission house
on the border of Invercombe's estate towards the West. Now,
Imagine for a moment that the few final necessary bonds
which would unite all of England are briefly forged. Imagine,
then, if we were to transmit Invercombe's force down the lines
in both directions—'

'You're talking about some kind of wrecking spell.'

'Indeed.'

'Which is what happened in the Falling.'

Barely for a moment did Alice Meynell seem uncomposed.
'That's history. There are—'

'After all you've done, you're expecting me to pass over
control of my . . .' Marion paused. '. . . of Invercombe, so that
you can wreak yet more damage?'

'Marion.' Alice Meynell's face radiated genuine sadness.
'There are many things we could talk about to do with what
did or didn't happen in the past. My poor son—who I believe
is with you there, although you've chosen not to mention
him—is in its thrall as much as any of us are. But he has always acted honourably in what he has tried to achieve. And
you will also be acting honourably if you do what I propose
now. But we must move on. Even in Invercombe, the clocks
must sometimes run. The spell I propose we use Invercombe's
power to create would not bring down a single building—or at
least only a very few which would soon fall anyway due to
some inherent weakness. Neither would it kill. Although, once
again, people die anyway, which is a fact you of all people
will understand . . .

'Think of these two armies, Marion, facing each other. My
forces, I admit to you in all honesty, are stretched. If we are to
attack, we must do so soon, and before the West's numbers
further entrench and increase. The West, on the other hand,
knows that it must cauterise this advance. In either event, both
sides must attack. Of course, such a large counterbalancing
movement as the West has performed will have weakened
their reserves on other fronts. My so-called masters may not
yet thank me for it, but I have given them the opportunity to
push towards Bristol from the north. One way or another, and

most likely tomorrow, the cannons will roar across this entire theatre of war. Endless blood will be spilt, much though both sides might protest that further slaughter is the last thing they desire.

'But consider this. Consider what would happen if all telephone lines in England were corrupted by the surge of a single spell. The main reckoning engines would instantly crash. Moments later, the power supply across all of England would also freeze. The trams would cease running, the trains would have to stop. In the great buildings, the lifts would jam. Everywhere, cold and lightless dark would soon reign. Pumps would cease working. Soon, there would be little fuel or water or gas. But more than that. My artillery-aimers, for example, who download their target information into numberbeads, would be entirely lost. The whole flow of data and electricity and information which lubricates a modern army would grind to a halt. I'm not saying that the guns wouldn't still fire, Marion. But, soldiers being the guildsmen that they are, there would be few enough of them once the flow of orders came to a halt. Do you see my point?'

'You're entirely wrong,' Marion said, 'about people not dying. My—the hospitals, so many systems which rely on power and information and order . . . Sewerage would back up. There would be chaos.'

'Ah—*chaos*!' Alice gave a merry laugh. 'So unlike this world we currently find ourselves in, eh? But I'm pleased that you believe me when I say that this thing is possible. Now let me tell you something else. You and I are not the only people heartily sick of this war. Think of poor Ralph. Think of the ordinary soldier and citizen. Think, even, of the people who followed you to Invercombe. They're all looking for new leadership, Marion, and for some other way. Why, otherwise, do they all chant your name? That disillusion isn't just something which the greatgrandmasters in their halls in London and Bristol are aware of—it's something they fear, and share. They, too, have lost loved ones and investments. Their guilds have weakened. Their authority has been compromised. This spell, the small destructive act which I am proposing, would give them the excuse they crave to change the course down which they are careering. In the shifterms when no proper war could be waged, and whilst the grids and systems are reconstructed, their only option would be to talk of peace.'

Peace—such a strange word to hear from the shapely lips of this creature. But she was persuasive, and the one thing Marion didn't doubt about Alice Meynell was that she, if anyone, could do these things. But there were obvious questions. 'Tell me, Greatgrandmistress. If this thing were to happen, what would you stand to gain from it?'

Alice smiled again. It was an acknowledgement, a sharing. *We two can speak frankly to each other. Out there—yes, Marion, I know you feel the same—we find nothing but dullards, followers and fools*. 'My guild, Marion, has been at least as ravaged by this war as any other. All this picking and unpicking, we might as well be done with it and reconstruct a new national grid. But that's incidental. I'm not the person I once was, Marion. I've come to accept that I, too, must change. And, being who I am, the world, as well, must change about me. For me, this advance is the last throw of the dice. I can't return to London as I was. The West may win eventually, but those who once urged prosecution of this war will only face recrimination. There will be trials, inquiries. Stones better left as they are will be upturned. And look at me. Look at me now. See who I am . . .'

The figure in the mirror seemed to thin before Marion's eyes. Alice Meynell was silvered glass, a trick of light and darkness. She was scarcely anything at all. 'I cannot go on as I am, Marion. I must change.'

'I presume you want to enter Invercombe. Why should—'

'Far from it. All of this can be accomplished by my staying here at Einfell and you remaining there at Invercombe. This is, after all, a technological Age. The spell itself can be transmitted easily enough. I imagine that Ralph, ill as he is, would be more than capable of overseeing such a thing. As I say, the link to the Eastern telephone system should be running very soon. In fact, I believe I can feel it now.' Alice gave a smile. She, the glass she was in, shivered. 'All that remains now is for you to link Invercombe back into the Western system by reactivating the transmission house which lies at the borders of your estate. I could tell you exactly what to do, but I'm sure Ralph could do so just as well. Of course, it's Telegrapher's work, and he'd have to reveal a few secrets, but, in a situation such as this, I hardly think that's a matter for concern.'

'So—we reconnect Invercombe to the Western telephone system, which will then be wrecked. And meanwhile I'm supposed to trust that you will allow the East to suffer the same fate?'

'Ah. Yes.' *You think exactly as I would* . . . 'As if this were all a ploy for me to hasten the East's victory! And why should *you* trust *me*, eh? But perhaps you trust Ralph—or at least trust him not to turn this into an act of military sabotage? As a Telegrapher, he will be able to tell just how much of England's telephone network is connected. If I were to attempt a clumsy feint, he would simply withhold the spell. In any case, Marion, that isn't what I want. What I want is an end to this war . . .'

Somewhere, the wind was blowing. Somewhere, Invercombe's clocks were chiming. But, for all that Alice Meynell had spoken of its shortage, time here balanced effortlessly on a single instant. There was much—above all, the purity of the greatgrandmistress's motives—that Marion doubted. But at the end of the day, it was down to this. She could either say yes. Or she could say no.

'One last thing, Marion. I'm not going to talk about the consequences of our not taking this course of action. You can make your own calculations. But for this spell to work—and I don't mean in some technical or guilded or political sense—it has to seem to be more than just some vast power cut. After all, the people of England have already had their lives disrupted by failure. The spell must appear to have *meaning*. It must, indeed, be more than what it is. I won't bore you with the detailed phrasing the spells requires, but, to the onlookers, which will of course be us all, it will come in three quick beats. Syllables. A single phrase . . .

Ma-ri-on.

'Across all of England, Marion. From every cable and device and machine, your name will be heard. Me, I'm just a greatgrandmistress. But you—you are legend. If this is to be done, and if it is to work, it must be done in your name, Marion Price, or not at all.'

Why . . .

But . . .

So many questions, but they were falling from her now, just as Marion Price herself was falling. The greatgrandmistress's logic was persuasive. It was near-seamless. And this damn thing that she had carried with her all the way to Invercombe, and which had grown and grown—by doing this, she could turn all the scrawled walls and the songs and the triple-beating guns and the pleading hands into something useful. In the process, she might even find out who she really was.

Marion heard something. A creaking, a ticking. She realised that it came from the ferocious pressure of her own hand as it gripped the dialling handle. 'How much time do we have?'

'Very little—hours. By morning, battle will begin in full. But you must get to that transmission house. I cannot do these things for you, Marion. I cannot arouse further suspicions by doing more than I have already done. But you need to speak to Ralph, Marion. He, too, has his role in this. Send him back here to this booth as soon as you can.'

'He's very ill.'

'But he's a fighter, isn't he? He's the son of his mother . . .'

'And what should I tell him?'

'Tell him . . .' Alice Meynell paused. Her expression changed. 'Tell him, we'll soon find out.'

Then the mirror hung blank. All Marion saw before her was herself.

There were already stirrings, for by now the near-presence of these two armies had been observed by others as well, but Marion found Ralph sitting at the long white table in the west parlour with the first course of soup cooling before him. He looked even paler now. Almost like Alice Meynell in the moment when the mirror had seemed to fail her.

'I've just been on the telephone,' Marion said, 'speaking to your mother.'

This was surely some joke, and Ralph attempted a smile.

Carefully, slowly, her heart once again racing, Marion sat down. The soup, sloppily ladled, remained uncollected, and voices grew louder in the inner hall as she explained. Even without these things she was telling Ralph, Invercombe was falling towards panic and disorder.

Ralph, to his credit, listened. The only times she had to pause were for his coughing spasms. There was nothing he didn't seem to understand.

'Do you trust her?' he said eventually.

Marion shook her head. 'I believe she's done terrible things. It's unnatural—no one is as well preserved as she is—everything about her is entirely wrong. I even think that she's more responsible than anyone else for this bloody war.'

Ralph's sunken eyes gazed at, and then through, her. He knew far more about Alice Meynell than he could admit to himself, let alone to her. And breath by breath, pulse by pulse, he was diminishing. Marion couldn't help selfishly wondering if he was up to this thing.

'Ralph, there was something she wanted me to say to you. Just a phrase—*We'll soon find out*.'

Ralph smiled. Slowly, he nodded. 'It was what we used to say to each other when we were travelling, wondering what the next place we came to would be like . . .' Hands slipping on the tablecloth, cutlery jingling, he climbed up from his chair. There were red spillages, Marion noticed, on the tablecloth, although the wine they had left untouched was white. 'We must get started . . .'

These were the things, he whispered—hands too weak to tremble, too frail to feel cold, laid on hers—that she must do to re-energise the transmission house on Invercombe's borders and open the way to the West.

'Funny,' she said to him. 'That folly—it always looked so appealing in the distance. Yet we never went there.'

The hands still kept their hold. 'You can't go alone.'

'Why draw attention to—'

'You don't *understand*, Marion. The two armies will be making reconnaissance, finding out resistances and the lie of the land.'

'We can't fight—that's the whole point.'

'They won't be looking to engage. If you come across a Western scout party in the darkness, all you need do is fire a few shots. They'll retreat, and report back. That's how it works.'

Ralph's flesh was heat now. Fierce and remote as the sun. All this talk of the chaos of battle, and suddenly he was explaining the whole thing as some courtly dance.

'Take some of the deserters with you, Marion. They've been soldiers, and they'll follow you anywhere.'

'But where's Klade . . . ?'

Guns were shouldered, bullets were counted, and the deserters passed along the lit terrace beside Invercombe's tall and beautiful windows as a shine of faces and metals, with the balehound trotting ahead and the ravener, the hackles of its huge and mangy pelt raised, loping warily behind. The other followers had gathered on the terrace to watch, and they chanted and cheered. Pipes gave their familiar discordant toot. A space formed around Marion and Ralph.

'How will you know when I've reached to the place?' she asked.

Lightning flickered. Ralph raised himself more upright. 'I'll know as soon as the connection is made.'

'And if nothing happens?'

He smiled. 'Then we'll be no worse off than we are.' Thunder boomed.

'So—'

In a whistling rush, a shell came to split the parterre gardens with light. The air grew solid in their faces and then fell away in a hissing suck as scraps of shrapnel, still writhing and aether-energised, tinkled down.

'That was bound to happen,' Ralph said calmly as vegetation sparked and burned. 'It could be the East, or more probably the West. The gunners are testing their aim, making themselves known. It won't damage the telephone lines— they're buried underground. Now go. Go . . . !'

Marion turned. She and the deserters headed off into the night, and then Ralph, who had sent many such groups into dark uncertainties, limped back inside the house with the other followers. Clearing the blockage in his throat, he issued instructions that everyone should move down into the servants' halls, where they would be safe from any stray shell. Not that he expected any significant bombardment, but he needed to be alone.

His feet dragged as he crossed the floor of the west parlour, where the candles which had been lit for their meal had long guttered out. The inner hall was emptier and brighter, blazing under the electric chandelier, and he was glad that he had to haul himself no further, and especially not ascend those stairs. His breath was loud in his head now. His heart was pounding. If anything, he felt yet more dreamily remote from this house than he had when he'd first entered it inside the fishtank of that helmet. In a few moments, he would speak again to his mother. It seemed quite impossible, yet he didn't feel a fraction of doubt. This was the work he had started that snowy day outside Hereford, and tonight, one way or another, he and it and the war would be ended for good.

Just a few more steps to reach the booth now. Then he could rest his body, exercise his mind. At least there were no more shells. Not yet, anyway. He wondered, indeed, if he'd lied to Marion about the intentions of these armies, and if it mattered, and just how much he really loved her, and what had happened to poor Klade, and how little any of them had left to lose. Then, vaguely, happily, he thought of Helen back in London, and how Flora and Augustus—Gussie—would probably sleep through all of this as London fell darkly quiet. And in the morning. Well, in the morning . . .

Ralph paused, swaying. He realised he wasn't alone. The changed figures Klade called the Shadow Ones had emerged from Invercombe's hidden spaces. Silvery-light as stirred fragments of dust, scented with sea and stone and Age-old wood, crossing the carpet in shifts and sighs, they struck him no longer as sad or terrible, but queerly beautiful. Ralph left the door of the telephone booth open, and their presence was around him as he dialled. All the pain passed from him as he made the connection to Einfell, and his head was filled with inexpressible song.

XVIII

Klade scurried across the flickering night landscapes of Inver-combe's grounds in the wake of Marion Price and the other Outsiders. A thunderous rushing came out of the sky. Trees, madly ragged with endless autumn, flared. Rages of wind bat-tered his face. But he was Klade and he was the Bonny Boy and this was the scene of battle. He was not deterred.

The sky split again in a white gash. Shadows splayed across the dying ground. The earth erupted into light, then smoke, then falling cascades of stones. Klade glanced back towards Inver-something. Joined by pillars of light and dark, it was now the fulcrum of earth and sky. The house was the war and it was the storm, and the earth was turning beneath his feet and the air hung solid as he ran. More light came, further off this time; a glowing rush. He found the other Outsiders as they cowered amongst the bushes amid curses and the click of guns.

'Don't shoot!' Marion Price's voice. 'Klade . . .' Her face was paler now amid the deep silence between the thunder-guns. A heart. A mask. 'You must go back.'

He shook his head.

'This isn't safe.' Her hand on his cheek. This time, he didn't flinch.

'Where *is* safe?' he said.

Some of the other Outsiders chuckled. He saw Marion Price smile. 'Then stay by me. We must move on.'

Klade had no idea where they were heading, although he knew that something vital must be accomplished with as much speed and stealth as was possible—something which would extinguish this war. Knew also, as if it needed knowing as the guns thundered their deep *Ma-ri-on* songs all around them, that they must do all that was necessary to protect Marion Price. And here ahead, on a slight rise, gloriously crystalline, rainbowed turrets raised like a beckoning hand.

This strange edifice of glassy stone seemed to move towards them across the wrecked ground. Almost there. The other Outsiders scanned the falling silence with the cold black eyes of their guns. For all its glinting strangeness, this building was no ghost, for a path led to its mock turrets. There was a door, even, towards which Marion Price, breaking from the protective corral of Outsiders, began to run. Klade ran with her as well, and it was in that moment that the darkness emptied in the flare of bullets.

Alice Meynell reached deep inside her portmanteau as, breathing its lost glamours, little more than a breath herself, she scooped up the wyreblack pages in her translucent hands. The ideographs, white swirls of aethered ink, comets, turning planets, circling stars, sang out to her. It was the same with the commonest spell a knife-grinder might cast as he honed a steel—that sense that what you were making had always waited, and you were simply drawing its perfection through the small wound your desire for it had made in the substance of the world—but never this strong. Not even in the keystone of the greatest building, or the powers which bound the moon to the earth. Not even in the greatest of all makings when the entire universe was willed by God the Elder himself. Although this, Alice imagined, as she ordered these flakes of falling night with senses she could no longer describe, must have been very much how He felt.

Doubt had never been something which had greatly afflicted her, but all the enterprises of her life seemed like abject wavering in comparison to now. Was the telephone on? Yes, of course it was on. Telephones, like the tides and the seasons and her continuing urge to be more of what she already was, had no state of off. But the mirror before her—hung inside what her eyes told her was an edifice of old, damp brick, although strangely ornamented, and lit by a bare single electric bulb—flared and sparked. The voices of the men within her near command, who had grown too fearful now to approach her directly, had keened like the calls of distant birds, and what was left of the old Alice Meynell dealt with their queries with a briskness which her old self would have admired. Western guns were lobbing in shells. Not a full assault, but a range-finding, a tuning-up, and she ordered them to make response from decoy positions whilst their main guns remained silent and unrevealed, just as the West's main guns undoubtedly were. When it came down to it, both sides in battle were essentially the same. The only thing which had ever mattered was who imagined they had won, and even that would soon be irrelevant.

Alice had had no reason to lie to Marion Price. She really had planned the exact consequences of the wrecking spell she had described. East and West, and lands beyond, would be brought to a paralytic halt. Most likely, peace would be sued for as well. England would probably be reunited. Even when judged by standards other than her own, there was much to be desired in the state which Alice planned to bring about. But, as always, such matters were incidental to her; cards you might pretend to possess according to how you wished to direct the flow of the game. It was logic which had always driven her. Sometimes, admittedly, it had taken her to degradations and sadnesses which—much like this war, or in facing her lost and ailing son—she believed she was capable of feeling much like anyone else. But Alice's difference, her beacon, her own personal Invercombe, had always been that she could see through such things to the greater truths beyond.

Now, she thought, as she poised herself in the waiting depths of the mirror, *I can even see through myself*. But, for all this situation's apparent strangeness, nothing but a clear and well-made path lay ahead. When the spell she would soon dictate to Ralph was cast, everything which she had promised Marion would happen. But there would be one last thing. She, or what she was to become, would also join with the spell and make that joyous leap into the networks, systems and reckoning engines on which this modern Age and the one which lay

beyond it would depend. She would become deathless. Pure
power. In essence, which was all she would be, the new Alice
Meynell would control this land. It was a giddy prospect, certainly. But she was sure she had neglected nothing. Carefully,
and for the last time, she consulted her portmanteau, and applied a little cream and foundation, dabbed some blusher to
her fading face. Then she remembered the green velvet box in
which she had long kept the trophies of her small conquests.
Buttons and brooches and hatpins and pendants, they mostly
seemed anonymous to her now, but she put them on in any
case. *These*, she thought with a final triumphant shudder as
she anointed her neck with the silver chain of a teardrop pendant, *are all the shackles I will soon cast off*.

Then the telephone began to ring, and Alice knew merely
from its tone that this call came from Invercombe, and that it
was Ralph. She smiled, happy as any mother might be that her
son had chosen to ring her, rather than it being necessary for
her to ring him.

How long had it been since he had last seen his mother? Ralph
had to stretch his brain to recall the time when he had sat with
her in the last summer warmth in the glassed-in gardens of her
London house, and the thought left him exhausted. He wondered how much of himself there was left, and what she would
make of the wraith he had become.

'Ralph.' As always, her eyes saw through him. And then,
and as in the old days, he felt some of the pains and doubts
which had beset him begin to dissolve. 'My darling. We're
nearly there now.'

'I've . . .' He realised as he paused that he was past coughing. He could barely hear the sound his voice was making, but
he knew that she heard. 'I've changed from the man I was.'

'Who would expect otherwise—after this war?'

He gave an inward shrug. More than ever, words seemed
unnecessary between them. He found, also, that he could
shape the figure he saw in the mirror before him into whatever
he wanted. Yes, he understood how Marion felt about Alice
Meynell. He could even dimly glimpse the bringer of revenge
and chaos which others might perhaps encounter in his mother's
shape. But that wasn't *her*. Not to him. He loved her, just as he

was now entirely certain his father had. It was the easiest, most natural thing in the world.

'How are Helen? Gussie? Flora?'

'They're all well, Ralphie. Or they were, and I'm sure they still are. They'll be better still when we get this thing done . . .'

But I'm worried. I can't last . . .

Ralph, you must never think like that. Remember all those long journeys across Europe . . .

The carriages, the foyers, the dinners on trays . . .

Her hand, reaching through the mirror, touched him. He breathed her fresh linen scent, and there was no pain at all. The Shadow Ones were with Ralph as well. They were the leaves of an endless book. They were light across the shore. As, through whispered chants and technical graduations and apertures and empowerments, Ralph broadened the bandwidth of the contact between Invercombe and Einfell and the open telephone systems of the entire East, he felt a lost and renewed sense of sharing with his mother, and a depth of closeness also with this house and all its purposes, which he would have loved to endlessly prolong. But part of him, the same part which had perhaps once lain in bed and battled fevers whilst the rest of him ranged across continents, felt the shudder of another shell. Then, with an urgency which affected him even in this remote and blissful state, all of Invercombe's clocks began to chime.

'These, Ralph, will unwind this war.'

The dark sheets of the spells of her portmanteau spilled with light. They looked to Ralph like the night sky, or the glitter of water when the summer sun is so bright that the troughs between each dazzling wavelet seem entirely black. He heard their chant. He felt their onrushing coolness. He breathed their salt. There were depths beneath him, and his lungs hurt.

This thing we're doing . . .

In a moment of doubt, the waters contracted to the shallow brightness of that paddling pool in the Kite Hills. He tasted bittersweet chlorine and salt.

Will it . . . ? I honestly don't know, Ralph. But . . .

A smile. Soft laughter. Hands. Protecting. Lifting.

'We'll soon find out.'

They both sang the spell together, and the Shadow Ones sang it as well.

Instinctively, Marion Price ducked, and Klade, clearly used to the whoosh of bullets, ducked with her as well. She crawled a few yards back towards a dip in the grass. Even the ravener, some part of its memory or instinct still working, had hunched down. Just ahead, in a series of yelps and soft socking sounds, the hapless and harmless balehound was being picked apart by bullets. The air rang and sang. Then there was silence.

Marion realised as she sucked back her breath that she was lying in a bowl of mud. The clump of earth and grass which loomed close to her face was all that lay between her and the guns which had flared ahead, and she wished that there was more. Should they really wait here? Then, as the silence stretched, she wondered if the soldiers ahead of them were still there, or were stealthily shifting closer. Perhaps Ralph was right—perhaps they'd seen them and retreated. But weren't the deserters supposed to have fired back first? She'd never realised how many uncertainties arose the moment someone started shooting at you.

Thunder rattled. More light rolled over them, glinting with icy brilliance on the folly which lay perhaps eighty yards ahead, then the lumpy ground around them exploded with rattling blasts. Shell cases pinged out, but Marion felt no inclination to move. She was afraid. It was that simple. It wasn't something you thought about. Your body did that all for you; the feeling washed straight up from your gut. But the fear wasn't *her*. After all, she was Marion Price. At that moment, bullets rained close to where she and Klade lay, spraying up stones and mud, and Marion breathed the same fear-smoke-and-mud stench which she had washed from many bodies in these years of war. So familiar, yet entirely new here. Even though the thunder seemed to have lessened and the guns had stopped firing again, her vision had sharpened to a near-supernatural extent. She could see Klade more clearly now than she had ever seen him. She touched his hand, and he smiled back at her. He and these deserters were doing this for *her*. And the folly was ahead. It was merely a matter of rearranging her thoughts until they made sense again.

The dark lit up as both sides started firing. To Marion's newly sensitised eyes, the bullets were thin trails of wyre-brightness, and she could distinguish the different bores of gun, and was aware of the greater power and purpose which the regular Western soldiers who lay between them and the folly were bringing to bear. Somebody shouted something, a flare drifted up, and they were bathed in a white light far more terrible than the short-lived brilliance of the shells. There was a particular concentration of fire against a nearby deserter, less lucky than she and Klade in the depth of the hollow they had crawled into. Jerked, puppet-like, he turned, rose, whitened, red-dened, then collapsed, scarcely recognisable but still hanging half-upright on the shattered remains of his bones. Casting lengthening shadows, the flare fell hissing to the earth. The situation, it struck Marion, was entirely hopeless. And soon there would be another flare.

Suddenly, instantly, shouting to Klade to stay put, she was up. The feeling, to be skidding, near-flying, across this tus-socked mud, was extraordinary. She fell into the space where the dead deserter squatted. Sliding, rummaging in a wet fall of flesh, she found the shape of his gun. Another flare was due any moment, but over there lay the place where the ravener knelt. Once more, she ran, and the giant creature snarled and shivered as she collided with its rank pelt. Even in this sleek blackness, she could clearly see the red of its eyes, the hooked curl of its black claws. Then came another flare, and the world turned white and was scarred by bullets' black trails. Someone began screaming, and Marion stroked the greasy hillocks of the ravener's spine and murmured through its stench to keep it calm and quiet. There was no doubt now in her mind that the Western soldiers had been ordered to protect this folly. She shifted her gun, feeling its runnels and rises. Just as the flare died, she rammed the snout into the ravener's flank. Bellowing, the crea-ture raised itself to its full height and staggered straight towards the folly. Marion also lunged, ducking left, skim-running, near-flying, sideways across the ragged earth as gunfire formed a blazing concentration on the ravener's silhouette. Sprays of blood burst back from it, but still it lumbered forwards. By her own zigzag route, Marion also kept moving. And the folly, from this new sideways angle, drew desperately near.

It was shaped like a castle, but its battlements were mere decorations, its arrow slits were blank—all quite useless for the purpose they mimicked. That was why these soldiers had had to dig their defence outside. But this was also their weakness, for it meant that they were exposed and essentially static. And their attention was turned outwards. All of these things, anyway, were what Marion hoped. The ravener had fallen dead. The downpour of bullets had become a sporadic shower.

The Western soldiers were close to her left now. She could hear them muttering to their guns. Then another flare went up, and all she could do was run. She collided with the amazing reality of the transmission house. Flakes of cement skidded beneath her fingers as she felt her way around it through the blinding white light. Then, suddenly, amazingly, there was a doorway, and she was falling through it, crashing down on her knees into puddled concrete. It was darker in here, but not entirely dark—not even as the flare died. There were stairs ahead. Her gun raised, her breath rasping, scarcely believing she was here, Marion began to climb.

The light grew stronger as the narrow spiral unwound. Voices came as well, and a changing yellow glow. The men's voices were urgent, but it was impossible to catch their exact words, and Marion didn't doubt that they would shoot in the instant they saw her, even if she had caught them unawares. Once more, her fingers traced the shape of her gun. She whispered silently in her head all the many prayers and spells she had heard moaned and murmured in the delirium wards as the brick pillar at the centre of the stairs curved away from her, upwards and inwards towards the light. This next inch, this next step, and she was certain they would come into view. But the moment lengthened.

Suddenly, she was at the edges of a lantern-lit room, and two men who had been squatting over something were turning towards her, their faces registering slow surprise as she raised her gun. The noise was incredible as the thing barked and leapt in her hands. The men were blown backwards, and the wall behind them exploded into red scrawls which dragged into long smears as they slid down. Her gun fell silent. The room shrank back. Remembering to breathe again, she moved forward. The odd thing was, these men weren't wearing uniforms, and neither did they seem to have guns. Inspecting them, Marion realised that they wore the talismans of the Western wing of the Great Guild of Telegraphers, and that the thing they had been squatting over was a toolbox. They were trying to disable this transmission house; *that* was what the Western soldiers outside were defending. What had Ralph said?—something about it being more difficult to entirely disconnect a transmission house than it was to enable it. Hoping that he was right, she tried to orient herself.

Even as gunfire rattled outside, there remained a dull, purposeful hum in this folly. It was like being inside a cramped version of the weathertop. Here, alarmingly close to where her ricocheting bullets had shattered the wall, were the main conductors. Here, in mushroom sprouts of anodised brass, were the registers of octaves and distance. Here, even, for this transmission house was an antique version of its type, was a small haft. Everything was different in many small details to the idealised device Ralph had attempted to describe to her, and yet, Marion realised as her fingers stroked the wires and metals, it was all essentially the same. There was nothing but that continuing hum as she began her work, then, with a sudden certain rush, she felt the nearness of Invercombe. No, its actual presence. For it was *here*, in dazzling leaps and bounds like an endless hall of mirrors, and she had no doubt that Ralph had established the connection. Marion smiled; it was impossible not to. She remembered the spell, the turns, the actions. And they remembered her. At the very time when she should have been anxious, she felt ridiculously calm. The only moment of panic came when she discovered that a fuse, a final keyshape to bridge the connection between West and the East, was missing. She looked around, registering the flat realities of this real place in which she found herself, and the continuing sound of gunfire, and the red-leaking bodies of the Western telegraphers which were slowly exuding their scents of death. Crouching, turning them over, feeling their sodden pockets, throwing aside a wallet, a cigarette lighter, Marion encountered a recognisably metallic lump and pulled it out, inserted it, male to female, into its home. The tone inside the transmission house grew louder. The task was nearly done.

Large, T-shaped and ceramic-handled, the final activating lever projected at 45 degrees from a slot in the wall, and there was a sense of weight even as she settled her hands around it; a feeling both strongly mechanical and yet marvellously magical. Marion's bloody fingers skidded off the handle's cracked white glaze as she pushed. The thing was even heavier than she thought. Wiping her hands down her coat, she leaned down with her full weight. Still, for a moment the lever held, then, the giving of something vast yet perfectly balanced, it moved. There was a mechanical *click*. Fractionally, the tone which filled the engine house rose. She stepped back. Something had changed, certainly, but she had no idea what. Something had changed outside as well. The gunfire had stopped.

Marion supposed that she had done her job, although the reek of death was getting stronger in here now. Automatically, in the way she would have done with any corpse, she laid out the bodies of the men. She straightened their guildpins and rearranged their clothes over the worst of their wounds. She closed their eyes. They were far younger than she'd thought, and had probably only ever plied their trade in this time of war. One was nursing a wispy moustache, the other bit his nails, and she didn't know what to feel about what she had done. It was silent outside: the deserters had lost the brave resistance they had put up on her behalf, and Klade—but she couldn't think that far. She picked up the gun again. The thing disgusted her now. But if she waited a little longer, the Western soldiers were sure to come up and finish off the job. But she was impatient. Gun raised, she headed back down the folly's tight spiral stairs.

It was still night outside, and her eyes were slow to adjust. She turned, aiming randomly as she limped out on to the slippery earth, and pulled the gun's trigger, but all she got from it was an impotent *click*. Then a ravener-like figure surged towards her from the dark. She cringed, then recognised its lopsided stance.

'We've won,' Klade lisped.

Four human deserters died along with the balehound and the ravener in what was to become known as the Battle of the Folly. Not one of the defeated Western soldiers—confused by the absence of any structured response from their attackers, and by their mad willingness to fight—had survived, although

Marion, as they trudged into the silent dark away from that raised, prohibitory hand, knew enough not to ask how or why.

That sound, that shift in tone, still haunted her as much as the deaths. It was like the change of key in the most aching part of a song; impossible to pin down. Had the war really ended? Had they done any of the things they were supposed to have done? She had no idea. Klade, in that moment of supposed victory, had drawn her against the large, surprisingly male shape of his body as she threw aside her gun, and she supposed she had hugged him back. But her head remained empty. Apart from the sense of that lever giving. Apart from this long, endless note . . . But the guns had stopped, and the sky was paling over the estuary in first anticipation of dawn. Dimly now, the shape of Durnock Head, and then that of the house, and its weathertop, were being revealed. Just as on every other day of its long existence, Invercombe was remaking itself.

Questions, questions, as they reached the gardens and the followers, drawn up by this new silence from their shelter in the servants' corridors, came streaming out to greet the returning party. But Marion hung back and, for once, they didn't seek her out. That sound, that song—there was some twist, something unmade, hanging within it which she fought to unravel. Then she remembered Alice Meynell's promise that the message, the wrecking spell, would come as three beats which would spell out her name. Ridiculous, really, to imagine such a thing. And vanity beyond all human scope. *Marion*. She tried to recall the sound. But the endless note she had cast into the telephone lines extinguished it. *Whatever else has been destroyed tonight*, she thought, pushing across the terrace towards the inner hall, *Marion Price has gone*.

The house felt empty. Not deserted, but discarded. No clock ticked or chimed as her footsteps trailed mud and worse across the carpets. Even as the windows, their curtains left open in last night's confusions, began to brighten, not a single shadow moved. The door of the telephone booth beneath the best stairs was ajar, and Ralph, forgotten, remained inside. After so much death, it was almost a surprise to find him alive, although slumped barely conscious over the dialling handle. She glanced towards the mirror as the people crowded around her. It was entirely blank.

Ralph felt hot and loose and light. 'The guns seem to have stopped,' she said as she helped him out of the booth, thinking of the junior members of his guild she had killed.

This, she thought as Ralph trembled against her, was the closest they had got to an embrace in all the angry years since she had left him in Sunshine Lodge, and part of her now realized that she was as guilty as he was in their separation, and that the true victim had been Klade alone. But crimes, neglects, wars, murders, once committed, could never be healed. All the rest was self-pity—the same pity she was feeling now.

Against his weak protests, she organised that he be carried up to his old room, then, unable to bear the silent, expectant gazes which surrounded her, she went outside. More and more light was coming now across the parterre gardens. The chain pools chuckled. Branch by topmost branch, the specimen trees were shimmering into life. She headed down the paths and crossed the springing turf and crouched by the seapool. Its waters slipped coolly through her fingers, but lingering curiosity made her still her hands to study the face which gathered on the surface as it smoothed. The rising sun had spread red banners across the sky, briefly turning the entire pool red as she washed the blood from her hands. Her face hung there, but it was quite unrecognisable. She headed on towards the shore.

Whatever Ralph had said was wrong: time really could go backwards, for Marion recognised a spring day when she saw and felt one; she knew its scents and sighs, and the wildness of this light, and the movements of those birds like risen flecks of foam. It would have been so easy just to stay here. Or to carry on walking, fleeing, along this shore, or to head straight into the forgetfulness of this incoming tide. What, after all, was holding her? Even for her son Klade, she knew by now that all she could ever feel was a dulled affection mingled with even duller regret. She wasn't his, and he wasn't hers, and no ships were out in the channel today, but at least the Severn Bridge still hung, a silvering of the light, a curtaining of the air.

Marion was too weary to stoop for cockles, or even to peel off her ruined boots. But again the light darkened and coalesced amongst the familiar rocks. Once more, a figure appeared, and she studied it calmly, for by now she was used to ghosts. Not Sally, no. Not Denise or Owen or her father or

Mam, or even quite the refracted image of Marion herself, although she recognised something in its aching stance. More a creature of the sea, it seemed to her as it picked its way between the shining rock-pools, than anything to be found upon the land. Living weed. Leavings of the shore. Mere driftwood and sail tarp. Perhaps a dying gannet.

'I thought this might be the place,' it murmured, 'to find you.' A hand trembled and tensed on a stick of driftwood, veins and bones tangling and untangling beneath loose and mottled skin. The face drooped around a lipless mouth, although the eyes inside their sagged blue pouches remained as calmly unsettling as ever. This was still Alice Meynell, even if she looked like an old shore-woman reduced to picking coal at the edge of the tide.

'You've changed . . .' Marion murmured, amazed.

Alice laughed. Her hair snagged out from her skull. 'Nothing like enough . . .'

'Last night—the spell. Do you know what happened?'

The hand which wasn't gripping the stick gave a trembling wave. 'Can't you hear? Where are the guns? Where are the ships? Why are we standing here? I'd credited you with more intelligence, even if you are just a shoregirl, than to doubt the evidence of your own senses. And Ralph's alive, isn't he? As if this house would ever let him die . . .'

'And you think the war has ended?'

'It was never that simple—but I imagine that in London and Bristol the processes which will lead in that direction are probably underway.' Another chuckle. 'My own forces, certainly, are in disarray.' Another wheeze. 'You've got what you wanted. And you don't even recognise it, or know what to do with it. You're so typical of . . .' As Alice searched for the word, a dewdrop formed and glistened on her hooked nose, was caught on the wind and blew away. She ground the tip of her driftwood stick deeper into the sand. 'We humans. We're all the same.'

'You *knew* that the folly would be defended. People *died* there. I killed . . .' Marion wiped her face. The shore receded in salty webs. 'I killed two men. Westerners of your own guild. They weren't even armed. And I—'

A brittle hand clutched on her arm. 'You did what was

necessary.' It gave a squeeze. 'What else could you have done? Did you think we could end an entire war without a little further bloodshed? Do you imagine that people are not dying now in the blackout cities? Just because we cannot hear guns, do you think they are not still firing? To reach the better, you must pass through the worst—did you not ever realise that, Marion Price, when your whole life screams out that very fact?'

'I've only ever tried to do what seemed best.'

'Best!' Alice sniffed, her eyes wandering over the gleaming bladderwrack. 'Yet you repaired the bodies of the fighting men who came back from the front, just as others made their bullets, or grew food to fill their bellies, so they could go back and fight again. Did you not imagine that you were as culpable as those who fired the guns? At least last night you briefly put all the self-justifying rubbish aside just for once and did something for *yourself*. Why, otherwise, did you ever come back to this house? And why did you let those people follow you? You did it because it was what you *wanted*, Marion Price. I'm sorry, by the way, that this whole enterprise didn't spell you your name as you'd wanted, but the spell was even stronger than I'd thought. But, you—you wanted to know what it felt like to have power, to have command. Life and death—those are the things you enjoy dealing with in what passes for your heart. All the rest is mere scenery. I don't even believe you can *love*, can you? No, not the way you'd want to. Not in the way you imagined love was felt by someone like my poor Ralph. Ah, *love*, Marion. Let *me* tell *you* about love . . .

'Love is the feeling which drives this shore. Love is the reason those seabirds are circling and calling to each other. Love is the raping solider, or the husband who goes off to war to kill other husbands. Love is the bee and love is the flower. Love is the prey a mother brings to her nest. Love is what brought those saddened women to Saint Alphage's. Love, as well, is most likely what kept your son at Einfell. Love, I would guess, is also the reason he probably feels so lost now. For love is the thing we use to dress up our lives with the appearance of meaning, or mourn for when it cannot be found. Love is what drove us to war, Marion. Love of place, love of person, love of self, love of things as they are. Love is blind instinct, Marion. It's the trick that nature plays upon its inventions to ensure that they copulate and protect their young. And you and I, Marion, through some fault we feel but cannot explain, imagine that we are immune to it. But let me tell you, we are not.

'How nice it would be, eh, to exist above it all in realms of pure power and spirit! Oh, yes, I share that urge, Marion. To take command of that unreasoning power which you and Ralph spent that summer attempting to define. Why should— what did you call it, Habitual Destiny?—control our lives? Surely we as reasoning creatures are above all that now? Last night, indeed. Last night . . .' In a spasm of trembling, and as the sand shone and loosened in the rising tide, Alice nearly fell. 'I fully believed I had the chance to become something else. Last night was everything I'd planned. Those faint shapes you encountered up at the house—the palest of the changelings, the ones closest to pure spell. They've gone this morning, haven't they?'

Marion waited. There was another swaying spasm; a baring of sparse teeth in a grimace or a smile.

'That could—*should*—have been me, Marion. The only thing I didn't tell you yesterday, Marion, was that I, too, was part of the spell. I planned to pass through the mirror, discard the husk you see before you entirely. But instead . . . Instead . . . Here I still am. Oh, it's no great mystery! I'm just an old woman, and I'd only look even more ridiculous if I plastered myself with scent and make-up. So why not be what I am? Whatever else I had last night, I stupidly lost. It fled into the mirror and left me here as you see me now, on this shore. And the funny thing is, Marion, I'm so, so tired I don't even bloody care.'

'You were like the Shadow Ones?'

'I'd changed, certainly. I believed I'd changed enough.' She wavered, nodded, considering. The tide, in its shining onwards rush, was sweeping closer to them. 'No, it wasn't *that* which stopped me. Haven't you been listening, girl? Isn't that what I've been trying to tell you? I was poised before the mirror. I was ready to take the leap at the moment you pulled that lever in the transmission house. But it was my own feebleness which stopped me. It was Ralph. It was . . .' She paused. Her face writhed. She spat the word out. '*Love*. I hesitated a moment too long last night, God help me Marion, because I didn't want to leave my son . . . All those years ago, when he was gripped by the worst of his illness, I had this wish, this prayer. Inside my head, I would scream, *Let it be me*. And last night, it came to me again, that same thought, and then it was too late . . .'

The glittering scraps which Marion had taken to be bits of foam or shell dangling from Alice's clothes and clinging to her stringy throat and ears, were, she now realised, expensive items of jewellery, beads, buttons . . .

'Perhaps you and I can walk out into this tide together, Marion. Or we could just stay here. Either way, the waters will take us soon enough. Can't you hear the tide's hissing! And you can push me down, Marion, or I will push you, and who cares which of us survives . . .'

Alice's hand was still gripping Marion's arm, but now in pleading support. It was hard, despite all the other emotions Marion knew she should have felt, not to feel pity for this old woman, who had fallen so far from the magnificent creature she had once been. She shook her head. 'There's been enough death.'

'There will *never* be enough death, Marion. That's the whole point . . .'

As Alice, one hand wavering on her stick and the other clasping Marion's arm, shuffled up the shore, it seemed at first that the tide might overtake them, but their reflections slowly dimmed as the waters thinned, then dissolved as they climbed towards the swing gate into Invercombe's blossoming gardens.

XIX

The signal which spread across East and West came not as a surge, but as a shift of tone. A mere change of key, and little enough if it had been mere sound, the spreading wave nevertheless rendered the machines and systems it encountered deaf to the spells of the guildspeople who commanded them. It was a new language, frustratingly close in every aspect of syntax to the one it had replaced, but impossibly difficult to understand and pronounce.

From the telephones, just as Alice Meynell had predicted, the signal surged into the reckoning engines, and from there into the power supplies, and soon suffused every other aethered device and material; meaning, in this advanced Age, almost everything. Even the many aspects of modern life unlinked from the main webs of communication became unworkable. Not only was there no electricity and no gas and no plumbing, but the song also carried itself on the air, and from hand to hand, and from the confused thoughts of one guildsman to another. Soon, other nations were suffering similar shutdowns, and even the weather-tops of ships in the remotest seas were becoming skittish before, in a last blaze of wind, they ceased. Or, more accurately, they became dormant, for guildsmen knew from the continued hum and thrum of their machines that life and power remained. What was lost was obedience.

There were deaths. There were riots. There were structural failures. But the song was more stubborn than it was destructive. Hallam Tower did not collapse, but its fixed beam remained glowing dark and light towards the West. The ziggurat of Westminster Great Park also remained entire. So did the Severn Bridge, and the halls in Bristol of the Merchant Venturers. Like the devices they housed, they were not destroyed; they had just become uncommunicative.

In such circumstances, with resort to travel by horse and dray—and even they were skittish—two days of waiting passed before the commanders of the Great Guilds of West and East made contact. Written communication remained difficult, so they met midway across England in Meriden. Inevitably, there was considerable distrust and rancour. But these men knew each other. They had shared families, lovers, railway carriages, gossip, restaurant tables, in better times before the war. Inevitably, as they shivered in the candlelit gloom of a deserted house which their soldiers, their guns impotent, guarded with the swords they had salvaged from guildhall museums, discussion soon focused not on the division of the spoils, but on how they might ensure that there might be any spoils left at all.

After a long shifterm of storms, the weather remained unseasonably calm in much of the West. At Invercombe, the waterwheel had frozen on its axle, but the weathertop continued to summon waves of warmth so strong that summer briefly reigned. Against Ralph's predictions, the trees and plants proved capable of budding, and the grass greened at an astonishing rate. Walls warmed. Even the shadows cast by the low winter sun seemed, by some refraction of the cloudless sky, to hang higher and brighter in the sky.

All instincts for tidiness amongst the followers were lost as the house's windows remained open and rugs were laid for picnicking upon the lawns, and then forgotten and trampled into the earth. Furniture was laughingly borne down the terraces. Soon, there were roses unbudding over chests of drawers and grandfather clocks chiming amid the hollyhocks. At night, the glamours and glows of the garden were far more

inviting than the unlit house, and many took to sleeping outside. If they slept at all, that was, amid the shameless love-
making which prevailed not just in Invercombe but across
much of England as old distinctions and rivalries were ren
dered briefly pointless. The night air was drenched in pollen
and murmurs, and grew softly alive with glimpses of limb and
petal; it sang with cries and gasps.

Ralph's old bed, his old room, were no longer the places
they had once been, and he persuaded a couple of the followers
to help carry him outside into the gardens, where the fervid air
had grown ridiculously warm. The place he settled on was by
the seapool, where a sofa from the peacock room had already
found its way. He lay down and looked up the sky. Butterflies,
roused early by the heat, rested on the flower-embroidered
cushions, and vines twined up from the quickening carpet of
grass as shadows played over him from the wavering trees. Invercombe breathed around him, and he breathed with it. Then
he heard footsteps. They came and went so slowly, and his
weary consciousness came and went with them, that he'd long
decided that they didn't really exist when a trembling shadow
began to inch its way over him.

'Ralph . . .'

The voice, the face, were almost entirely different. But he
smiled. For Ralph knew that it was finally time to humour
the mumbling old creature his mother had become, even if
he could never quite forgive her, and 'Old Alice' soon became
a familiar figure at Invercombe, wandering to and from the
house bearing trembling trays of food to her recovering son,
or sitting talking with him just as she had always done on their
long-ago journeys across Europe, which was now almost all
that she remembered.

Amid this green riot, the house felt damply old. You could hear
the creaks and gives as ivy tore and old timbers and stones settled. The best stairs were no longer straight, and blisters of
falling plaster were revealed as tapestries were hauled from the
walls to make bedlinens for the lovers in the citrus grove. Marion explored the new emptiness of these rooms, or sat for long
hours in the telephone booth, where the mirror still hung reflec-
tionless. There was an odd sense of life without its beckoning

darkness, as if something was happening either too quickly or slowly for her to notice. The gardens, for all that daisies were jauntily pushing up through the terrace paving and moonivy now clothed the statues, held less appeal to her; she grew tired of disturbing the bodies she so often found coupling on the beds they had brought out, and headed for the shore. Here, summer also briefly reigned, although the waters she waded beyond the edge of her familiar space of rocks grew suddenly cold and Wales dissolved into the mist which hung beyond this core of warmth. Invercombe might be losing its chimneys, but her shore was unchanged, and she wandered barefoot, although the sense remained—and more especially at twilight or as she moved back through the gardens—that she was still being watched.

On the fourth morning, when the early roses had already lost their petals and the later sallows were fully in flower, she encountered Ralph. He was up and walking the gardens, albeit with the aid of a stick, and he looked better, even if he had aged with a rapidity which almost matched his increasingly weak and incoherent mother.

'Ah, Marion!'

Like two guests at a party who felt that they should know each other, there was a moment's awkwardness as they stood together in the scented sunlight, but she managed a smile even as she noticed the greys at the edges of his hair, the dryings and draggings of his face. He was no longer the old Ralph and it was only with wry sadness that she realised they were standing on the close walk just beyond the pyrepoppies amid which they had once made ecstatic love. Falling into step, they wandered along the paths. Everything seemed quieter today, and they both agreed that there were fewer followers here now. If, indeed, that was how any of them still thought of themselves.

'Fresh people have come to Invercombe, as well as those who have left,' Ralph said. 'After all, who cares about guild warning signs now? And they're bringing the most extraordinary rumours. It's said that all of the main reckoning engines are still working, but that they're not in anyone's control. And did you know a crude postal system's been started between London and Bristol? Riders, men on foot, or with carts. Can you imagine—we're going back three Ages!'

'People can't just dance and make love.'

'They can't, can they? And you know, I still haven't got the faintest idea whether that's a pity or not. For what it's worth . . .' His steps slowed beneath the green shade of the pinetum. 'For what it's worth, Marion, I've sent a letter to my wife back in London. The Elder knows whether it will ever get there, but I'll keep writing and sending them until I get there myself to ask Helen if she wants me back.'

'There's little to keep you here, now, Ralph. Not unless you count your mother, and I suppose she belongs in the East as well, if she ever belongs anywhere.'

'That isn't what I mean, Marion. I just wanted to say . . . I just wanted to tell you how much I loved you.' He laughed. 'There!' He stopped and turned, gesturing to the green-lit trees about them. 'I've said it! And look, not one single thing about the world has been changed.'

'That's not true,' Marion said. 'I loved you as well. It's just . . .'

'Something we could never find a word for?'

Unthinkingly, neither of them seeming to lead the other but the moment happening to a will of its own, they embraced. Marion laid her head against Ralph's shoulder. No longer with the remote bedside manner of old, but with a twinge of a sexual urge, she felt the shape of his body. They kissed, and Ralph laid his hand across her right breast. But, even in this radiant garden, it was only a ghost of their old passion, and they soon drew apart.

'So . . . You'll be leaving?'

'No.' Ralph shrugged. 'Or not quite yet. The guildsmaster part of me, the husband and father part, wants to get back to London as soon as possible. But the rest of me feels that there's still something here at Invercombe which hasn't been done. After all, this is where the spell was sent out from. And there have been, as I say, the oddest rumours. So I think I'll just wait here for another few days to regain my strength.'

'Have you seen Klade?'

Some of the old greyness and worry reasserted itself over Ralph's features as he shook his head.

Klade was difficult for Marion to find for the very reason that he was often close by, watching and following her. With so-called followers frolicking half-naked through the greenery, he found a cherishable sense of security at the edge of the quieter places where she moved, in the silences and the distant shine of her silhouette as she walked the shore, and in her startled, absent gaze when he stumbled as he followed her back towards the house through the flower-lit pathways at nightfall.

Sometimes, he watched the other followers as well, and witnessed their breathy fumblings and listened to their liquid grunts. With his mother and father—and a wasted creature who claimed to be his grandmother—so near, Klade told himself that he was no longer alone. But alone was how he felt, especially as Inver-something began to take on some of the scents and disorders of Einfell. He missed Ida. He missed the Big House and the Ironmasters. He missed the Shadow Ones. He missed their song. Really, all the comfort he had left was Marion Price, for she and he were, Klade decided as he followed her, alike in so many ways. In their wandering wonderingness. In their need, which he respected, to be alone.

Picking up her trail as she headed towards the shore by some unthinking route, tasting the dewy grass which had been shaped by her bare feet, he watched as she and the man who was his father met and talked. Their words were drowned by the sigh of the trees, but soon, he was sure, they would beckon him from the patch of shadow where he crouched. Together, they would all Laugh and Hug and Dance in the sunlight. But instead they ceased their talking and put their mouths together just like all the others. Klade watched in disappointment, and yet was saddened when they stepped apart. In his distress, Klade remained crouching in the same spot even as Marion Price walked closer to him along a turn of the path.

'Ah . . . Klade.' There was that odd look in her eyes as he straightened up. 'There's something I want you to help me with.' She used the smile he'd seen her give to Outsiders and followers when she wanted a job done. 'It's a bit of a grim task, but there are graves which need digging for the soldiers who died at the folly. You need have nothing to do with their bodies . . .' As if Klade hadn't seen bodies. 'I just need some help with digging the holes.'

He followed her across an expanse of flowers and grass to a musty shed, where she found two spades. As his flat, sharp blade slid into Invercombe's earth, it seemed to Klade they were preparing to bury the war itself. Noon passed. The day proved not quite so warm as the one which had preceded it, but it was hot work. When a hole grew deep, Marion Price, her hands warm and slippery with sweat and earth, helped him out, and Klade did the same for her. He gripped her waist as she leaned against him, and the sigh of the trees, the colour of the sky, deepened. In the golden mid-afternoon, with eight wormy spaces of shadow laid out in the greensward, he noticed that the flowers of late summer had already bloomed and would soon be dead. Striking his spade, he rested his arms and watched as Marion began to cut the next grave's turf.

'I'm glad we've done this together, Klade. It's no recompense, but something's always better than nothing . . .' The trees chanted. Sweat had shaped and darkened her blouse. Klade knew the differences of a woman's body from his own well enough by now, and he was puzzled by his unreasoning desire to discover the exact nature of his mother's. 'And I— this is a terrible thing to say, but I had a sister who took ill and died very quickly when I was young. And when I see Ralph . . . Well, I wonder why he was spared and she wasn't.' She laughed. Sensing where his gaze was settled, her fingers redid the loosened buttons on her blouse. 'As if I'm still expecting to find some sense in the world.'

'There isn't.'

Her stance altered. 'You should ignore my rambling, Klade. You have youth, health, plenty of time. Ralph will be able to help you start a new life when he leaves Invercombe far better than I ever could. Just remember that that old woman isn't the sweet old lady that I know she seems. It's a—'

'Why are you afraid of me?'

She wiped back her hair. 'But I'm not.'

The scent of bared earth grew stronger as he walked towards her around the line of graves.

'Klade—I don't understand . . .'

But she did. After all, if his father and all the other followers could do these things, why not Klade? And he loved Marion Price. Of that much he was certain. And surely she, as his mother, must love him as well? His hands reached for her and she stumbled back, tripping over her fallen spade, and Klade stumbled with her, conscious of her resistance, but also that he was big and that she was small, and how once he'd gripped her arms and pushed her all the way down into this fragrant autumn turf, she'd be unable to escape until he had done all the things that he wanted. But surely this was not the way love was supposed to be, for she was shouting for him to let her go as she twisted this way and that away from his seeking mouth, then slammed her elbow into the side of his skull. Klade shook his head, seeing stars. As his sight cleared, the vision of this fear-struck female, her eyes wide and her mouth slack with terror, made him loosen his grip. In a series of kicks and squirms and giving resistances, Marion Price crawled away from him.

Saddened, exhausted, his face pressed against the scented earth, he lay listening to the softening thud of her departing feet. His hand lolled over the meadow grass into one of the graves, and it seemed logical that he should roll the rest of the way into it. For he was the Bonny Boy, and the soft earth surrounded him. He curled up as the air cooled and it grew entirely dark. Then it began to rain.

Leaves dropped and clogged the pathways and drifted down the gullies into pools where they joined with all the petals and seeds and rotting fruit and dead insects of Invercombe's quick seasons, causing overflows and blockages which widened into chain-mailed puddles within which wardrobes warped and paddled their lion's feet, whilst precious tapestries leaked rainbows of dye.

Marion spent the night crouched and shivering on the weathertop's iron gantry, looking out across the lightless dark. Every now and then, as the wind roared up and the rain washed more heavily against her, she felt the structure give another ominous shift. This, for the first time, was ordinary weather, brought here to Invercombe by nothing more unusual than the prevailing winds. She wondered what Ralph was waiting here for, and then if he hadn't perhaps already gone back to his life and his family without saying goodbye. She wondered, as well, why she'd remained here for so long herself. But the world beyond, as the high gantry creaked and dripped and, in a series of triumphant rushing roars, the River Riddle began to tear the water-race far beneath her apart, still seemed empty and unformed. Going out there would be like walking into a mirror. It would be like throwing herself off this drop.

The night was long, but she found that she was still crouched on the bare wet iron, her hands blued and her jaw rattling, at the coming of dawn. Naked tree by naked tree, bare grey field by bare grey field, the warless winter landscape of Somerset revealed itself through the continuing downpour. It seemed at first to Marion that it was entirely deserted, but then she saw a stutter of yellow moving between the black hedgerows. Two lights. Yellow, unwavering. She climbed to her feet and watched as the headlights of England's only functioning car clawed towards Invercombe.

Silver-spoked wheels crackled across the wet gravel as it pulled up beside Invercombe's front door. Wipers stopped sweeping, headlights blinked off, and two men of military bearing, although they wore no recognisable uniform, bustled out. Suspiciously, they eyed Invercombe's gutter-weeping frontage, its bare trees. After an exchange of nods, they opened the car's rear door, and a figure in a dark green cloak emerged. Standing to its full height, it cast back its hood and looked around with eyes of unfathomable grey.

Silus had never been to Invercombe before, yet he felt he knew this place almost too well. In a lopsided attempt at orderliness, a few buckets had been placed inside beneath the worst drippings and leakings in the great hall, but many of them had overflowed, and loose windows banged, and the predominant smell was of wet plaster and spoiled carpets. This was much like Einfell, even down to the sense of things which needed doing, but most probably would never be done. But he could tell that the house was not merely ailing, but dying. The song, what remained of its foundation spell, was a mere whisper, easily drowned by the choppy surgings of the tides in the deep tunnels against which it had long fought. And the Shadow Ones had gone.

Silus felt that he knew these faces as well. Yes, this was the man who had once nearly died here, then taken command of much of the Eastern forces during their recent pointless war, and then nearly died again. He seemed bright enough now, although

Silus could tell that the disease had weakened him, and that he would live to no great age. And this, surely, was the girl this man had once loved—Klade's mother, the famous Marion Price who had become so much of a legend it was hard to believe that she was really standing before him, and all the more so when she looked this drenched and pale, and her thoughts were so wary and confused. Clearly, though, things had played themselves out here in a way which went back to the times when this third figure he now saw approaching, this stoop of flesh borne on a rattling stick whom he knew he should recognise but truly didn't, had once reigned over his desires in a way which now scarcely seemed credible. Silus wanted to ask Alice and Ralph and Marion about Klade, who was surely nearby, but at the same time there was this dread darkness, a near-falling, which made him hesitate. He'd had his fill of bad news lately. And of pain. Above all, he was prepared to take his time.

It was suggested that they take what would surely be the house's last meal in Invercombe's gently collapsing west parlour. After some debate, Silus's two minders, the one appointed by Bristol's Merchant Venturers and the other by London's Great Guilds, who distrusted each other far more than they distrusted him, agreed. The gaps in the windows were wedged with damp-swollen cushions, and candles were placed at the end of the table where the plaster had not yet fallen in. Tins of food were decanted, cold and unheated, upon harlequin plates, and there were jugs of the rainwater from the overbrimming butts to drink, and Silus was content, for this was exactly how he and poor lost Ida had once lived.

Amid the tick of rain and of cutlery, he attempted to explain himself. It always seemed such a difficult task in front of a human audience, but in truth there was little enough to relate, even if he used his mouth to speak. There was his so-called enlistment along with many others into the Western needs of war. There were the weary years of travel and work. Then his capture by the East. He lifted his cloak a little further from his arms to display the silvered tracks of the electrodes they had used in their questioning of him. *See, I, too, now have my Mark.* To Silus, it seemed a fine, rich joke, but no one else ever smiled, and they did not do so now. The fact was, he supposed, that they feared him.

'After that, I was taken East. There were months of boredom. A tiny cell, with a single bulb was all I had left to sing to. Then came the night of the changed song, and in an instant, everything went dark. People were screaming. The guards could no longer work the locks. But it all seemed to me a small enough thing . . .'

But it was also large: he'd known that as soon as he'd led his captors and fellow inmates out into the chaotic London night where all the windows and streetlamps were entirely dark. He knew it now. Even if he and the other changed, Chosen—however you cared or cared not to term them— who emerged blinking and shrieking from their hiding places and their corrupted locks and broken chains had taken the task of undoing the song as some pressing debt, it would be the work of years. But Silus, who had once been a man of power, still recognised its substance when he held it in his changed hands, and step by step, tier by tier, he ascended the councils of the guilds as the city dissolved into riot in the days which followed. He explained time and again how the shift in pitch was something he and all the other Chosen could whistle, hum, sing, dance to as easily as the humblest ditty. He was presented with frozen axles. He made them turn. More tentatively, a small electric generator in one of the lesser guildhouses was produced. It, too, came to life. More warily yet, he was transported to a small reckoning engine at the relay house of one of the lesser guilds, which was of greater significance to them than those who brought him there were prepared to admit. This task he refused, until various conditions regarding the treatment of the other Chosen were met. Of course, the guildsmen could have killed him, or put him back in cheap, unaethered chains, but then where would they have been? And he had already established contact with the presence of the Shadow Ones who somehow no longer seemed to exist as flesh, but deep within the core of the country's networks. Slowly, the Chosen were regathering, but this time they would not be bonded by any conditions other than of their own making. It was all merely a matter of patience and time. That, and a few further requests.

'For once, Alice, I was ruthless in a way I think you would

applaud and recognise. But I am also entirely content that I've done the right and necessary thing . . .'

The old woman looked at him blankly across the table, and Silus realised that her sight was poor, and that she probably found it hard to hear his lisping voice over the noise she made in eating. Of the two of them, Alice was now by far the most changed. She was like this leaking, dripping house; a lost and dying spell. Soon, he knew, he would have to rouse himself and start the process of unpicking England's frozen note, just as he had promised the guilds of London and Bristol. But even then, even when the wheels finally started spinning and the generators began to hum, their spells would not be the ones their old masters recognised, or would ever be able to learn. On one thing, Silus explained in all frankness, he was determined. From now on, the working of aether would remain in the hands of those who had felt it and had suffered from it the most. It seemed, he suggested to the tired faces at this table, a fair exchange.

A thing of clotted mud, Klade had roused himself from the grave in which he'd been lying and crawled through the estate in the first shinings of winter dawn. One last sight of the house, he told himself, and he would be gone. Invercombe was already so empty. Most of the followers had left, driven away by this foul weather and the prospect beyond of a changed world, and every one of Inver-something's chimneys had fallen. Still, it was with considerable surprise that he encountered the fine and purposeful machine which stretched before the front door. He touched its drop-beaded chromes and leathers and sniffed the warm salts of its engine and listened to its odd, faint song. How had it managed to get here at all, when nothing was supposed to work?

Klade saw a gleam spreading across the terraced paving from the west parlour. He heard voices through the rain, and he felt something more. Something lost. Something familiar. A presence—and a voice which was like the spitting of the rainspout above him, yet made him grind his muddy hands across his face. Klade stumbled over the squishy lawns and hunched where the rain thudded over the dead black leaves of an umbrellifer. From here, he could see through the fractured panes of the French windows, but those inside could not see him, or sense him, either—not even Silus, who sat at the head of the table making gestures which Klade recognised by now as signifying command.

He could crouch here for ever, or he could beat at that window and beg to be let in. Silus would give a snaky smile, and he and his Bonny Boy, who really had grown, would finally be reunited, but Klade now understood that that wasn't what happened to the lad in the song. For the Bonny Boy grew because he was buried in a hole like the ones he and Marion had dug yesterday, and all Klade needed to do to be the same was to wait for the roots and the worms to have their fill of him. He could think of far worse things than turning into flowers and leaves. Like the changed look in people's eyes whenever they saw him. Like the terrified gasps and squirms of Marion Price beneath him yesterday. Or being with Silus, and yet never quite being with him at all. Just as he had never quite been with Ida, or with Fay, or even with the Ironmasters as they beat their metal hands and sang their jolly songs. Just as he had never been or belonged with anyone or anything either inside or outside Einfell.

The trees, the rain, the voices, the candlelight, flickered across the teeming gardens. Moving out from his patch of shadow, then further around the house, Klade came to a space of lawn where forgotten washing still dripped, and entered the house through the servants' quarters, and picked his way past mould-flowering frames, and felt for stairways, and headed down.

It grew dark. No longer the hiss of the storm, but the deeper moan of the restless salt water which had long surged below Invercombe filled his ears. On hands and knees, then on his belly in the wet blackness, he wormed his way amid the groaning stone. It was difficult work. Dangerous, as well. Not that danger mattered to him, but these passages were teetering on collapse, and with them would go the entire headland, the gardens, the house. Another day, another few hours, and he would have left it too late. But, glistening in shifting blotches before his eyes, a little light began to come. This, as far as he could tell, was something resembling the direction his father had led him a few days before, even if the stones tilted and echoed into spaces he couldn't comprehend. For a moment, the slippery ceiling both in front and behind him seemed to press irresistibly down, and Klade was certain that he really would be buried, but then, with a sideways shift which the very push of the land seemed to be urging upon him, he was standing near-upright in a corridor, and light and the sound of waves and the feel of the salt air showed him the way.

Here, in this small chamber in the cliffs, nothing had changed. Klade, washed and stripped of his rotting clothes by his struggles amid the grasping rocks, gazed at the alcove. Two glass vials still glowed and flickered. They pulsed with the heave of the sea. His father had talked about power and money when he had shown him these things. That, and something about a thumb eater, and a life ahead for Klade which he'd known even then that he'd never be able to live. He lifted a vial. He felt the charge of its light, the roar of its song. For this was aether, brought here from far away in the days before he was even born, when Marion Price and Ralph Meynell had briefly imagined they loved each other, and the sad old creature people called Old Alice had done things which no one seemed able to forgive. For this was aether, and this moment was his.

Some resistance to the stopper, then it was open, and the vial brimmed dark and sang out to him as he lifted it to his lips. Klade's hand trembled in a final moment's human uncertainty. Then he drank, and all he saw was light, all he heard was song.

XX

Bristol Boneyard, on a spring morning in the first year of this new and still nameless Age, was a surprisingly beautiful place. As Marion walked up between the larger memorials, the faces and voices of those whom they had been built to commemorate no longer called out to her, and the crushed fragments of marble of the white path were silent. The spells which had been infused into the stones had faded, and their resurrection was no one's priority, least of all the Chosen, and perhaps not even the grieving families which had once had them cast at such expense. But this seemed to her, as Bristol murmured and smoked below in all its varieties of life, to be no bad thing. It was time the dead were left buried; time for those still living to be allowed to live.

The small monument lay amid a field which, neglected as well, had become a sweep of high grass and flowers. It was of plain black marble, and not particularly well cut or engraved, for stonemasons, like every other variety of guildsperson, were having to relearn their trade. But its rough unevenness seemed appropriate, and her fingers, as they traced the chipped engraving, liked the cool finality of the stone.

Here lie the bodies of
Sally Price
Who lived and died before this Age
And her father
Bill Price
'Dad'—a proud shoreman

Then, in slightly smaller and even rougher script:

Here also lies
Marion Price

The faintly flattened track which lay between the wavering bluebells and seedheads told her that others had come this way. Perhaps they were the fellow followers, or soldiers or riverfolk Marion Price had once tended, or those who had read about her in the Western papers and brought one of the cheap amulets which bore her face. But there were few enough of them, and Marion felt no particular alarm at the thought that she might be discovered here, and less still that she would be recognised, or that anyone now would really care.

Straightening up, she scanned the meadow this graveyard had become. The reason life grew so wildly and well here, she realised, was due to the number of times this earth had been turned over to accommodate the dead of the war. England's soil had been especially well-fertilised in recent years, as she supposed Noll would have sardonically pointed out, although the thought no longer struck her as sad, or poignant, or even humorous. It was just the way the world was.

People had grown almost as tired of Marion Price, and of the recent war with which she would always be associated, as she had herself. They were grateful to put aside such things, and the songs which went with them, and to believe that she had died in the shift of powers which had brought about this exhausted peace. Even for her, the memories of what had happened at Invercombe were confused, although she could never forget the blood of those two dead telegraphers, or the changed note of the song. Now, when people talked about the end of the war, the sudden collapse of power and technology seemed part of an inevitable drift towards peace. The Great Guilds of East and West, it was said, had already been sending out tentative feelers that winter, and the powers of mainland Europe had lost interest in the battle being fought in their backyard, and the prospect of further years of war seemed intolerable. But, Marion reminded herself, it had also seemed intolerable then. Yet the war had gone on.

Slowly, her lengthening pepper-and-salt hair tied back, and the warm breeze flapping at her loose brown clothes, she headed back down the faint path towards the grainy city. The smells of Bristol's smokes, its sounds, were entirely different this spring. The trams hung useless on their rusting gantries, whilst, according to a recent letter from Ralph, those in London were pulled by horses, and looked even more ridiculous. And yet their movement, all of this world's slow resurrection, was heartening. Food was still in short supply and of poor quality, but it was obtainable, and the water pipes and the sewerage processing, at least in the cities, just about functioned during some times of each day. People had worked to bring these things about in a way that they had rarely worked before.

Marion left the lower reaches of the Boneyard, and entered the streets of Bristol. If anything, they were even louder and busier than before, although now with processes of rebuilding and the rickety hammerings of the few patched and nurtured engines which had now been persuaded to work without the cossetings of aether. Many of the buildings, as their structures were unpicked back to their keyplates, were encased in rickety scaffolding, and buckets of rubble were being hauled whilst bonfires burned and smoke and grit hazed the morning air. Everywhere, there was work. All that was missing, the changed essential key which she still believed the pulling of that lever in the folly at Invercombe had brought about, was the familiar ululating chants of guildsmen's songs.

Past the Dings, and the gulls were still circling over the Avon, and Upmeet Market teemed and stank as it always had. This being Bristol, as well, there were faces of every shade, accents of every hue, and disbelieving curses in a dozen dialects at the ridiculous prices which were being quoted. Many of the fine bottles of wine, Marion noticed as the stallholder smiled back at her and tapped his nose, bore no labels. Quite how the shaky public services got their share of all this private enterprise was a mystery, but then she supposed that that had always been the way in the West. And here was a bearpit where an old ravener from the war was billed as tonight's big attraction, and a few early dollymops were parading their low-cut wares up and down the Sty, and beyond that the massed spars of ships in Saint Mary's Quay waited for a shift in the tide and a change in the wind now that their weathertops were impotent. But, as Marion could tell from her old shoregirl instincts and the thinly gathering clouds, a good breeze would come by this afternoon.

Noll still worked at the Bristol Infirmary, and she knew that she owed him a visit. But, as with Ralph, she much preferred writing and receiving letters to meeting people face to face. She liked the spongy softness of the pulpy recycled paper and the sooty ink, and the slowness of each envelope's journey, and the vague thought it might not arrive at all. Funnily enough after the rampant unpredictability of war, uncertainty was one thing which she and all the other citizens of England had had to remain used to in this strange new peace. Uncertainty, indeed, was one of the words Noll was now toying with as he set about the task of bringing the lost and refound theory of Habitual Adaptation to public acceptance, although it seemed to Marion that the words would eventually find their place to describe some quite different phenomenon in this new Age. And she remembered as well what Alice Meynell had said about love in their last coherent conversation. She was left now with the uneasy thought that the greatgrandmistress had been some ultimate expression of what humans could become if they submitted solely to the forces she and Ralph had once sought to define. But something had been missing, a lost fragment of the equation which had spread and darkened until all that was left was greed. To Alice, a final leap into the pure power and intelligence of the reckoning engines had probably seemed inevitable, but to Marion that fatal jump which she had made last winter from the glass balcony of her crazed and creaking guildhouse seemed yet more inescapable.

What had been missing in Alice Meynell, Marion thought as she turned into the great buildings of Boreal Avenue, was the human spirit which drove this city, even though its fountains no longer played down the tiered front of the Hall of

Wheelwrights. It was the same spirit which gave Ralph and
Noll pleasure in their correspondence about a theory within
which their own burgeoning friendship could never be entirely
explained. For Noll, who now claimed a senior professorship in
the tentative reorderings of Bristol's university, the study of life
was a career, whilst for Ralph it remained a hobby to which,
now as ever, he was unable to devote the time he would have
wished. But that seemed right to Marion as well, for Ralph, who
was now often credited as the first senior guildsperson to seek
peace, remained head of what was still being termed the Great
Guild of Telegraphers—even though the telephone system
didn't work. Undeniably, the juggling act of keeping the suddenly distant bits of England in contact was important work. He
wrote frequently of coming up to Bristol, but the journey now
took the best part of two days, and he was anxious not to risk
his health, nor to be away from his family. Marion, writing
back, told him to rest, and that Flora and Gussie were the most
important work of all.

At the far end of Boreal Avenue, the great building which
had once been called the Halls of the Merchant Venturers rose
above the smoke and soot. Always an extraordinary edifice, it
had become even more extraordinary now. The coralstone
which had reached its final froths and filigrees sixty years before had started to regrow. The building was now hatted, spired
and mushroomed with new turrets and flooded with huge, near-
translucent veins, which glowed and pulsed at night across this
lantern-lit city like the beating of a huge heart. Some people
found what they now called the House of the Chosen sinister in
its dizzily shifting configurations, but Marion thought it beautiful. If it reminded her of anything at all, it was of a massively
barnacled rock. In London, the old green ziggurat of Westminster Great Park had undergone a similar, although probably entirely different, transformation under Silus's command, and
was said by Ralph to be even more incredible. But he was a
Londoner; he would say that.

There were fencings across what had once been a major
thoroughfare, and the humans who patrolled there carried examples of that rare thing in this new Age: working guns. Here
as in many cities, there had been riots and ill-organised attempts at stormings, and the walls nearby were scrawled with

obscenities about the fairies, the goblins, the devils, although Marion noticed that only untainted stone glowed on the final flourishes of the edifice itself, and she felt a questioning resistance which would have made her hesitate to come closer to this place even without the guard's half-levelled gun.

'Any relation?' he asked after glancing down at the scrap of paper she'd presented.

She shook her head. 'There are lots of Prices.'

Those who passed by along Boreal Avenue quickened their step or made the signs of their old guilds as they saw the guard shrug and let her through into the House of the Chosen. The building's main arch, partly that of the old structure she remembered visiting when she'd come here to argue about yet another blockage in medical supplies, had grown into a gravity-defying rainbow of stone. The Chosen, she thought, know how to impress us humans. Amongst the many things they are not, is stupid—or naïve.

The light changed. The city faded. Was that a huge crystal bird moving overhead? But it was only one of Bristol's old trams hanging on the rail which had once entered this building, or the jewelled ornament which the tram had become. And it was moving once again with smooth purpose, although Marion had no idea how, or why, or to where.

She knew something of these changed halls. But each time she'd come was different. The lights, the shapes, the colours, were as restless in their movements as those who dwelt here, and the House of the Chosen really did feel like a pumping heart to her now that she was inside it, and was borne along its marvellous arteries. She saw figures, and the mis-shapes of figures. There was so much glass, or some other kind of veiling, that it was difficult to be sure. Once, the monstrous shape she saw looming towards her began to hesitate just as she did, and she was confronted with a distorted reflection of herself. Through fairground rises and turns, past seeming natural caverns and odd glimpses of the old halls—busts, portraits, a porter's trolley—she suddenly found herself inside what was recognisably one of the old meeting rooms of the Merchant Venturers' Halls. She remembered these panelled walls, and her impotent frustration as the men before her blandly refused to accept her plans. Nearly the same old Bristol still lay beyond the window, although the

cathedral's main tower was now somewhat tilted, and the long
table before her was dusty and empty, and the panelling had
dampened and warped, and the parquet clattered loosely as she
walked across it towards the hunched figure of her son. She
imagined that Klade had chosen this place partly as reassurance,
and also a memory, and perhaps as a point about the shift of
roles, and maybe also as a joke, and no doubt also for other
many reasons, for the ways of the Chosen are never the ways of
ordinary mankind.

'It's a beautiful morning. Spring really is here . . .'

. . . is here . . .

Marion paused. Each time she came here, she told herself
that she had become used to the combined sense of her son
talking through his barely altered voice, yet also directly into
her head. But the feeling was both intimate and strange, and it
always took a moment to adjust.

'Funny,' she said, 'how we see the same changes of the
season every year, and yet we're still surprised by them.'

It's part of what we are.

'Yes.' She smiled, relaxing just a little. 'It is, isn't it? All
of us.'

Klade, now that her eyes had adjusted to the room's dulled
gleams, still looked a little like the lad of old. That, she supposed, must always have been the hardest thing for the families who had once bravely come to the place they used to call
Einfell to visit their changed relatives. That, and to know that
they knew what you saw, and understood what you were thinking. As dark as Silus was light, Klade's flesh seemed partly
sea-wet stone and partly the greyed skin of the wary lad she
had first encountered beside the followers' bonfires. His eyes,
for all that they had hollowed, deepened, widened, still made
her think of Ralph.

'And what have you been doing?'

. . . doing?

'This and that,' she said. 'Writing letters.'

Finding out the names of those two dead telegraphers . . . ?

'That as well.' Their families now possessed much of the
money Marion had carelessly accumulated from the pamphlets which had once poured out in her name, although they
would never know where it had come from.

Marion and Klade talked for a while of the Price family.
Brave and unjudging as always, Owen had come to this House
of the Chosen last shifterm before he set sail for Spain. So,
after much fussing and hesitation, had Denise. She even
claimed she liked it here—after all, she was entirely used to
wandering within other people's dreams. But Mam, who now
lived in the small shoreside cottage in Luttrell Marion had
bought for her, had only ever been to Bristol once, and that
was to take Sally to the Boneyard. Frail as she was, she was
unlikely to ever come to this city again.

'And what about you?'

. . . you?

Marion shrugged. Slowly, in a cold breath, Klade nodded
his cliff-like face. One of the many good new things about being with her son was the absence of any need to explain how
she felt. He always knew. And for the first time in her life, she
hadn't been doing anything—that was the whole point. But
even as she thought this, she felt pangs of her old guilt.

'Perhaps it's the spring.'

'You humans are such restless creatures.' *You only have to
look outside at this city . . .* 'But that's what I wanted to talk to
you about, Marion. So much has happened in so little time.
We are still getting endless requests from the guilds to mend
this or that, with threats of dire or terrifying consequences if it
is left unmended. Only yesterday I was told that five thousand
people will die with the imminent breaking of Clifton Dam.'

'Then they should be moved.'

'That's exactly what I told them. And it isn't beyond the
wit of man to have the valley drained, but of course they want
it both and every way. They want their spells to work again,
and they want their electricity, as if it's something we've taken
and can give them back. It's a natural force—it's been there
all along. *That's* what I want them to understand. If they really
knew how their own generators worked, if they had them reconstructed or remade, then they would have as much power
as they would ever need. They would never need to come to
the Chosen again . . .'

'But they will still come to you, Klade, and to every other
one of your kind.'

'That is precisely why I wanted to speak to you. I'll be frank. I need the help of someone who can act as a proper intermediary. Someone used to dealing with the guilds. Someone they can respect and talk to without the words stopping in their throats. Someone who, as far as is humanly possible, has an understanding of what it feels like to be on both sides.'

Me?

'Who else could I mean? I know, I know, that Marion Price is supposed to have died. But she could be resurrected again. It would add to your . . . glamour. People would listen to you, Marion, in a way that they will never ever listen to the likes of me.'

I'm not Marion.

Who are you, then?

It would be all too easy to think some vague answer which Klade would understand far better than she did herself. But she cleared her throat. 'That's the one thing I never expect to find out.'

A deep gush of laughter registered within her. 'You're right.' *How could I disagree . . .* 'And perhaps this work was never meant for you. Perhaps someone else deserves a chance.'

What a shame we no longer have the Beetle Lady . . .

Or the ravener . . .

Or the balehound . . .

Or Ida, who was once so dear to me . . .

'I love you, Klade. You know that, don't you?'

The rocky head moved a little. The huge mineral hands lay upon her, although they remained light as ghosts. Her Bonny Boy truly had grown. *I love you, too.* 'But I'll never grow tired of hearing that phrase.'

'Neither will I.'

Marion looked around her. The room had a damp, homely smell. It reminded her a little of the old cottage at Clyst, and also of the fading days of Invercombe.

'So . . . What do you plan to do now?'

It was Klade's turn to hesitate. 'I suppose that first we must entrench. I hate to use military terms, but I fear they will always be appropriate in the world of men. People will never trust us, and we will always be half the bogey-man, half an un-wanted answer to their prayers. It wasn't us who destroyed the old guilds. They did that themselves by splitting into territo-rial loyalties during the Civil War. Once people knew that town and family came before guild, it could never be the same. But at least now we Chosen can begin to define what is ours. I've done a little research. One of our kind also played a pivotal role at the end of the last Age. Her name was Anna Winters, and she founded the place which came to be known as Einfell where I was raised. But she could have done much more. There were moments when she held the balance of power, and she chose to let it slip. She didn't want to be what she was, and I cannot believe that that way ever leads to hap-piness. At least I made a conscious choice, and I am glad I did. As for Einfell, it was never that old village, or even some fairy myth. The Beetle Lady was right. The place we were seeking lay beyond even Invercombe, and now that's gone as well . . .'

'Some people are calling this Einfell.'

'This is just another building. The truth is always else-where. And the real Einfell isn't somewhere you can stand in.' *Not, at least, in the flesh you're wearing, Mother. It lies there . . .*

Klade gestured, and Marion saw that a mirror hung in what had previously been the furthest, dimmest corner of this long room. It remained dark for a moment, then brightened, and the reflection of a beautiful young woman, scarcely more than a girl, smiled out at them as she combed her lustrous ebony hair.

'What's it like to be in there?'

I don't know. That's one step even I can't yet fully make.

Drawing whatever presence they had seen back into unimaginable matrices of the reckoning engines, the mirror faded to black. Outside, in a lesser fading, Marion saw that clouds were coming in over Bristol on a freshening breeze.

'I need to go now. I'm sorry—'

Don't be sorry. Not for anything.

She smiled. 'Then I'm not.'

'And where are you going?'

'I'm still not quite sure. But I nearly am.'

'That's good. And you'll keep in touch?'

Klade's hand, his whole heavy arm, reached towards her, and she clasped it, and raised it to her face, and stroked it, and kissed it, and tasted tidal rock, and salt.

Always.

Then the dream shifted, and she was outside, and walking briskly towards her lodgings. The old silos and sugar warehouses were still partly abandoned, but the small new shoots of lesser buildings and stills and mashing houses were starting to rise from their ruins. Prices of the small amounts of sugar which were starting to arrive from the Fortunate Isles were still exorbitant, especially as the East's beloved bittersweet had proved impossible to grow without the endless nurturing of spells. Some said the demand would never return—after all, people had lived for years with little enough sweetness in their lives—but, thinking of Denise, Marion rather suspected that it would.

Sunshine Lodge still smelled and felt pretty much the same. There, in room 12A, she stuffed her few belongings into an old canvas bag and signed herself out in the book which the woman in the hairnet presented to her. **M. Price** with a slur on the M, so it could have been a W or an N or a U—or perhaps even an S. For Marion was dead, and Price was a common enough name. And who wanted to think about the past? As she walked towards the docks, she decided that how she lived from now on would be a far better memorial for her lost and joyful sister than anything a stonemason would ever be able to create. For Sally had loved and laughed unthinkingly and unselfishly, and the old, fading Marion was determined she would try to live her life in the same way. She would sleep when she slept and wake when she woke, and cry when she felt like crying. She would learn how to laugh as well. Even thinking those thoughts made her step quicken, and she smiled up at the sky, and chuckled out loud, and nearly fell over a bundle of ropes.

'Why . . . If it isn't the Price girl!'

Turning, Marion saw that a large black woman was sharing a bench with a pair of gulls. Her hair was a ball of white now, and her features had puffed and thinned a little, but she was still recognisably Cissy Dunning. Marion sat down beside her in place of the rising, complaining gulls.

'The Price girl,' Marion said. 'Is that really how you still think of me?'

Cissy smiled. 'You wouldn't believe all the things I've heard about you since. Thinking you're still the way you were back in that summer at Invercombe is part of what's kept me sane.'

'You look well.'

'You mean old—you might as well go on and say it.'

'In that case, Cissy, you can say it about me as well . . .'

The two women laughed, and for those who walked past along the docks, their manner and conversation would have seemed no more than what it was: two women, one black, one white, one entering middle age and the other leaving it, catching up on old times just as many Bristolians now did. At least Cissy was alive, and had managed to get by since leaving Invercombe. Alice Meynell, as good as her word, had allowed her to find further work in other houses, and then war had intervened, and her skills in organising food and accommodation had been in even more demand.

'Before then, I'd thought my job was looking after houses. But I discovered it was people I'd always been taking care of, although it was a hard enough way to have to learn. Houses fall . . .' She nodded back in the direction of the extraordinary new spires of the House of the Chosen. 'Even the biggest.'

Cissy said she'd have retired by now if her guild had honoured her pension. The way things were, though, she still had to work. And she often thought about Invercombe. Yes, she'd been there, or to the space of onrushing sea which was mostly all that remained now. She'd even heard the stories the mariners and the shorefolk were telling, and laughed at their wildness. Invercombe never had been some fairy palace. The only ghosts which had ever haunted it were the ones people saw in their own heads. No, what she missed was the real place, the cools of its corridors and the gleams of its windows and soft warmth of its gardens and the laughter of its busy maids. And Weatherman Ayres—she missed him as well, and missed the life they'd planned to lead, although he'd have been off on some Western frigate at the first sign of war, stubborn man that he'd been. Most likely, she'd probably still be sitting on this same bench, and still without a proper pension, and still grieving for him, and wondering how long she'd manage to keep bending with *her* hips.

'You've never thought of going back to the Fortunate Isles?'

Cissy wrinkled her nose. 'There's *another* place I go to in my thoughts. Me and Weatherman Ayres often walk those white sands. But the real islands, from all I hear, are in as big a mess as we are here. Sure, they've abolished what the East still likes to call slavery. But there's less work to be done, and less pay, which makes for harder living by any arithmetic. People talk about *England* over in the Fortunate Isles the way we used to talk about them over there. Those ships you see leaving won't just be coming back with cane. There'll be more and more people with my colour skin heading for England, and we won't be content with just sweeping the streets to see where all the gold's gone that was supposed to be hidden underneath.'

'It'll be good for the country.'

'Ha! You try telling that to the average guildsman. Stealing jobs—I've heard it already. And then there's this new damn fool theory—if you read the papers, you may have heard it— that we're all risen from apes instead of being the Elder's good creations, and all life's about is who kicks the strongest. And there's meetings where they'll tell you that the likes of us African people are a whole lot nearer cousins to the apes than you whites.'

'That isn't—'

'No, no,' Cissy insisted, either stubbornly or wilfully misinterpreting the objection. 'It's true. The posters are everywhere. Look.' She nodded towards a wall behind them. 'There's one over there.'

The two women fell silent. It had, after all, been a long time.

'Well . . .' By shuffles and rises, Cissy made to stand. 'This won't get things seen to.'

Helping her, Marion took her hands, and Cissy swayed for a moment, catching her breath. 'You'd have made a good steward, you know. Such a waste . . .' Chuckling to herself, shaking her head, she turned and waddled off on her failing hips.

It was early afternoon, and the docks were busy, departures and loadings hurrying to make the most of the prevailing winds and tide. Sails boomed, ropes slithered, cargoes rolled, but still it seemed strangely silent without the accompanying

smoky rush of endless engines. The ships which had bravely
forgone sail entirely were now being dismantled for their ores
in the breakers' yards, although there were, Marion noticed as
she walked on, a few loud and leaky vessels which ran on engines entirely devoid of the strengthenings of aether. Klade
was right; the less the Chosen helped, the more humanity
would prosper.

There was no doubt that trade had shrunk. Offers for deckhands, which had once been chalked on blackboards beside
gangplanks, were now scarce. Berths were rare as well, for the
big passenger vessels that had limped back into port generally
hadn't limped out again, and people were as anxious to leave
England as they ever had been, despite what Cissy said. Beyond
the loading runs and slipways, where the old smells of bilge and
molasses still prevailed, leaned many unwanted and often dras-
tically unseaworthy vessels, some of which, in what looked like
a vain hope, had drippingly painted signs on their hulls offering
them for sale. One particular vessel took her attention. It was
small, and turned the tip of its single high mast in seemingly
impatient figure-eights as the tide snaked around it.

She found the unemployed mariner who claimed to be its
owner playing cards in an old shed nearby. Negotiations were
swift. Marion was certain she'd got no bargain, and even wondered if she wasn't conspiring in theft, but at least she knew
enough mariners' phrases to keep the old man on his toes. The
deal was done. They spat on their palms, shook hands. Heading back to her vessel after buying water and supplies, Marion
found him checking ropes and rusty fixings and muttering
spells which no longer worked. But the little ship seemed sea-
worthy, and they both agreed that its main liability was the
weathertop which, stained with acids and rusts and engine ice,
sat uselessly in the middle of the deck. After some work with
a spanner, and much wrenching and splintering, they had the
thing loose and set it rolling across the deck. Trundling overboard, it vanished with a large splash.

Marion pulled out at mid-afternoon with a few other last
vessels on the departing tide along the Avon Cut. Bells
clanged. Shouts were exchanged. Then through the open locks,
and the deeper currents beyond Avonmouth, and the stronger
pull of the winds, and all Bristol shrank. She could sense the

keel seeking direction, she could feel the rudder's need. This was where the Severn and the tides of the channel met amid changing scents and dimpled water. Sea or river? But the vessel was a far more capable craft than the cabin boat she had once navigated down from Bewdley, and she let its prow surge south and west towards the widening estuary. On one side lay Wales, those towns and mountains she had still never visited, and on the other the hills of the West rolled green and verdant under breezy flickers of sunlight. The Severn Bridge still hung entire across the quickening currents, a frozen spell, even if it no longer glowed at night. There was talk that it would be reopened to traffic by this summer, although men would have to learn how to climb and paint its gantries in place of the gargoyles the ailing Guild of Beastmasters was not able to create. Like many such structures, it was more strongly built than its designers had ever been allowed to credit. Funnily enough, Marion thought, considering how everything now depended on unavoidable physics, life was still all a matter of belief.

Beyond here, although there were many banks and buoys to navigate, and land still enclosed the Bristol Channel's horizons, Marion was unmistakably at sail on the sea. She tacked, and the prow bobbed and cut, and the boom swung over the deepening waves. There was much flotsam about from the storms of last winter, both natural and man-made, and huge brown islands of weed glowed as they decayed with an eerie phosphorescence which had nothing to do with magic. Marion could feel, smell, that it would be a good year for the shorefolk.

Now, as the currents turned boisterous, and just when the coastline to her left should have been most familiar to her, it grew strange. Clarence Cove had widened, and all that was left of Durnock Head was a white-tipped crashing of waves. Hauling in the rudder, Marion steered as close as she dared. The huge new cliffs were rougher and more sheer, but there was little else left to show where Invercombe had once stood, for even the wider outreaches of the edges of its estate had slipped and changed. Still, peering down over the side as she checked for obstructions and her vessel danced over the waves, she was sure for a moment that she saw pathways down there amid the wavering marine life, and gesturing statues, and the golden glow of a weathertop, and the flashing tall windows of the house which she still visited often in her dreams. But the seabirds feeding their offspring on this season's new bounty swooped wildly about her in agitated screams, and these waters were unmapped, and dangerously unbuoyed. Tilting the rudder, loosening the sail, she headed back towards deeper waters. South, and west.

Ian R. MacLeod was born in Birmingham in the United Kingdom and has lived most of his life there. His short fiction has appeared in *Interzone*, *Asimov's*, and *Fantasy & Science Fiction*, and been widely anthologized and translated. He is the winner of two World Fantasy Awards.

THE ULTIMATE IN FANTASY!

From magical tales of distant worlds to stories of those with abilities beyond the ordinary, Ace and Roc have everything you need to stretch your imagination to its limits.

Marion Zimmer Bradley/Diana Paxon

Guy Gavriel Kaye

Dennis McKiernan

Patricia McKillip

Robin McKinley

Sharon Shinn

Katherine Kurtz

Barb and J. C. Hendees

Elizabeth Bear

T. A. Barron

Brian Jacques

Robert Asprin

penguin.com

**Explore the outer reaches
of imagination—don't miss these authors
of dark fantasy and urban noir that take you
to the edge and beyond.**

Patricia Briggs	**Karen Chance**	**Anne Bishop**
Simon R. Green	**Caitlin Kiernan**	**Janine Cross**
Jim Butcher	**Rachel Caine**	**Sarah Monette**
Kat Richardson	**Glen Cook**	**Doug Clegg**

penguin.com

Penguin Group (USA) Online

What will you be reading tomorrow?

Tom Clancy, Patricia Cornwell, W.E.B. Griffin,
Nora Roberts, William Gibson, Robin Cook,
Brian Jacques, Catherine Coulter, Stephen King,
Dean Koontz, Ken Follett, Clive Cussler,
Eric Jerome Dickey, John Sandford,
Terry McMillan, Sue Monk Kidd, Amy Tan,
John Berendt…

You'll find them all at
penguin.com

Read excerpts and newsletters,
find tour schedules and reading group guides,
and enter contests.

Subscribe to Penguin Group (USA) newsletters
and get an exclusive inside look
at exciting new titles and the authors you love
long before everyone else does.

PENGUIN GROUP (USA)
us.penguingroup.com